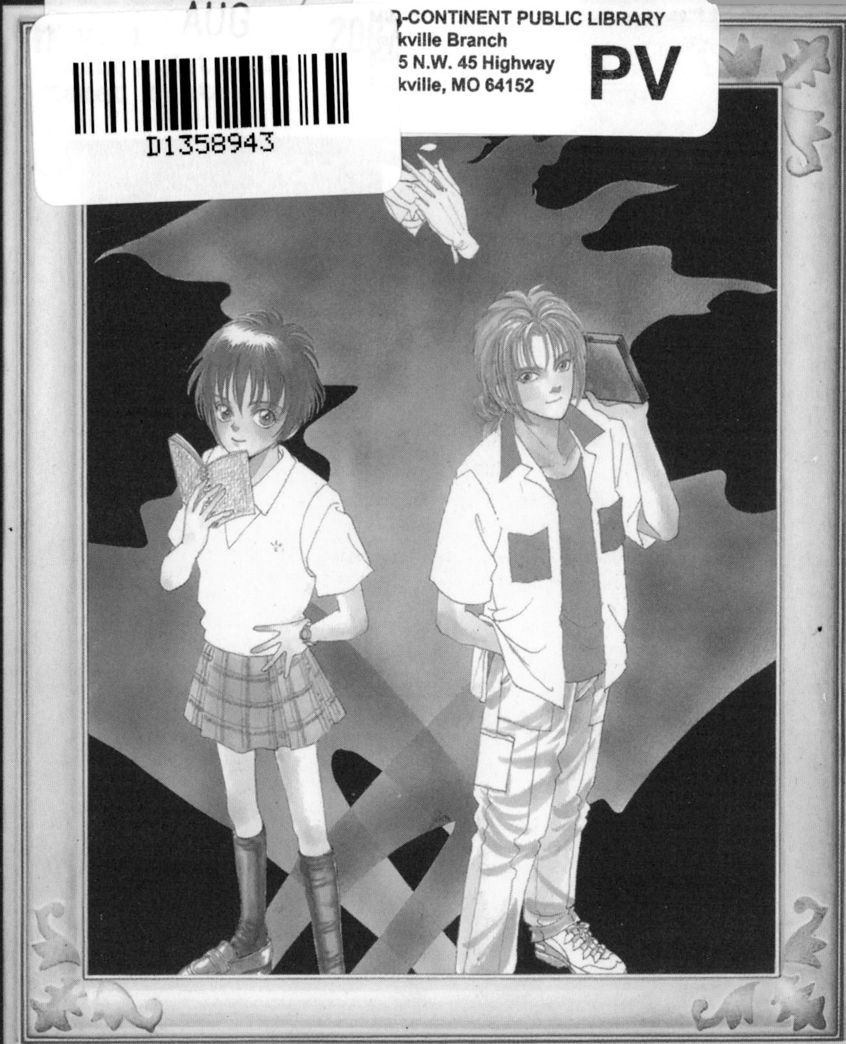

KAMEN TANTEI

Kamen Tantei Volume 1
Created by Matsuri Akino

Translation - Mike Kiefl
English Adaptation - Patrick Neighly
Retouch and Lettering - Courtney Geter
Production Artist - Fawn Lau
Cover Design - John Lo

Editor - TIm Beedle
Digital Imaging Manager - Chris Buford
Production Manager - Elisabeth Brizzi
Managing Editor - Vy Nguyen
Editor-in-Chief - Rob Tokar
VP of Production - Ron Klamert
Publisher. - Mike Kiley
President and C.O.O. - John Parker
C.E.O. and Chief Creative Officer - Stuart Levy

A  Manga

TOKYOPOP Inc.
5900 Wilshire Blvd. Suite 2000
Los Angeles, CA 90036

E-mail: info@TOKYOPOP.com
Come visit us online at www.TOKYOPOP.com

ISBN: 1-59816-499-6

First TOKYOPOP printing: September 2006
10 9 8 7 6 5 4 3 2 1
Printed in the USA

Volume 1

By
Matsuri Akino

HAMBURG // LONDON // LOS ANGELES // TOKYO

RAMEN TANTEI™

Contents

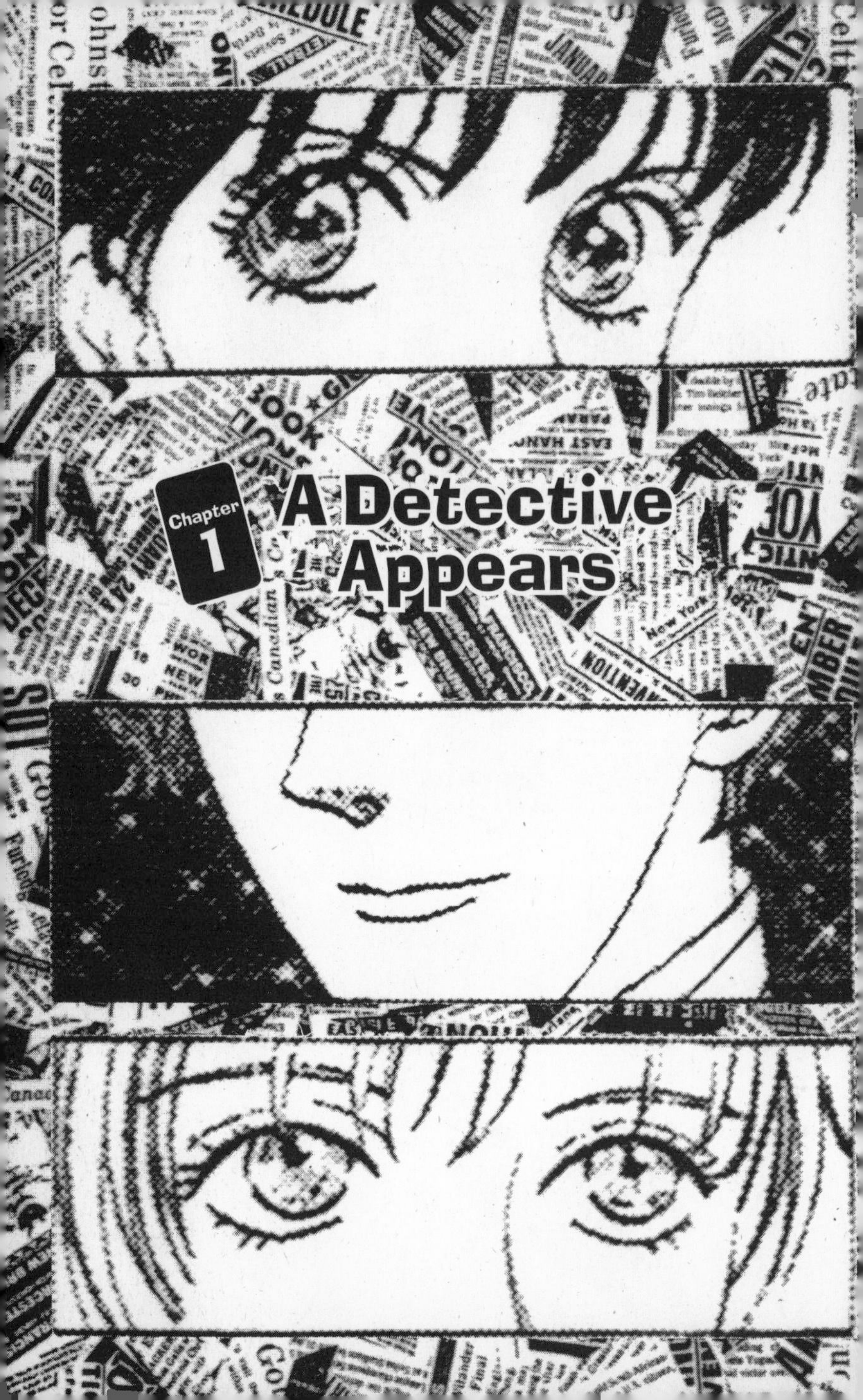
Chapter 1
A Detective Appears

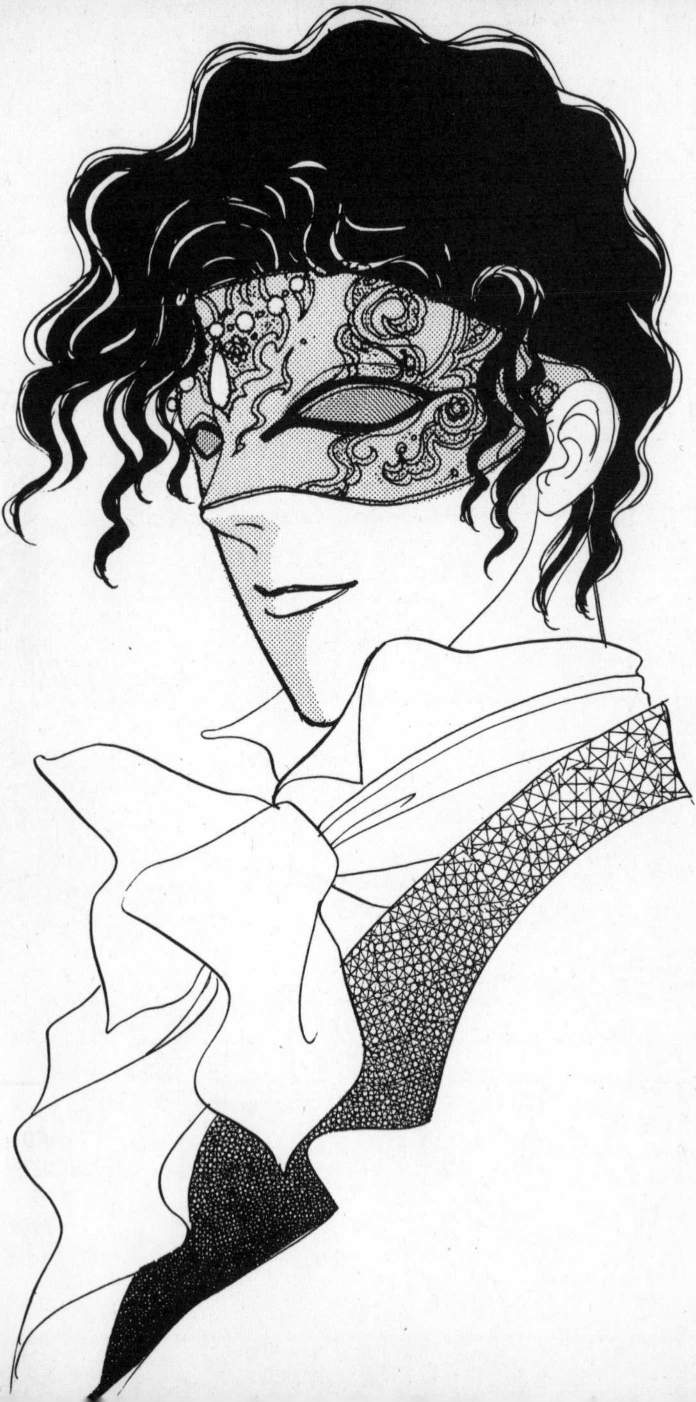

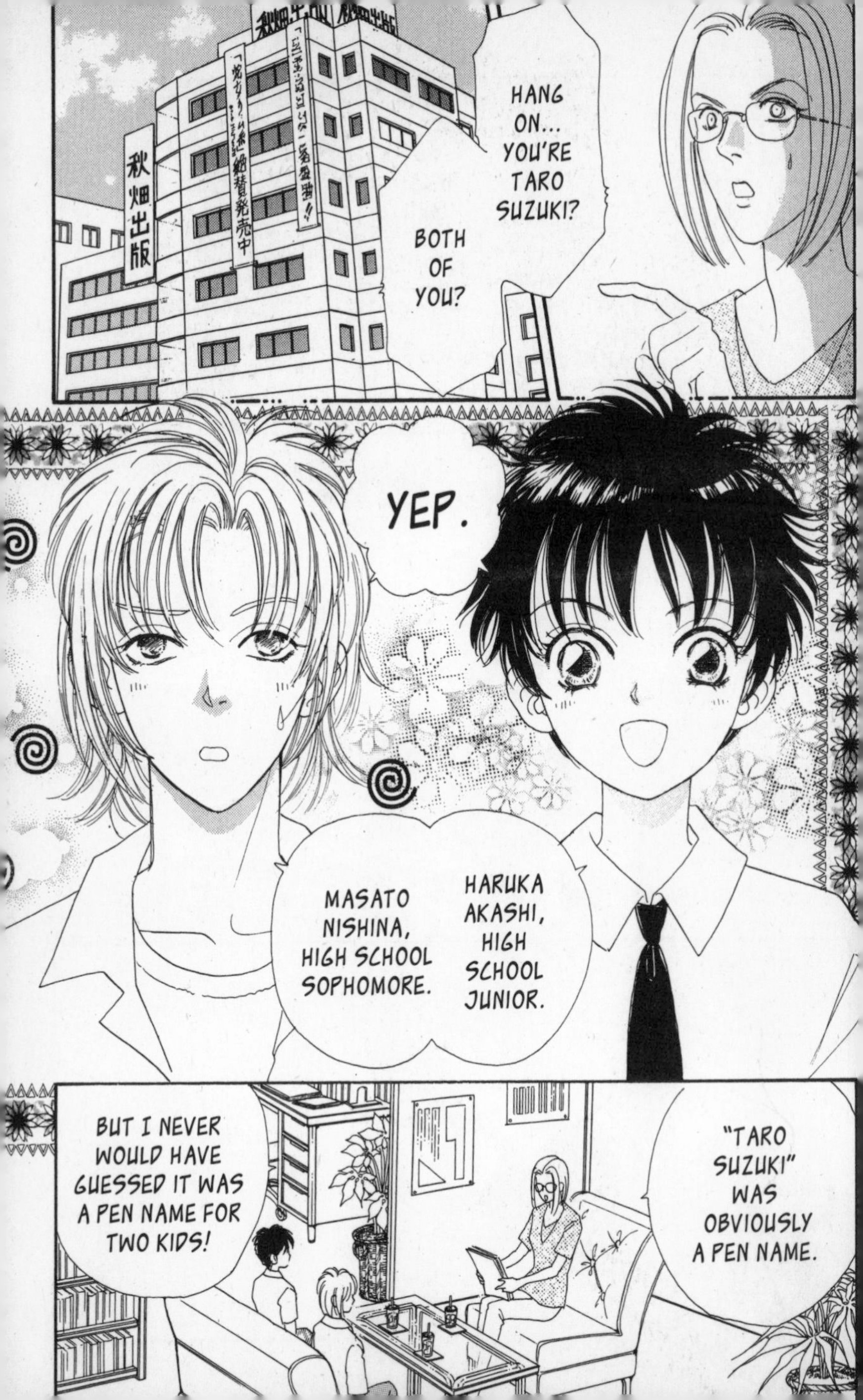

HANG ON... YOU'RE TARO SUZUKI?
BOTH OF YOU?
秋畑出版
YEP.
MASATO NISHINA, HIGH SCHOOL SOPHOMORE.
HARUKA AKASHI, HIGH SCHOOL JUNIOR.
"TARO SUZUKI" WAS OBVIOUSLY A PEN NAME.
BUT I NEVER WOULD HAVE GUESSED IT WAS A PEN NAME FOR TWO KIDS!

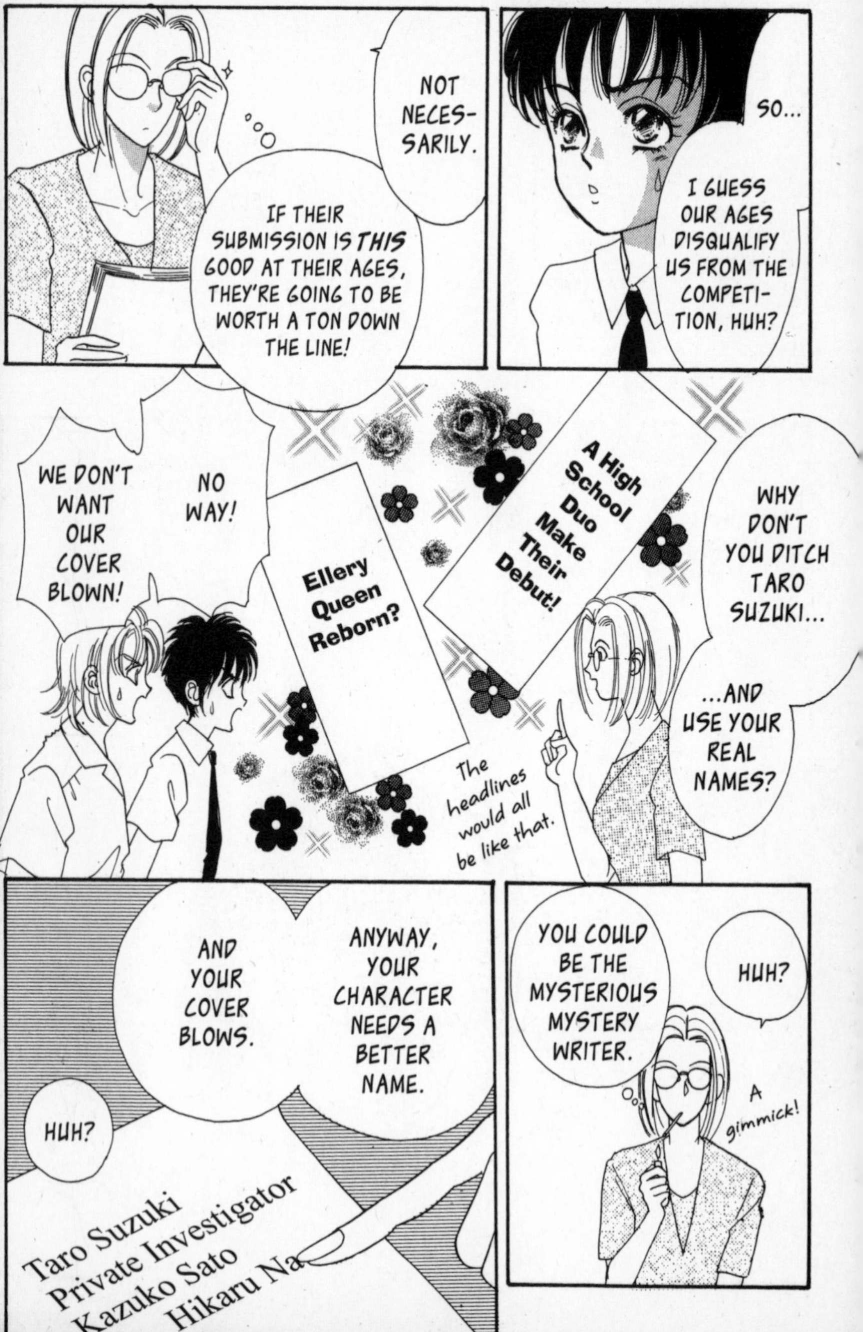
SO...
I GUESS OUR AGES DISQUALIFY US FROM THE COMPETITION, HUH?
NOT NECES-SARILY.
IF THEIR SUBMISSION IS *THIS* GOOD AT THEIR AGES, THEY'RE GOING TO BE WORTH A TON DOWN THE LINE!
WHY DON'T YOU DITCH TARO SUZUKI...
...AND USE YOUR REAL NAMES?
A High School Duo Make Their Debut!
Ellery Queen Reborn?
The headlines would all be like that.
NO WAY!
WE DON'T WANT OUR COVER BLOWN!
HUH?
YOU COULD BE THE MYSTERIOUS MYSTERY WRITER.
A gimmick!
ANYWAY, YOUR CHARACTER NEEDS A BETTER NAME.
AND YOUR COVER BLOWS.
HUH?
Taro Suzuki
Private Investigator
Kazuko Sato
Hikaru Na

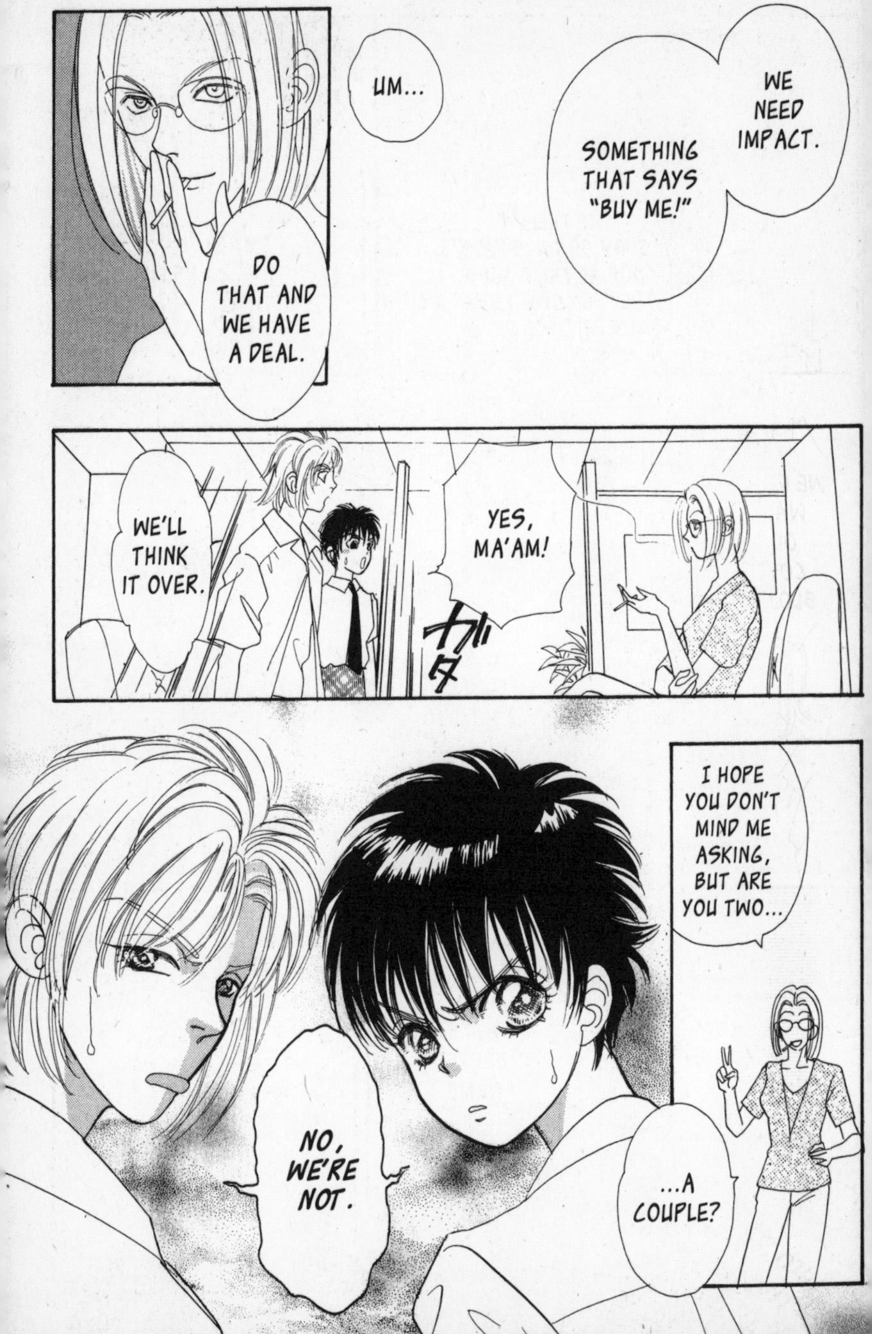
WE NEED IMPACT.
SOMETHING THAT SAYS "BUY ME!"
UM...
DO THAT AND WE HAVE A DEAL.
YES, MA'AM!
WE'LL THINK IT OVER.
ガタ
I HOPE YOU DON'T MIND ME ASKING, BUT ARE YOU TWO...
...A COUPLE?
NO, WE'RE NOT.

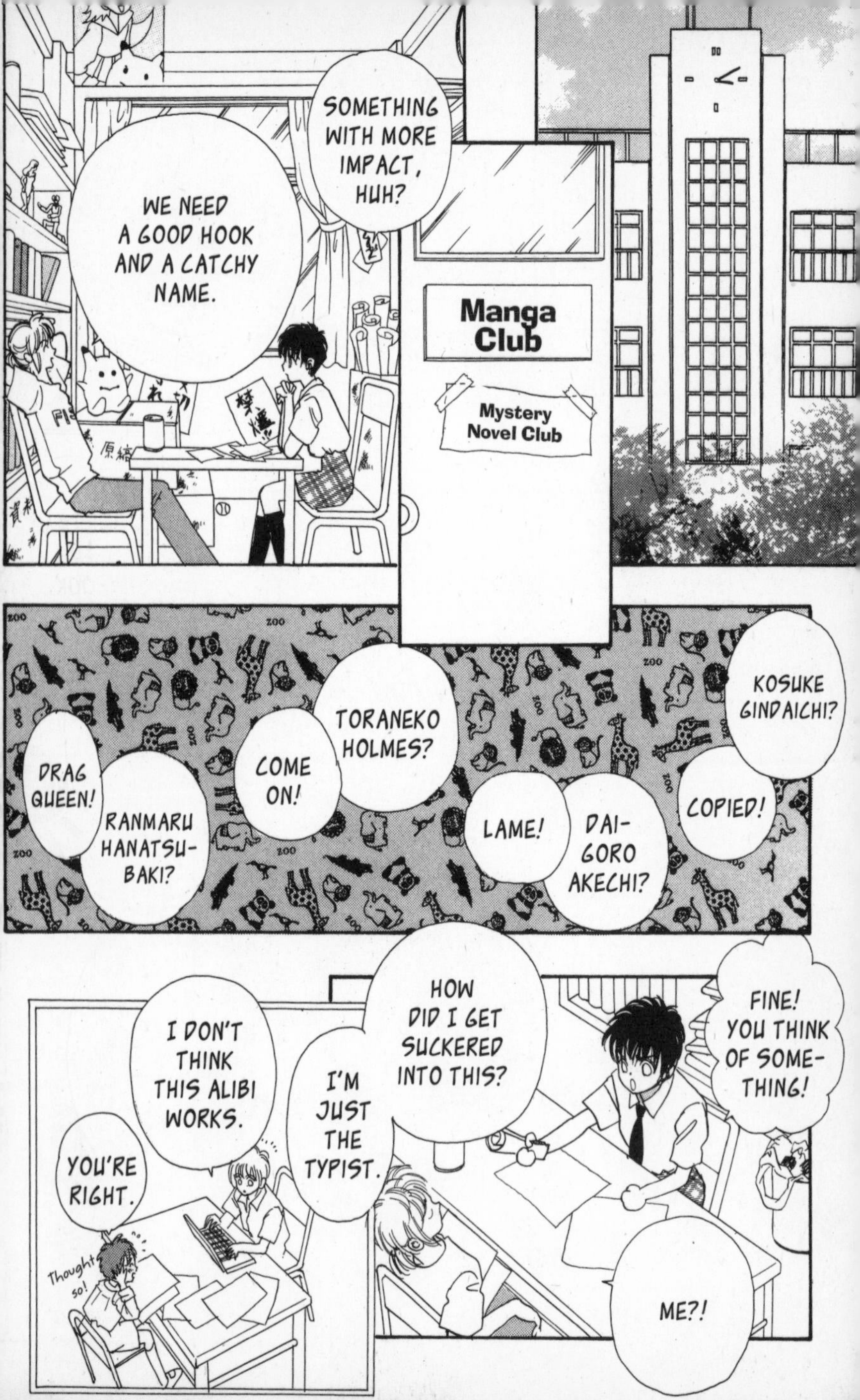
Manga Club
Mystery Novel Club
SOMETHING WITH MORE IMPACT, HUH?
WE NEED A GOOD HOOK AND A CATCHY NAME.
KOSUKE GINDAICHI?
COPIED!
DAI-GORO AKECHI?
LAME!
TORANEKO HOLMES?
COME ON!
RANMARU HANATSU-BAKI?
DRAG QUEEN!
FINE! YOU THINK OF SOME-THING!
HOW DID I GET SUCKERED INTO THIS?
ME?!
I DON'T THINK THIS ALIBI WORKS.
YOU'RE RIGHT.
Thought so!
I'M JUST THE TYPIST.

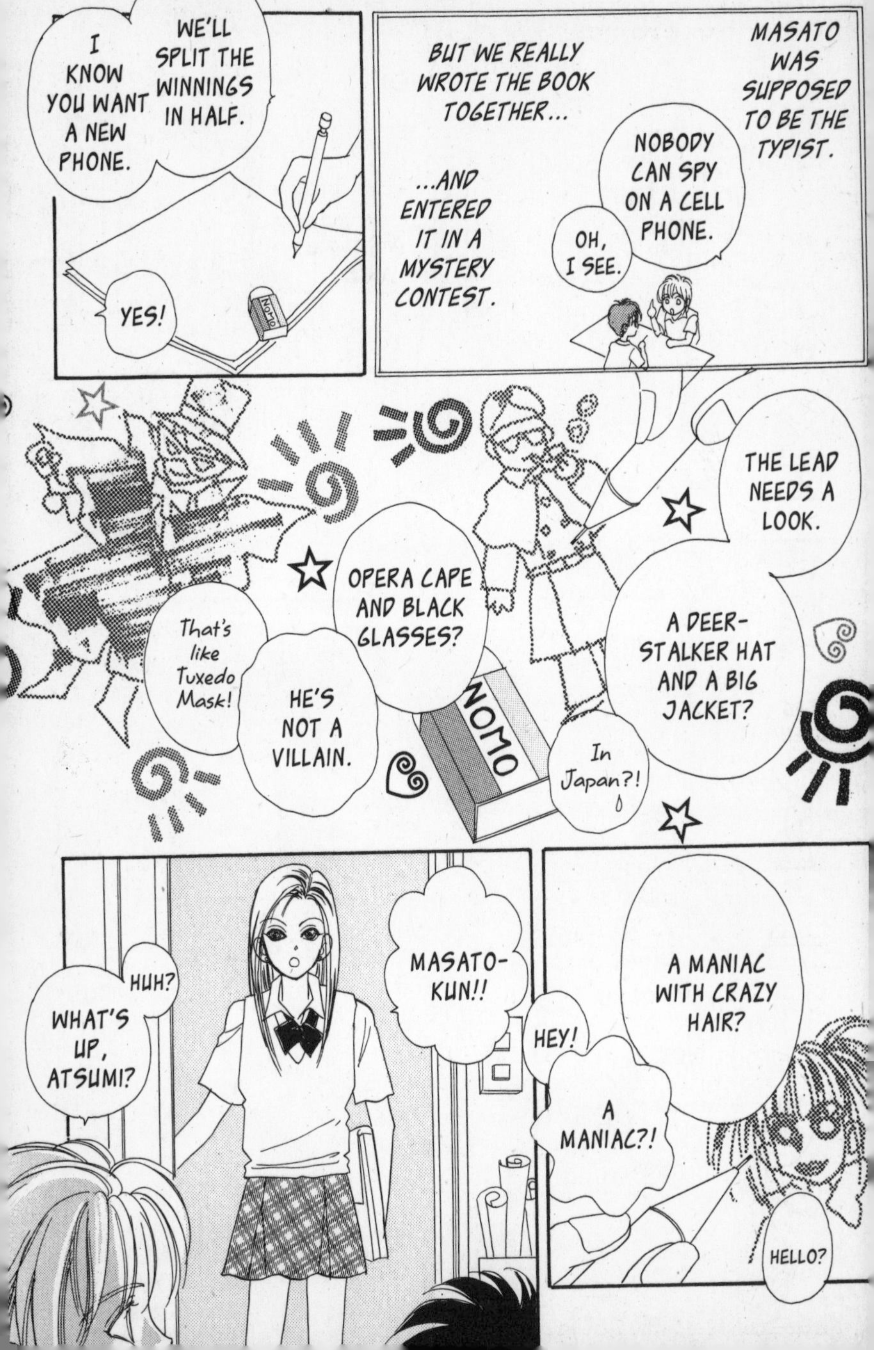
MASATO WAS SUPPOSED TO BE THE TYPIST.
BUT WE REALLY WROTE THE BOOK TOGETHER...
NOBODY CAN SPY ON A CELL PHONE.
OH, I SEE.
...AND ENTERED IT IN A MYSTERY CONTEST.
WE'LL SPLIT THE WINNINGS IN HALF.
I KNOW YOU WANT A NEW PHONE.
YES!
NOMO
THE LEAD NEEDS A LOOK.
A DEER-STALKER HAT AND A BIG JACKET?
In Japan?!
OPERA CAPE AND BLACK GLASSES?
NOMO
HE'S NOT A VILLAIN.
That's like Tuxedo Mask!
A MANIAC WITH CRAZY HAIR?
HEY!
A MANIAC?!
HELLO?
MASATO-KUN!!
HUH?
WHAT'S UP, ATSUMI?

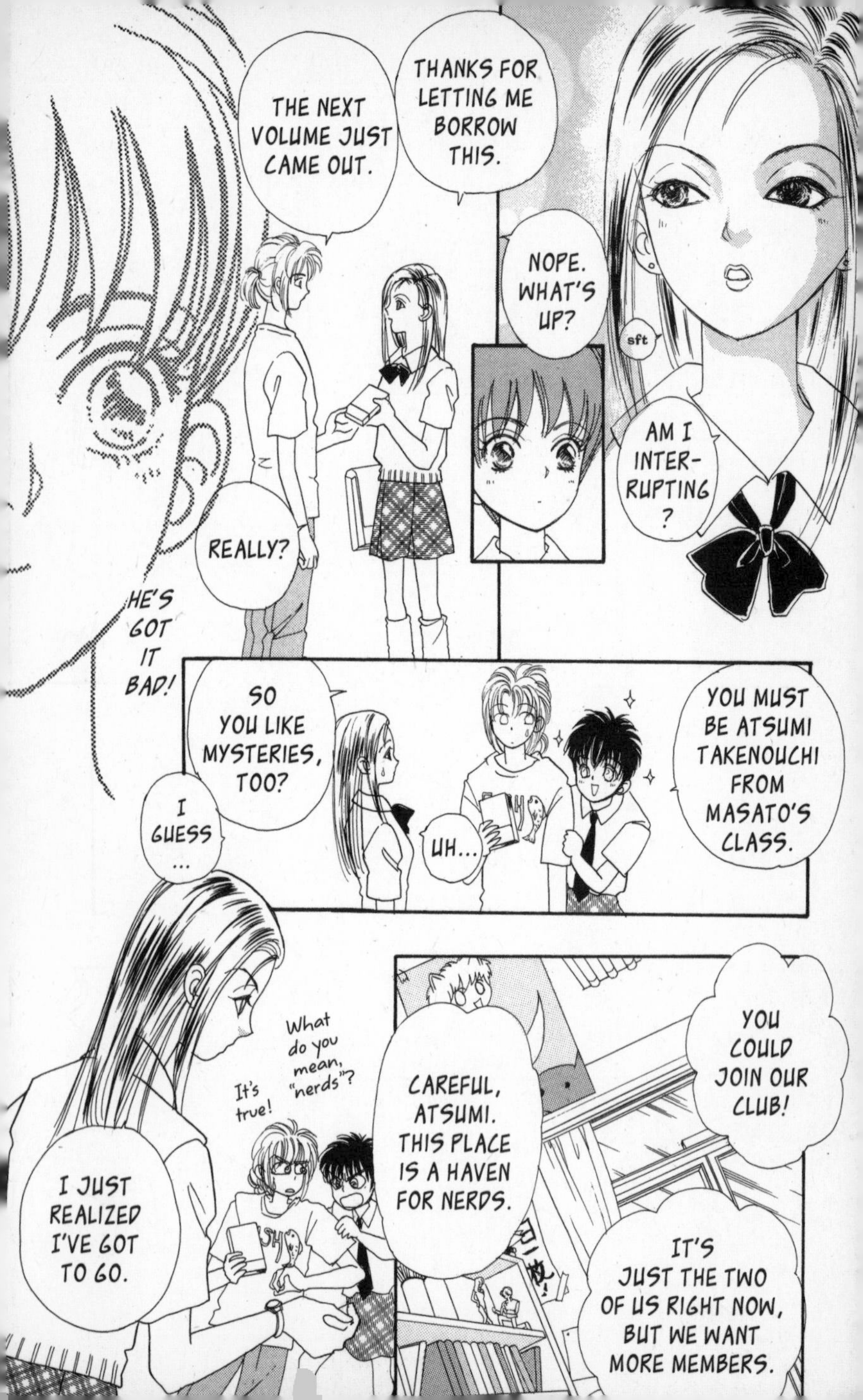
AM I INTER-RUPTING?
sft
NOPE. WHAT'S UP?
THANKS FOR LETTING ME BORROW THIS.
THE NEXT VOLUME JUST CAME OUT.
REALLY?
HE'S GOT IT BAD!
YOU MUST BE ATSUMI TAKENOUCHI FROM MASATO'S CLASS.
SO YOU LIKE MYSTERIES, TOO?
UH...
I GUESS...
YOU COULD JOIN OUR CLUB!
IT'S JUST THE TWO OF US RIGHT NOW, BUT WE WANT MORE MEMBERS.
CAREFUL, ATSUMI. THIS PLACE IS A HAVEN FOR NERDS.
What do you mean, "nerds"?
It's true!
I JUST REALIZED I'VE GOT TO GO.

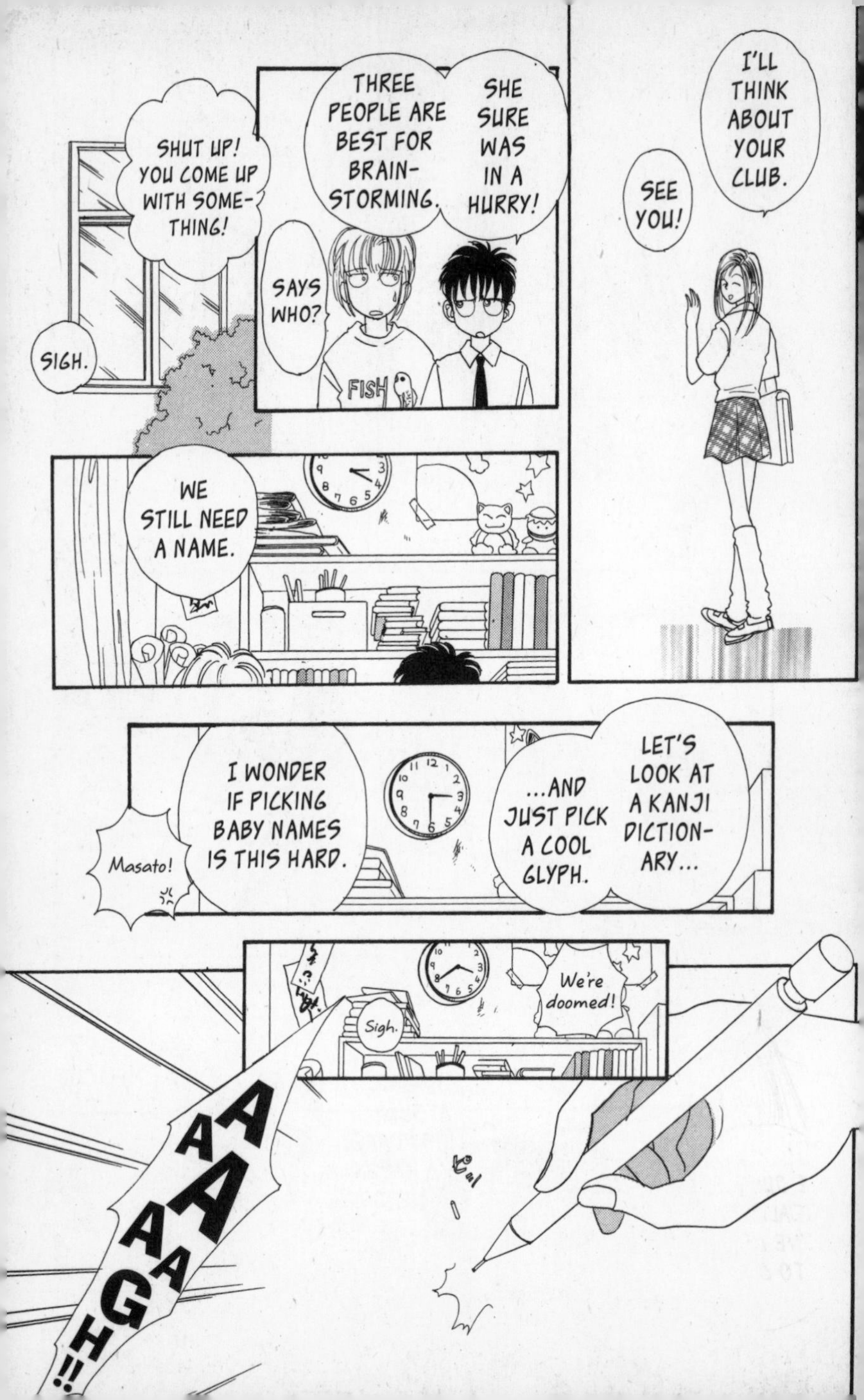
I'LL THINK ABOUT YOUR CLUB.
SEE YOU!
SHE SURE WAS IN A HURRY!
THREE PEOPLE ARE BEST FOR BRAIN-STORMING.
SAYS WHO?
SHUT UP! YOU COME UP WITH SOME-THING!
SIGH.
FISH
WE STILL NEED A NAME.
LET'S LOOK AT A KANJI DICTION-ARY...
...AND JUST PICK A COOL GLYPH.
I WONDER IF PICKING BABY NAMES IS THIS HARD.
Masato!
We're doomed!
Sigh.
AAAAAAGH!!

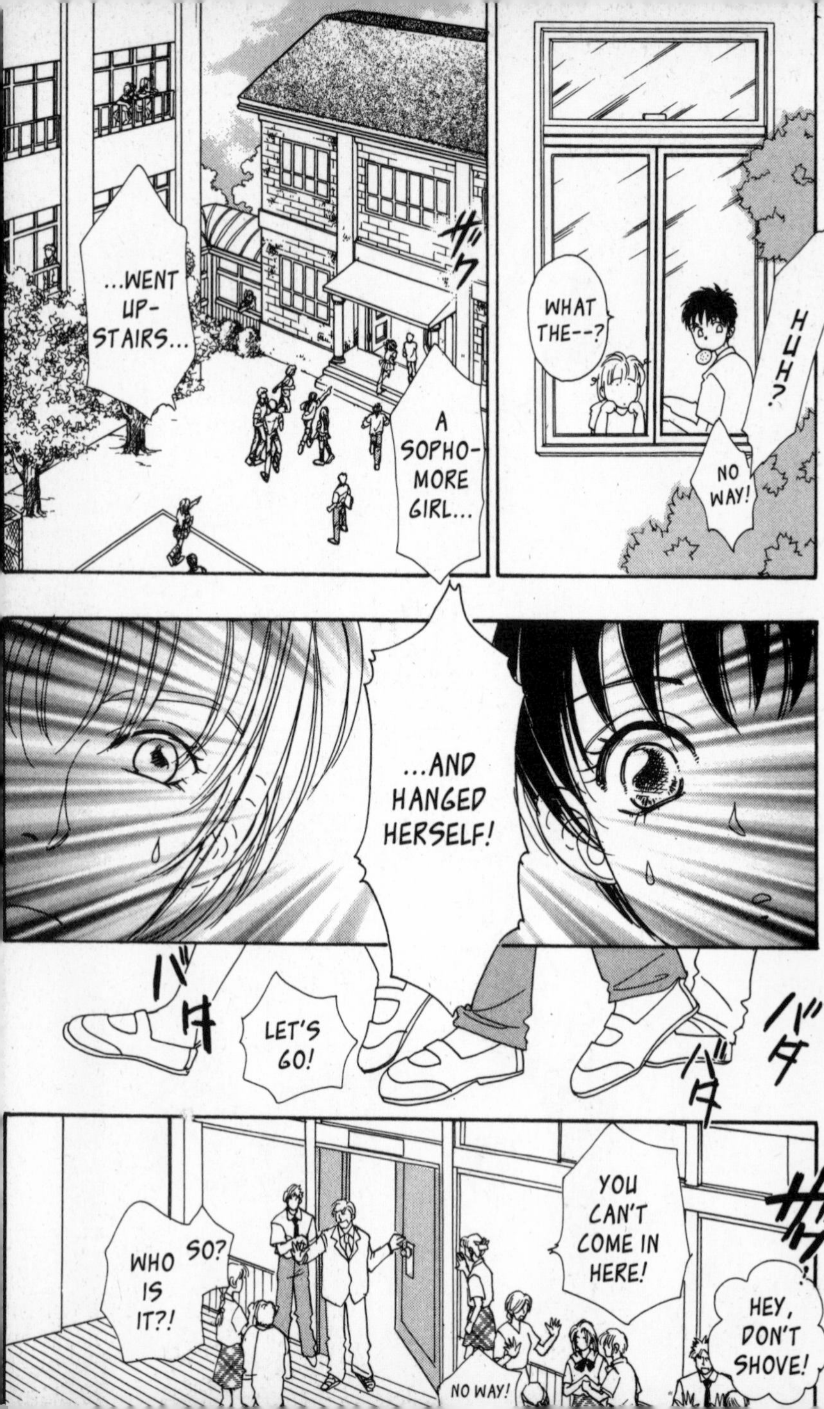
HUH?
WHAT THE--?
NO WAY!
ザワ
A SOPHO-MORE GIRL...
...WENT UP-STAIRS...
...AND HANGED HERSELF!
バタバタ
LET'S GO!
バッ
ザワッ
YOU CAN'T COME IN HERE!
HEY, DON'T SHOVE!
NO WAY!
SO?
WHO IS IT?!

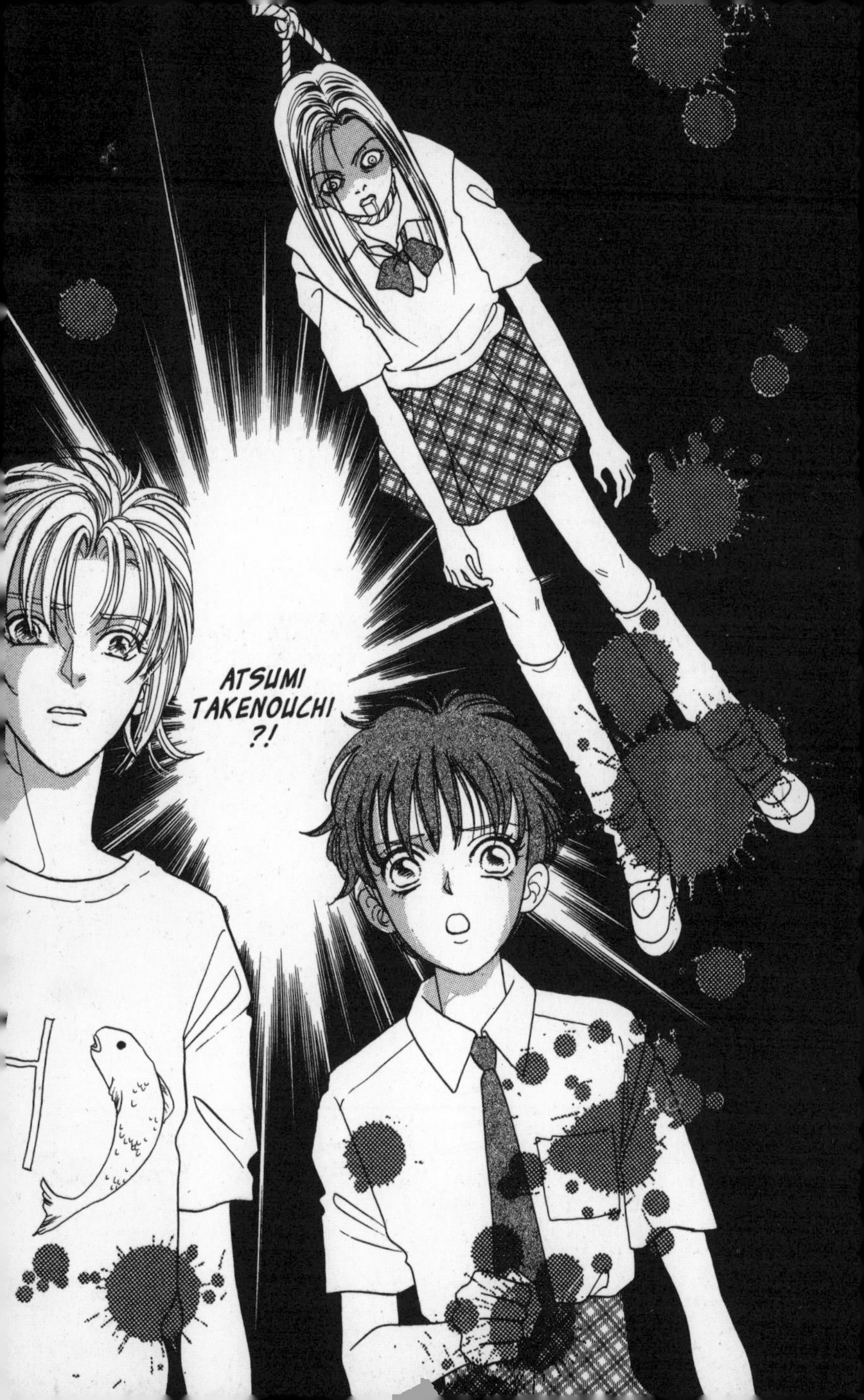
ATSUMI TAKENOUCHI ?!

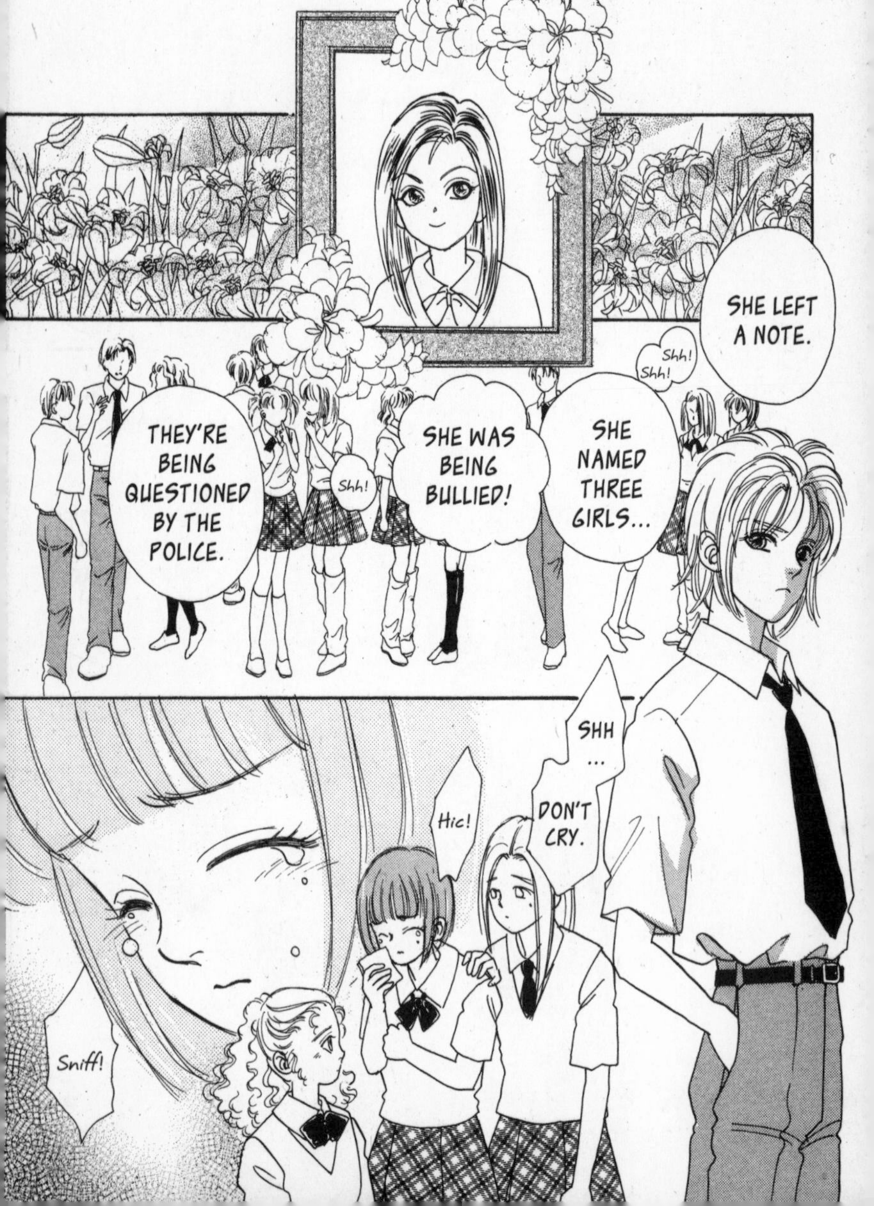
SHE LEFT A NOTE.
Shh! Shh!
SHE NAMED THREE GIRLS...
SHE WAS BEING BULLIED!
Shh!
THEY'RE BEING QUESTIONED BY THE POLICE.
SHH ...
DON'T CRY.
Hic!
Sniff!

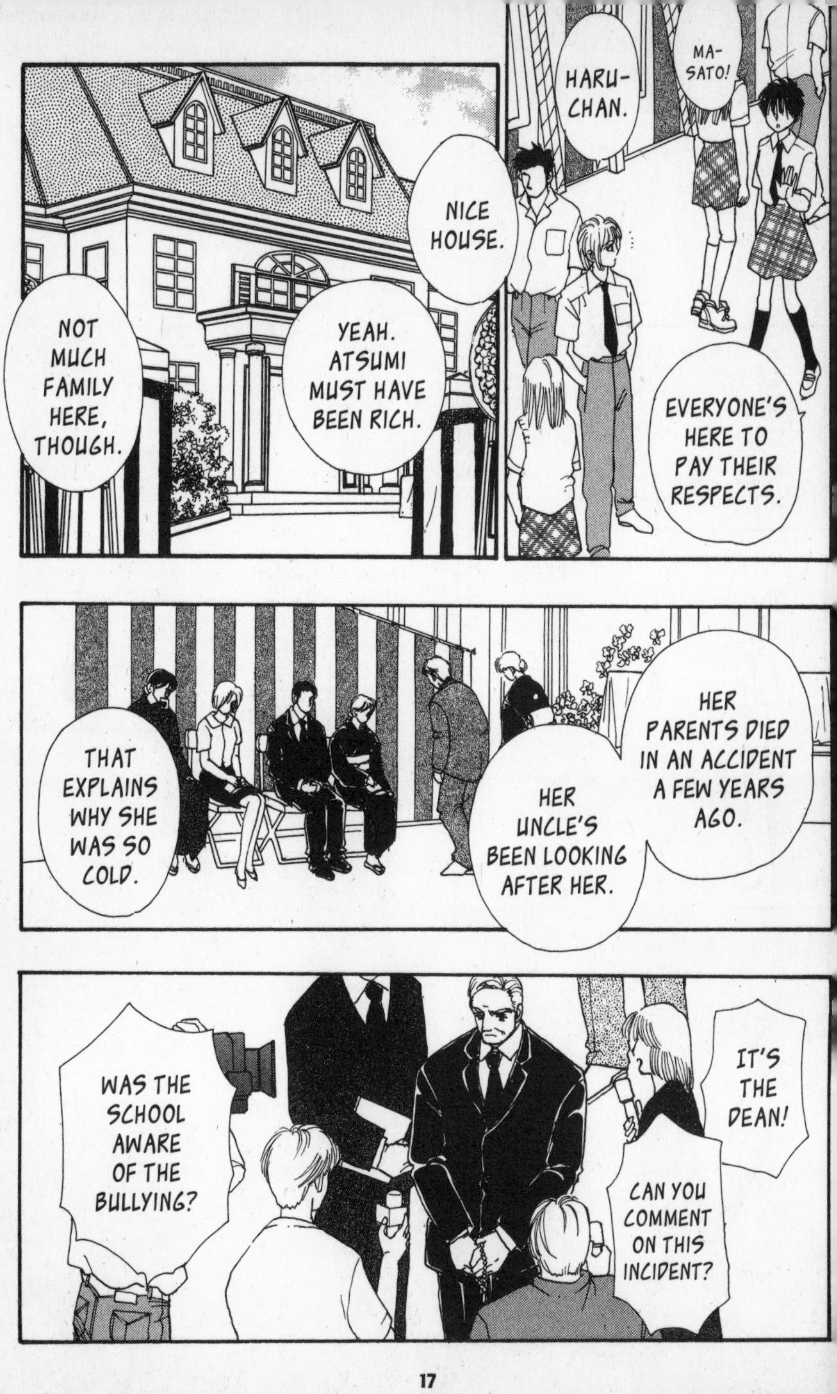
MA-SATO!
HARU-CHAN.
EVERYONE'S HERE TO PAY THEIR RESPECTS.
NICE HOUSE.
YEAH. ATSUMI MUST HAVE BEEN RICH.
NOT MUCH FAMILY HERE, THOUGH.
HER PARENTS DIED IN AN ACCIDENT A FEW YEARS AGO.
HER UNCLE'S BEEN LOOKING AFTER HER.
THAT EXPLAINS WHY SHE WAS SO COLD.
IT'S THE DEAN!
CAN YOU COMMENT ON THIS INCIDENT?
WAS THE SCHOOL AWARE OF THE BULLYING?

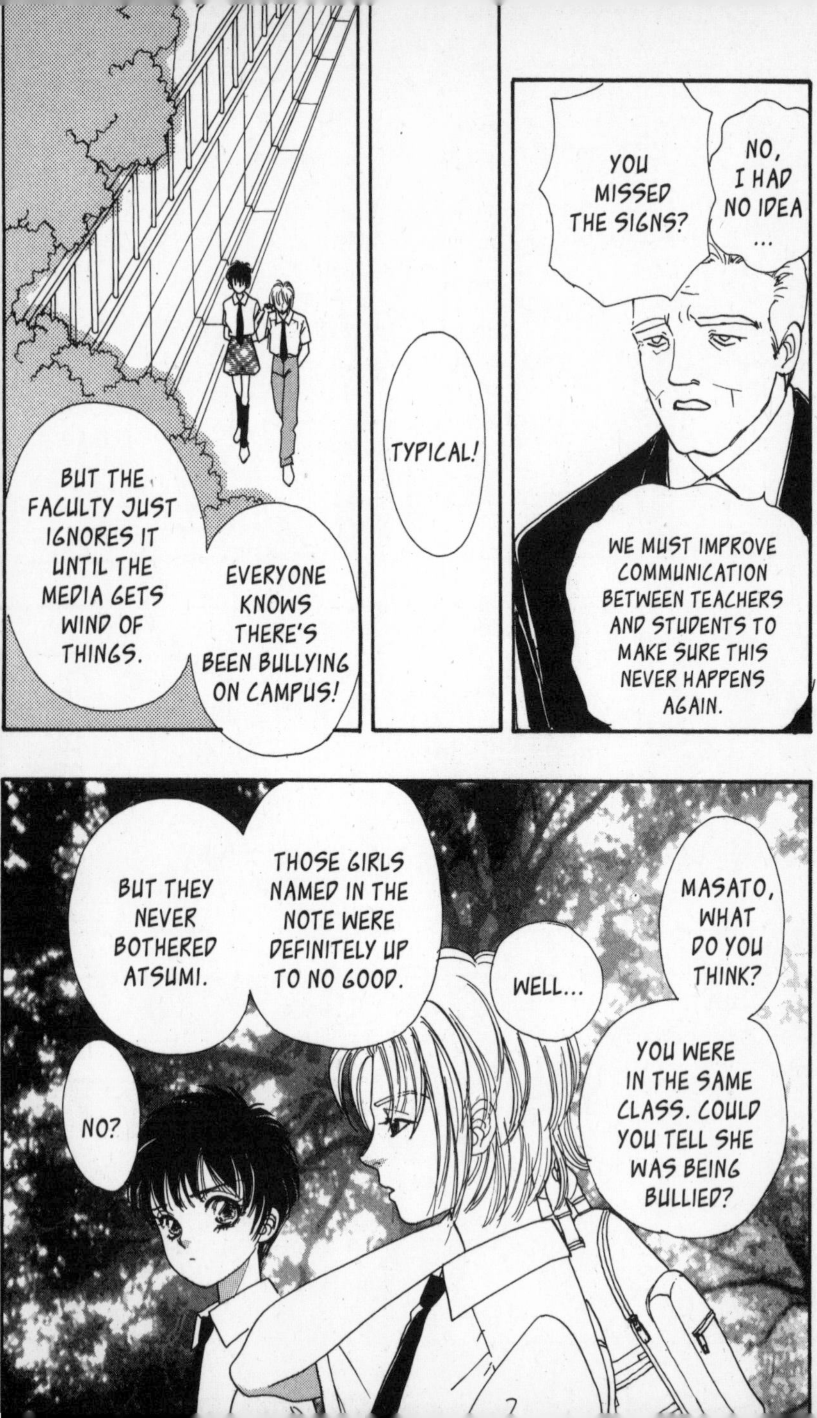
YOU MISSED THE SIGNS?
NO, I HAD NO IDEA ...
WE MUST IMPROVE COMMUNICATION BETWEEN TEACHERS AND STUDENTS TO MAKE SURE THIS NEVER HAPPENS AGAIN.
TYPICAL!
EVERYONE KNOWS THERE'S BEEN BULLYING ON CAMPUS!
BUT THE FACULTY JUST IGNORES IT UNTIL THE MEDIA GETS WIND OF THINGS.
MASATO, WHAT DO YOU THINK?
YOU WERE IN THE SAME CLASS. COULD YOU TELL SHE WAS BEING BULLIED?
WELL...
THOSE GIRLS NAMED IN THE NOTE WERE DEFINITELY UP TO NO GOOD.
BUT THEY NEVER BOTHERED ATSUMI.
NO?

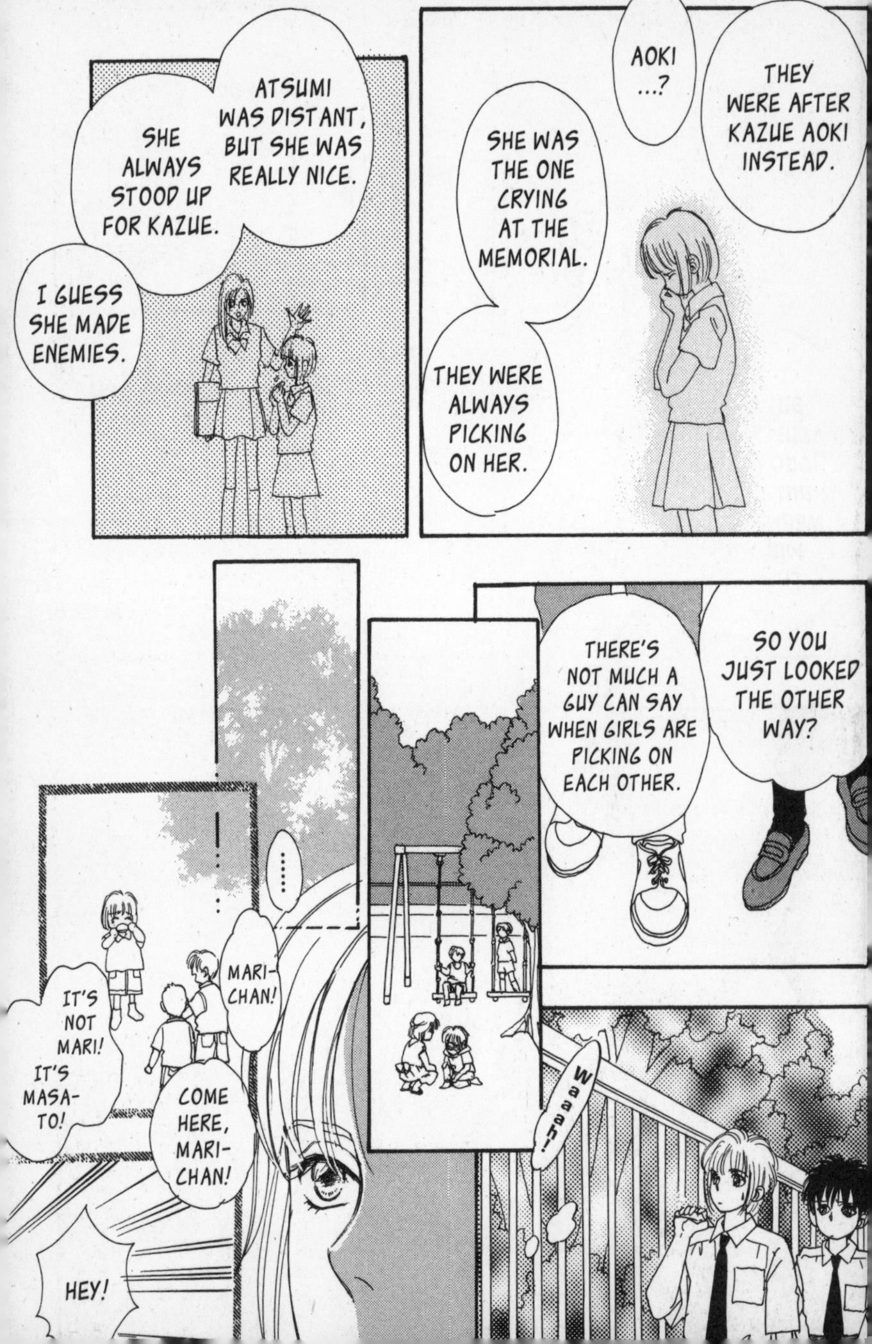
THEY WERE AFTER KAZUE AOKI INSTEAD.
AOKI ...?
SHE WAS THE ONE CRYING AT THE MEMORIAL.
THEY WERE ALWAYS PICKING ON HER.
ATSUMI WAS DISTANT, BUT SHE WAS REALLY NICE.
SHE ALWAYS STOOD UP FOR KAZUE.
I GUESS SHE MADE ENEMIES.
SO YOU JUST LOOKED THE OTHER WAY?
THERE'S NOT MUCH A GUY CAN SAY WHEN GIRLS ARE PICKING ON EACH OTHER.
Waaah!
!...
......
MARI-CHAN!
IT'S NOT MARI! IT'S MASATO!
COME HERE, MARI-CHAN!
HEY!

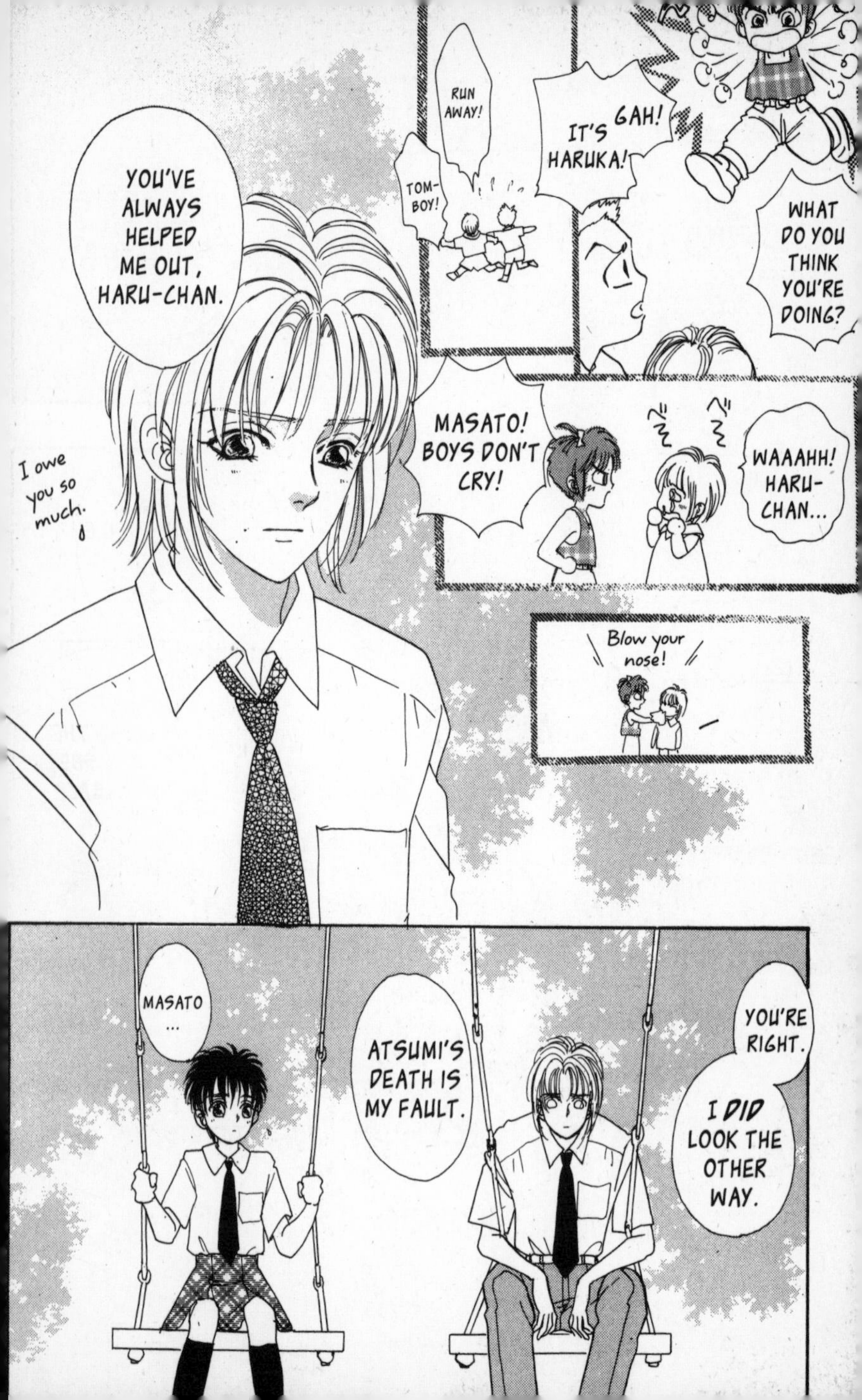
GAH! IT'S HARUKA!
WHAT DO YOU THINK YOU'RE DOING?
RUN AWAY!
TOM-BOY!
WAAAHH! HARU-CHAN...
MASATO! BOYS DON'T CRY!
Blow your nose!
YOU'VE ALWAYS HELPED ME OUT, HARU-CHAN.
I owe you so much.
YOU'RE RIGHT.
I *DID* LOOK THE OTHER WAY.
ATSUMI'S DEATH IS MY FAULT.
MASATO ...

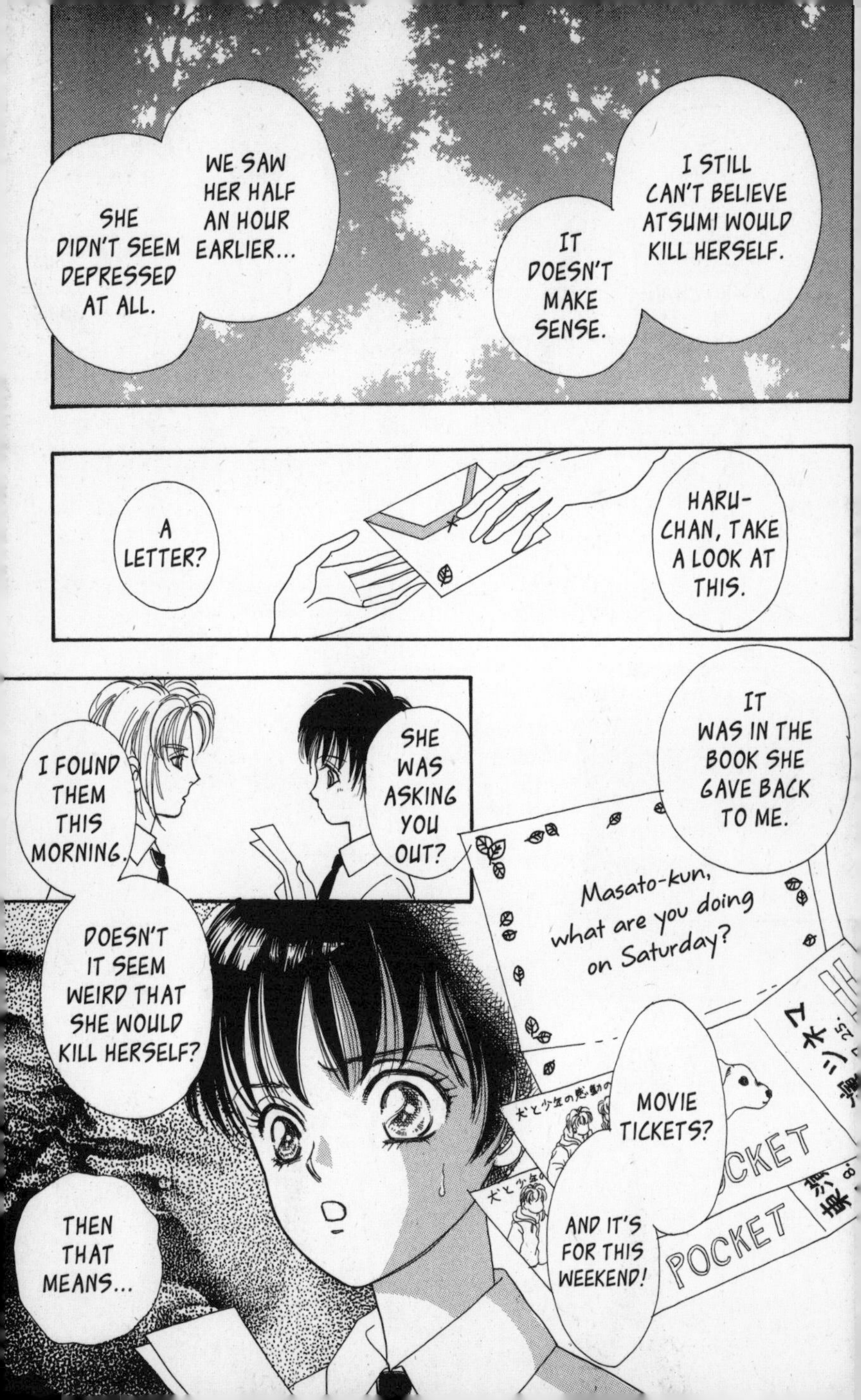
I STILL CAN'T BELIEVE ATSUMI WOULD KILL HERSELF.
IT DOESN'T MAKE SENSE.
WE SAW HER HALF AN HOUR EARLIER...
SHE DIDN'T SEEM DEPRESSED AT ALL.
HARU-CHAN, TAKE A LOOK AT THIS.
A LETTER?
IT WAS IN THE BOOK SHE GAVE BACK TO ME.
Masato-kun, what are you doing on Saturday?
SHE WAS ASKING YOU OUT?
I FOUND THEM THIS MORNING.
MOVIE TICKETS?
AND IT'S FOR THIS WEEKEND!
POCKET
POCKET
DOESN'T IT SEEM WEIRD THAT SHE WOULD KILL HERSELF?
THEN THAT MEANS...

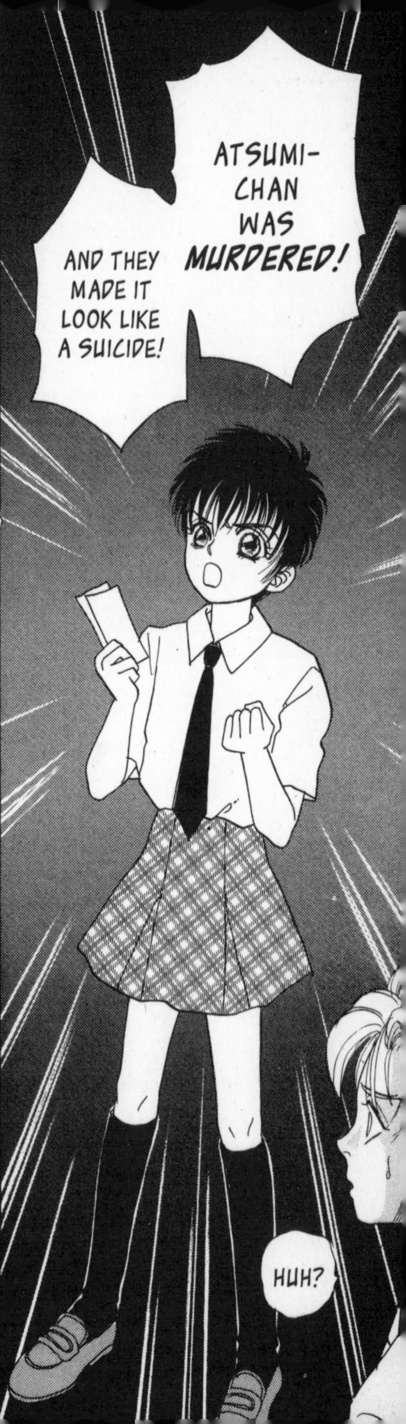
ATSUMI-CHAN WAS MURDERED!
AND THEY MADE IT LOOK LIKE A SUICIDE!
HUH?

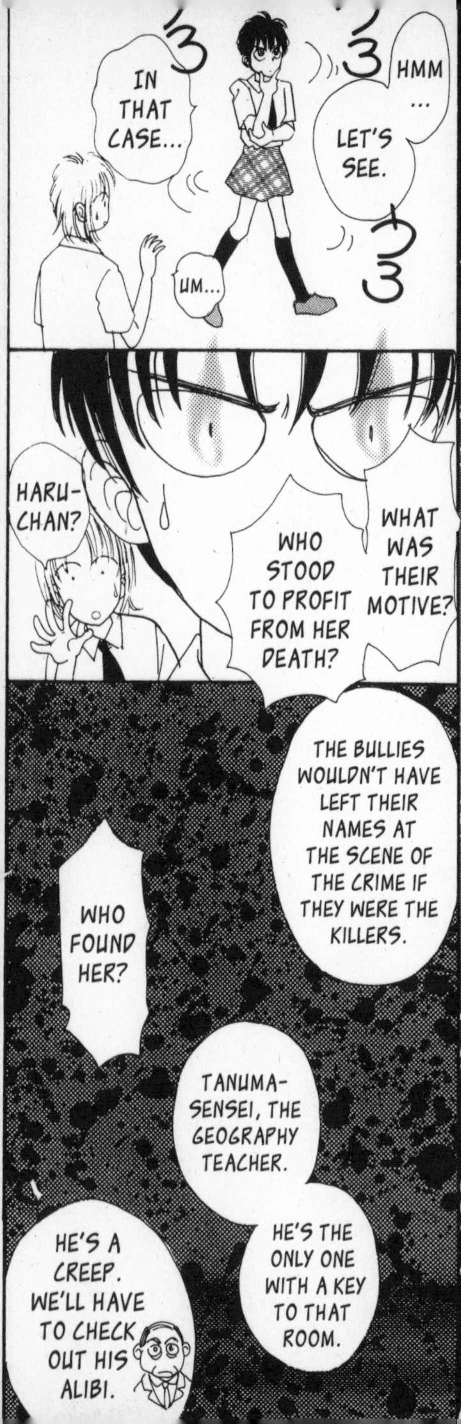
HMM ... LET'S SEE.
IN THAT CASE...
UM...
WHAT WAS THEIR MOTIVE?
WHO STOOD TO PROFIT FROM HER DEATH?
HARU-CHAN?
THE BULLIES WOULDN'T HAVE LEFT THEIR NAMES AT THE SCENE OF THE CRIME IF THEY WERE THE KILLERS.
WHO FOUND HER?
TANUMA-SENSEI, THE GEOGRAPHY TEACHER.
HE'S THE ONLY ONE WITH A KEY TO THAT ROOM.
HE'S A CREEP. WE'LL HAVE TO CHECK OUT HIS ALIBI.

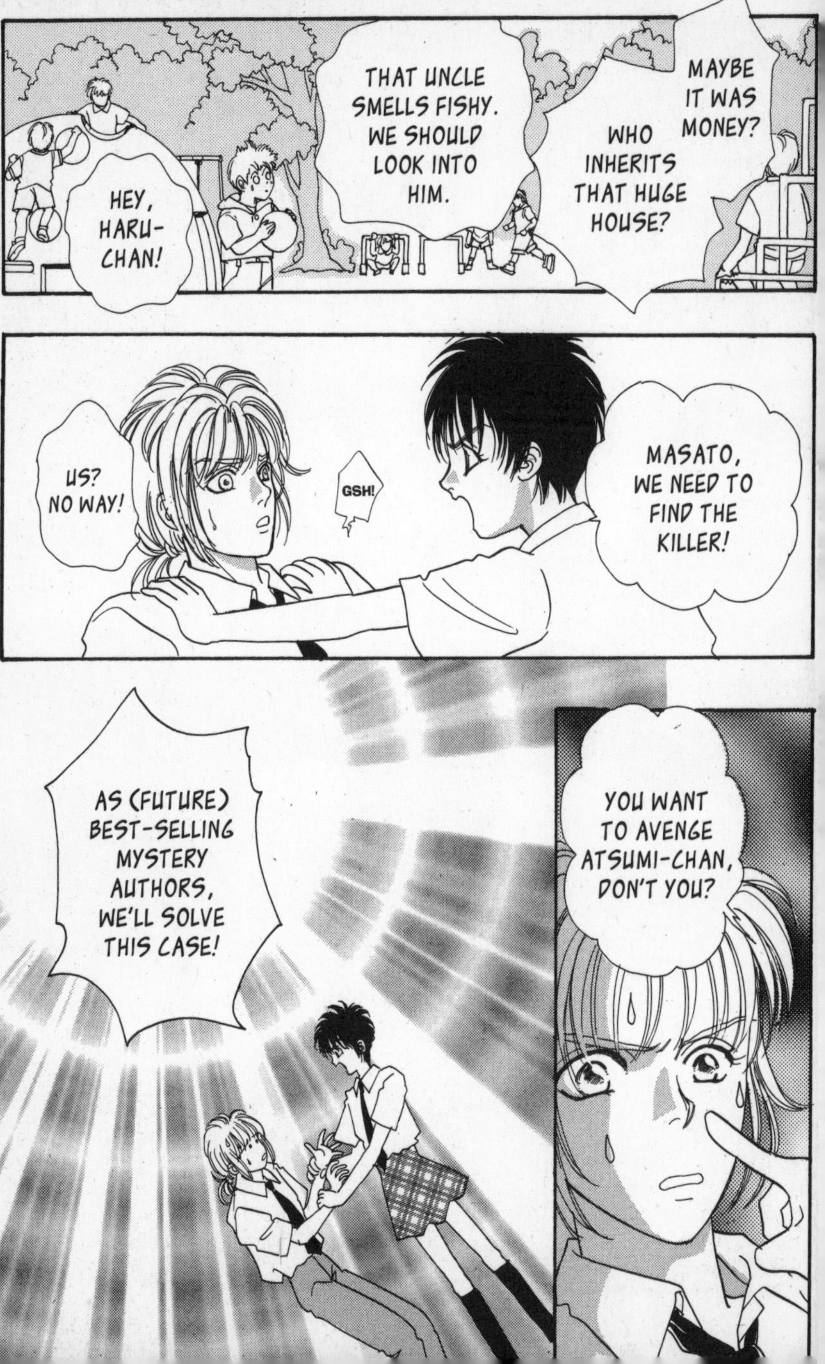
MAYBE IT WAS MONEY?
WHO INHERITS THAT HUGE HOUSE?
THAT UNCLE SMELLS FISHY. WE SHOULD LOOK INTO HIM.
HEY, HARU-CHAN!
MASATO, WE NEED TO FIND THE KILLER!
GSH!
US? NO WAY!
YOU WANT TO AVENGE ATSUMI-CHAN, DON'T YOU?
AS (FUTURE) BEST-SELLING MYSTERY AUTHORS, WE'LL SOLVE THIS CASE!

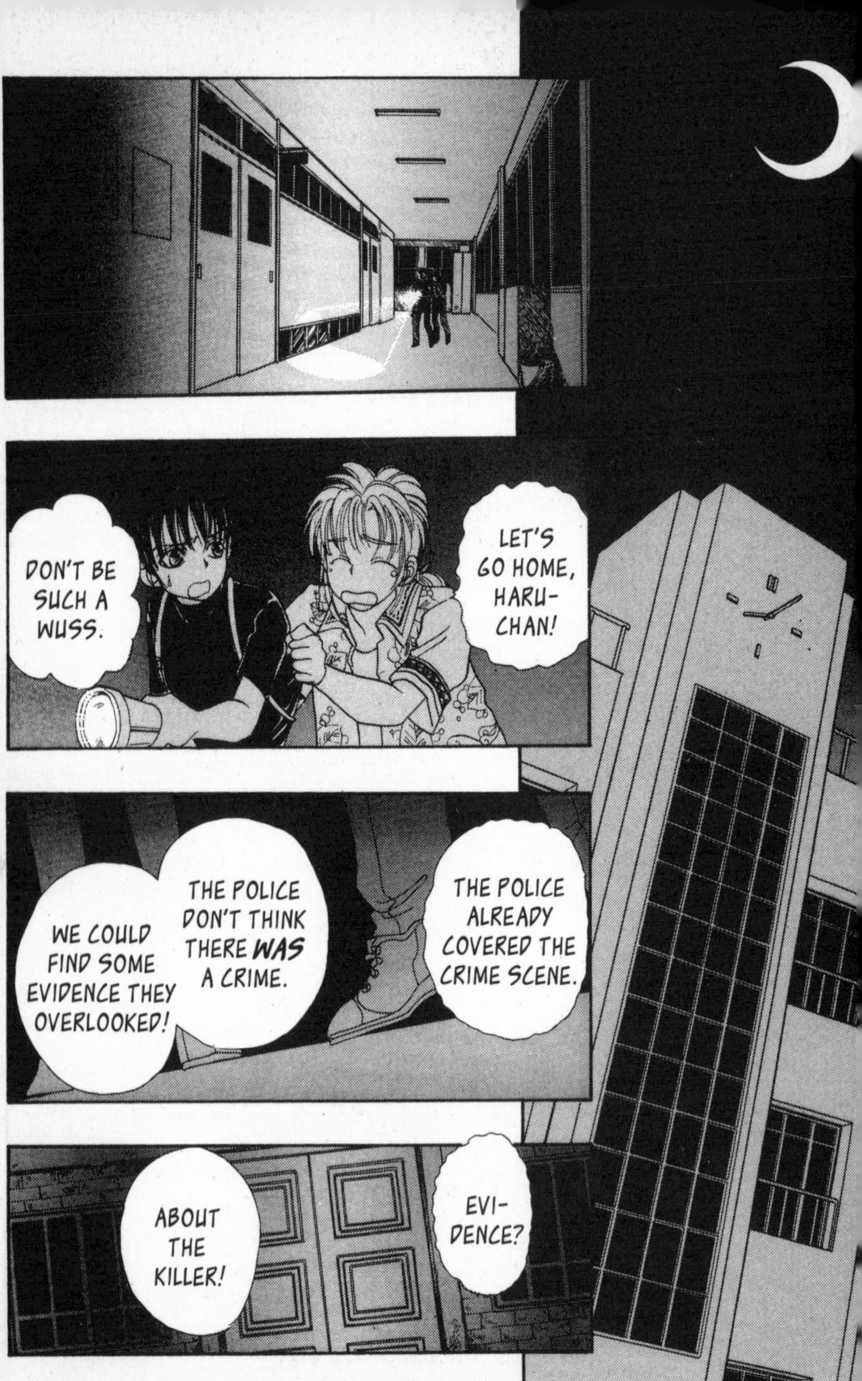
LET'S GO HOME, HARU-CHAN!
DON'T BE SUCH A WUSS.
THE POLICE ALREADY COVERED THE CRIME SCENE.
THE POLICE DON'T THINK THERE *WAS* A CRIME.
WE COULD FIND SOME EVIDENCE THEY OVERLOOKED!
EVI-DENCE?
ABOUT THE KILLER!

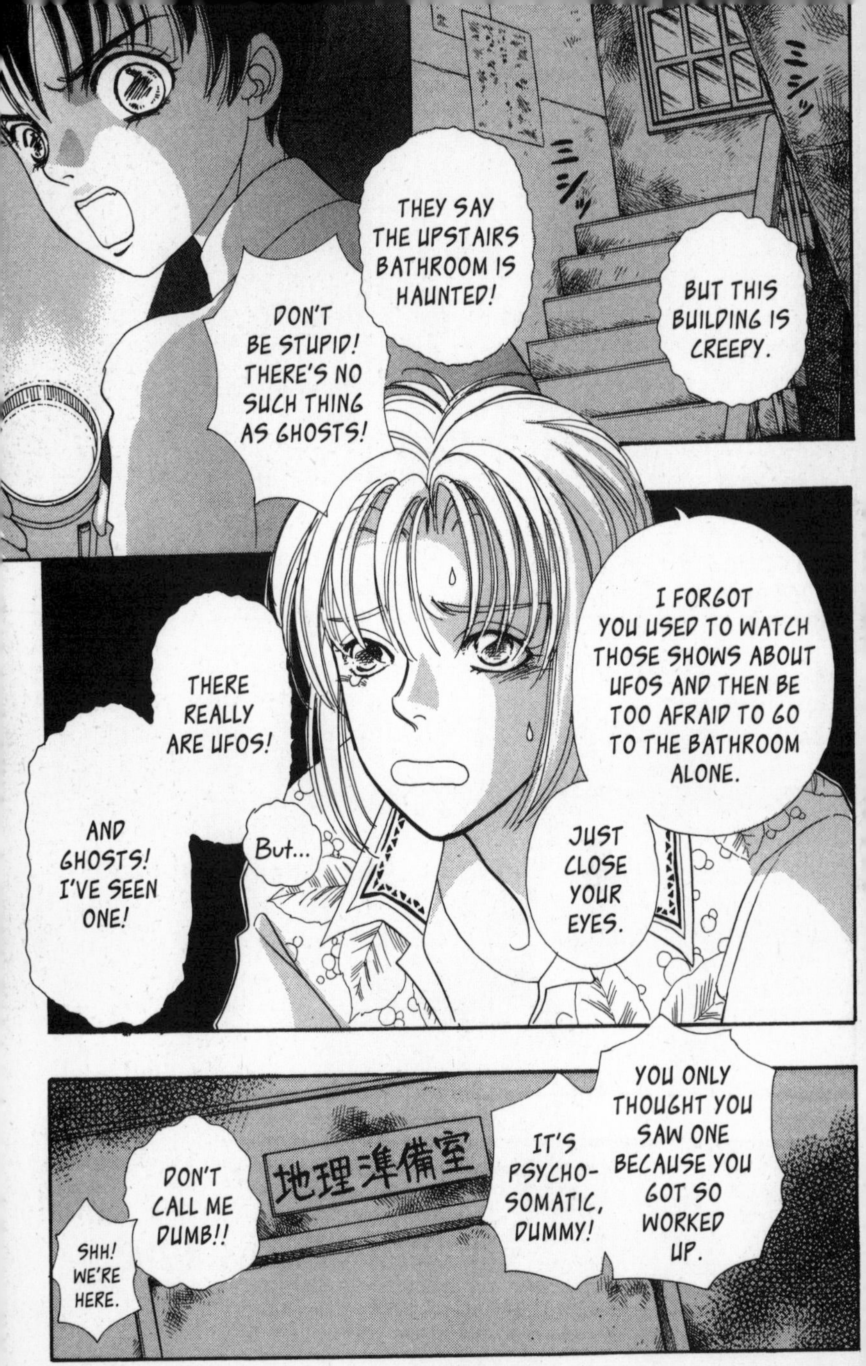

ミシッ
ミシッ
BUT THIS BUILDING IS CREEPY.
THEY SAY THE UPSTAIRS BATHROOM IS HAUNTED!
DON'T BE STUPID! THERE'S NO SUCH THING AS GHOSTS!
I FORGOT YOU USED TO WATCH THOSE SHOWS ABOUT UFOS AND THEN BE TOO AFRAID TO GO TO THE BATHROOM ALONE.
JUST CLOSE YOUR EYES.
But...
THERE REALLY ARE UFOS!
AND GHOSTS! I'VE SEEN ONE!
YOU ONLY THOUGHT YOU SAW ONE BECAUSE YOU GOT SO WORKED UP.
IT'S PSYCHO-SOMATIC, DUMMY!
地理準備室
DON'T CALL ME DUMB!!
SHH! WE'RE HERE.

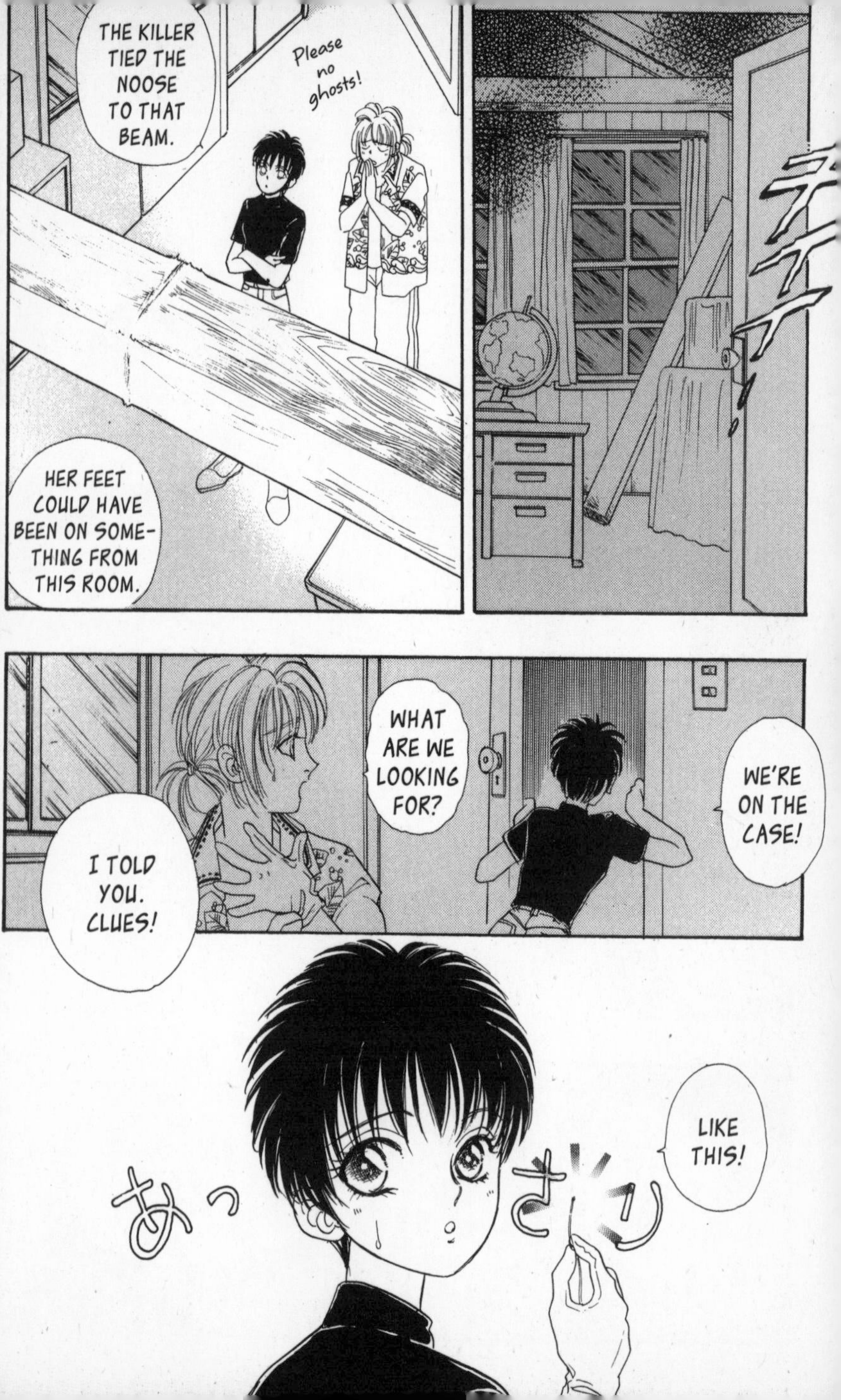
Please no ghosts!
THE KILLER TIED THE NOOSE TO THAT BEAM.
HER FEET COULD HAVE BEEN ON SOME-THING FROM THIS ROOM.
WE'RE ON THE CASE!
WHAT ARE WE LOOKING FOR?
I TOLD YOU. CLUES!
LIKE THIS!
あっさり

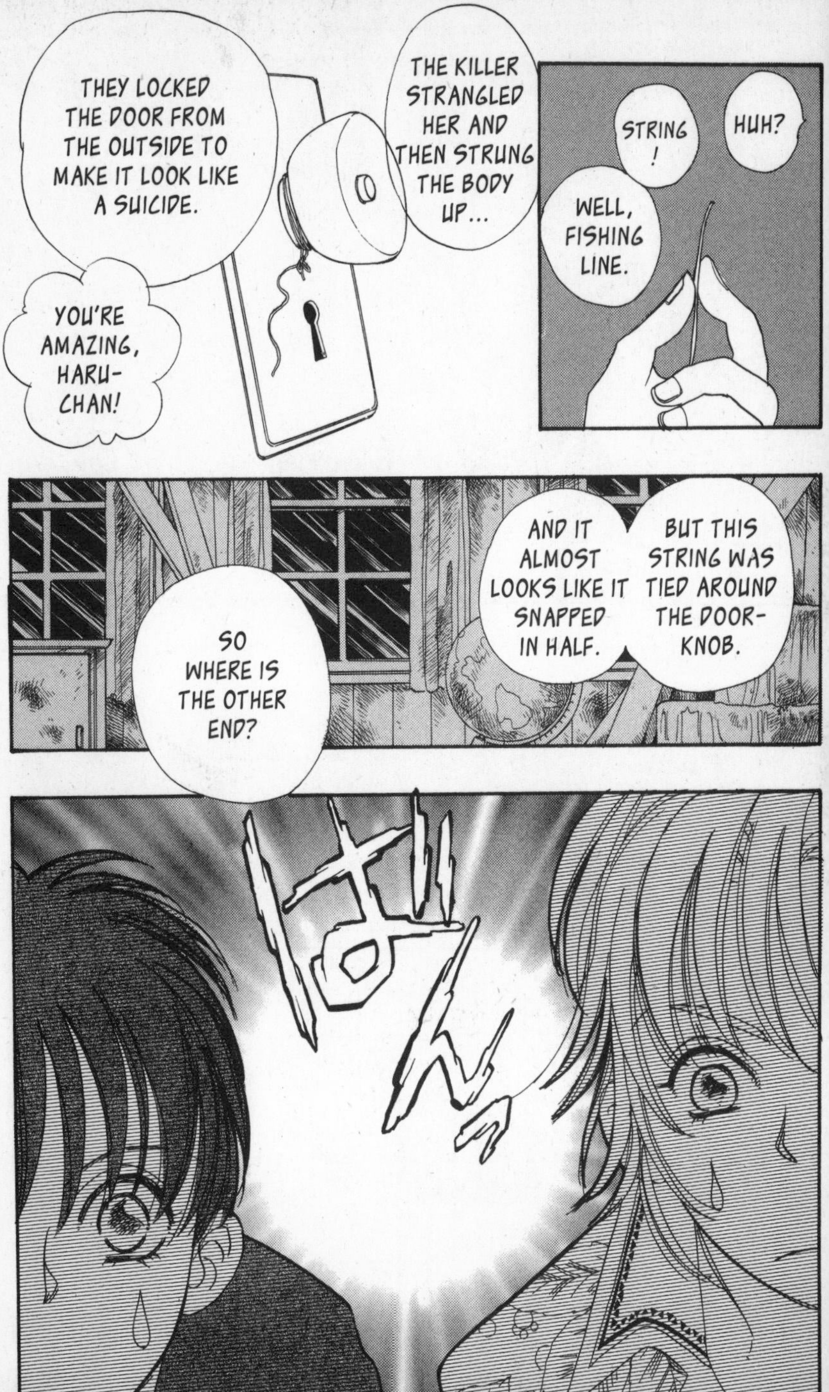
HUH?
STRING!
WELL, FISHING LINE.
THE KILLER STRANGLED HER AND THEN STRUNG THE BODY UP...
THEY LOCKED THE DOOR FROM THE OUTSIDE TO MAKE IT LOOK LIKE A SUICIDE.
YOU'RE AMAZING, HARU-CHAN!
BUT THIS STRING WAS TIED AROUND THE DOOR-KNOB.
AND IT ALMOST LOOKS LIKE IT SNAPPED IN HALF.
SO WHERE IS THE OTHER END?

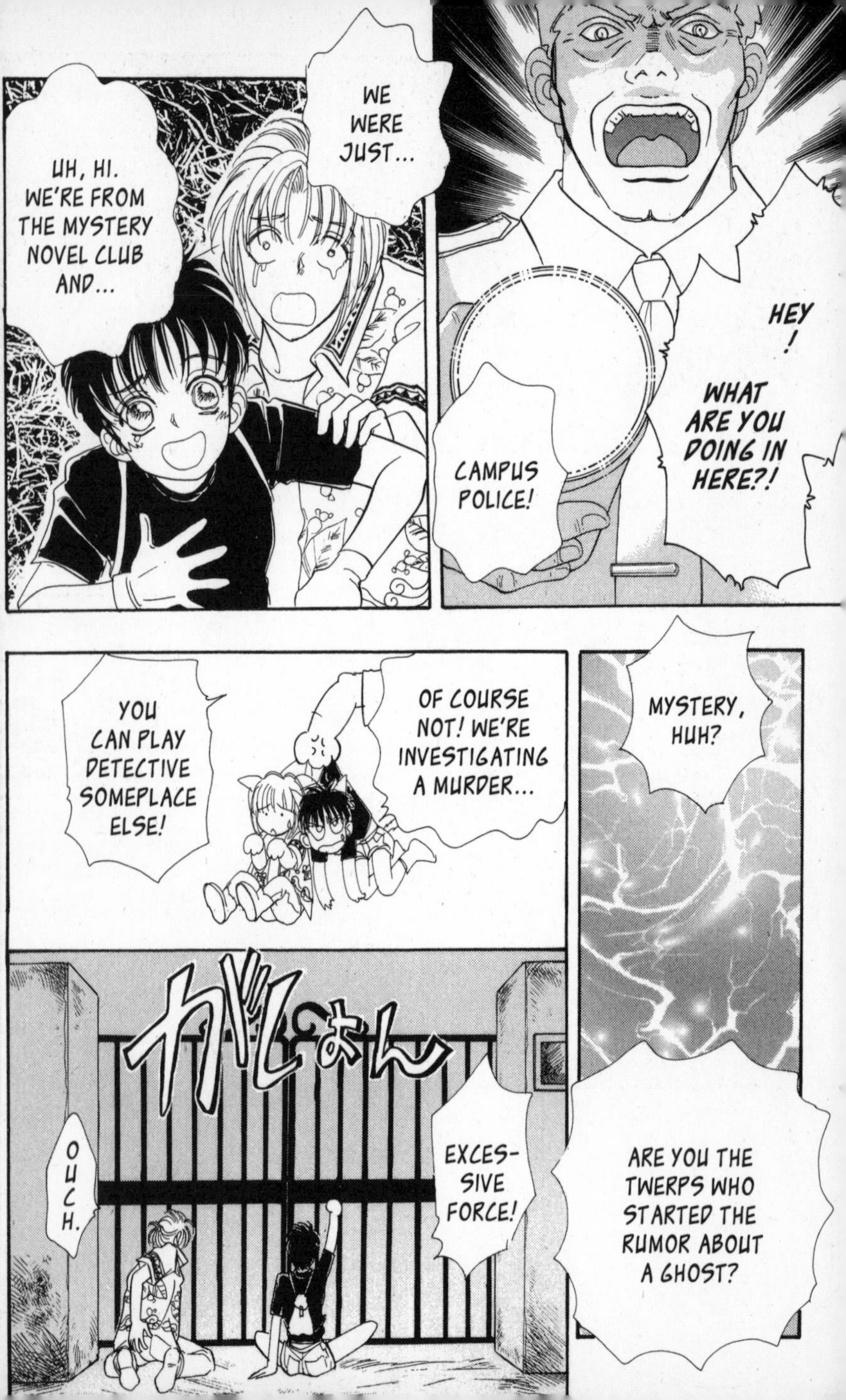
HEY! WHAT ARE YOU DOING IN HERE?!
CAMPUS POLICE!
WE WERE JUST...
UH, HI. WE'RE FROM THE MYSTERY NOVEL CLUB AND...
MYSTERY, HUH?
ARE YOU THE TWERPS WHO STARTED THE RUMOR ABOUT A GHOST?
OF COURSE NOT! WE'RE INVESTIGATING A MURDER...
YOU CAN PLAY DETECTIVE SOMEPLACE ELSE!
EXCES-SIVE FORCE!
OUCH.

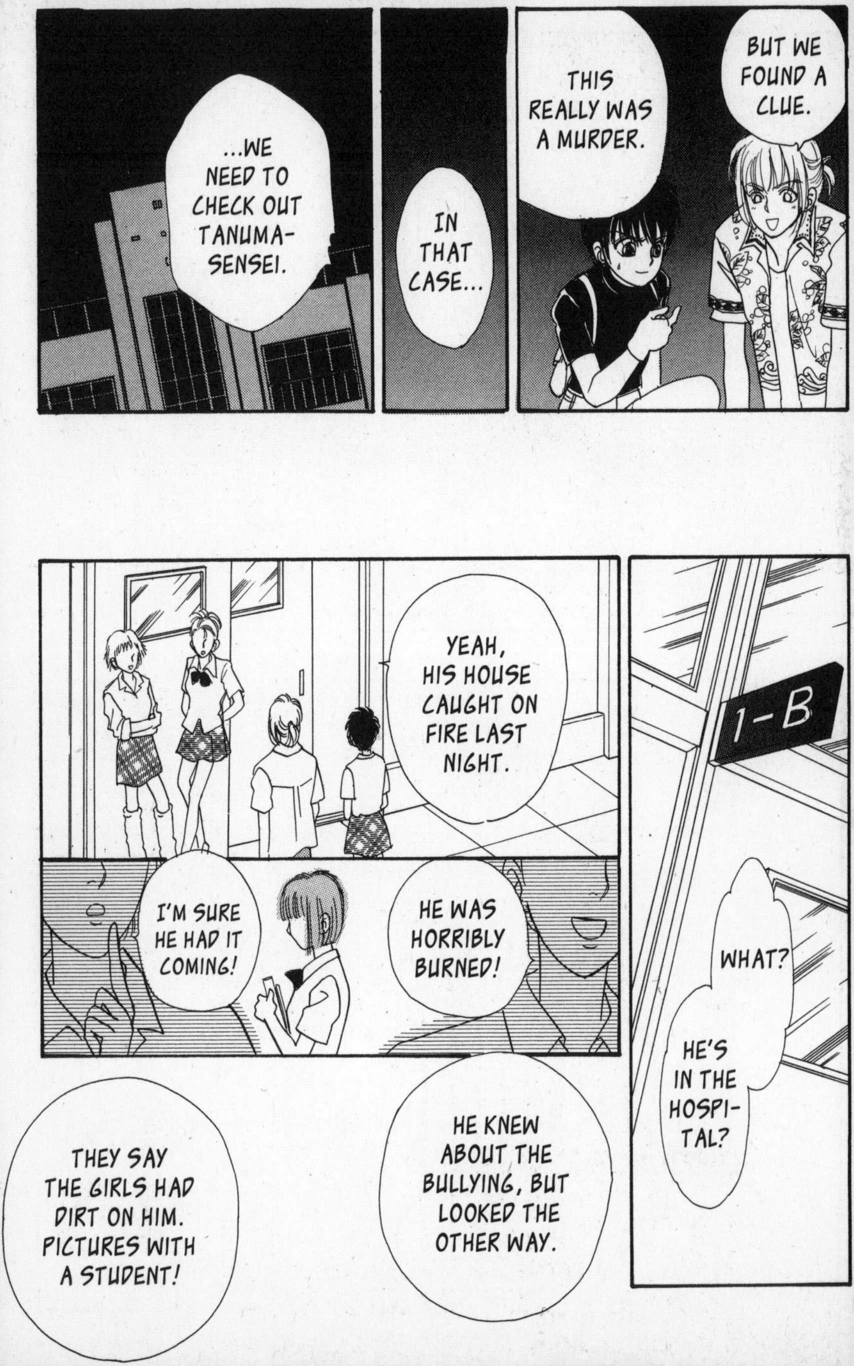
BUT WE FOUND A CLUE.
THIS REALLY WAS A MURDER.
IN THAT CASE...
...WE NEED TO CHECK OUT TANUMA-SENSEI.
WHAT?
HE'S IN THE HOSPITAL?
1-B
YEAH, HIS HOUSE CAUGHT ON FIRE LAST NIGHT.
HE WAS HORRIBLY BURNED!
I'M SURE HE HAD IT COMING!
HE KNEW ABOUT THE BULLYING, BUT LOOKED THE OTHER WAY.
THEY SAY THE GIRLS HAD DIRT ON HIM. PICTURES WITH A STUDENT!

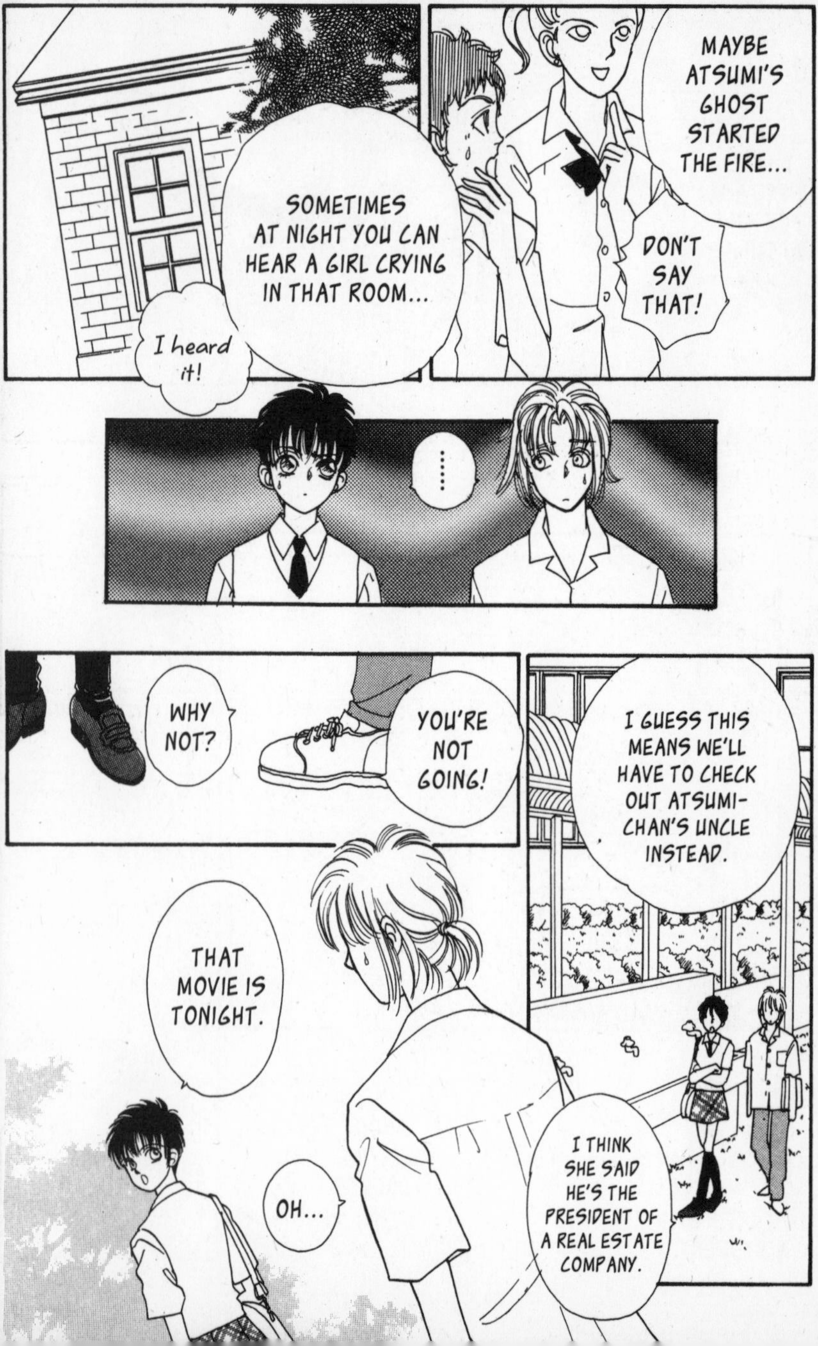
MAYBE ATSUMI'S GHOST STARTED THE FIRE...
DON'T SAY THAT!
SOMETIMES AT NIGHT YOU CAN HEAR A GIRL CRYING IN THAT ROOM...
I heard it!
......
I GUESS THIS MEANS WE'LL HAVE TO CHECK OUT ATSUMI-CHAN'S UNCLE INSTEAD.
I THINK SHE SAID HE'S THE PRESIDENT OF A REAL ESTATE COMPANY.
YOU'RE NOT GOING!
WHY NOT?
THAT MOVIE IS TONIGHT.
OH...

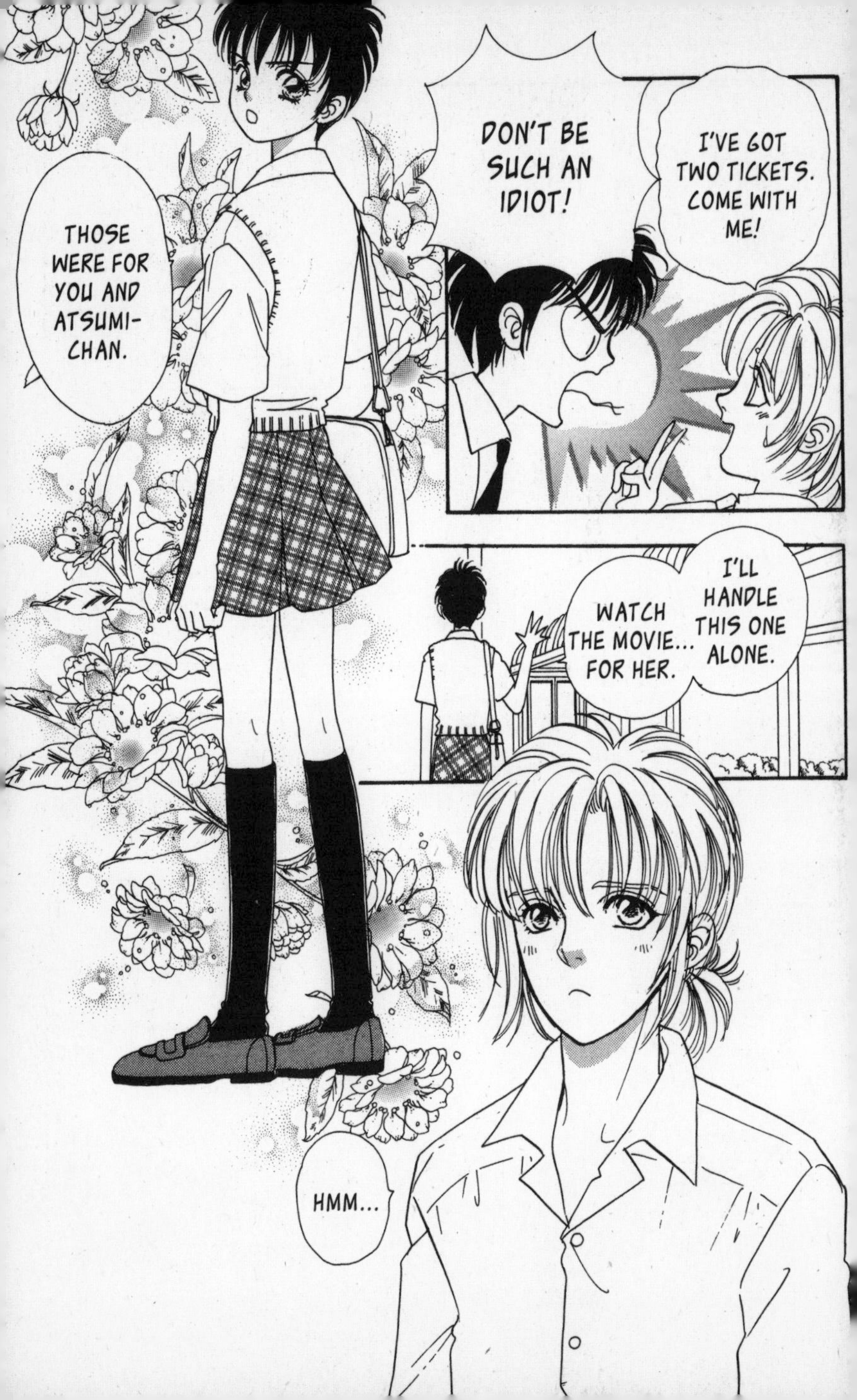
I'VE GOT TWO TICKETS. COME WITH ME!
DON'T BE SUCH AN IDIOT!
I'LL HANDLE THIS ONE ALONE.
WATCH THE MOVIE... FOR HER.
HMM...
THOSE WERE FOR YOU AND ATSUMI-CHAN.

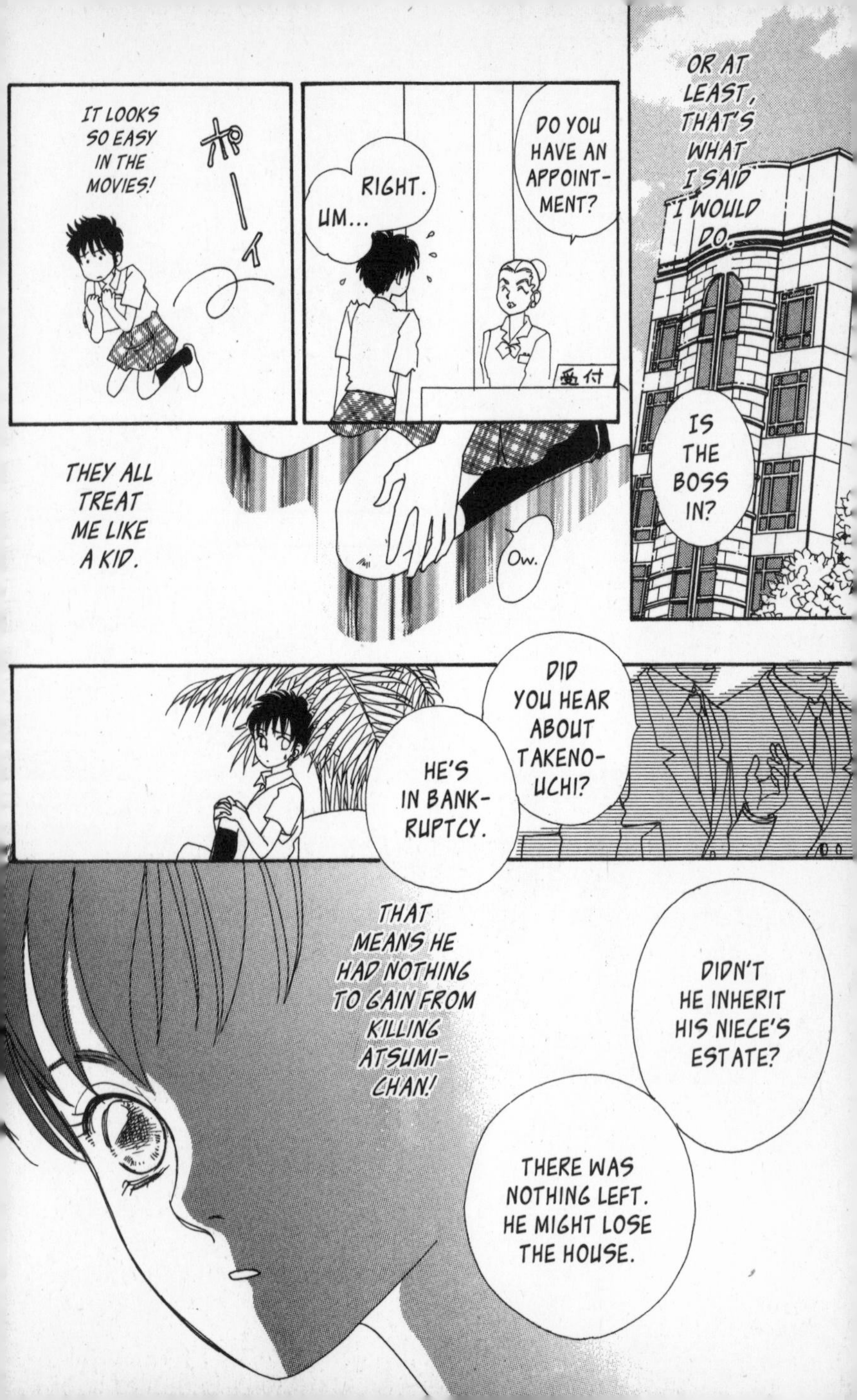
OR AT LEAST, THAT'S WHAT I SAID I WOULD DO.
IS THE BOSS IN?
DO YOU HAVE AN APPOINTMENT?
RIGHT. UM...
受付
IT LOOKS SO EASY IN THE MOVIES!
ポーイ
Ow.
THEY ALL TREAT ME LIKE A KID.
DID YOU HEAR ABOUT TAKENOUCHI?
HE'S IN BANKRUPTCY.
DIDN'T HE INHERIT HIS NIECE'S ESTATE?
THERE WAS NOTHING LEFT. HE MIGHT LOSE THE HOUSE.
THAT MEANS HE HAD NOTHING TO GAIN FROM KILLING ATSUMI-CHAN!

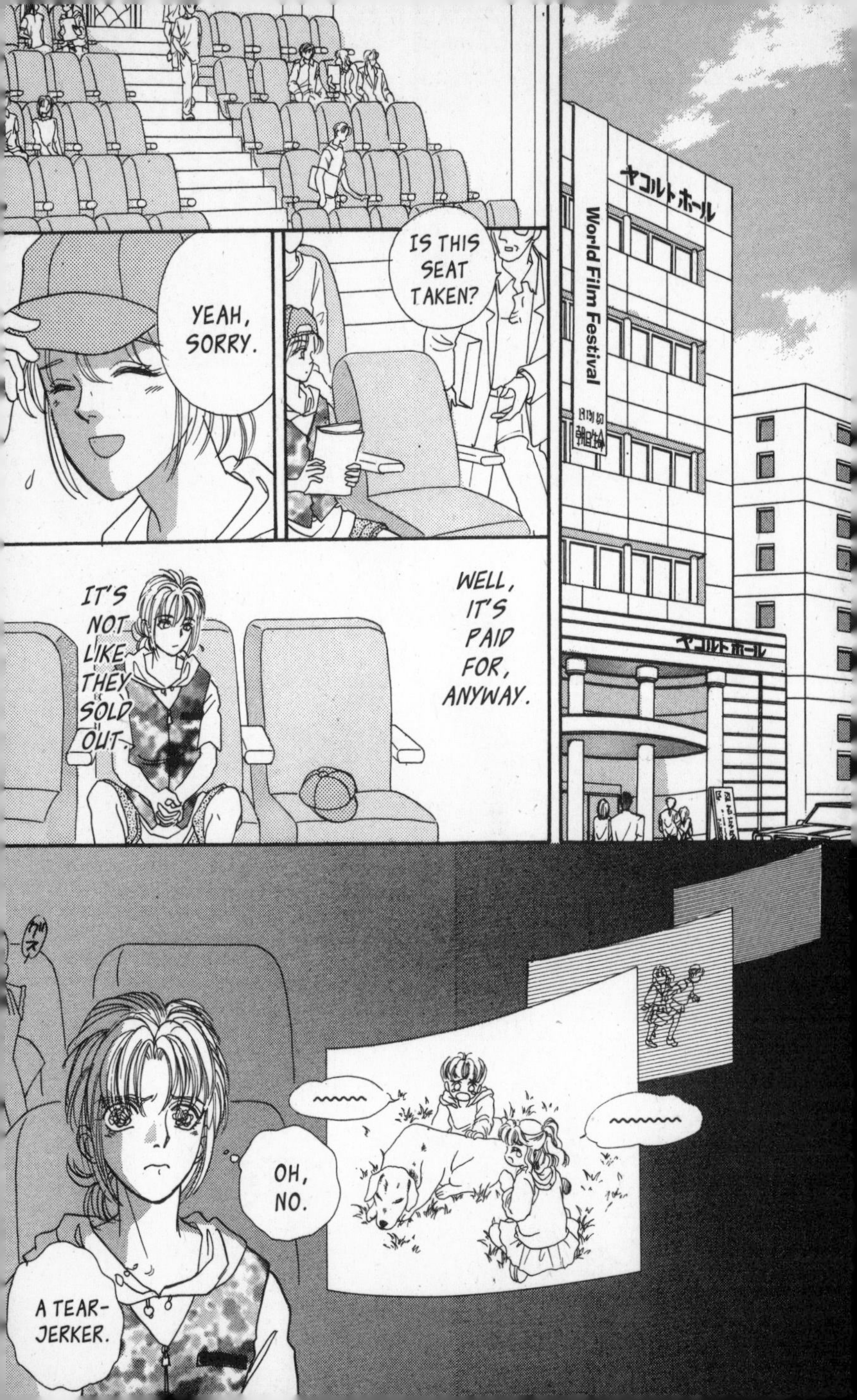

ヤコルトホール
World Film Festival
ヤコルトホール
IS THIS SEAT TAKEN?
YEAH, SORRY.
WELL, IT'S PAID FOR, ANYWAY.
IT'S NOT LIKE THEY SOLD OUT.
OH, NO.
A TEAR-JERKER.

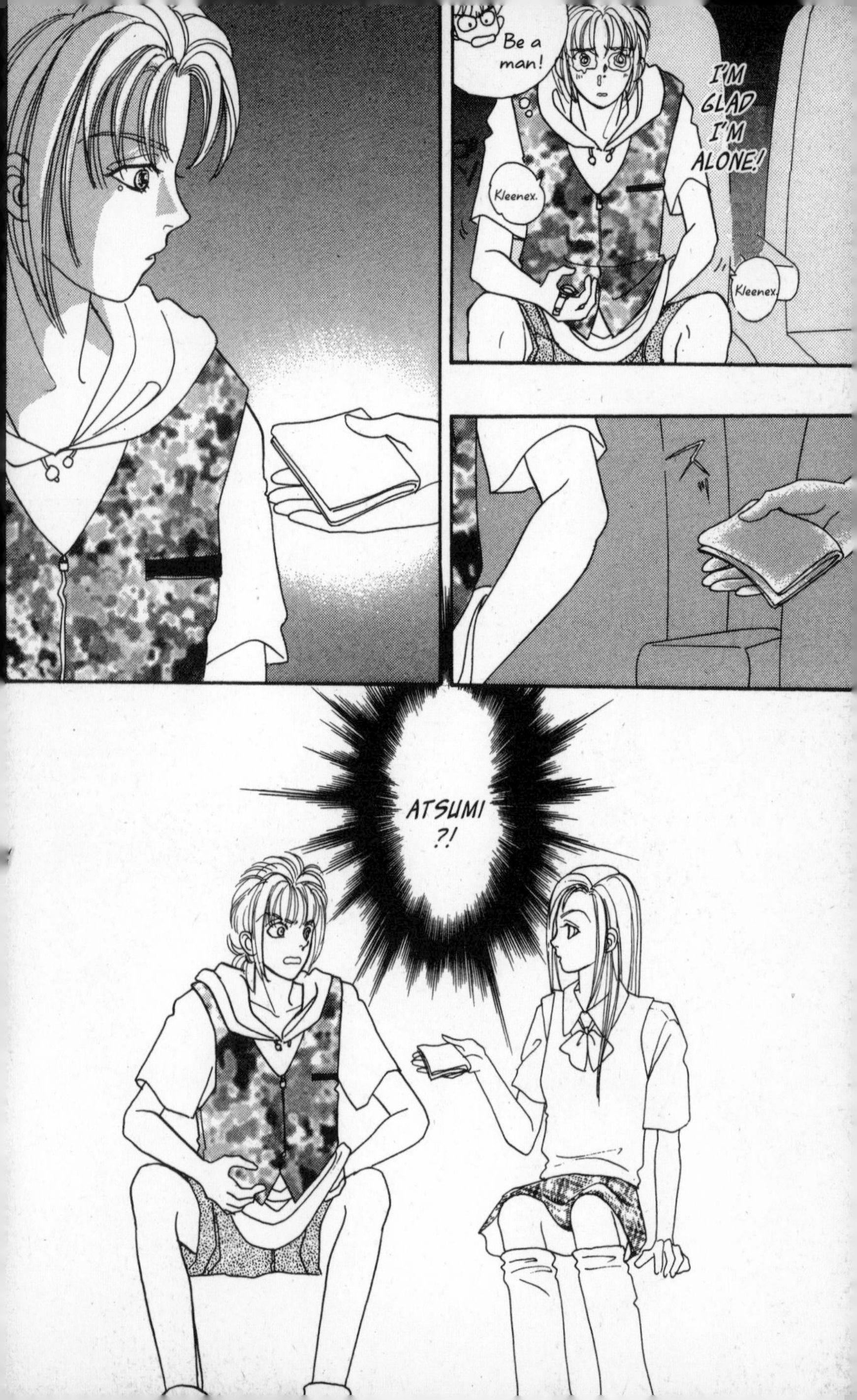
I'M GLAD I'M ALONE!
Be a man!
Kleenex.
Kleenex.
ATSUMI ?!

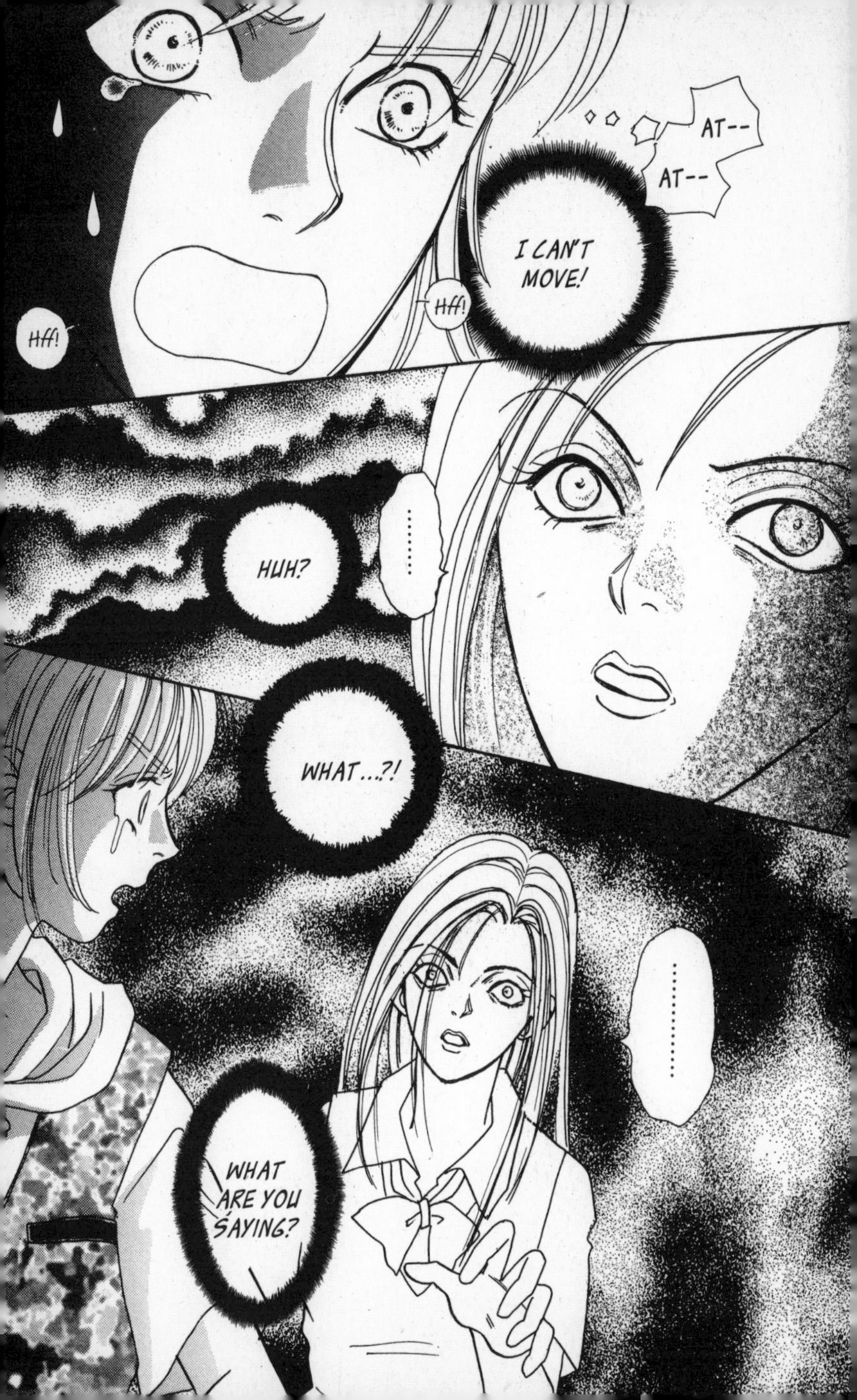
AT--
AT--
I CAN'T MOVE!
Hff!
Hff!
......
HUH?
WHAT...?!
......
WHAT ARE YOU SAYING?

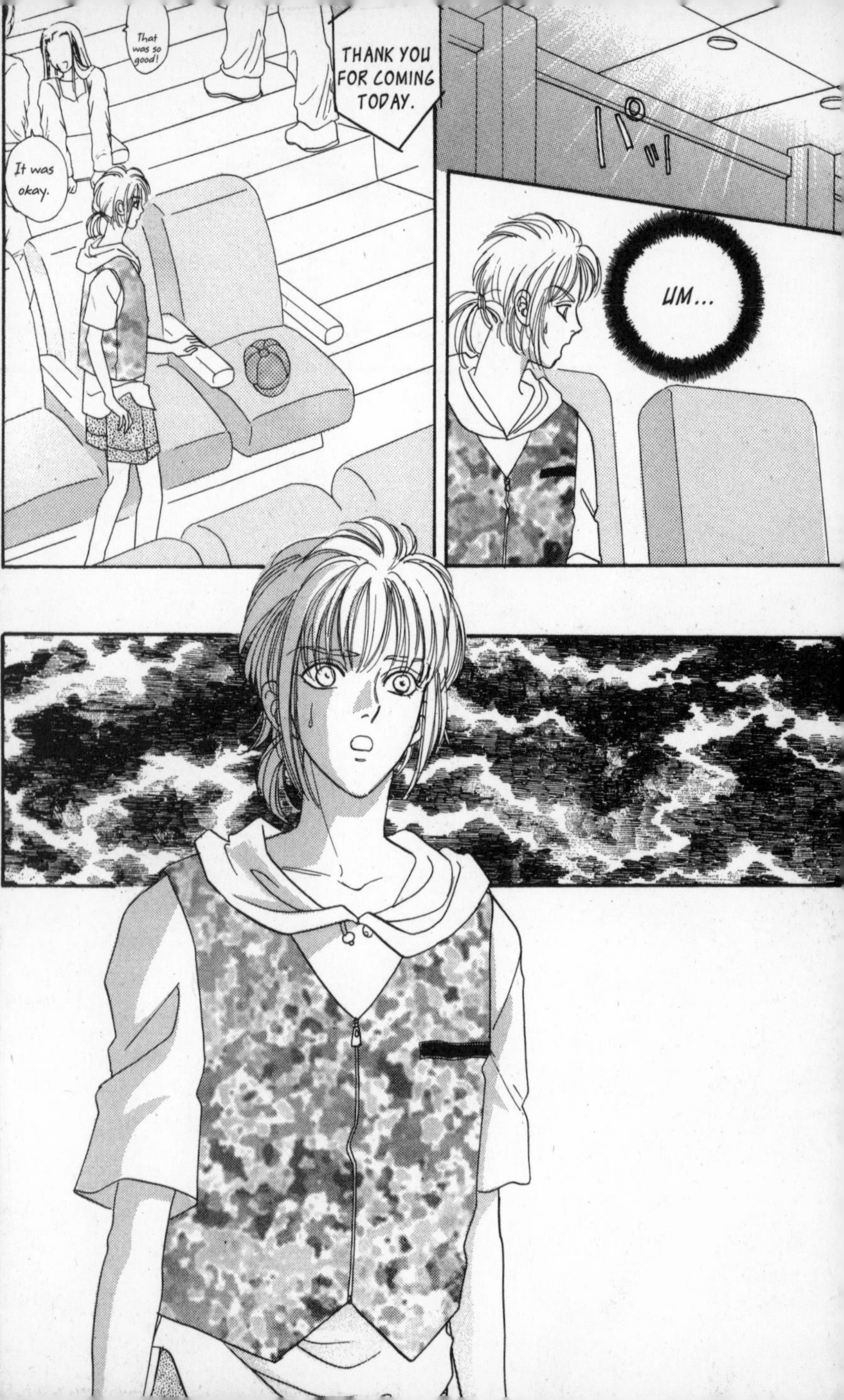
パッ
UM...
THANK YOU FOR COMING TODAY.
That was so good!
It was okay.

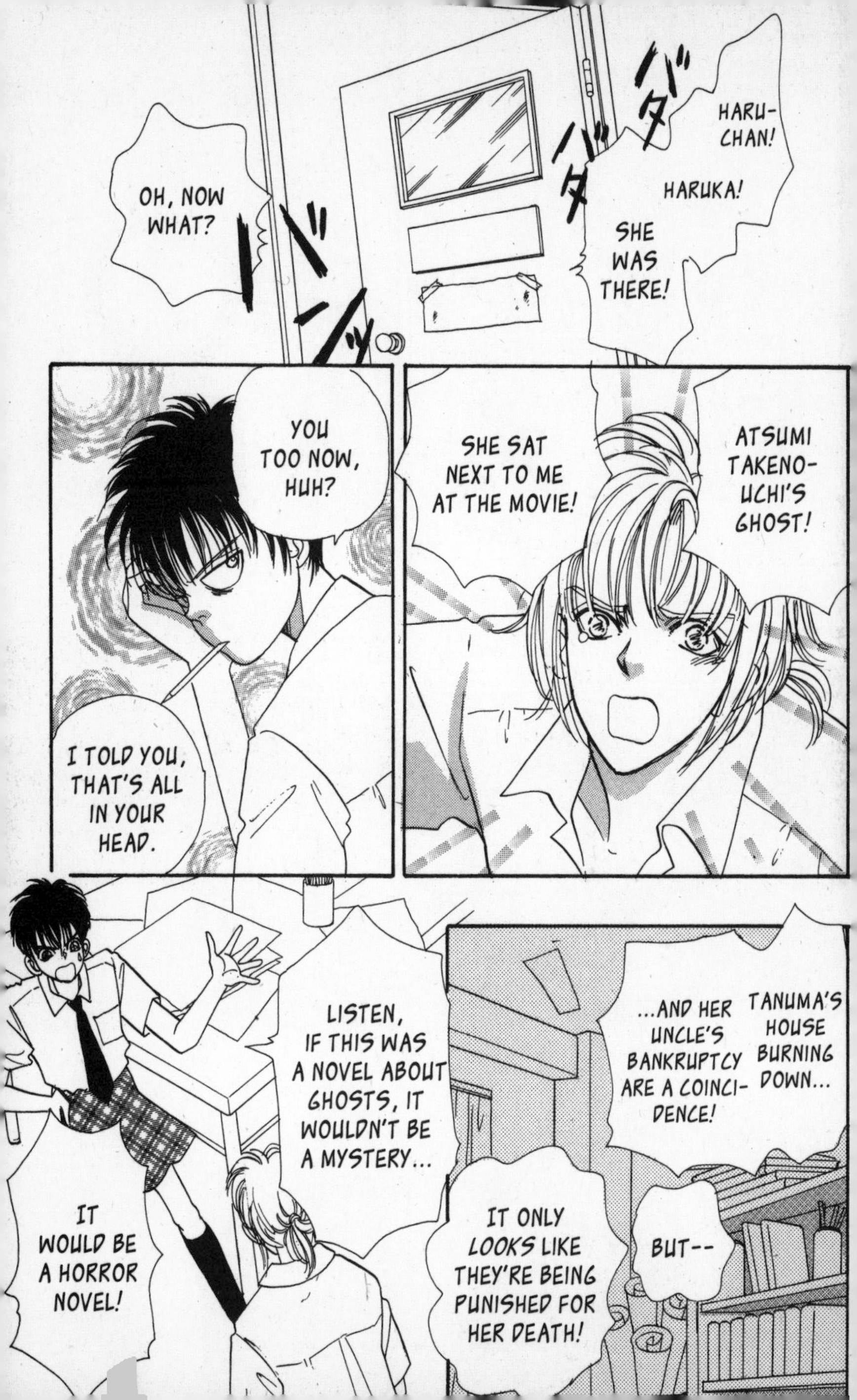
バタ バタ
HARU-CHAN!
HARUKA!
SHE WAS THERE!
バンッ
OH, NOW WHAT?
ATSUMI TAKENO-UCHI'S GHOST!
SHE SAT NEXT TO ME AT THE MOVIE!
YOU TOO NOW, HUH?
I TOLD YOU, THAT'S ALL IN YOUR HEAD.
TANUMA'S HOUSE BURNING DOWN...
...AND HER UNCLE'S BANKRUPTCY ARE A COINCI-DENCE!
BUT--
IT ONLY *LOOKS* LIKE THEY'RE BEING PUNISHED FOR HER DEATH!
LISTEN, IF THIS WAS A NOVEL ABOUT GHOSTS, IT WOULDN'T BE A MYSTERY...
IT WOULD BE A HORROR NOVEL!

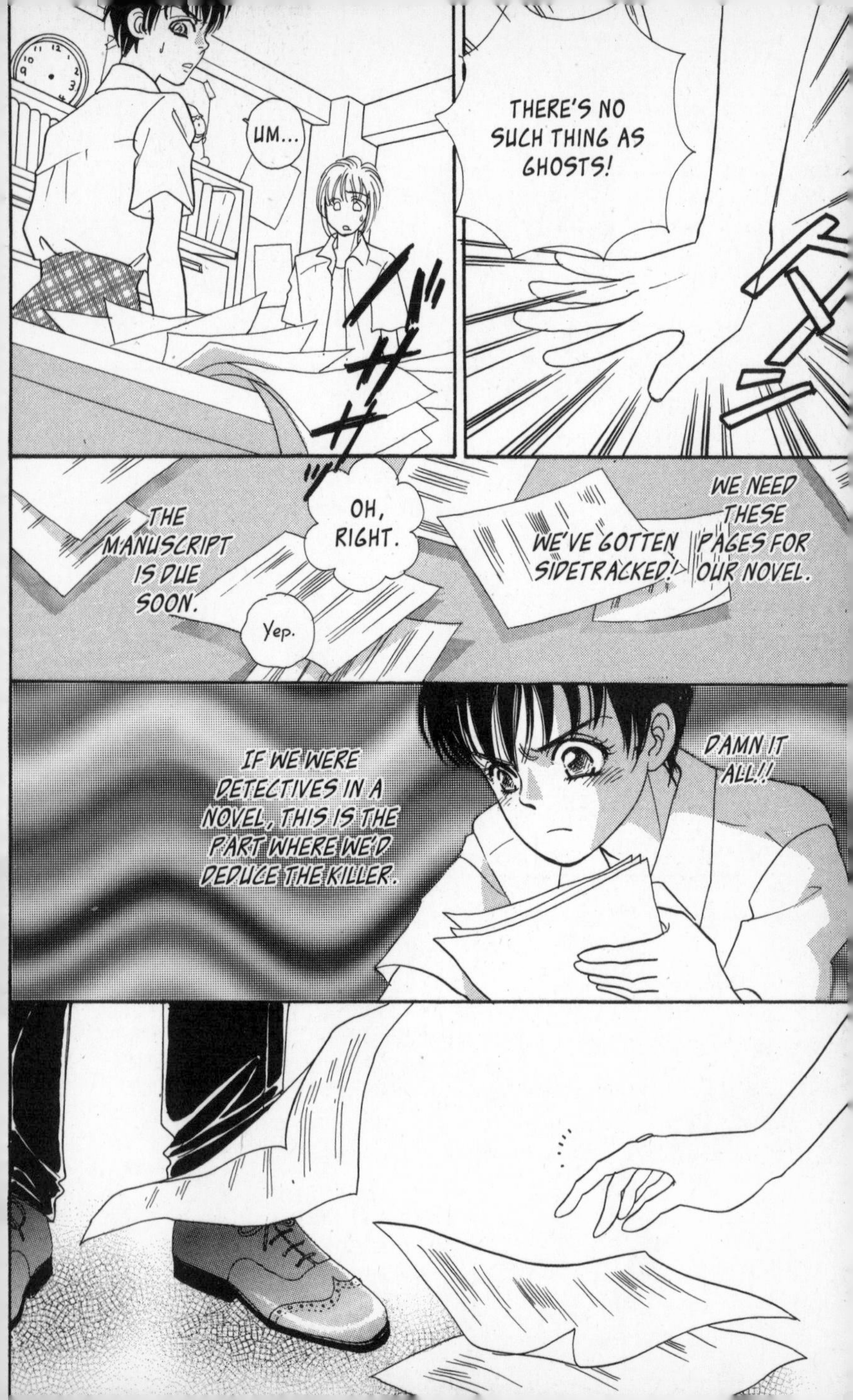
THERE'S NO SUCH THING AS GHOSTS!
UM...
WE NEED THESE PAGES FOR OUR NOVEL.
WE'VE GOTTEN SIDETRACKED!
OH, RIGHT.
THE MANUSCRIPT IS DUE SOON.
Yep.
DAMN IT ALL!!
IF WE WERE DETECTIVES IN A NOVEL, THIS IS THE PART WHERE WE'D DEDUCE THE KILLER.

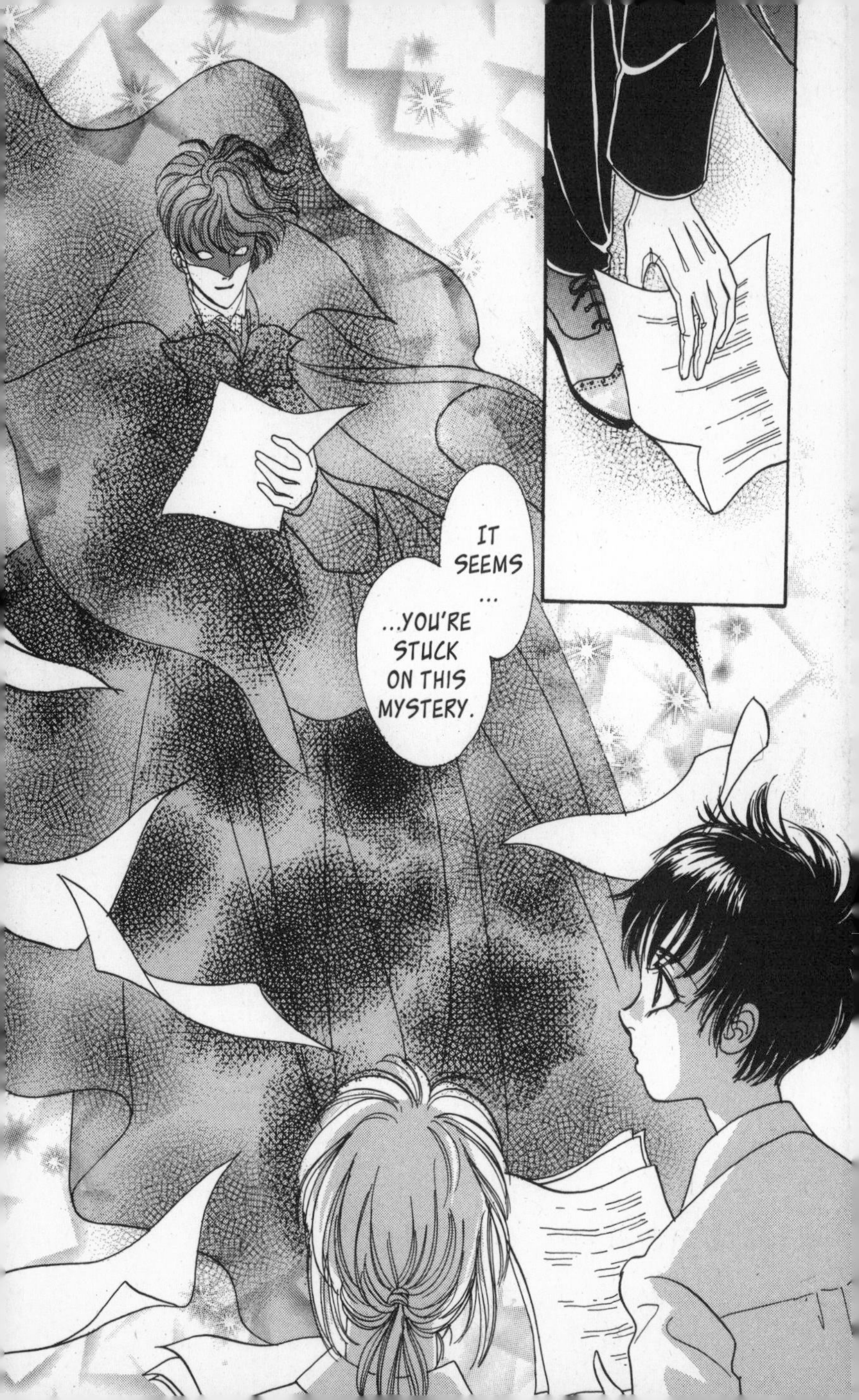
IT SEEMS ...
...YOU'RE STUCK ON THIS MYSTERY.

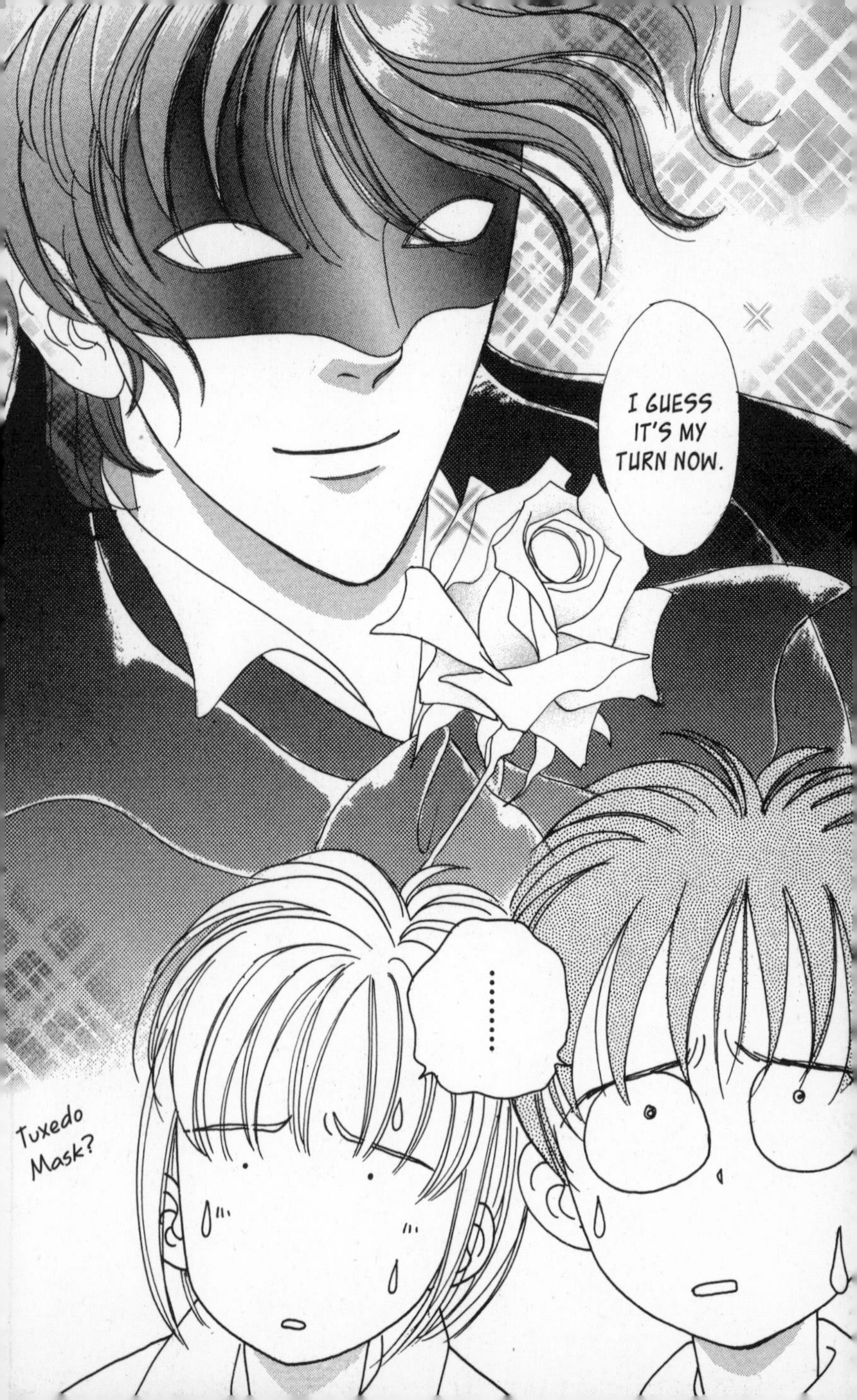
I GUESS IT'S MY TURN NOW.
......
Tuxedo Mask?

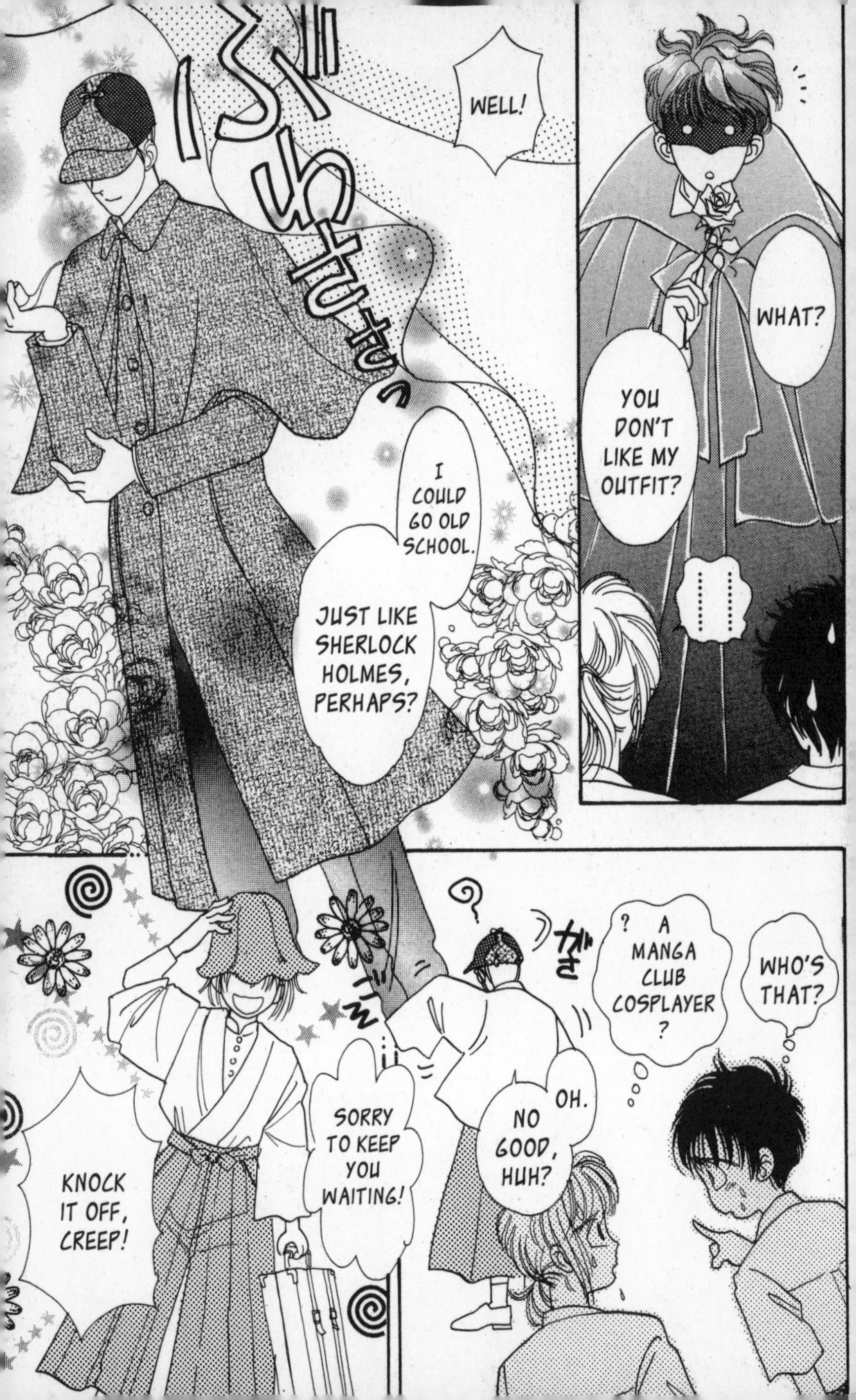
WHAT?
YOU DON'T LIKE MY OUTFIT?
......
WELL!
I COULD GO OLD SCHOOL.
JUST LIKE SHERLOCK HOLMES, PERHAPS?
WHO'S THAT?
? A MANGA CLUB COSPLAYER ?
OH.
NO GOOD, HUH?
SORRY TO KEEP YOU WAITING!
KNOCK IT OFF, CREEP!

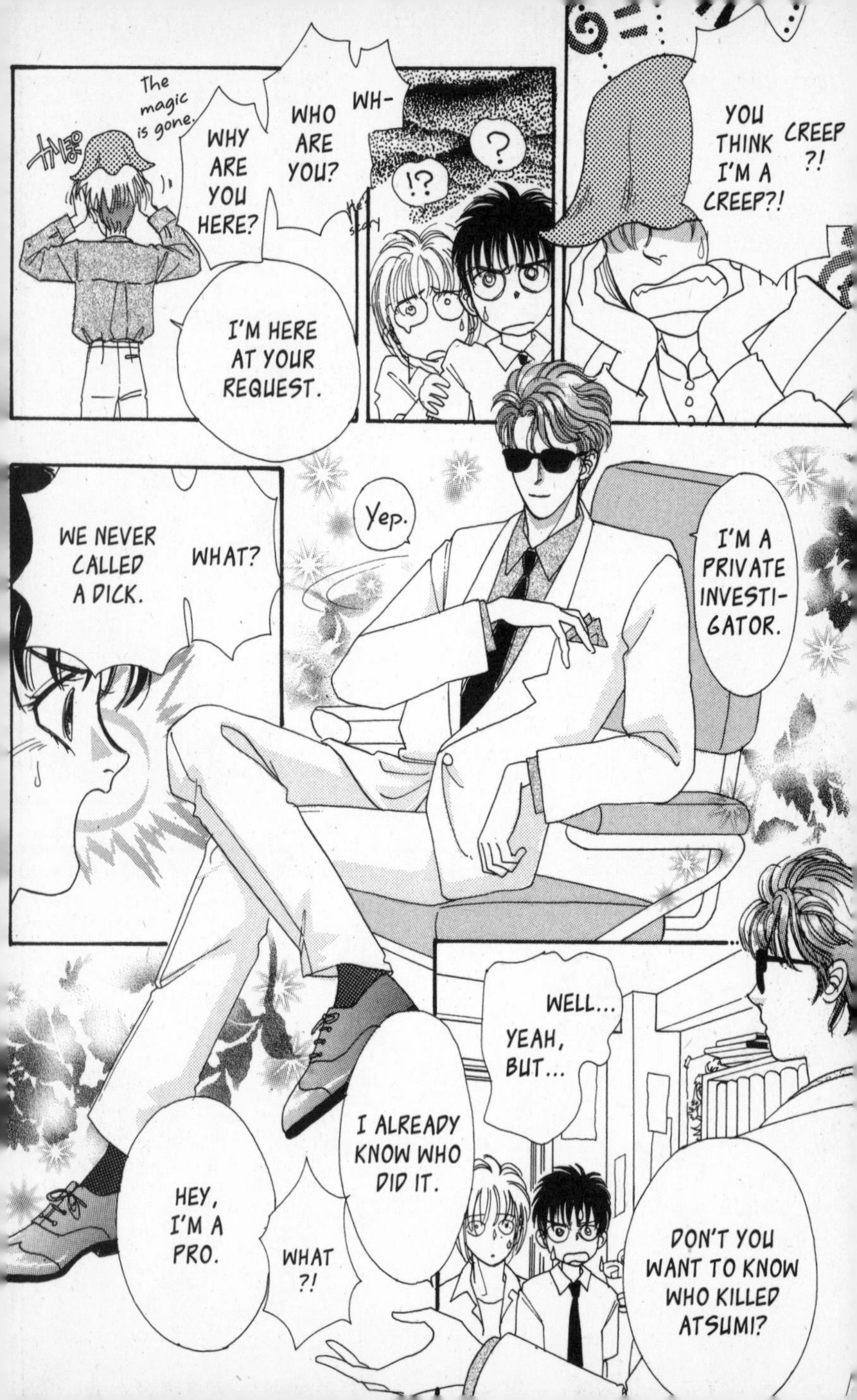
CREEP ?!
YOU THINK I'M A CREEP?!
WH-
?
!?
WHO ARE YOU?
WHY ARE YOU HERE?
The magic is gone.
I'M HERE AT YOUR REQUEST.
I'M A PRIVATE INVESTIGATOR.
Yep.
WHAT?
WE NEVER CALLED A DICK.
WELL... YEAH, BUT...
DON'T YOU WANT TO KNOW WHO KILLED ATSUMI?
I ALREADY KNOW WHO DID IT.
WHAT ?!
HEY, I'M A PRO.

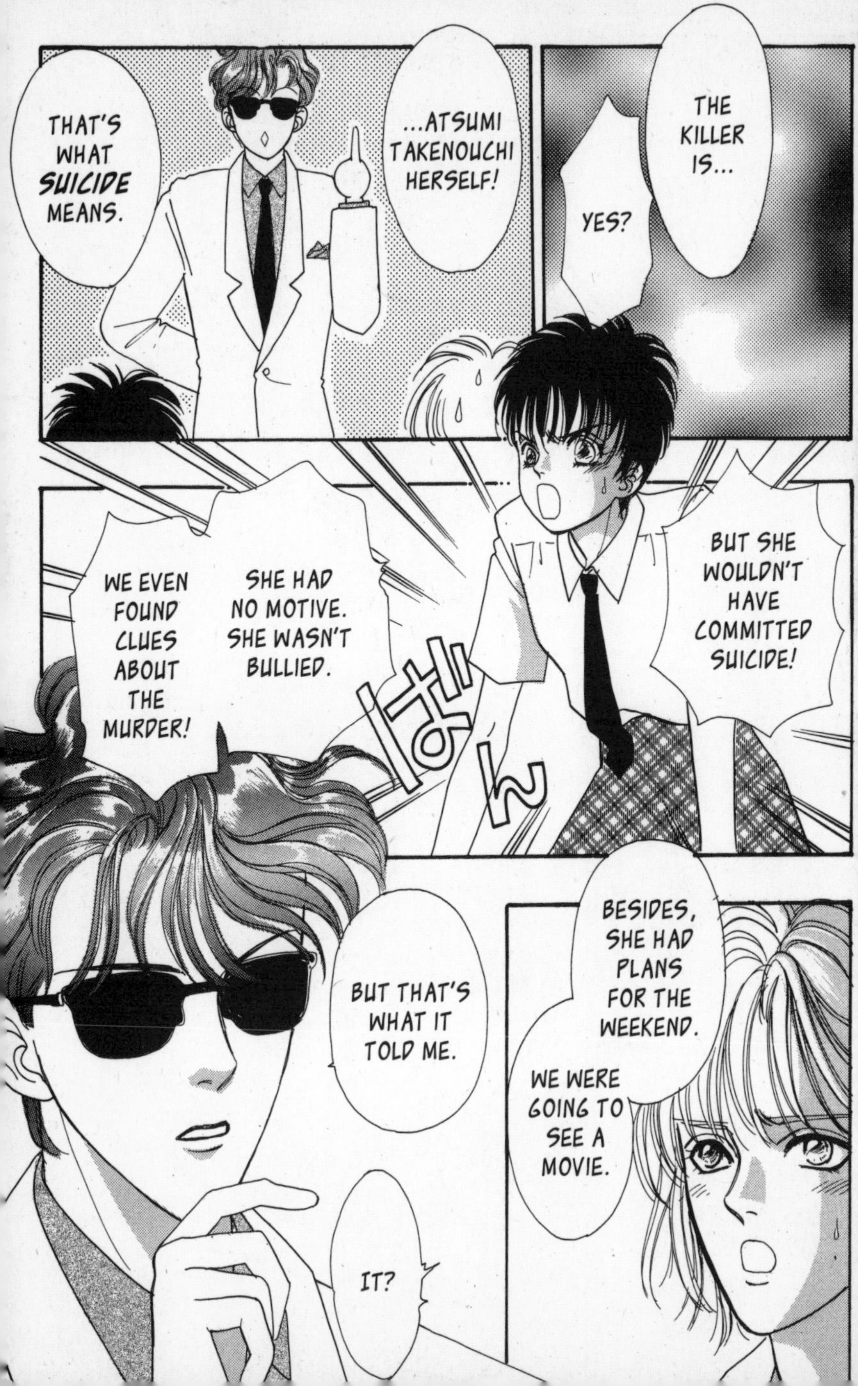
THE KILLER IS...
YES?
...ATSUMI TAKENOUCHI HERSELF!
THAT'S WHAT SUICIDE MEANS.
BUT SHE WOULDN'T HAVE COMMITTED SUICIDE!
SHE HAD NO MOTIVE. SHE WASN'T BULLIED.
WE EVEN FOUND CLUES ABOUT THE MURDER!
ばん
BESIDES, SHE HAD PLANS FOR THE WEEKEND.
WE WERE GOING TO SEE A MOVIE.
BUT THAT'S WHAT IT TOLD ME.
IT?

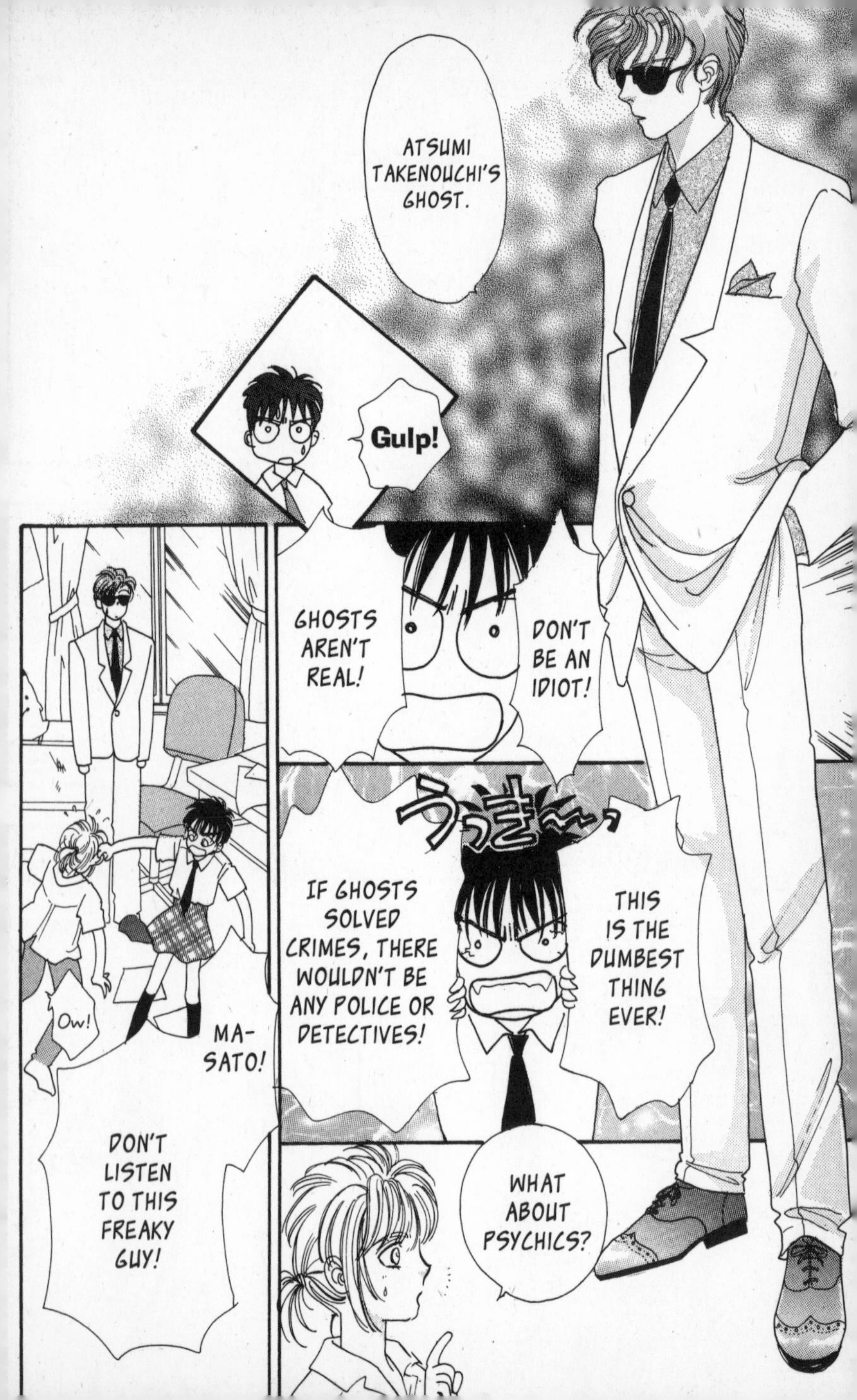
ATSUMI TAKENOUCHI'S GHOST.
Gulp!
DON'T BE AN IDIOT!
GHOSTS AREN'T REAL!
うっき〜〜っ
THIS IS THE DUMBEST THING EVER!
IF GHOSTS SOLVED CRIMES, THERE WOULDN'T BE ANY POLICE OR DETECTIVES!
WHAT ABOUT PSYCHICS?
MA-SATO!
Ow!
DON'T LISTEN TO THIS FREAKY GUY!

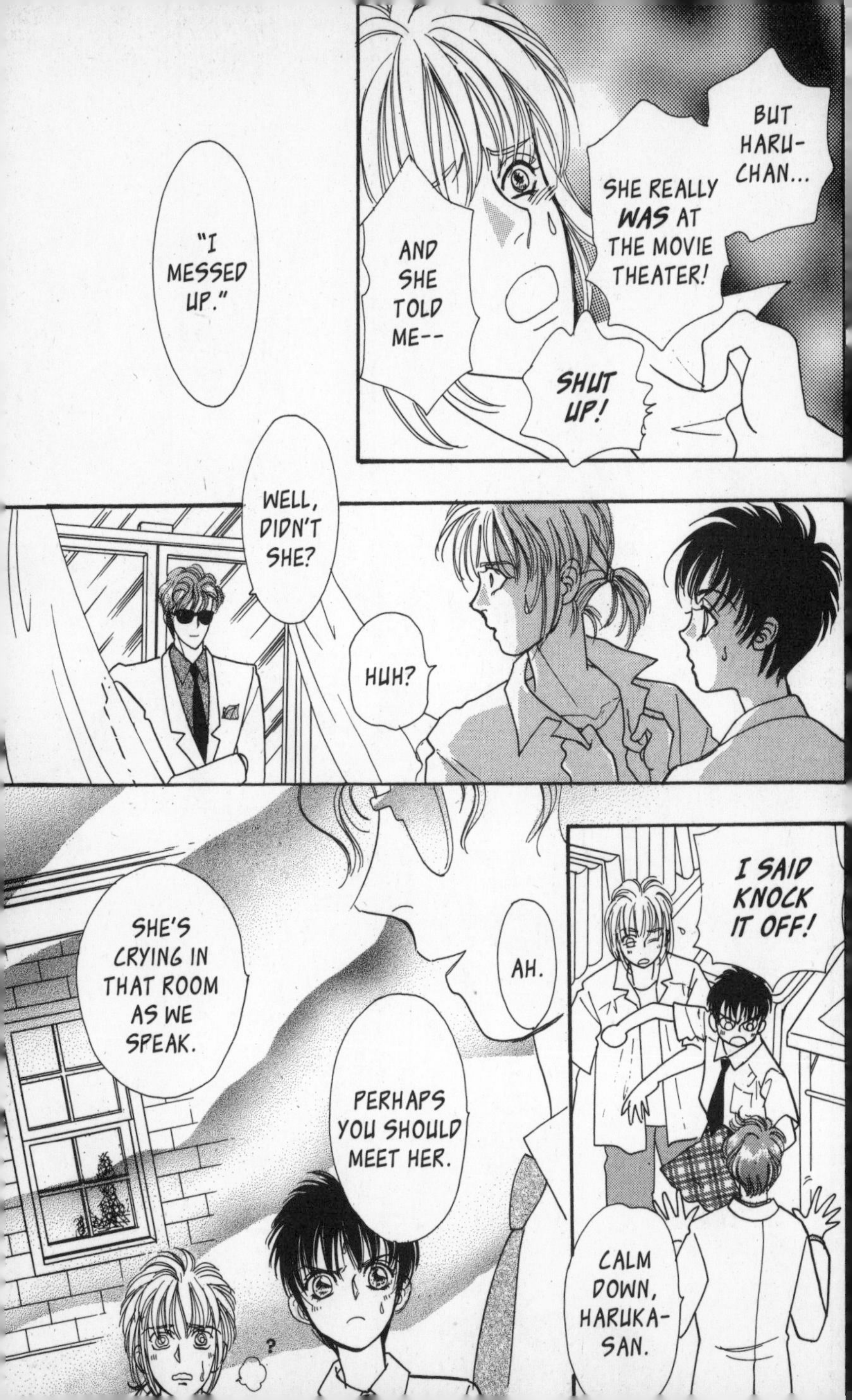
BUT HARU-CHAN...
SHE REALLY *WAS* AT THE MOVIE THEATER!
AND SHE TOLD ME--
SHUT UP!
"I MESSED UP."
WELL, DIDN'T SHE?
HUH?
I SAID KNOCK IT OFF!
CALM DOWN, HARUKA-SAN.
AH.
SHE'S CRYING IN THAT ROOM AS WE SPEAK.
PERHAPS YOU SHOULD MEET HER.

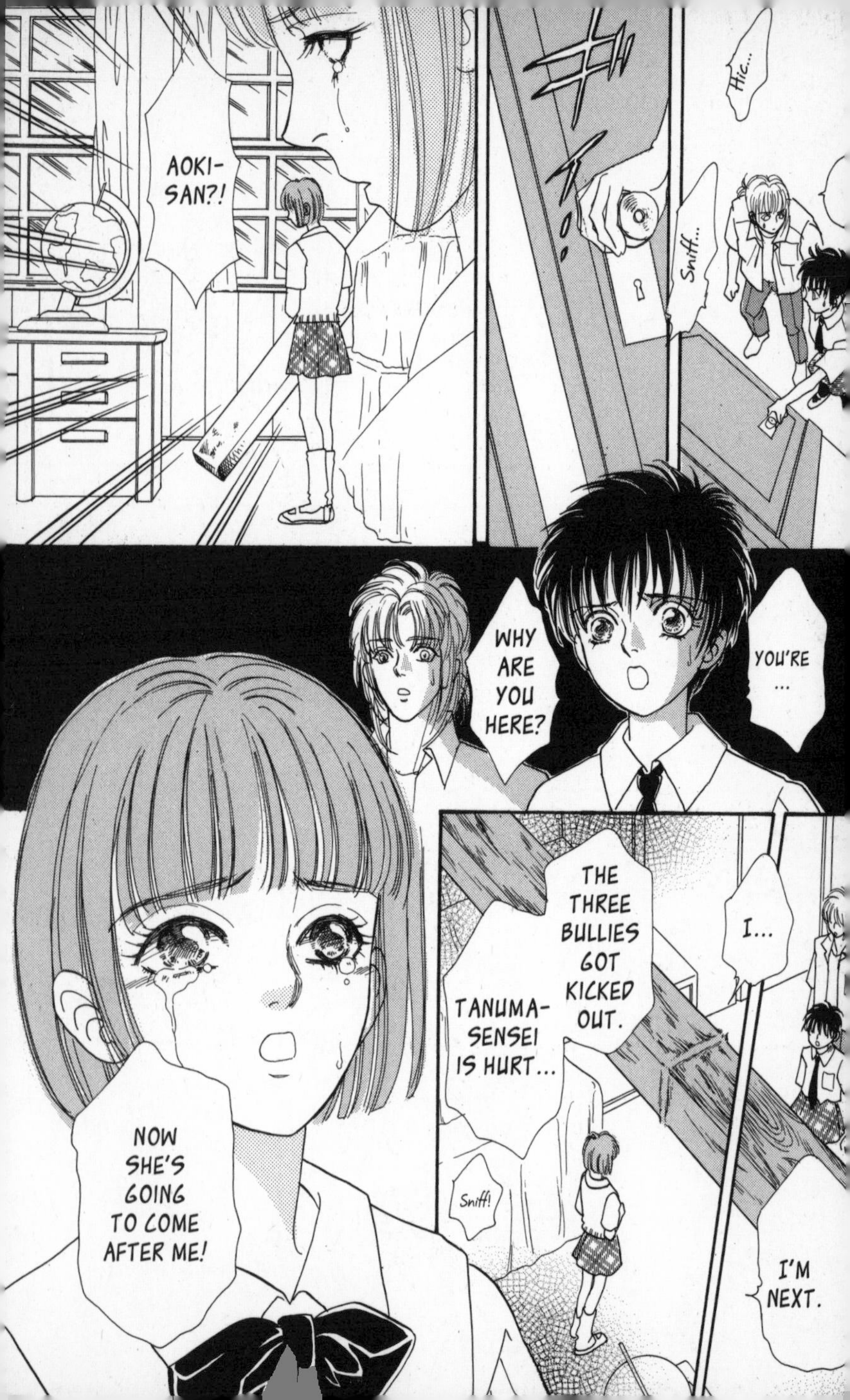
Hic...
Sniff...
AOKI-SAN?!
YOU'RE ...
WHY ARE YOU HERE?
I...
I'M NEXT.
THE THREE BULLIES GOT KICKED OUT.
TANUMA-SENSEI IS HURT...
Sniff!
NOW SHE'S GOING TO COME AFTER ME!

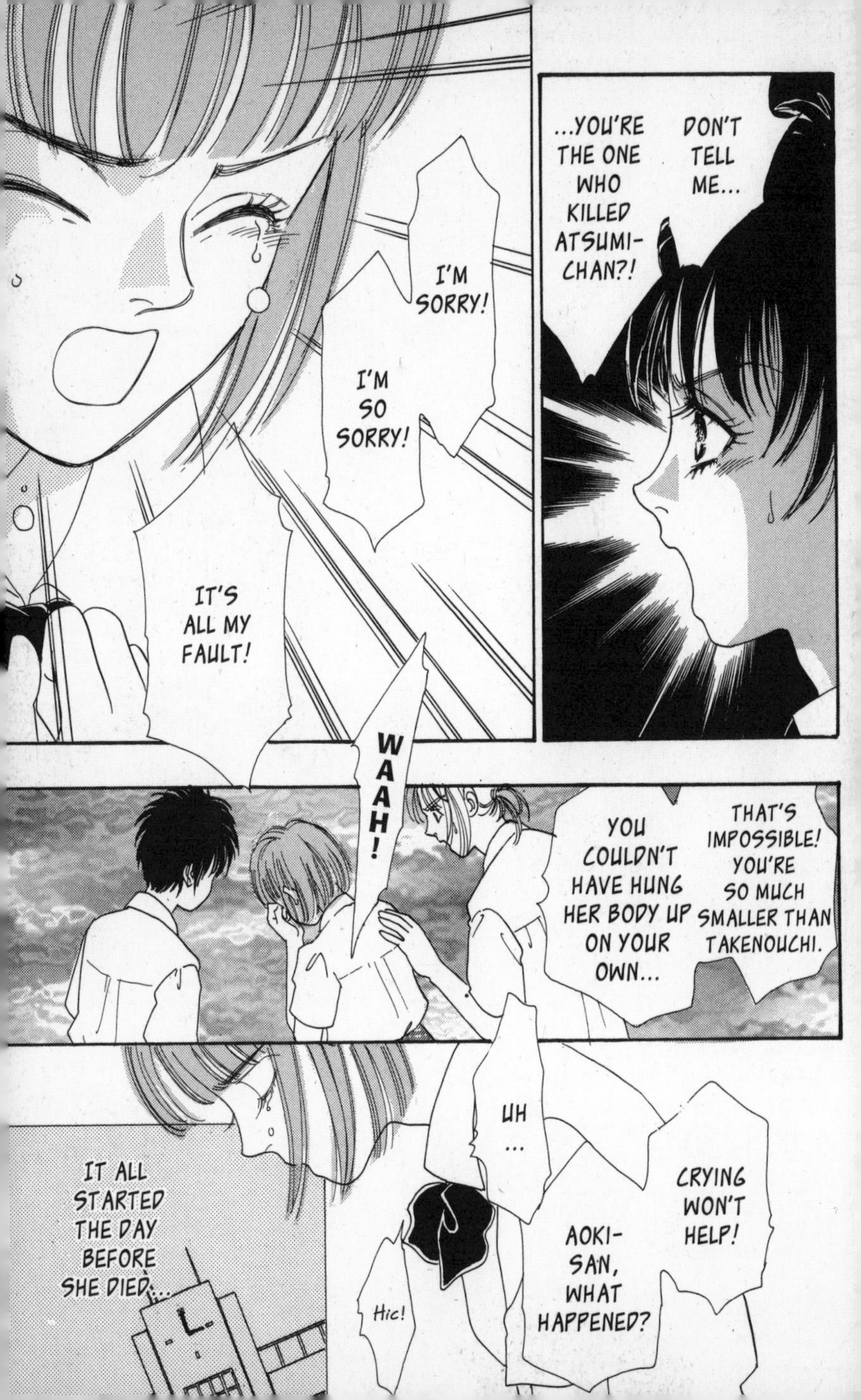

DON'T TELL ME...
...YOU'RE THE ONE WHO KILLED ATSUMI-CHAN?!
I'M SORRY!
I'M SO SORRY!
IT'S ALL MY FAULT!
WAAAH!
THAT'S IMPOSSIBLE! YOU'RE SO MUCH SMALLER THAN TAKENOUCHI.
YOU COULDN'T HAVE HUNG HER BODY UP ON YOUR OWN...
CRYING WON'T HELP!
AOKI-SAN, WHAT HAPPENED?
UH ...
Hic!
IT ALL STARTED THE DAY BEFORE SHE DIED...

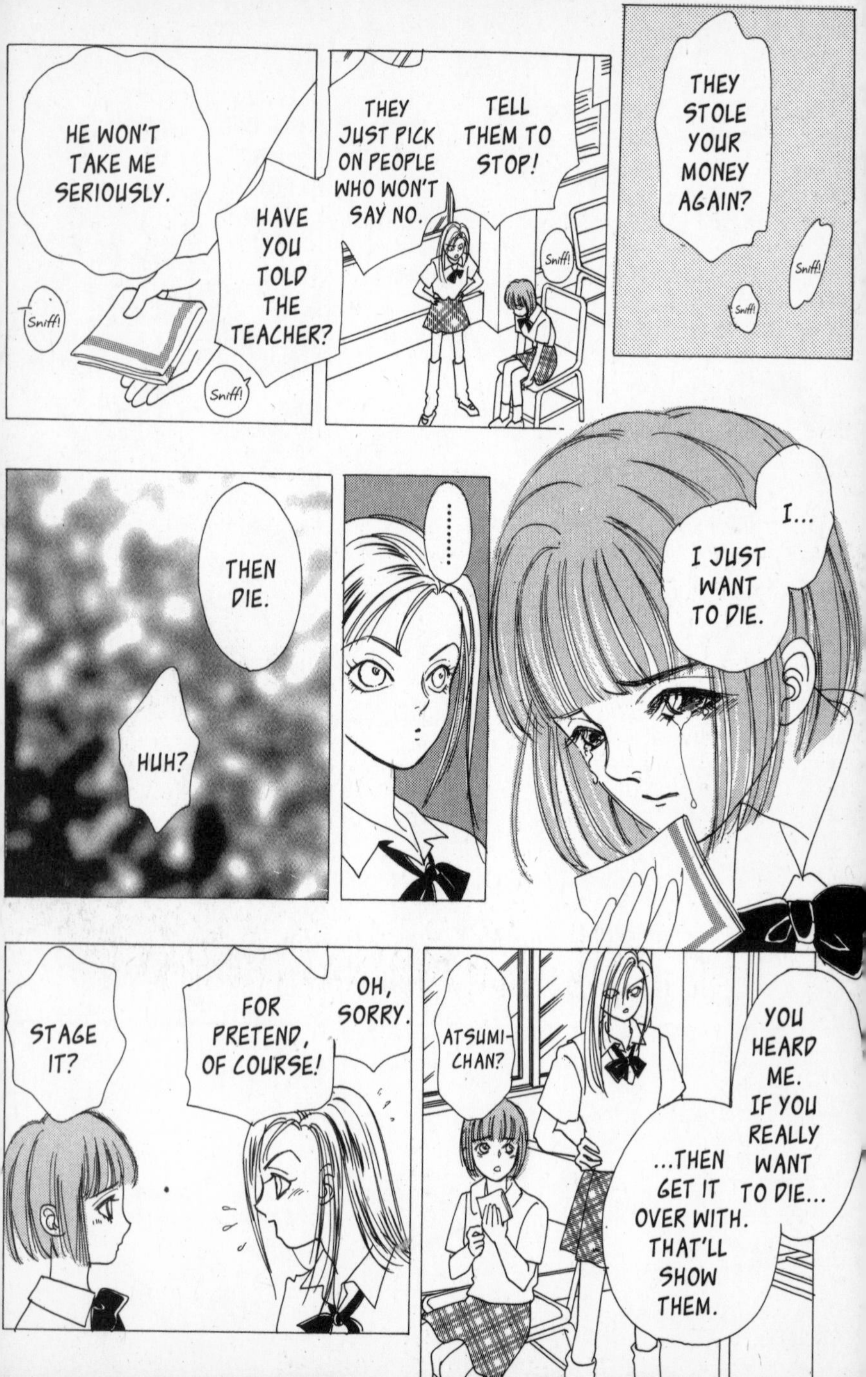
THEY STOLE YOUR MONEY AGAIN?
Sniff!
Sniff!
TELL THEM TO STOP!
THEY JUST PICK ON PEOPLE WHO WON'T SAY NO.
Sniff!
HAVE YOU TOLD THE TEACHER?
HE WON'T TAKE ME SERIOUSLY.
Sniff!
Sniff!
I... I JUST WANT TO DIE.
....
THEN DIE.
HUH?
YOU HEARD ME. IF YOU REALLY WANT TO DIE...
...THEN GET IT OVER WITH. THAT'LL SHOW THEM.
ATSUMI-CHAN?
OH, SORRY.
FOR PRETEND, OF COURSE!
STAGE IT?

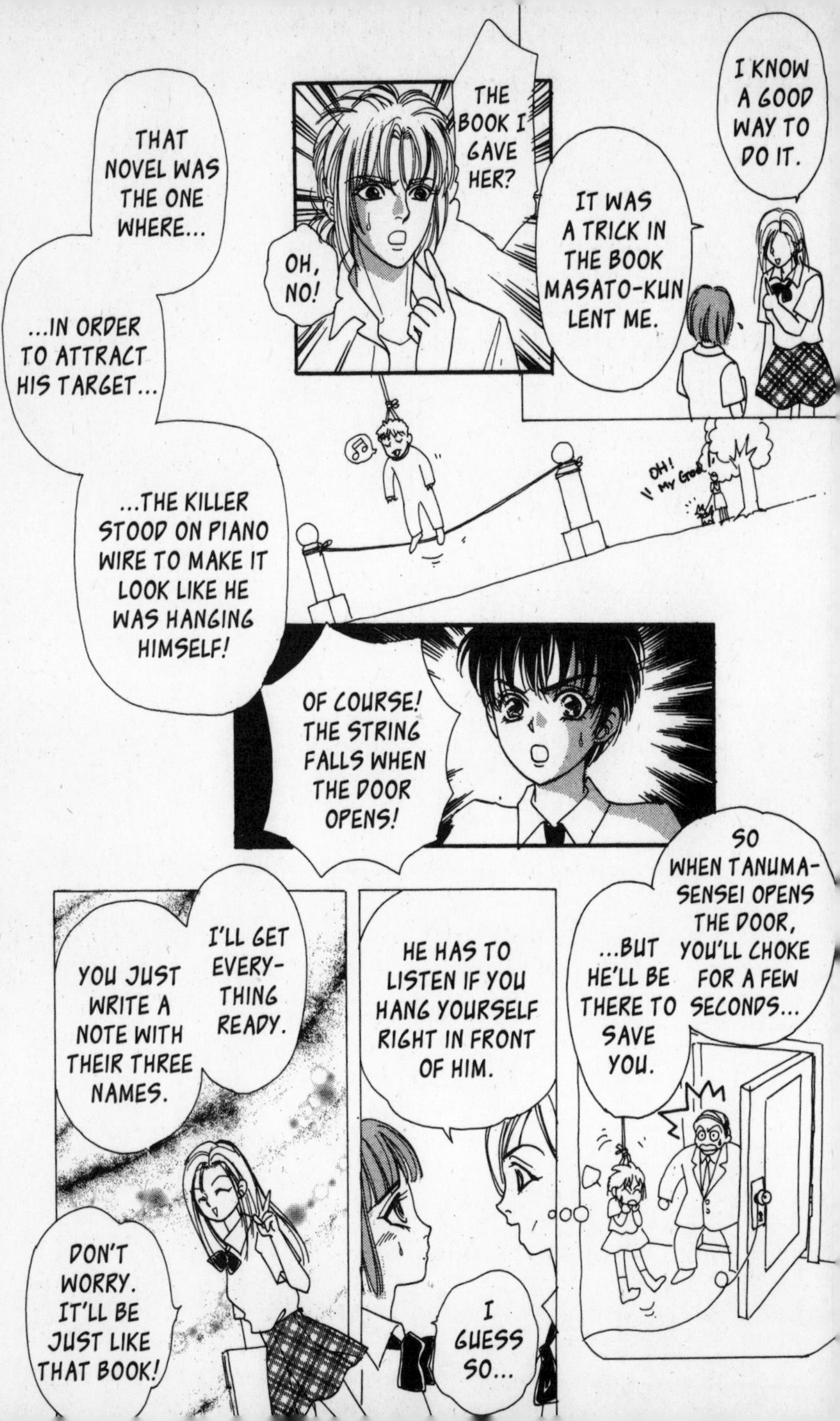
I KNOW A GOOD WAY TO DO IT.
IT WAS A TRICK IN THE BOOK MASATO-KUN LENT ME.
THE BOOK I GAVE HER?
OH, NO!
THAT NOVEL WAS THE ONE WHERE...
...IN ORDER TO ATTRACT HIS TARGET...
OH! My God!
...THE KILLER STOOD ON PIANO WIRE TO MAKE IT LOOK LIKE HE WAS HANGING HIMSELF!
OF COURSE! THE STRING FALLS WHEN THE DOOR OPENS!
SO WHEN TANUMA-SENSEI OPENS THE DOOR, YOU'LL CHOKE FOR A FEW SECONDS...
...BUT HE'LL BE THERE TO SAVE YOU.
HE HAS TO LISTEN IF YOU HANG YOURSELF RIGHT IN FRONT OF HIM.
I GUESS SO...
I'LL GET EVERY-THING READY.
YOU JUST WRITE A NOTE WITH THEIR THREE NAMES.
DON'T WORRY. IT'LL BE JUST LIKE THAT BOOK!

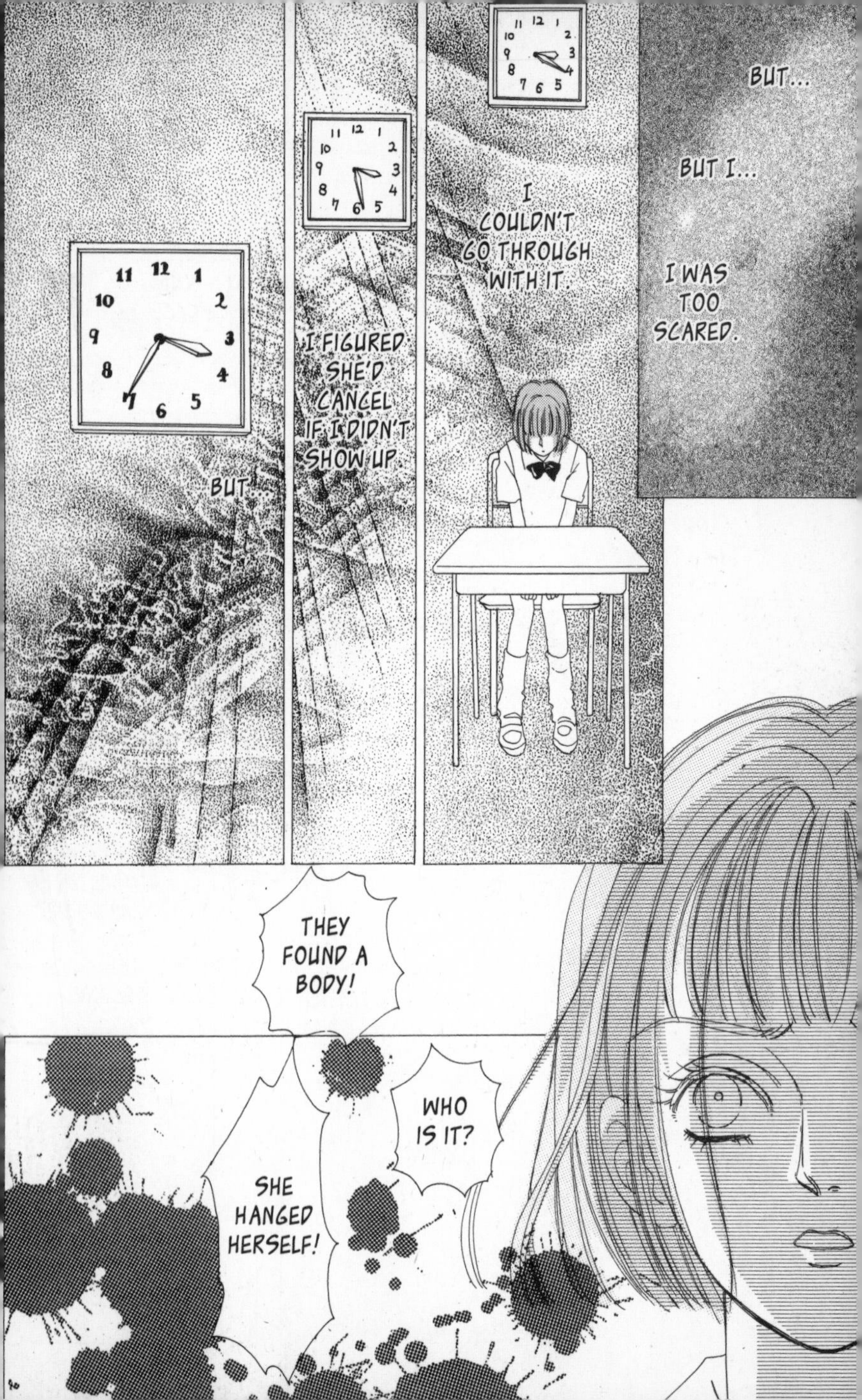
BUT...
BUT I...
I WAS TOO SCARED.
I COULDN'T GO THROUGH WITH IT.
I FIGURED SHE'D CANCEL IF I DIDN'T SHOW UP.
BUT...
THEY FOUND A BODY!
WHO IS IT?
SHE HANGED HERSELF!

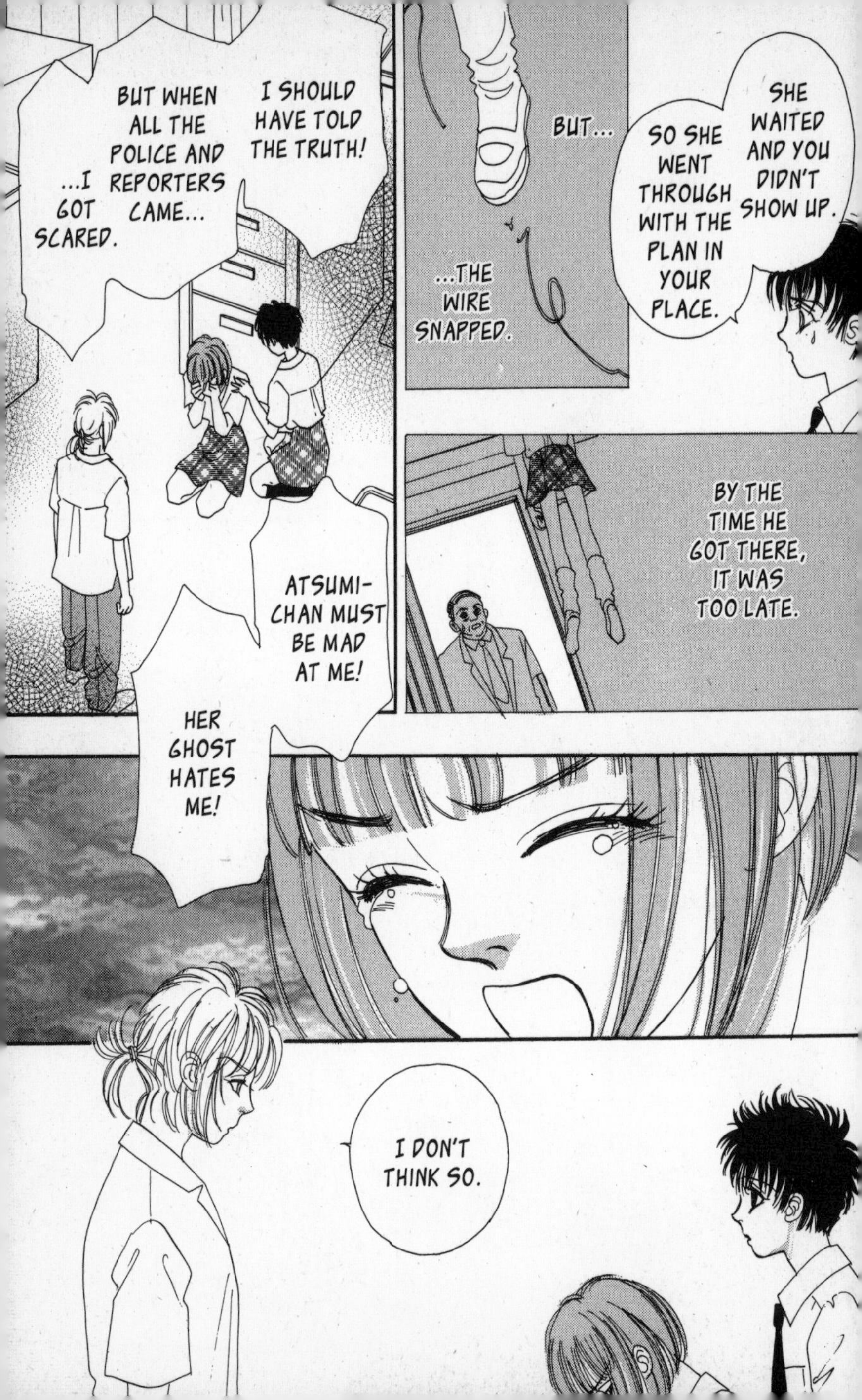
SHE WAITED AND YOU DIDN'T SHOW UP.
SO SHE WENT THROUGH WITH THE PLAN IN YOUR PLACE.
BUT...
...THE WIRE SNAPPED.
BY THE TIME HE GOT THERE, IT WAS TOO LATE.
I SHOULD HAVE TOLD THE TRUTH!
BUT WHEN ALL THE POLICE AND REPORTERS CAME...
...I GOT SCARED.
ATSUMI-CHAN MUST BE MAD AT ME!
HER GHOST HATES ME!
I DON'T THINK SO.

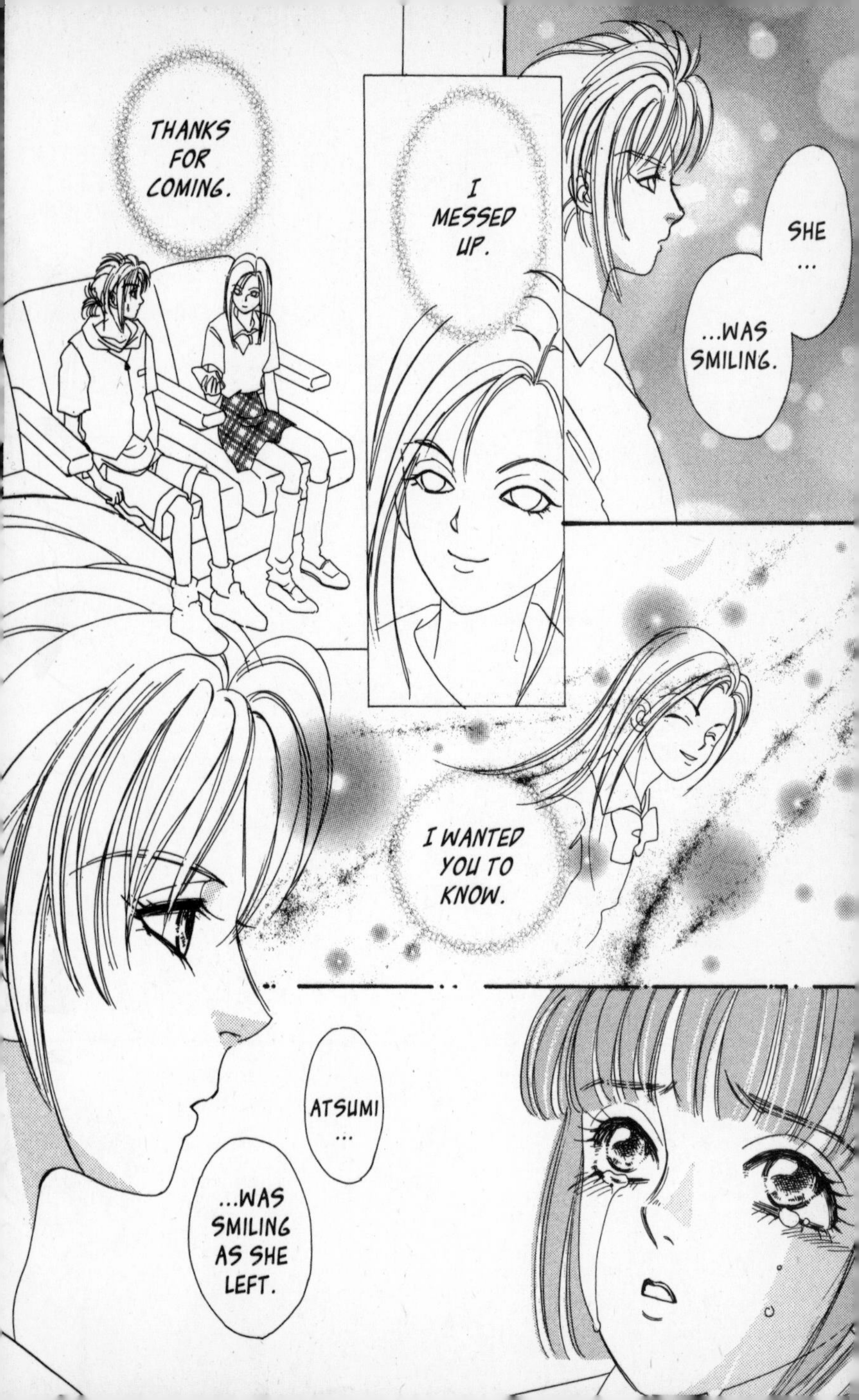
SHE ...
...WAS SMILING.
I MESSED UP.
THANKS FOR COMING.
I WANTED YOU TO KNOW.
ATSUMI ...
...WAS SMILING AS SHE LEFT.

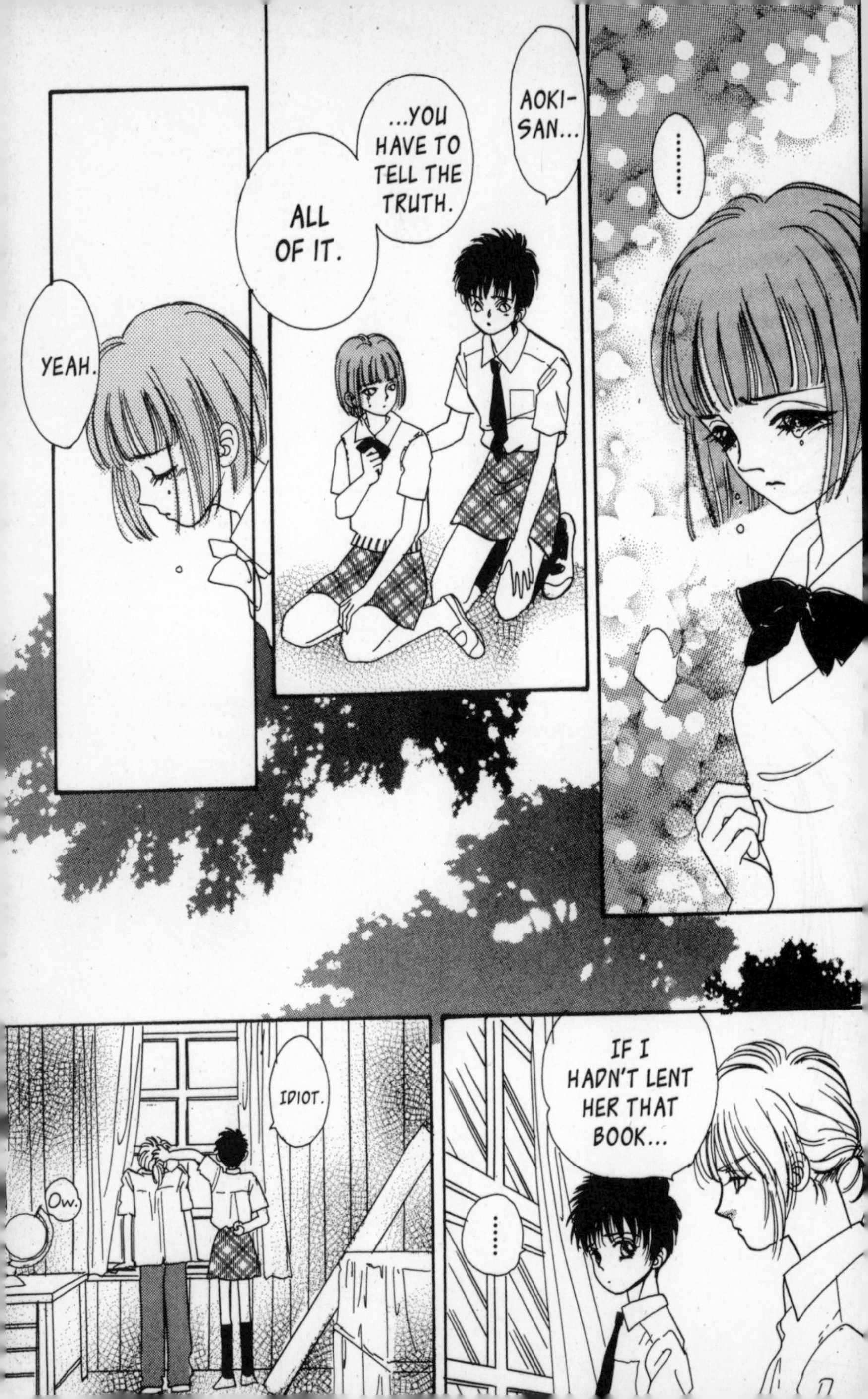
......
AOKI-SAN...
...YOU HAVE TO TELL THE TRUTH.
ALL OF IT.
YEAH.
IF I HADN'T LENT HER THAT BOOK...
......
IDIOT.
Ow.

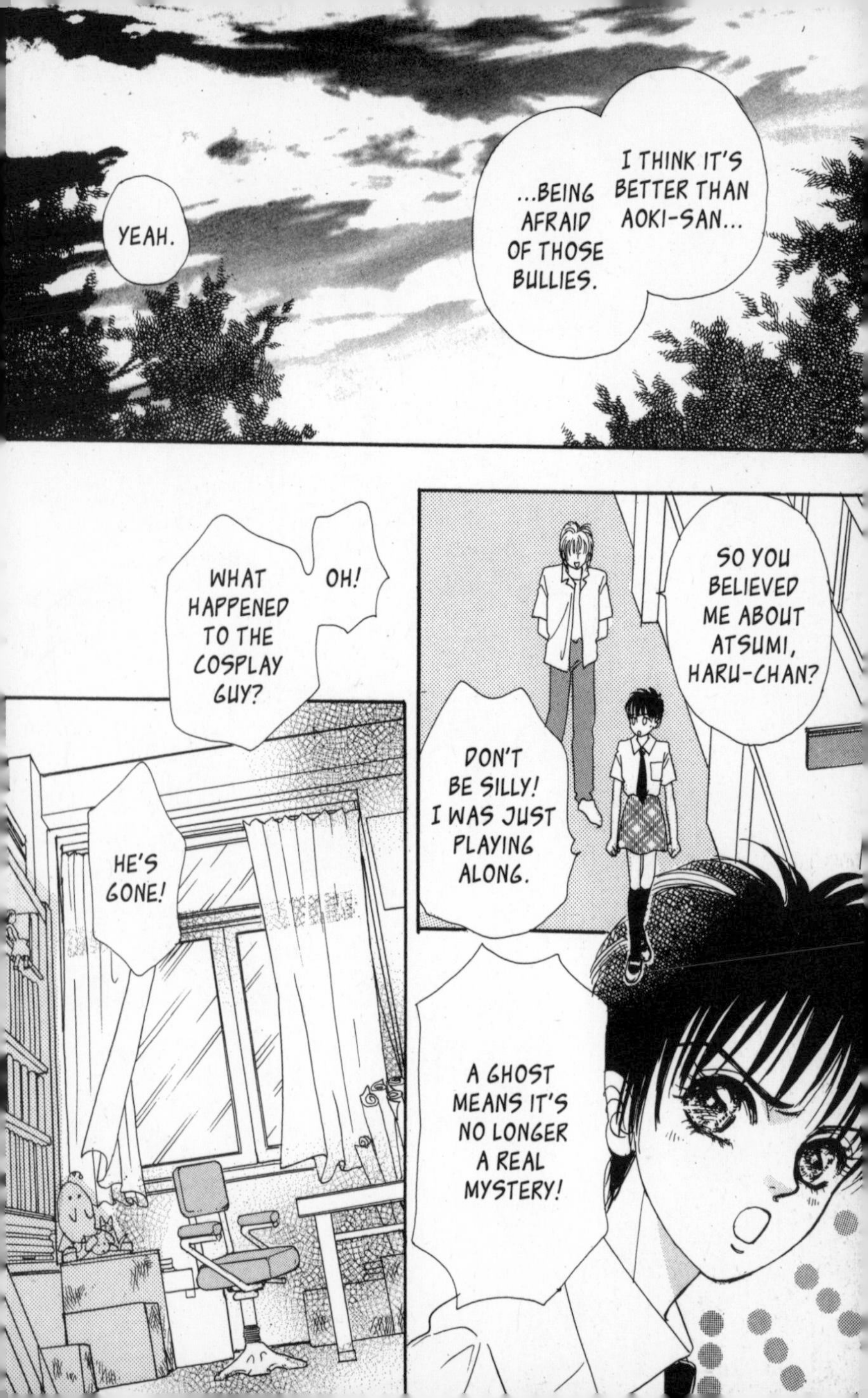
I THINK IT'S BETTER THAN AOKI-SAN...
...BEING AFRAID OF THOSE BULLIES.
YEAH.
SO YOU BELIEVED ME ABOUT ATSUMI, HARU-CHAN?
DON'T BE SILLY! I WAS JUST PLAYING ALONG.
A GHOST MEANS IT'S NO LONGER A REAL MYSTERY!
OH!
WHAT HAPPENED TO THE COSPLAY GUY?
HE'S GONE!

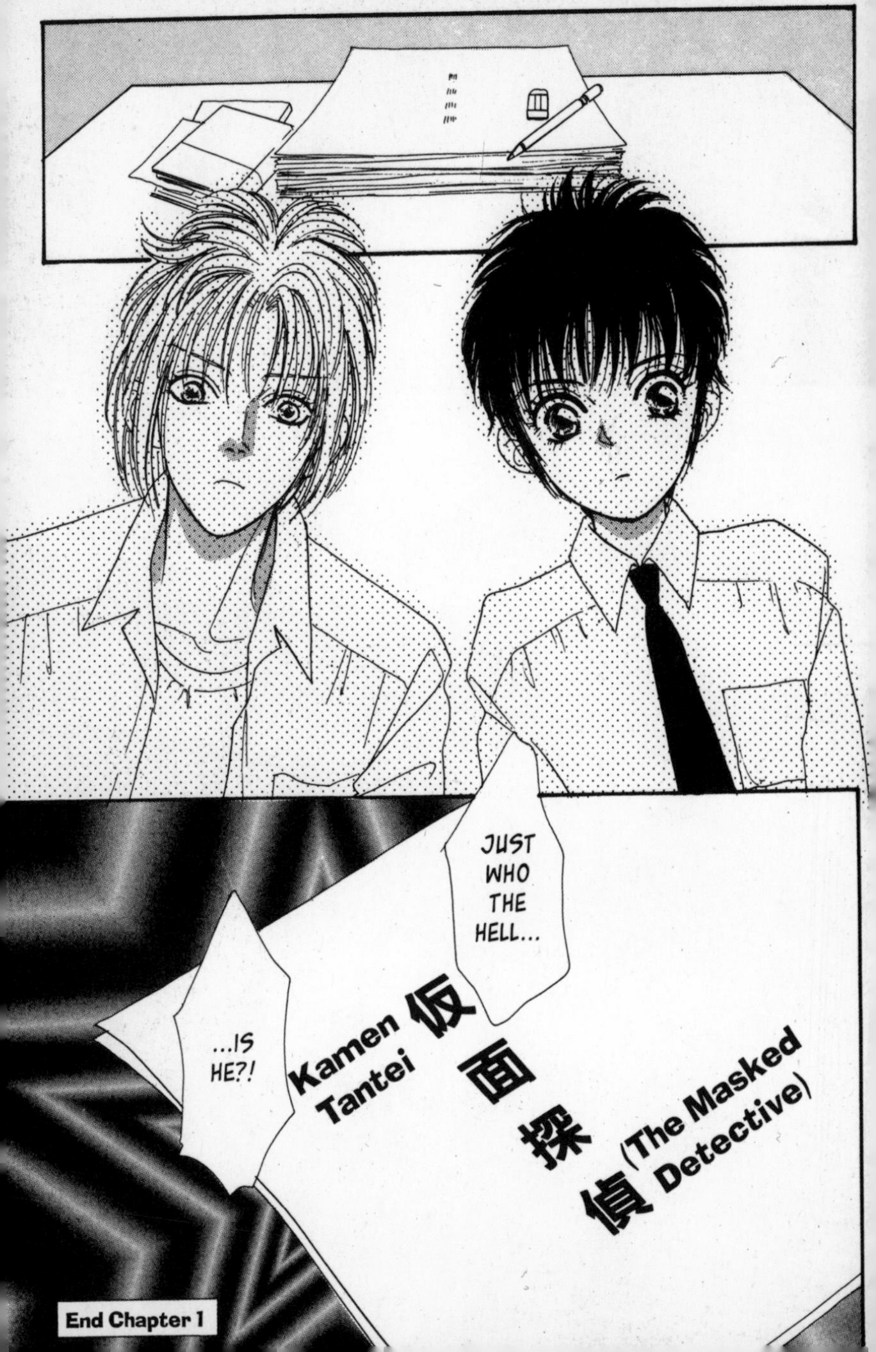
JUST WHO THE HELL...
...IS HE?!
Kamen Tantei 仮面探偵 (The Masked Detective)

End Chapter 1

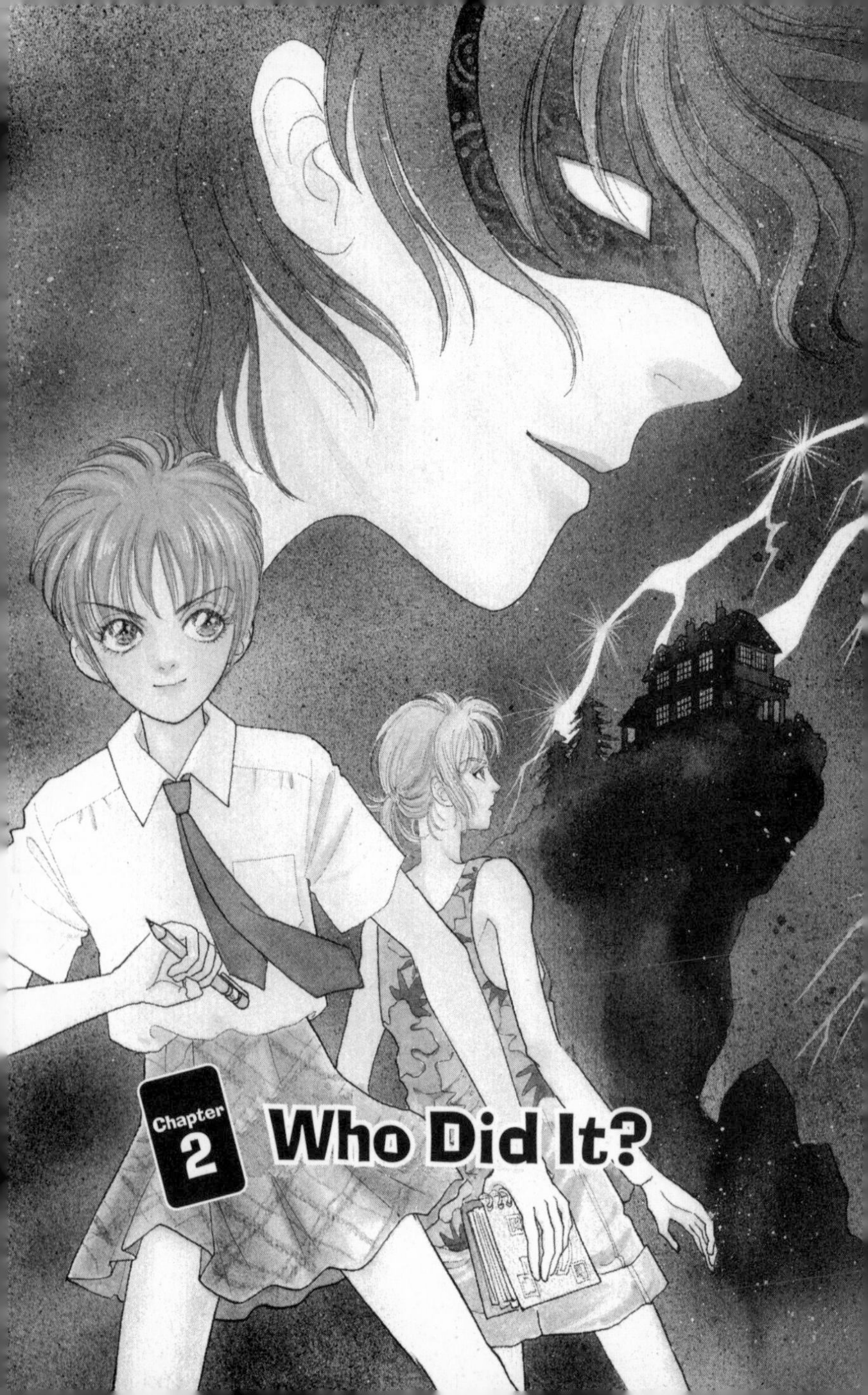
Chapter 2
Who Did It?

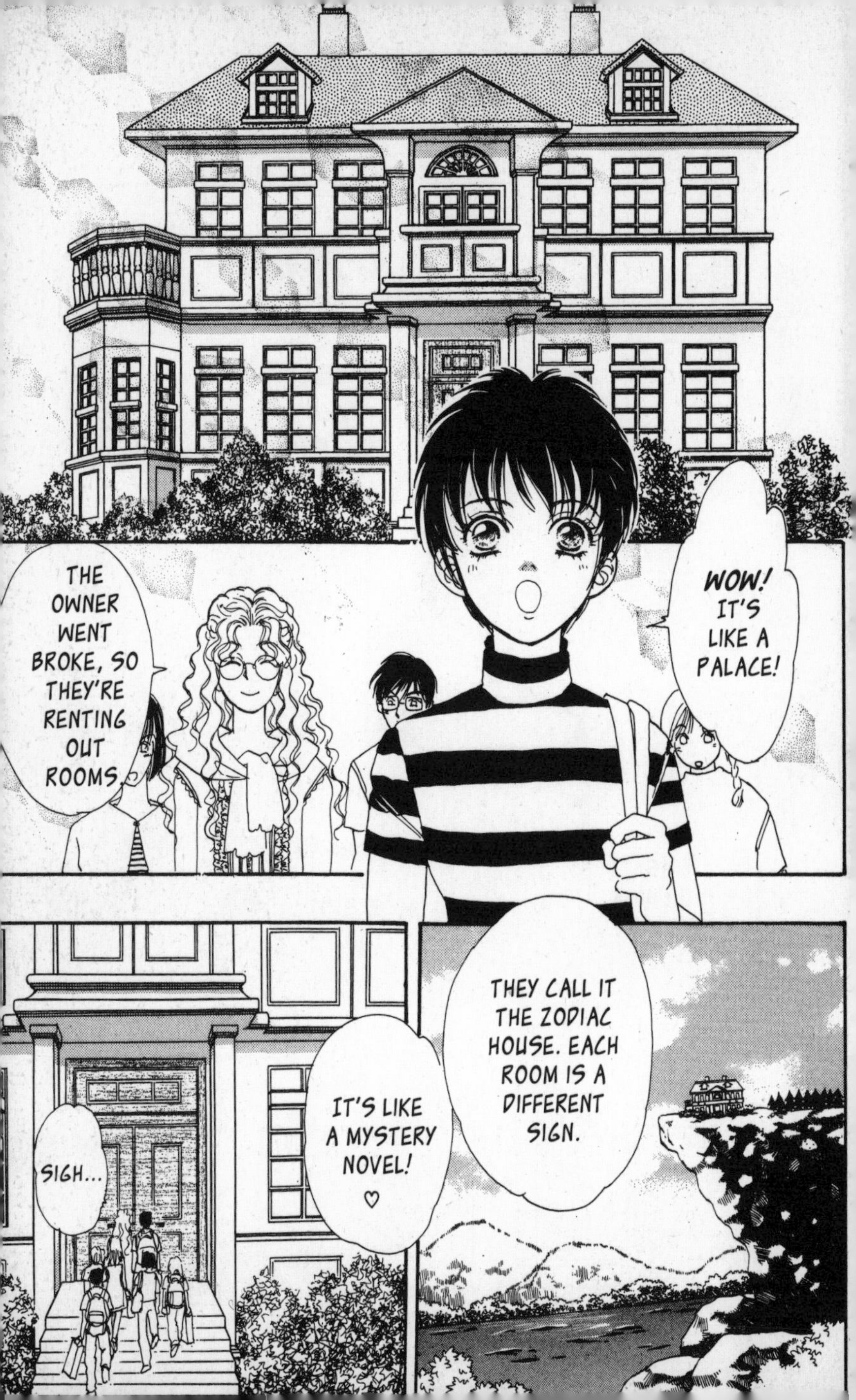
WOW! IT'S LIKE A PALACE!
THE OWNER WENT BROKE, SO THEY'RE RENTING OUT ROOMS.
THEY CALL IT THE ZODIAC HOUSE. EACH ROOM IS A DIFFERENT SIGN.
IT'S LIKE A MYSTERY NOVEL! ♡
SIGH...

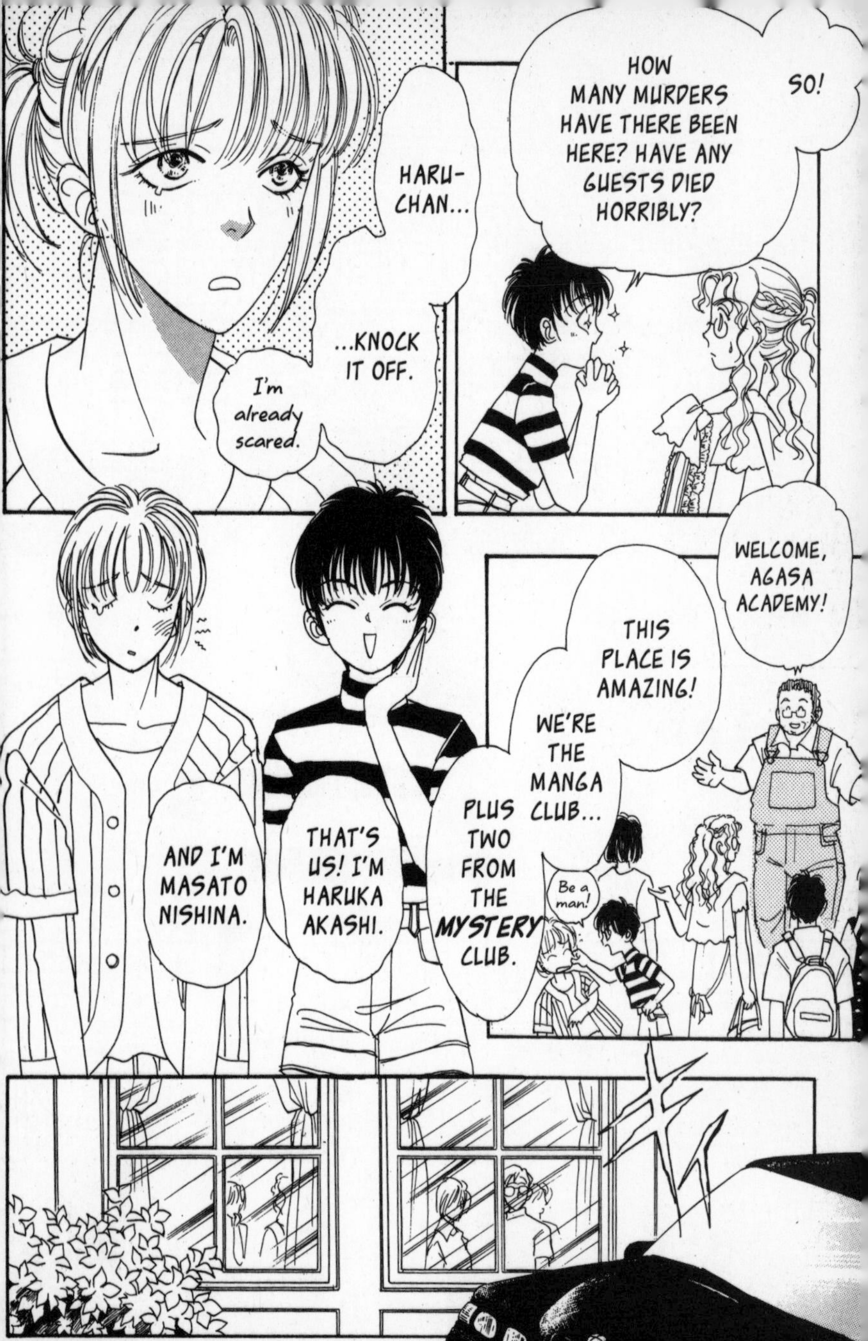
SO!
HOW MANY MURDERS HAVE THERE BEEN HERE? HAVE ANY GUESTS DIED HORRIBLY?
HARU-CHAN...
...KNOCK IT OFF.
I'm already scared.
WELCOME, AGASA ACADEMY!
THIS PLACE IS AMAZING!
WE'RE THE MANGA CLUB...
Be a man!
PLUS TWO FROM THE MYSTERY CLUB.
THAT'S US! I'M HARUKA AKASHI.
AND I'M MASATO NISHINA.

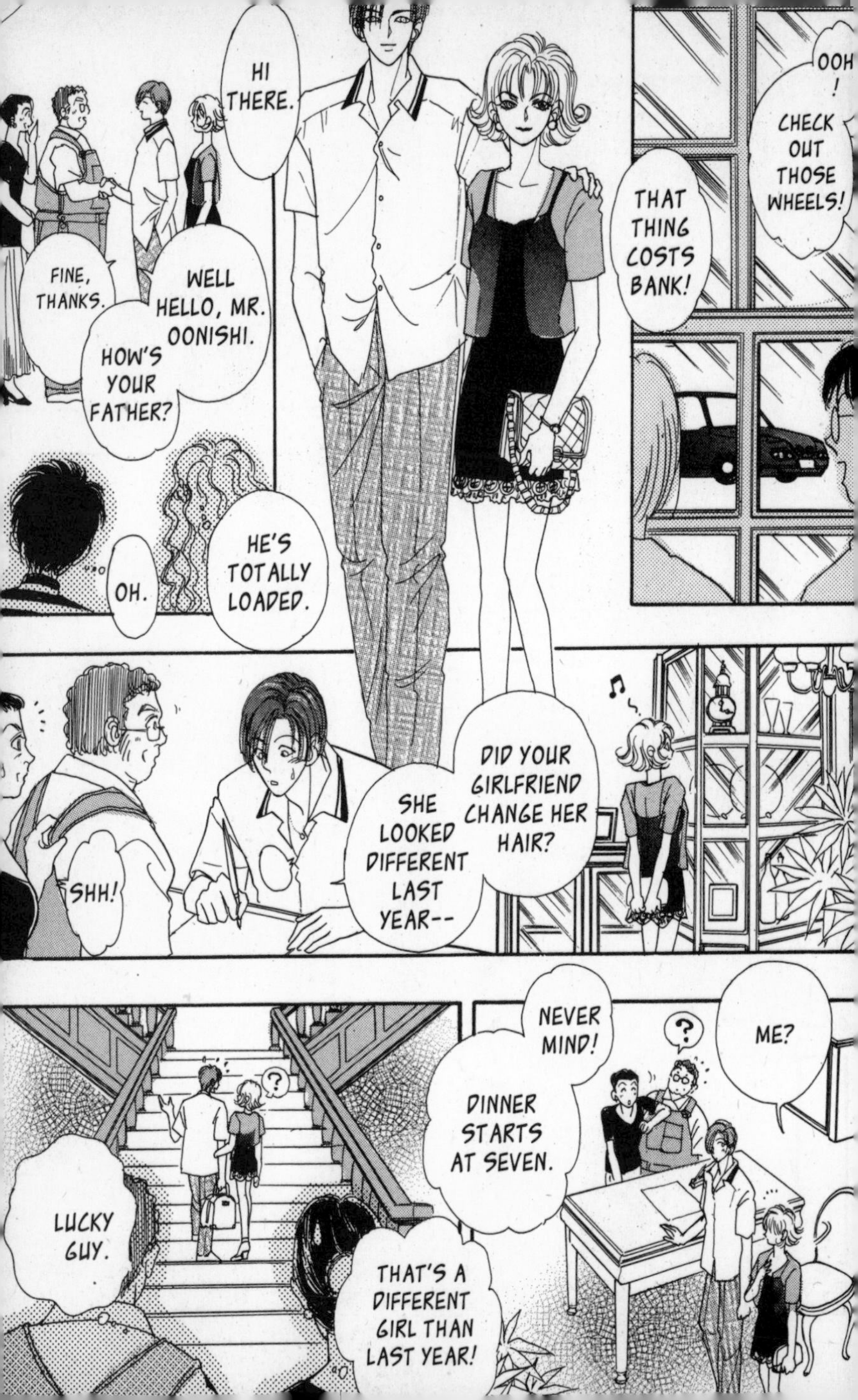
OOH! CHECK OUT THOSE WHEELS!
THAT THING COSTS BANK!
HI THERE.
WELL HELLO, MR. OONISHI. HOW'S YOUR FATHER?
FINE, THANKS.
HE'S TOTALLY LOADED.
OH.
DID YOUR GIRLFRIEND CHANGE HER HAIR?
SHE LOOKED DIFFERENT LAST YEAR--
SHH!
ME?
NEVER MIND!
DINNER STARTS AT SEVEN.
THAT'S A DIFFERENT GIRL THAN LAST YEAR!
LUCKY GUY.

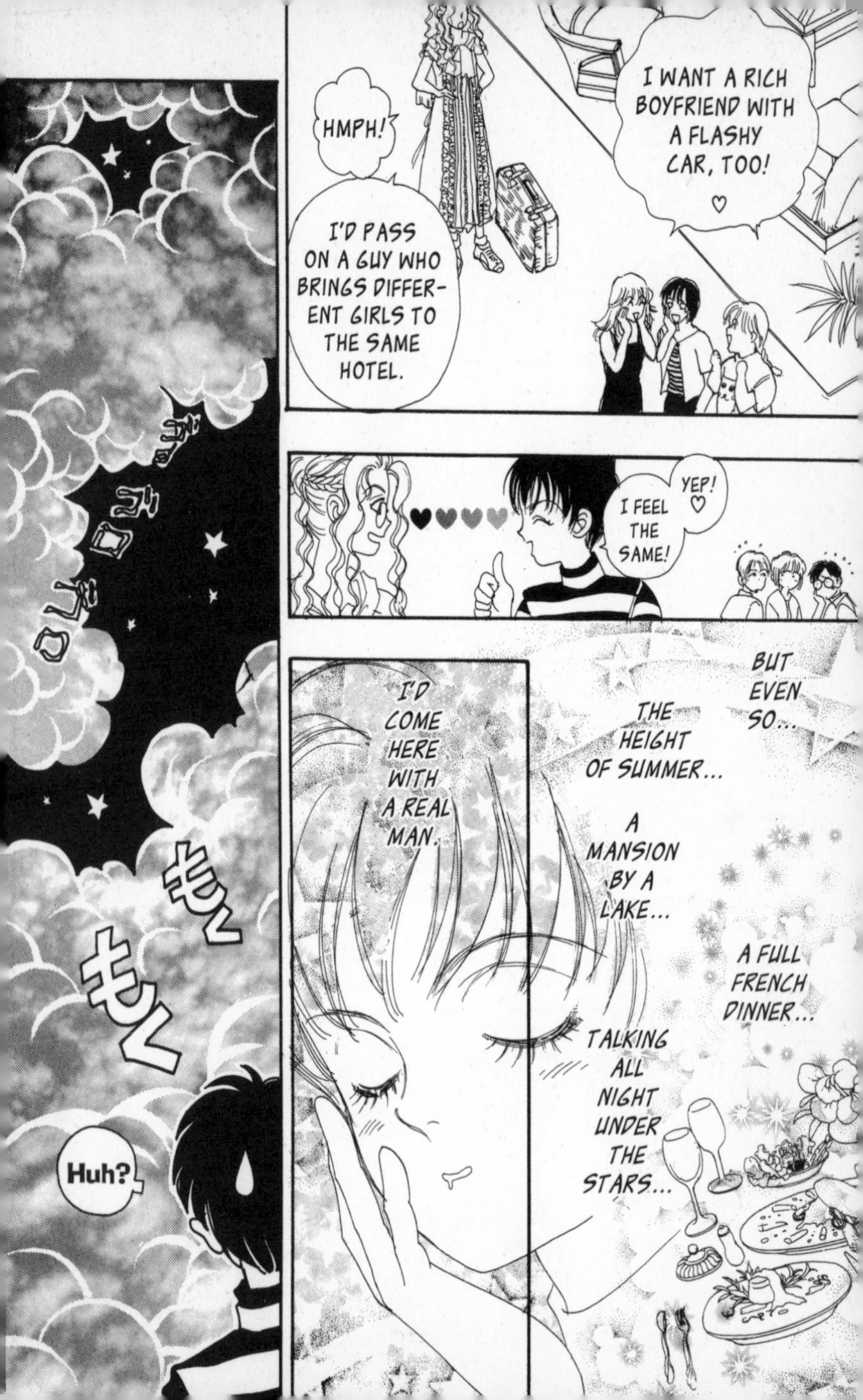
I WANT A RICH BOYFRIEND WITH A FLASHY CAR, TOO! ♡
HMPH!
I'D PASS ON A GUY WHO BRINGS DIFFERENT GIRLS TO THE SAME HOTEL.
YEP! ♡
I FEEL THE SAME!
BUT EVEN SO...
THE HEIGHT OF SUMMER...
A MANSION BY A LAKE...
A FULL FRENCH DINNER...
TALKING ALL NIGHT UNDER THE STARS...
I'D COME HERE WITH A REAL MAN.
ゴロゴロ
もく もく
Huh?

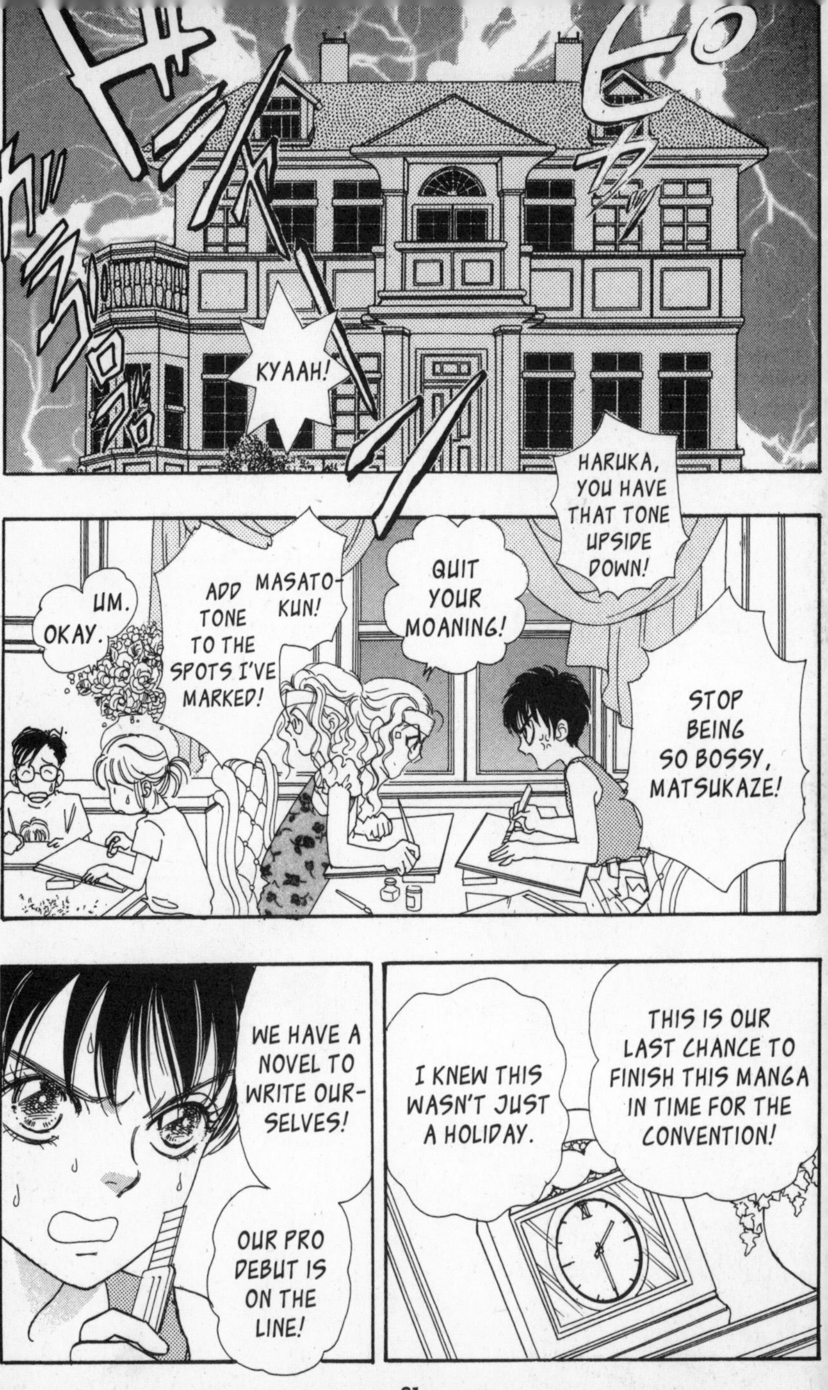
KYAAH!
HARUKA, YOU HAVE THAT TONE UPSIDE DOWN!
STOP BEING SO BOSSY, MATSUKAZE!
QUIT YOUR MOANING!
MASATO-KUN! ADD TONE TO THE SPOTS I'VE MARKED!
UM. OKAY.
THIS IS OUR LAST CHANCE TO FINISH THIS MANGA IN TIME FOR THE CONVENTION!
I KNEW THIS WASN'T JUST A HOLIDAY.
WE HAVE A NOVEL TO WRITE OUR-SELVES!
OUR PRO DEBUT IS ON THE LINE!

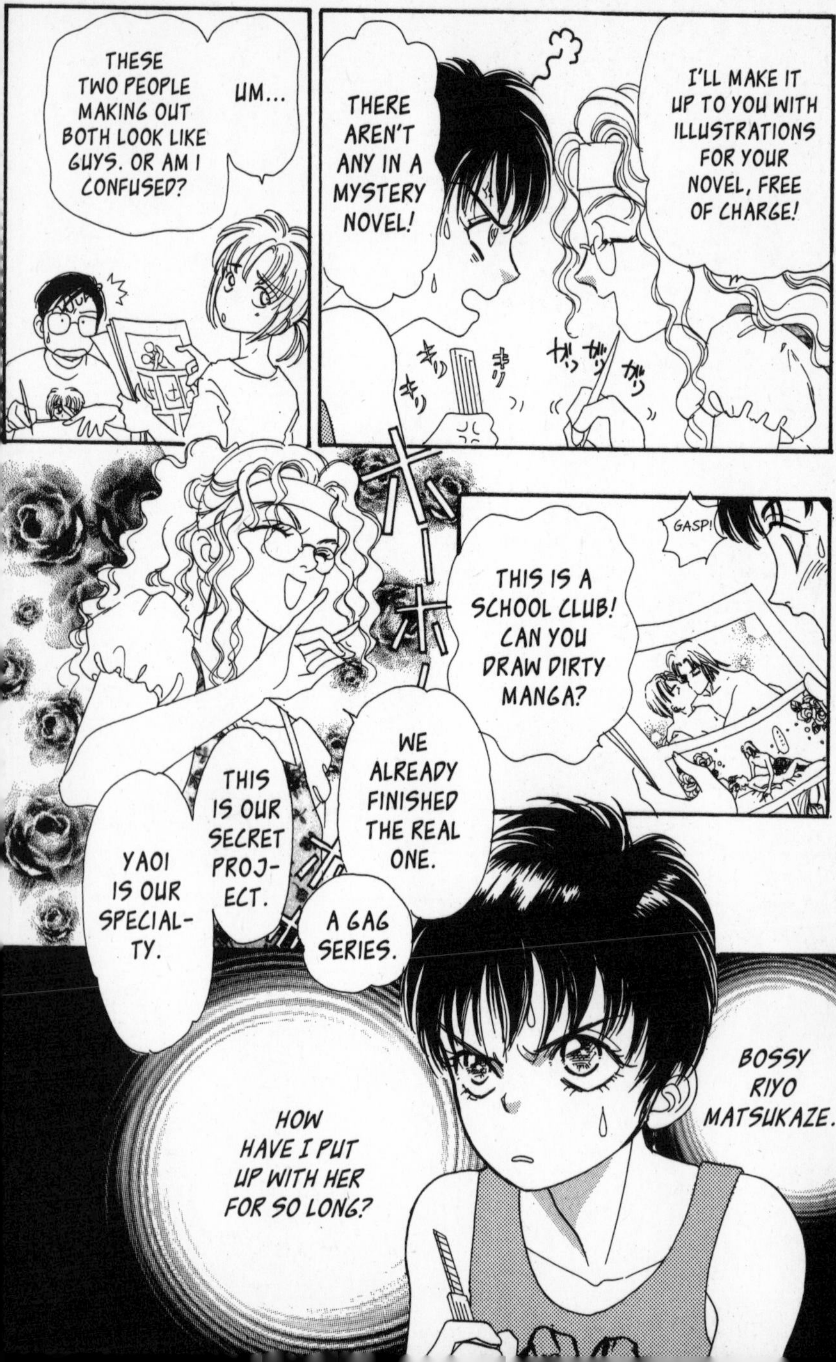
I'LL MAKE IT UP TO YOU WITH ILLUSTRATIONS FOR YOUR NOVEL, FREE OF CHARGE!
THERE AREN'T ANY IN A MYSTERY NOVEL!
UM...
THESE TWO PEOPLE MAKING OUT BOTH LOOK LIKE GUYS. OR AM I CONFUSED?
GASP!
THIS IS A SCHOOL CLUB! CAN YOU DRAW DIRTY MANGA?
WE ALREADY FINISHED THE REAL ONE.
A GAG SERIES.
THIS IS OUR SECRET PROJ-ECT.
YAOI IS OUR SPECIAL-TY.
BOSSY RIYO MATSUKAZE...
HOW HAVE I PUT UP WITH HER FOR SO LONG?

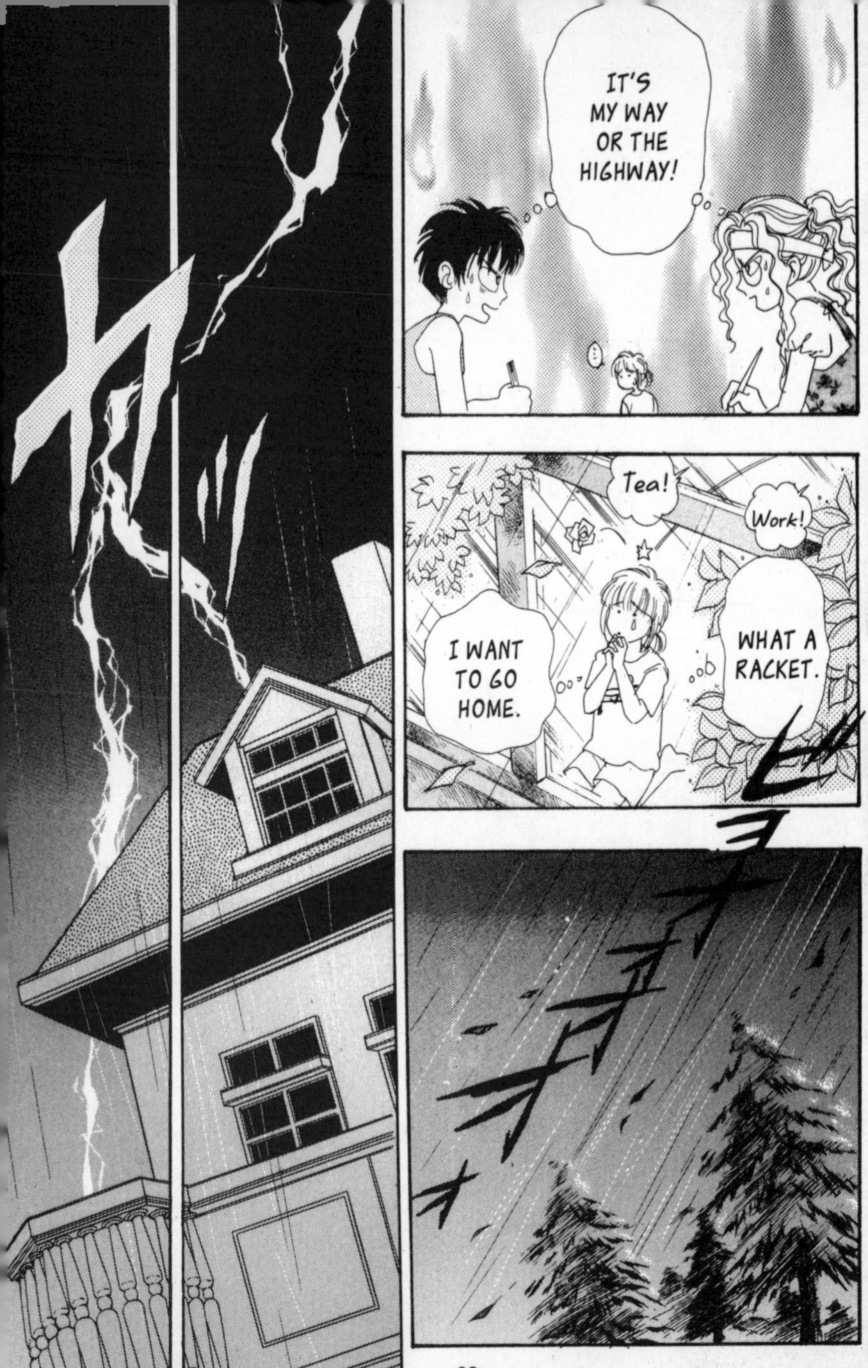
IT'S MY WAY OR THE HIGHWAY!
...
Work!
Tea!
WHAT A RACKET.
I WANT TO GO HOME.

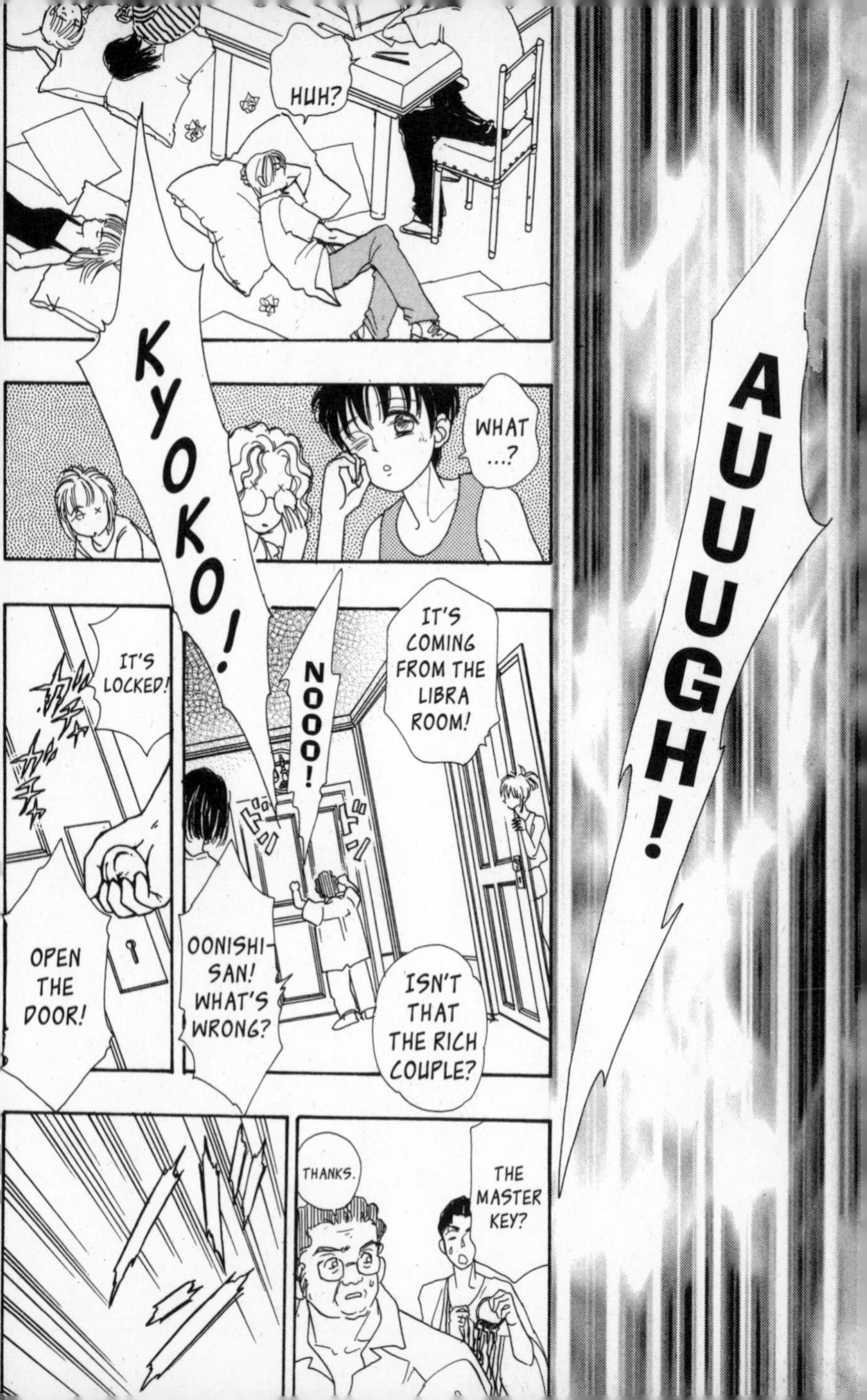
AUUUGH!
HUH?
KYOKO!
WHAT ...?
IT'S COMING FROM THE LIBRA ROOM!
NOOOO!
ISN'T THAT THE RICH COUPLE?
OONISHI-SAN! WHAT'S WRONG?
IT'S LOCKED!
OPEN THE DOOR!
THE MASTER KEY?
THANKS.

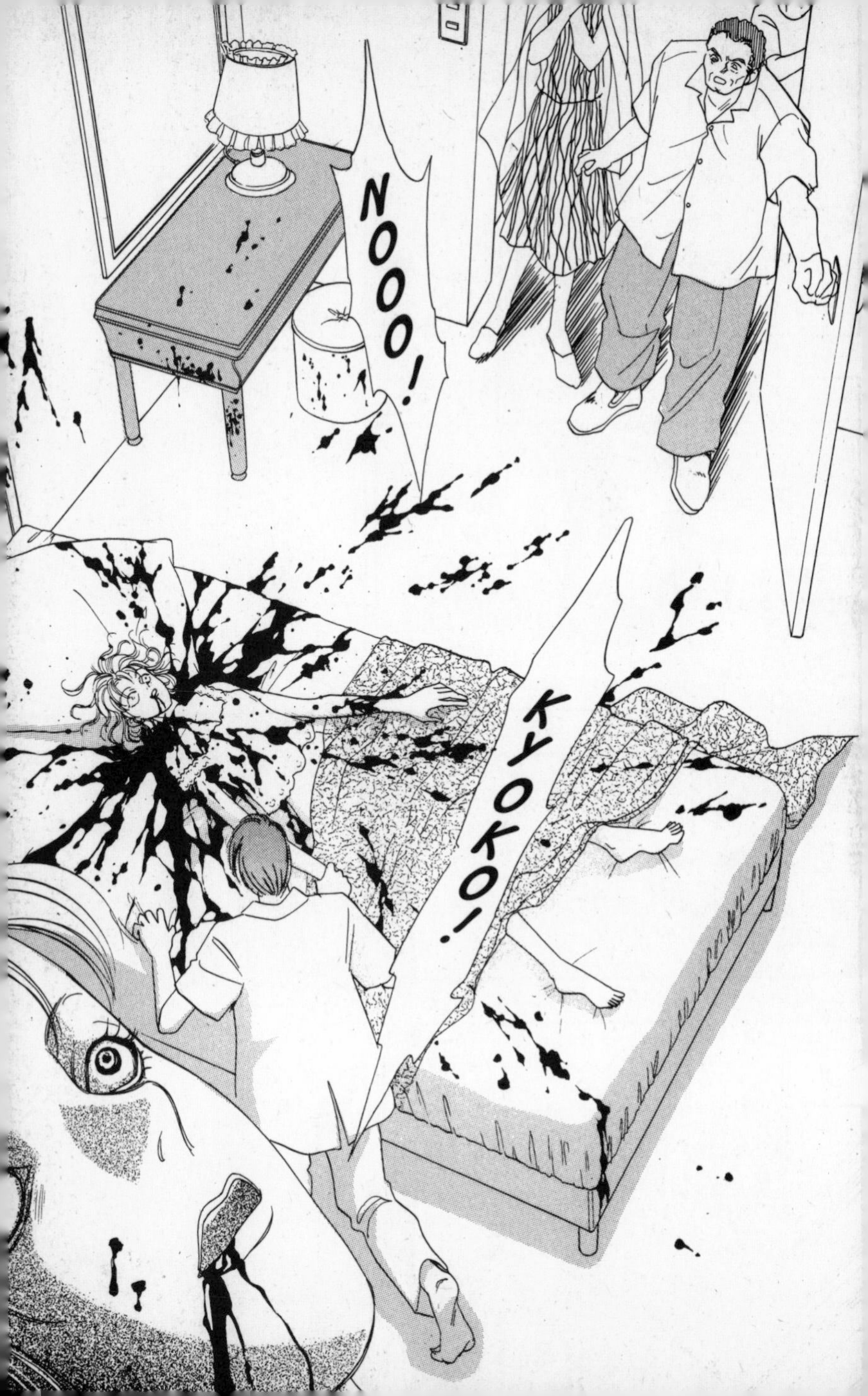
NOOOO!
KYOKO!!

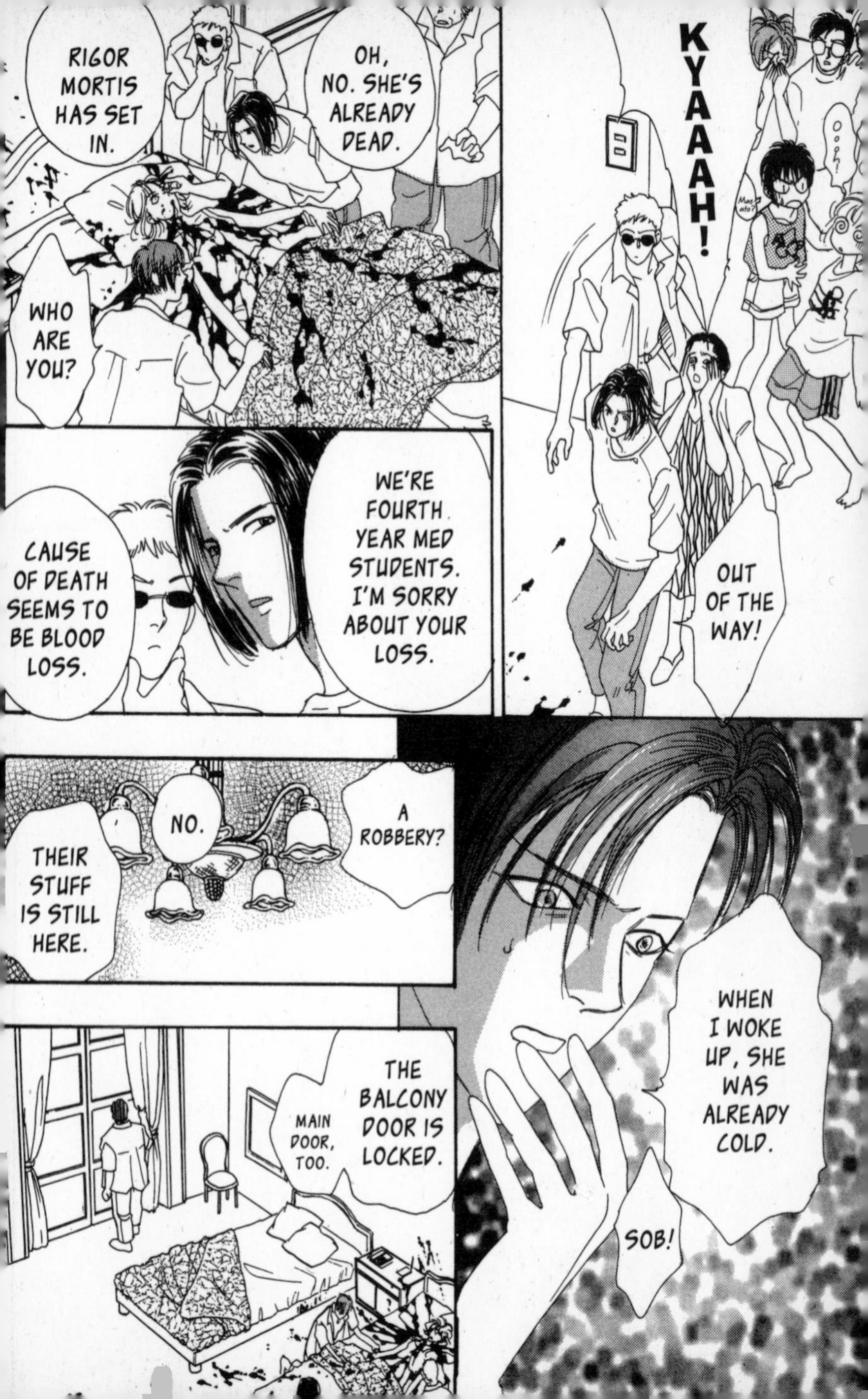
KYAAAH!
Masato?
OUT OF THE WAY!
OH, NO. SHE'S ALREADY DEAD.
RIGOR MORTIS HAS SET IN.
WHO ARE YOU?
WE'RE FOURTH YEAR MED STUDENTS. I'M SORRY ABOUT YOUR LOSS.
CAUSE OF DEATH SEEMS TO BE BLOOD LOSS.
WHEN I WOKE UP, SHE WAS ALREADY COLD.
SOB!
A ROBBERY?
NO.
THEIR STUFF IS STILL HERE.
THE BALCONY DOOR IS LOCKED.
MAIN DOOR, TOO.

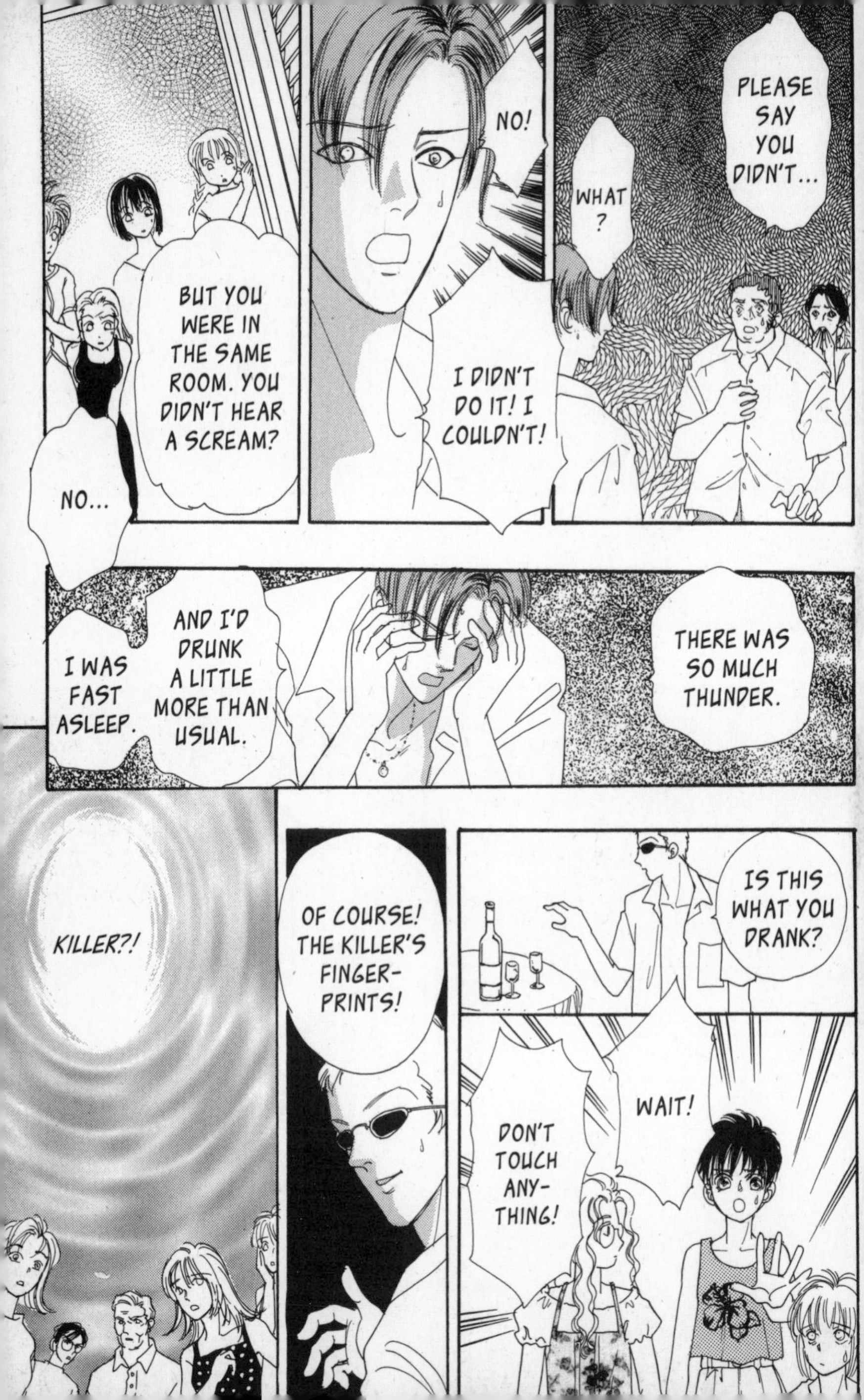
PLEASE SAY YOU DIDN'T...
WHAT?
NO!
I DIDN'T DO IT! I COULDN'T!
BUT YOU WERE IN THE SAME ROOM. YOU DIDN'T HEAR A SCREAM?
NO...
THERE WAS SO MUCH THUNDER.
AND I'D DRUNK A LITTLE MORE THAN USUAL.
I WAS FAST ASLEEP.
IS THIS WHAT YOU DRANK?
WAIT!
DON'T TOUCH ANY-THING!
OF COURSE! THE KILLER'S FINGER-PRINTS!
KILLER?!

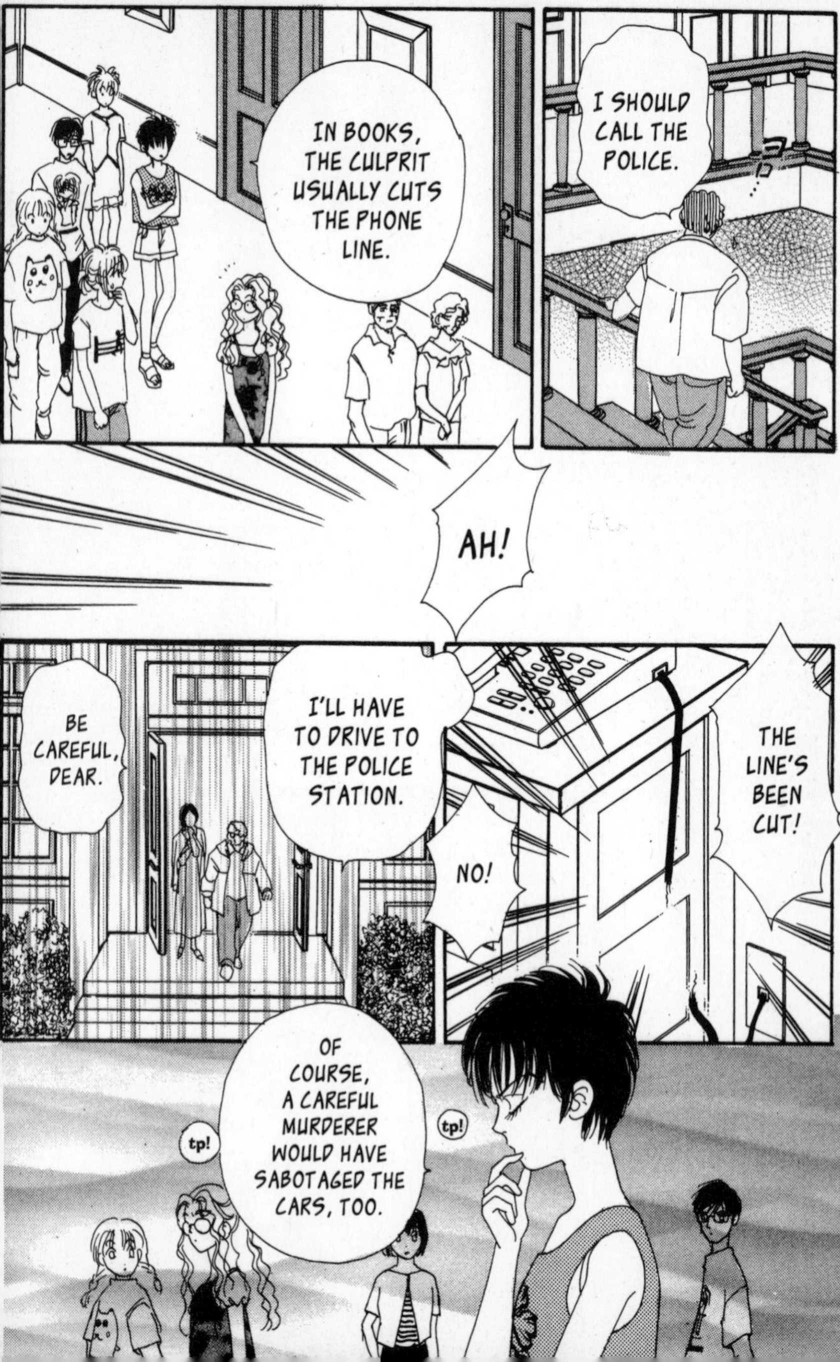
I SHOULD CALL THE POLICE.
IN BOOKS, THE CULPRIT USUALLY CUTS THE PHONE LINE.
AH!
THE LINE'S BEEN CUT!
NO!
I'LL HAVE TO DRIVE TO THE POLICE STATION.
BE CAREFUL, DEAR.
tp!
OF COURSE, A CAREFUL MURDERER WOULD HAVE SABOTAGED THE CARS, TOO.
tp!

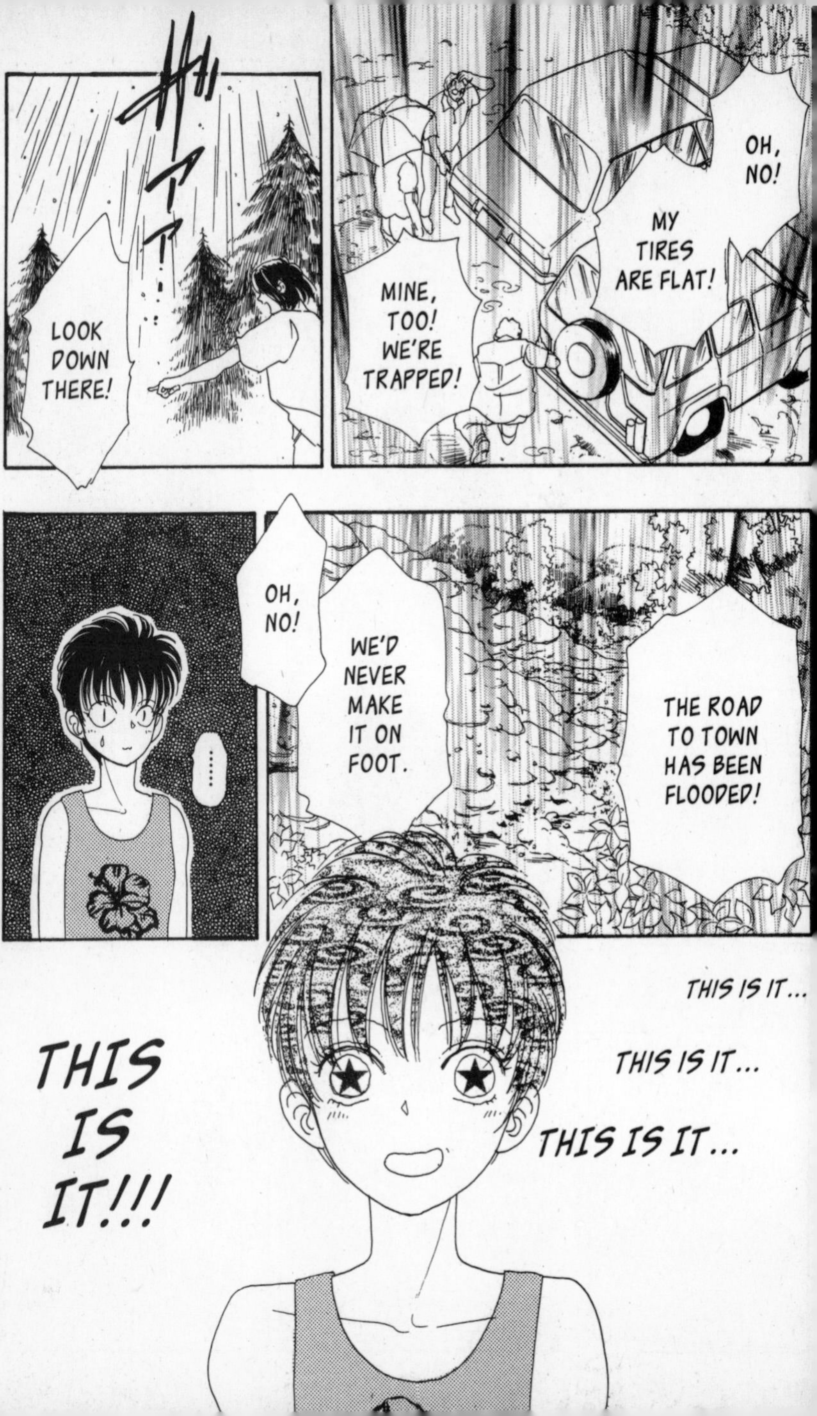
OH, NO!
MY TIRES ARE FLAT!
MINE, TOO! WE'RE TRAPPED!
LOOK DOWN THERE!
THE ROAD TO TOWN HAS BEEN FLOODED!
WE'D NEVER MAKE IT ON FOOT.
OH, NO!
......
THIS IS IT...
THIS IS IT...
THIS IS IT...
THIS IS IT!!!

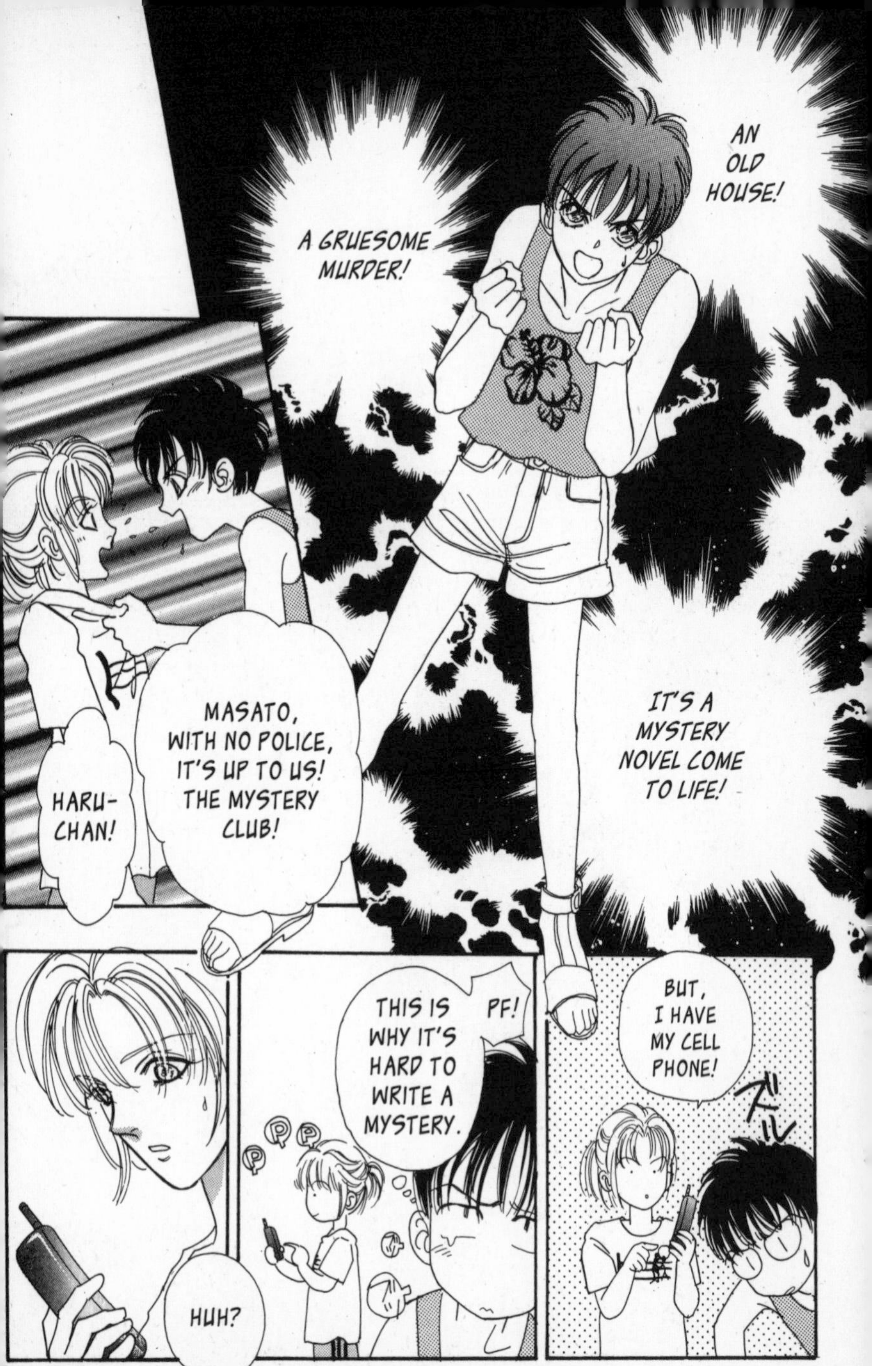
AN OLD HOUSE!
A GRUESOME MURDER!
IT'S A MYSTERY NOVEL COME TO LIFE!
MASATO, WITH NO POLICE, IT'S UP TO US! THE MYSTERY CLUB!
HARU-CHAN!
BUT, I HAVE MY CELL PHONE!
PF!
THIS IS WHY IT'S HARD TO WRITE A MYSTERY.
HUH?

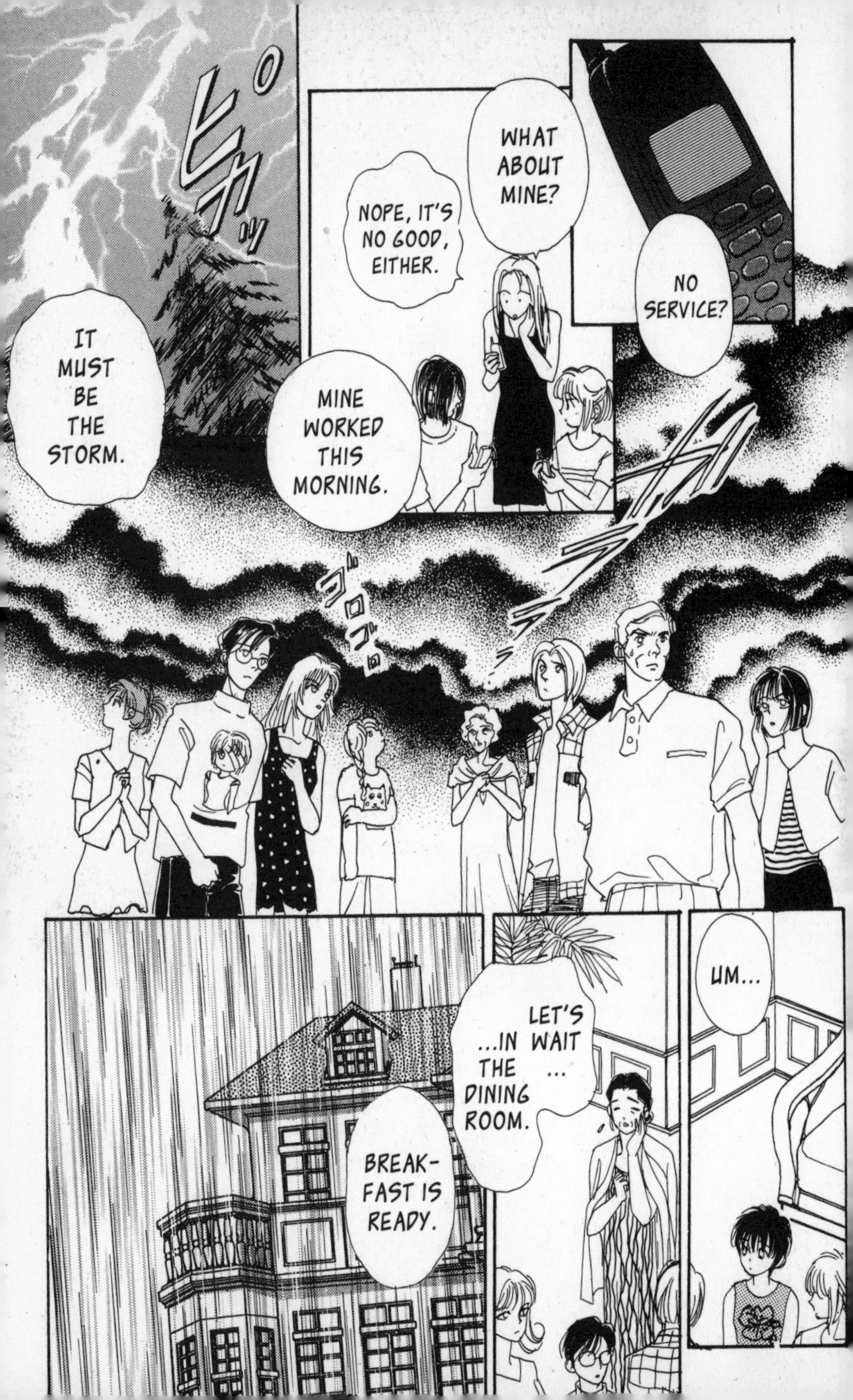
NO SERVICE?
WHAT ABOUT MINE?
NOPE, IT'S NO GOOD, EITHER.
MINE WORKED THIS MORNING.
ピカッ
IT MUST BE THE STORM.
ゴロゴロ
UM...
LET'S WAIT ...
...IN THE DINING ROOM.
BREAK-FAST IS READY.

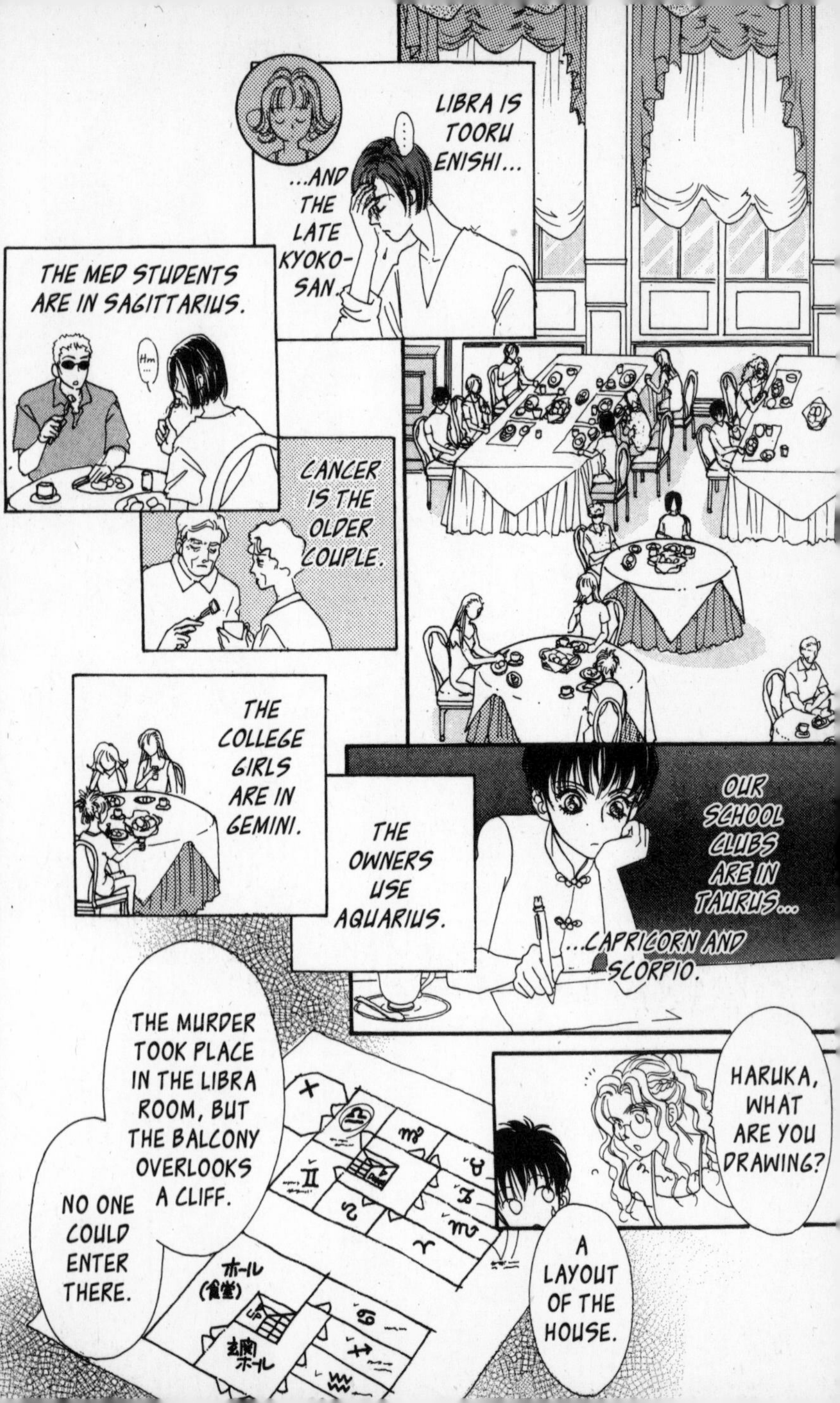

LIBRA IS TOORU ENISHI...
...
...AND THE LATE KYOKO-SAN.
THE MED STUDENTS ARE IN SAGITTARIUS.
Hm...
CANCER IS THE OLDER COUPLE.
THE COLLEGE GIRLS ARE IN GEMINI.
THE OWNERS USE AQUARIUS.
OUR SCHOOL CLUBS ARE IN TAURUS...
...CAPRICORN AND SCORPIO.
HARUKA, WHAT ARE YOU DRAWING?
A LAYOUT OF THE HOUSE.
THE MURDER TOOK PLACE IN THE LIBRA ROOM, BUT THE BALCONY OVERLOOKS A CLIFF.
NO ONE COULD ENTER THERE.
ホール
(食堂)
玄関ホール

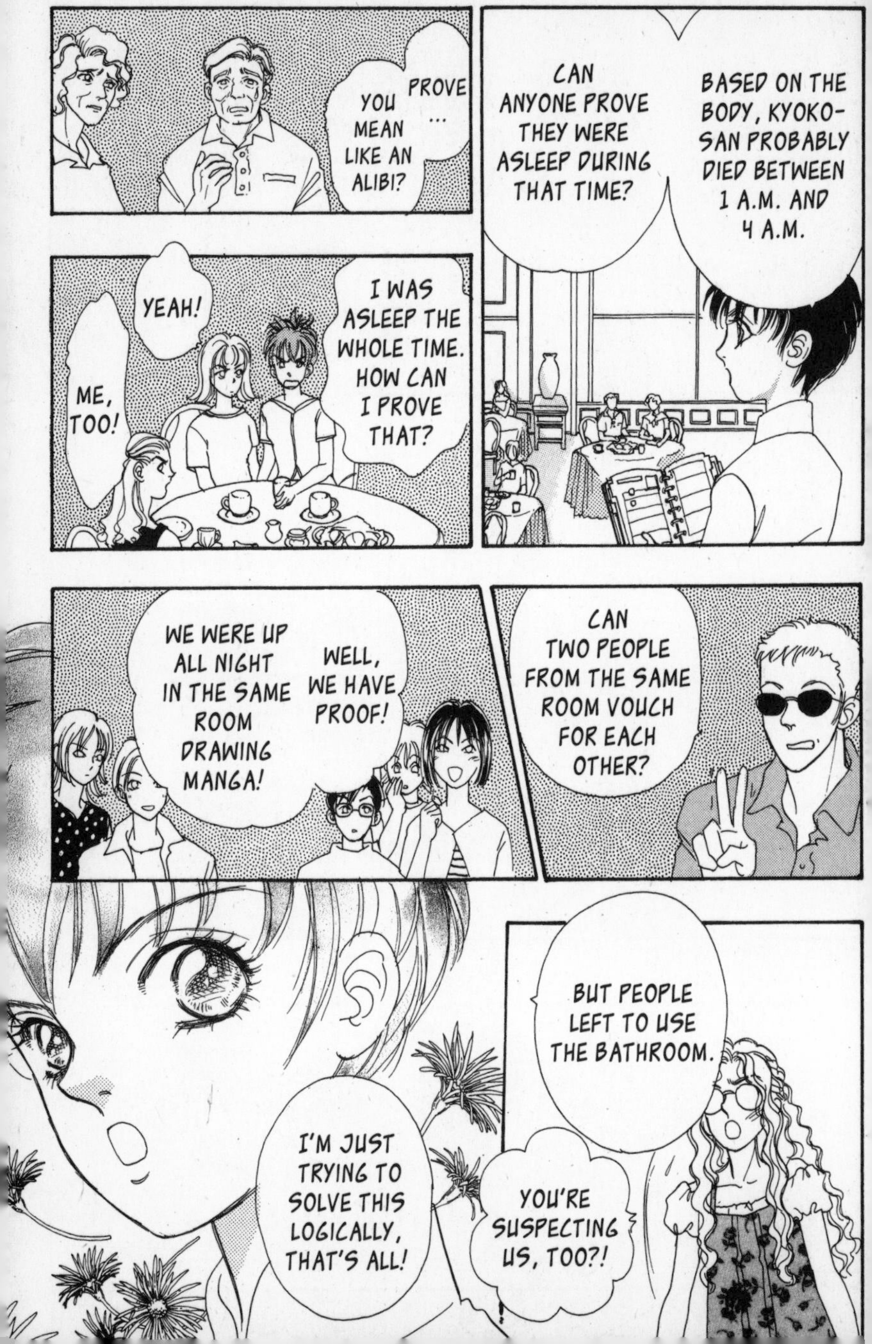
BASED ON THE BODY, KYOKO-SAN PROBABLY DIED BETWEEN 1 A.M. AND 4 A.M.
CAN ANYONE PROVE THEY WERE ASLEEP DURING THAT TIME?
PROVE...
YOU MEAN LIKE AN ALIBI?
I WAS ASLEEP THE WHOLE TIME. HOW CAN I PROVE THAT?
YEAH!
ME, TOO!
CAN TWO PEOPLE FROM THE SAME ROOM VOUCH FOR EACH OTHER?
WELL, WE HAVE PROOF!
WE WERE UP ALL NIGHT IN THE SAME ROOM DRAWING MANGA!
BUT PEOPLE LEFT TO USE THE BATHROOM.
YOU'RE SUSPECTING US, TOO?!
I'M JUST TRYING TO SOLVE THIS LOGICALLY, THAT'S ALL!

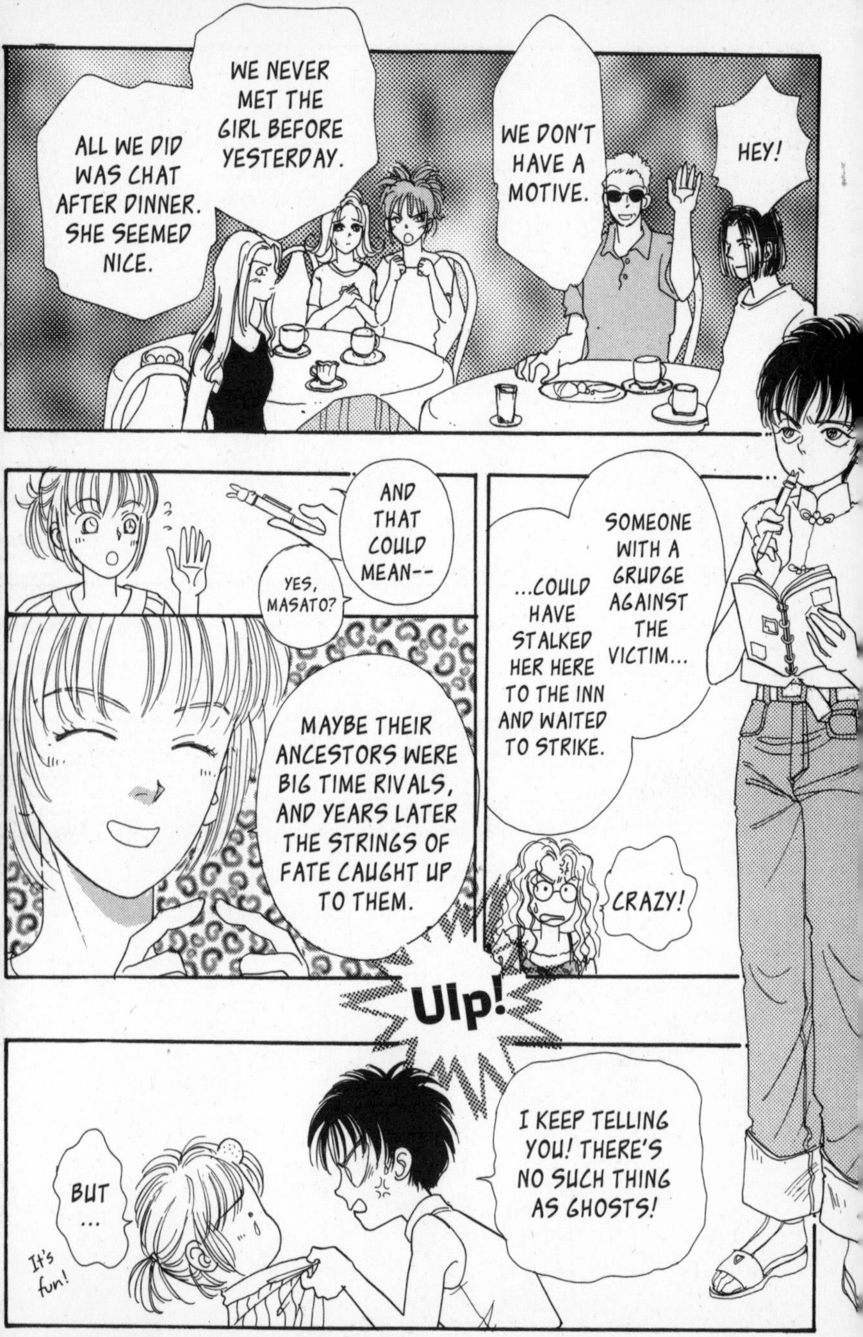
HEY!
WE DON'T HAVE A MOTIVE.
WE NEVER MET THE GIRL BEFORE YESTERDAY.
ALL WE DID WAS CHAT AFTER DINNER. SHE SEEMED NICE.
SOMEONE WITH A GRUDGE AGAINST THE VICTIM...
...COULD HAVE STALKED HER HERE TO THE INN AND WAITED TO STRIKE.
CRAZY!
AND THAT COULD MEAN--
YES, MASATO?
MAYBE THEIR ANCESTORS WERE BIG TIME RIVALS, AND YEARS LATER THE STRINGS OF FATE CAUGHT UP TO THEM.
Ulp!
I KEEP TELLING YOU! THERE'S NO SUCH THING AS GHOSTS!
BUT ...
It's fun!

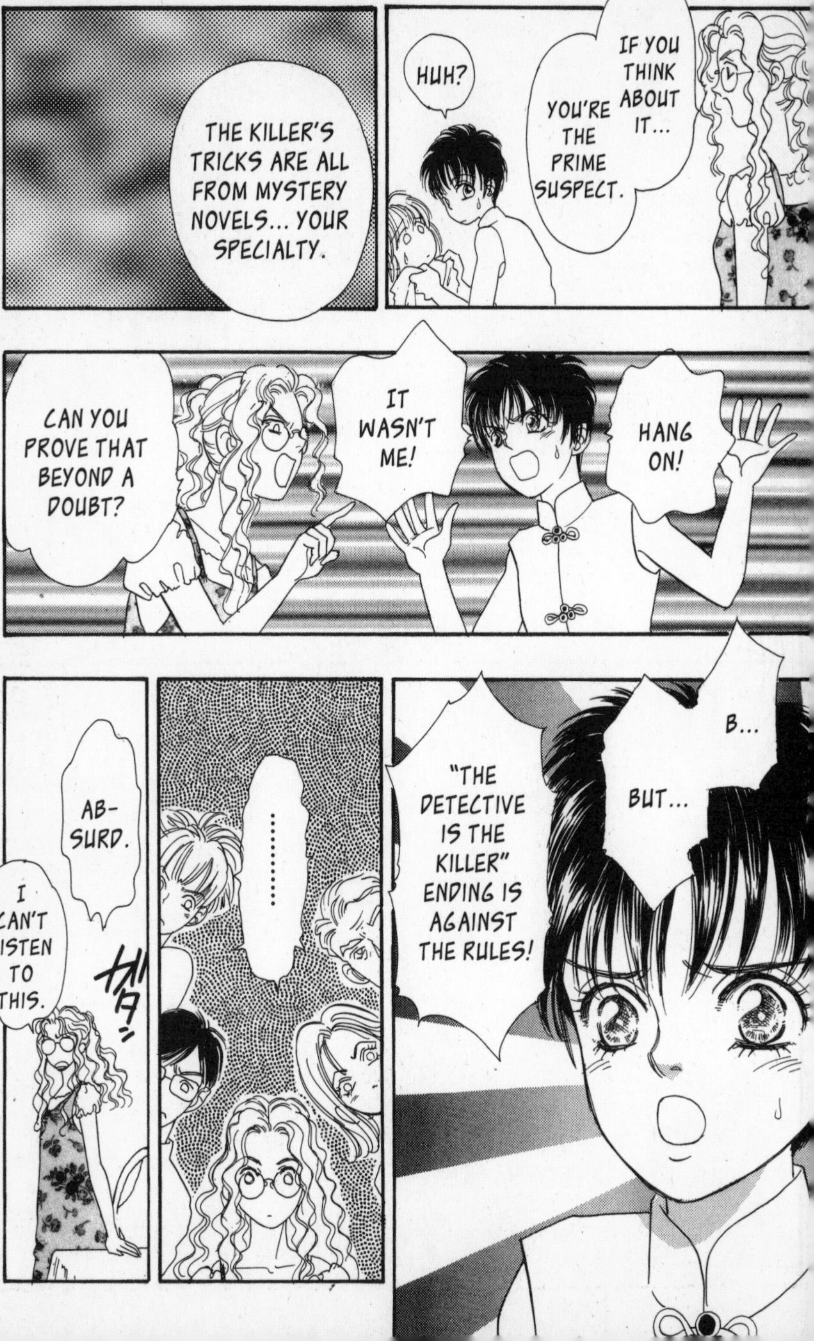
IF YOU THINK ABOUT IT...
YOU'RE THE PRIME SUSPECT.
HUH?
THE KILLER'S TRICKS ARE ALL FROM MYSTERY NOVELS... YOUR SPECIALTY.
HANG ON!
IT WASN'T ME!
CAN YOU PROVE THAT BEYOND A DOUBT?
B...
BUT...
"THE DETECTIVE IS THE KILLER" ENDING IS AGAINST THE RULES!
......
AB-SURD.
I CAN'T LISTEN TO THIS.

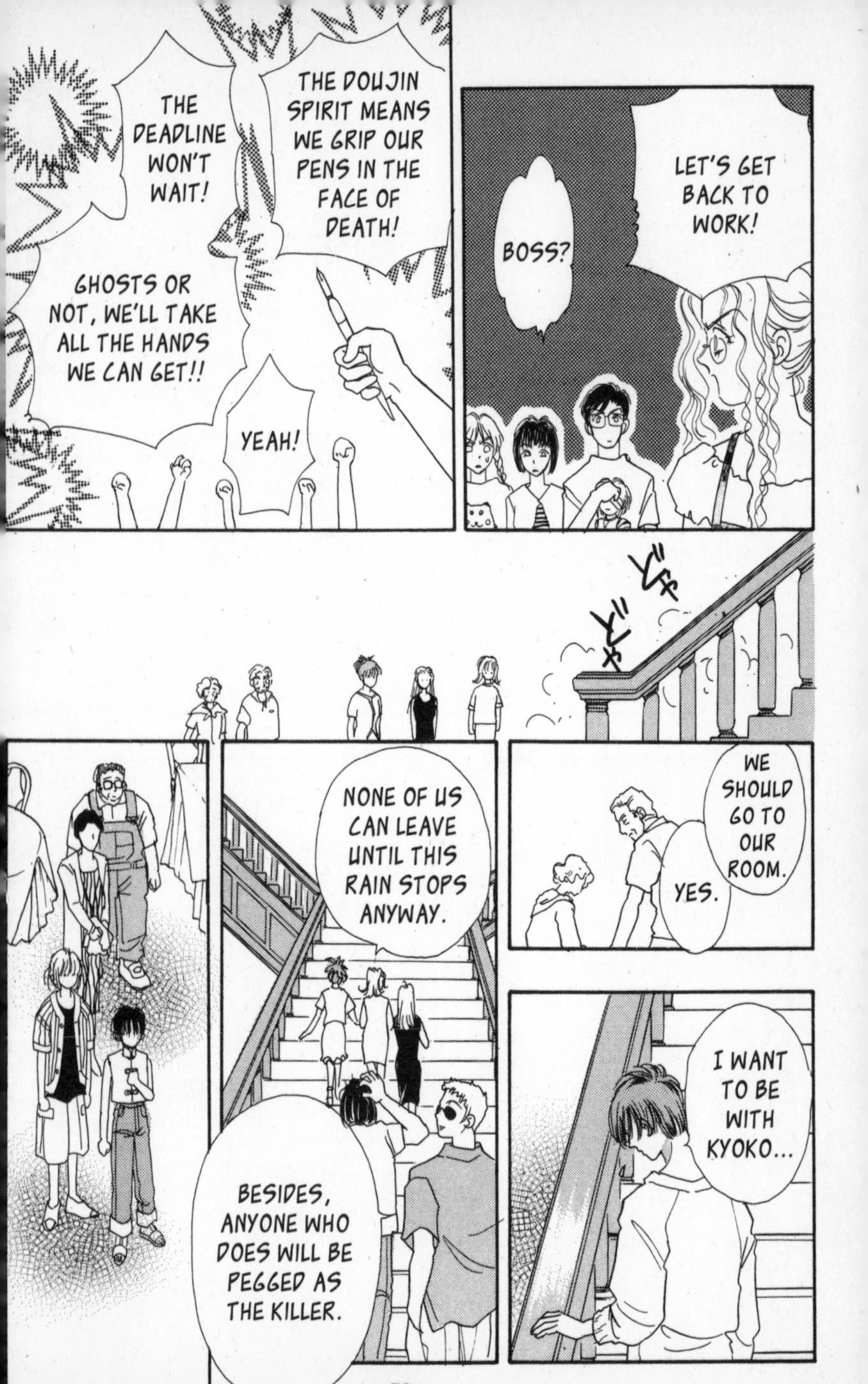
LET'S GET BACK TO WORK!
BOSS?
THE DOUJIN SPIRIT MEANS WE GRIP OUR PENS IN THE FACE OF DEATH!
THE DEADLINE WON'T WAIT!
GHOSTS OR NOT, WE'LL TAKE ALL THE HANDS WE CAN GET!!
YEAH!
ドヤ
ドヤ
WE SHOULD GO TO OUR ROOM.
YES.
I WANT TO BE WITH KYOKO...
NONE OF US CAN LEAVE UNTIL THIS RAIN STOPS ANYWAY.
BESIDES, ANYONE WHO DOES WILL BE PEGGED AS THE KILLER.

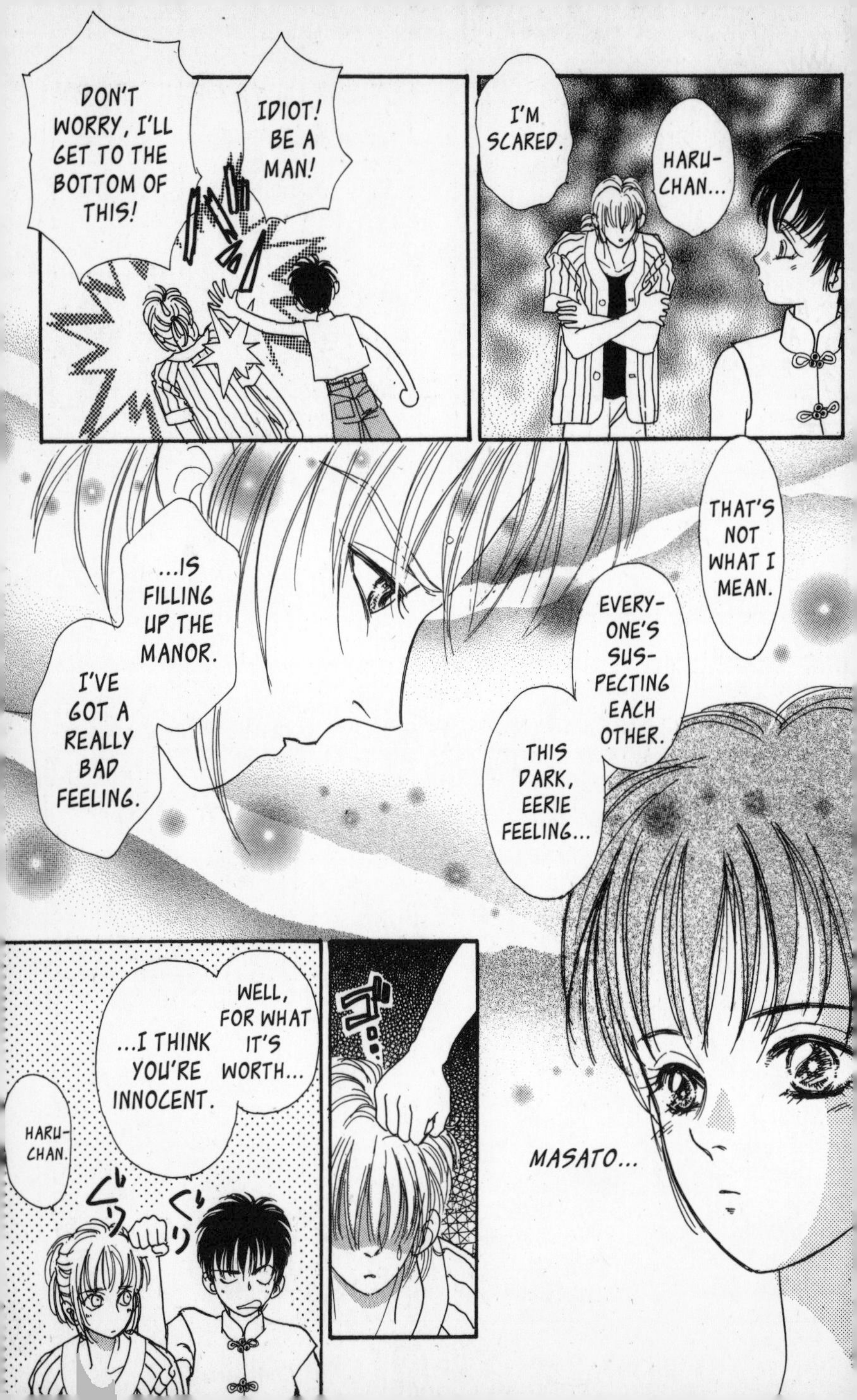
HARU-CHAN...
I'M SCARED.
IDIOT! BE A MAN!
DON'T WORRY, I'LL GET TO THE BOTTOM OF THIS!
THAT'S NOT WHAT I MEAN.
EVERY-ONE'S SUS-PECTING EACH OTHER.
THIS DARK, EERIE FEELING...
...IS FILLING UP THE MANOR.
I'VE GOT A REALLY BAD FEELING.
MASATO...
WELL, FOR WHAT IT'S WORTH...
...I THINK YOU'RE INNOCENT.
HARU-CHAN.

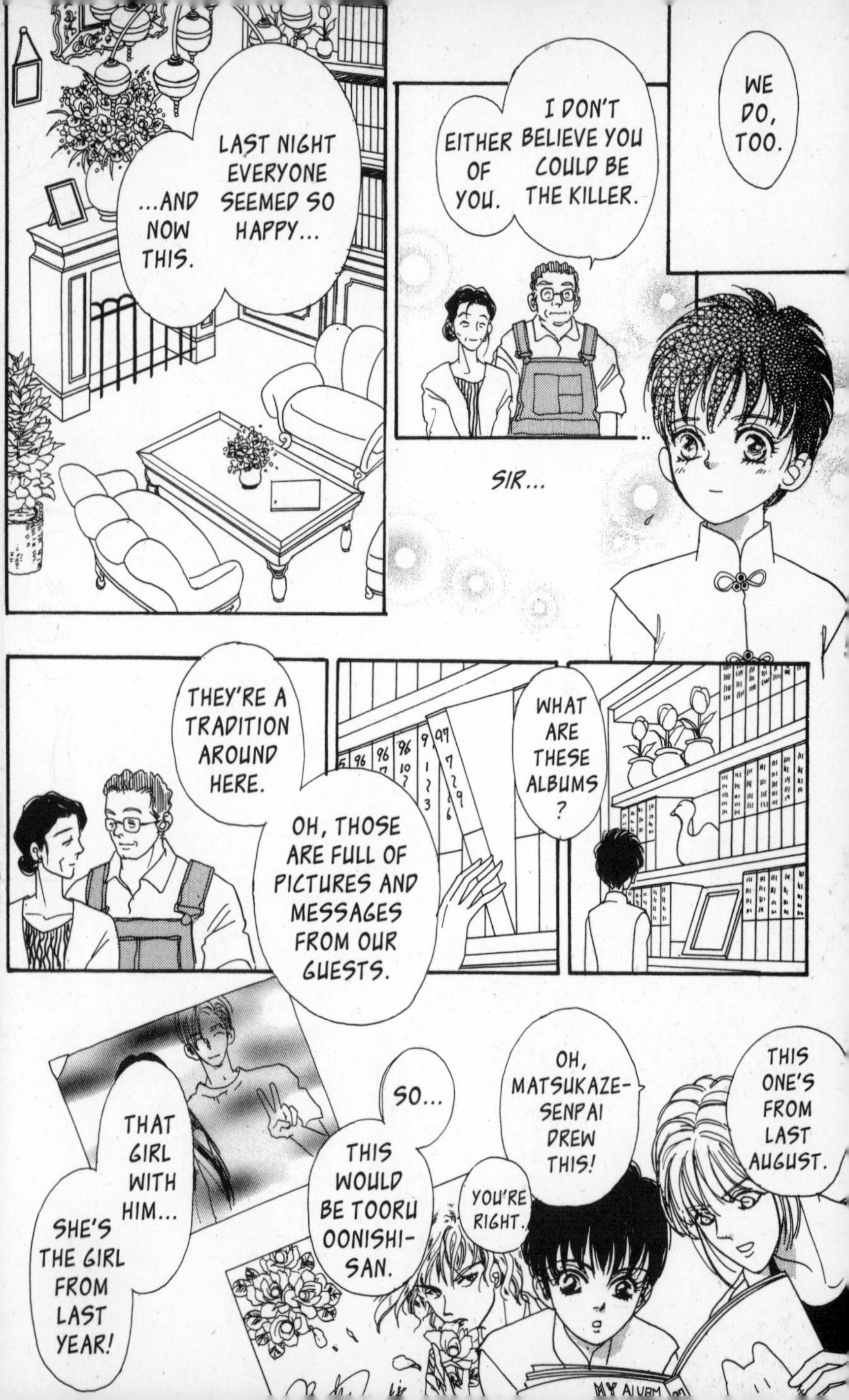
WE DO, TOO.
SIR...
I DON'T BELIEVE YOU COULD BE THE KILLER.
EITHER OF YOU.
LAST NIGHT EVERYONE SEEMED SO HAPPY...
...AND NOW THIS.
WHAT ARE THESE ALBUMS?
OH, THOSE ARE FULL OF PICTURES AND MESSAGES FROM OUR GUESTS.
THEY'RE A TRADITION AROUND HERE.
THIS ONE'S FROM LAST AUGUST.
OH, MATSUKAZE-SENPAI DREW THIS!
YOU'RE RIGHT.
SO...
THIS WOULD BE TOORU OONISHI-SAN.
THAT GIRL WITH HIM...
SHE'S THE GIRL FROM LAST YEAR!

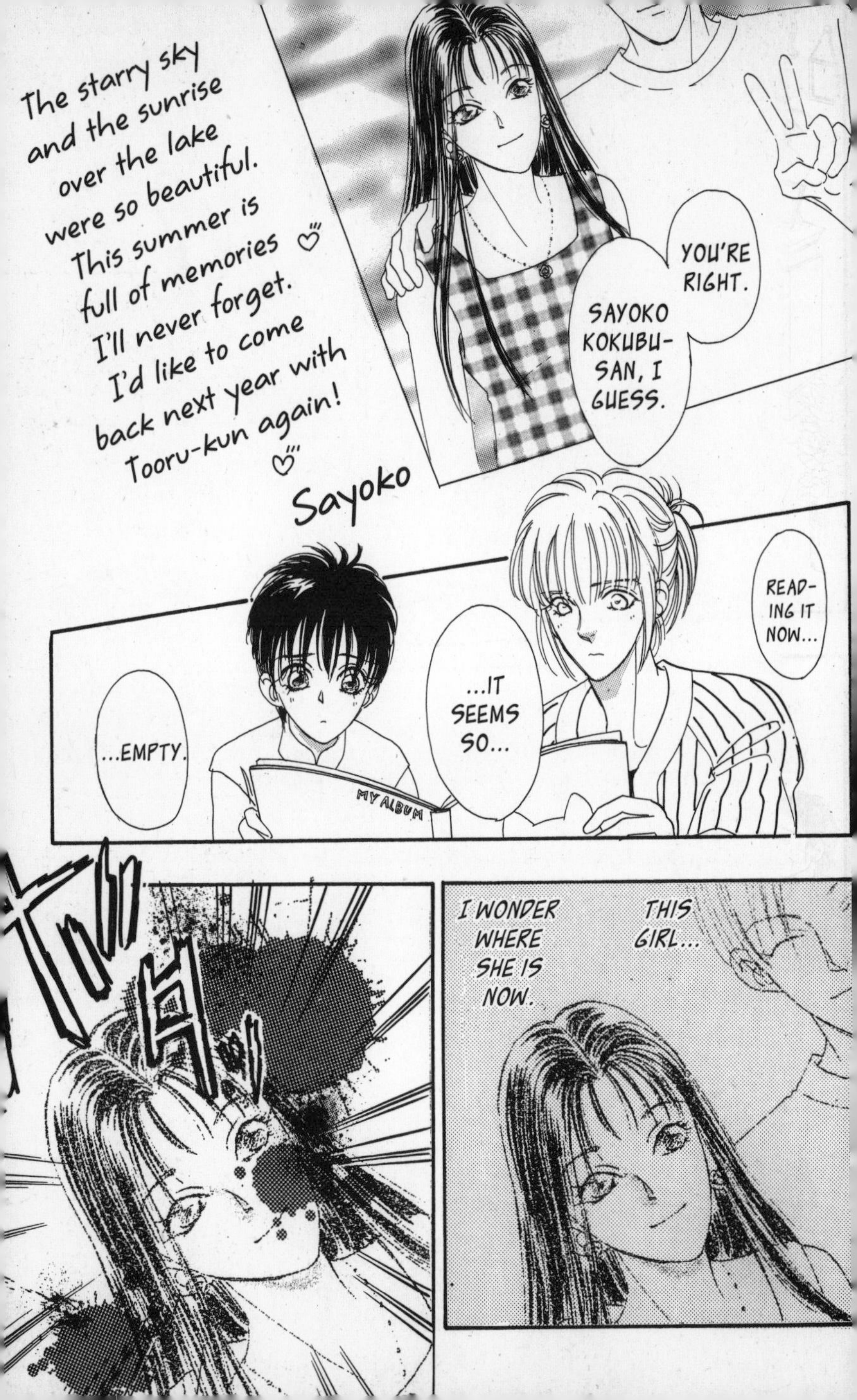
YOU'RE RIGHT.
SAYOKO KOKUBU-SAN, I GUESS.
The starry sky and the sunrise over the lake were so beautiful. This summer is full of memories I'll never forget. I'd like to come back next year with Tooru-kun again!
Sayoko
READING IT NOW...
...IT SEEMS SO...
...EMPTY.
THIS GIRL...
I WONDER WHERE SHE IS NOW.

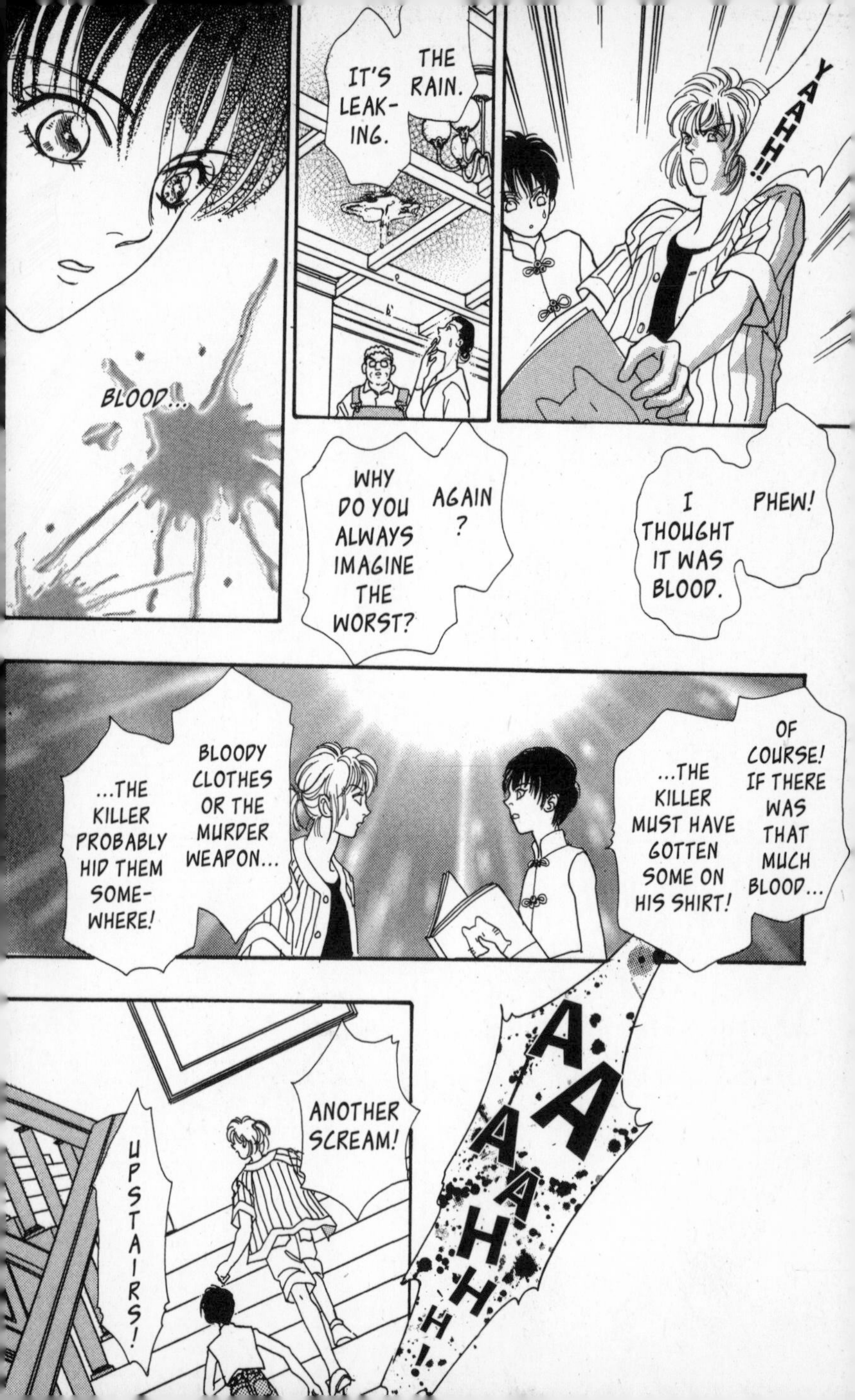
YAAHH!!
THE RAIN.
IT'S LEAKING.
BLOOD...
PHEW!
I THOUGHT IT WAS BLOOD.
AGAIN?
WHY DO YOU ALWAYS IMAGINE THE WORST?
OF COURSE! IF THERE WAS THAT MUCH BLOOD...
...THE KILLER MUST HAVE GOTTEN SOME ON HIS SHIRT!
BLOODY CLOTHES OR THE MURDER WEAPON...
...THE KILLER PROBABLY HID THEM SOMEWHERE!
AAAAHHHH!
ANOTHER SCREAM!
UPSTAIRS!

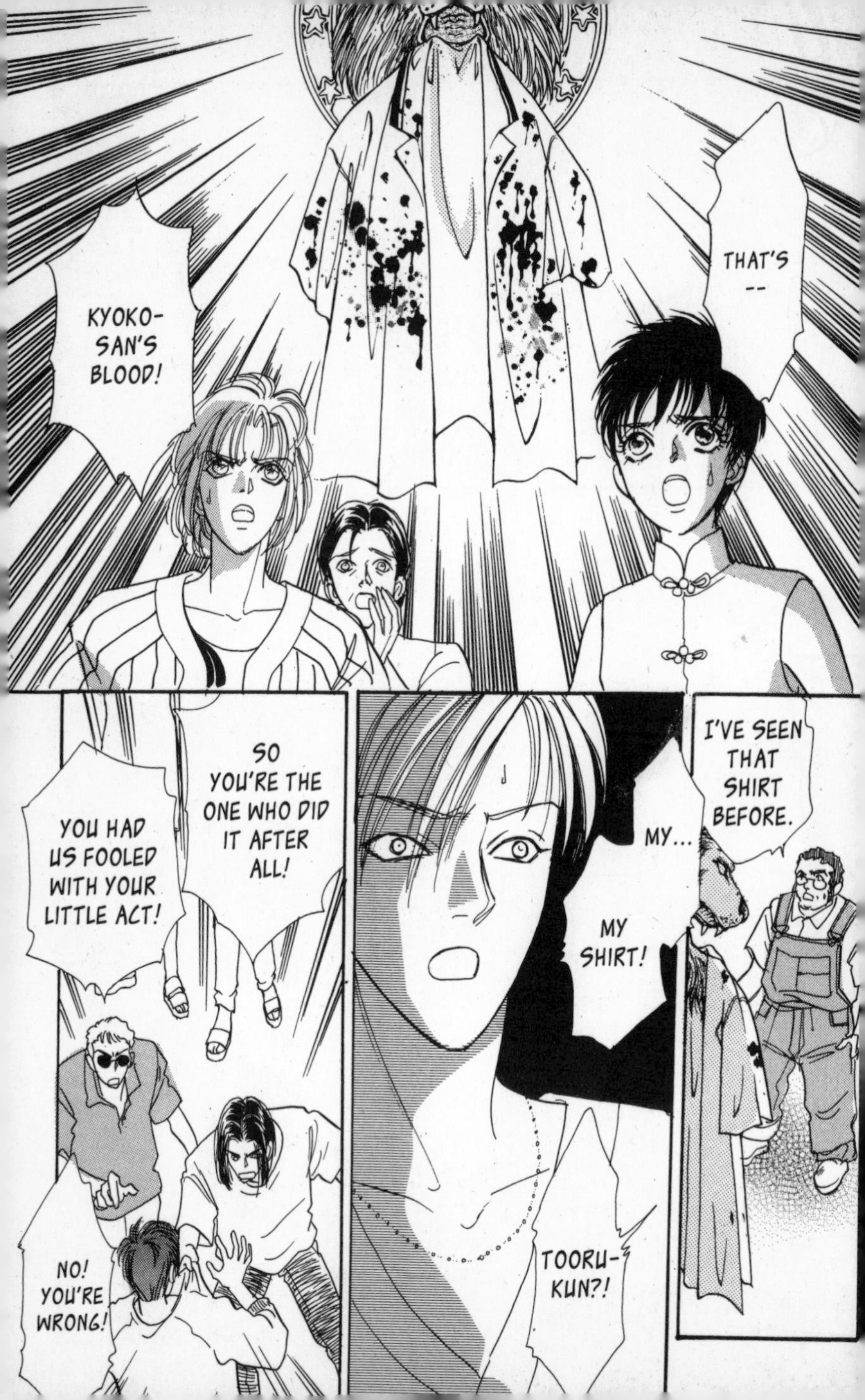
THAT'S --
KYOKO-SAN'S BLOOD!
I'VE SEEN THAT SHIRT BEFORE.
MY...
MY SHIRT!
TOORU-KUN?!
SO YOU'RE THE ONE WHO DID IT AFTER ALL!
YOU HAD US FOOLED WITH YOUR LITTLE ACT!
NO! YOU'RE WRONG!

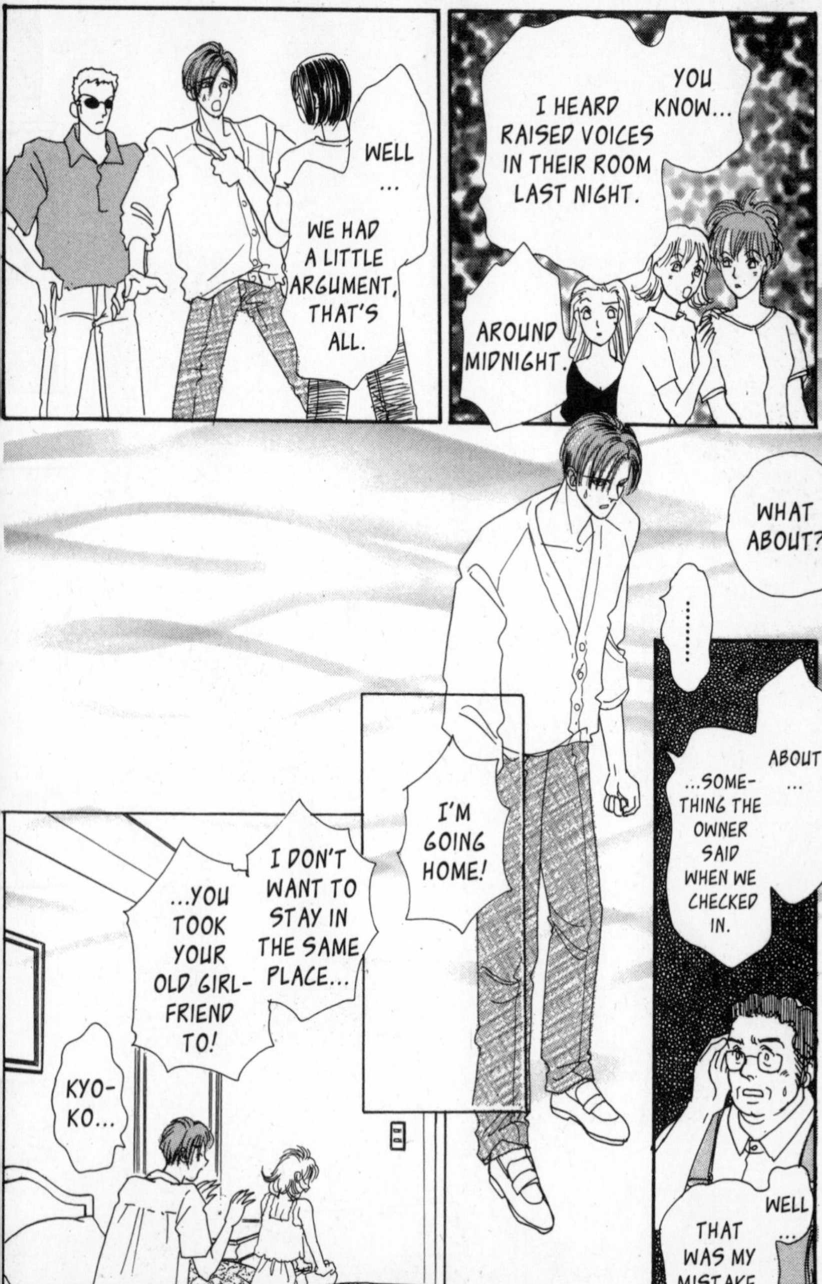
YOU KNOW...
I HEARD RAISED VOICES IN THEIR ROOM LAST NIGHT.
AROUND MIDNIGHT.
WELL ...
WE HAD A LITTLE ARGUMENT, THAT'S ALL.
WHAT ABOUT?
......
ABOUT ...
...SOME-THING THE OWNER SAID WHEN WE CHECKED IN.
WELL ...
THAT WAS MY MISTAKE.
I'M GOING HOME!
I DON'T WANT TO STAY IN THE SAME PLACE...
...YOU TOOK YOUR OLD GIRL-FRIEND TO!
KYO-KO...

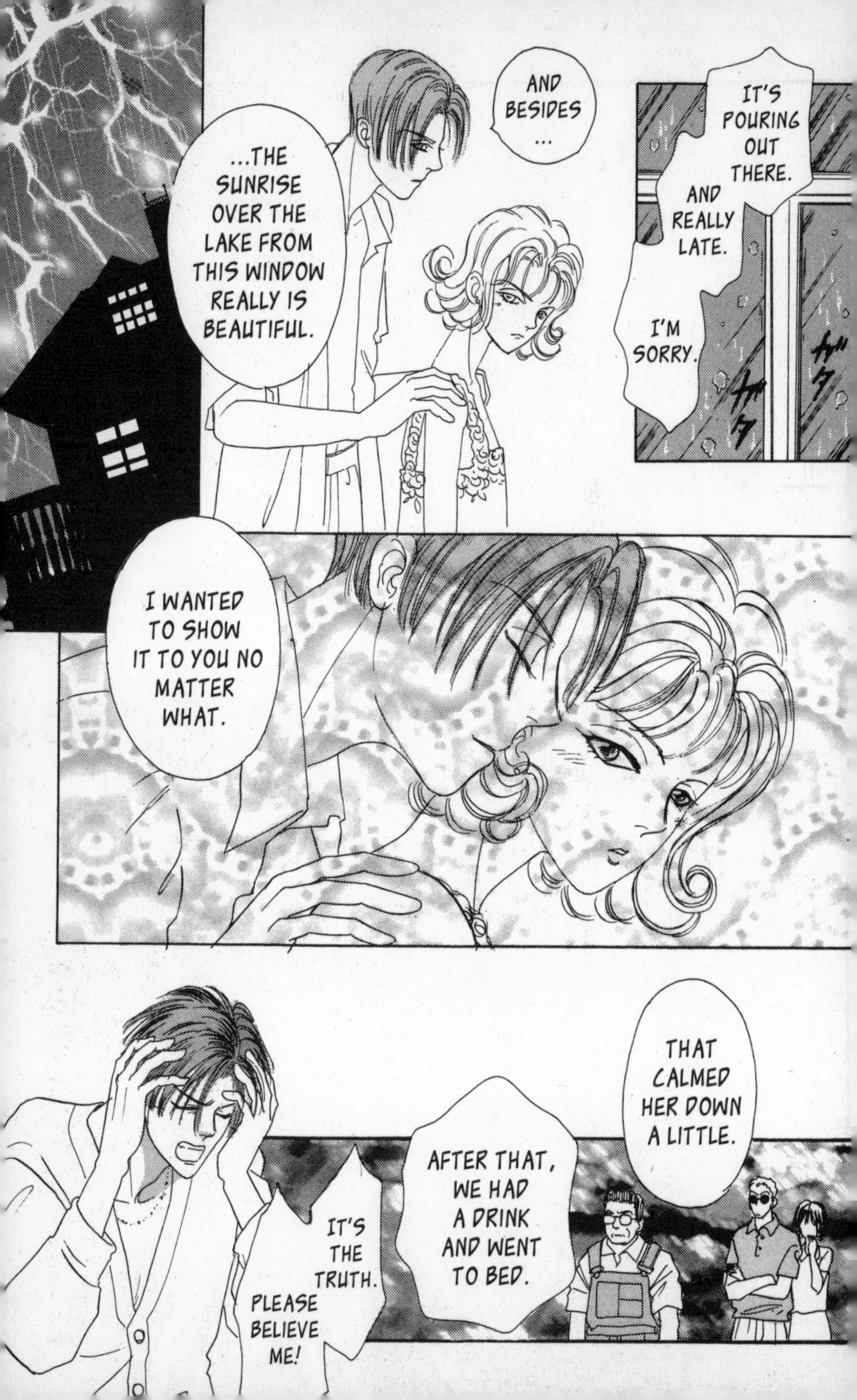
IT'S POURING OUT THERE.
AND REALLY LATE.
I'M SORRY.
AND BESIDES ...
...THE SUNRISE OVER THE LAKE FROM THIS WINDOW REALLY IS BEAUTIFUL.
I WANTED TO SHOW IT TO YOU NO MATTER WHAT.
THAT CALMED HER DOWN A LITTLE.
AFTER THAT, WE HAD A DRINK AND WENT TO BED.
IT'S THE TRUTH.
PLEASE BELIEVE ME!

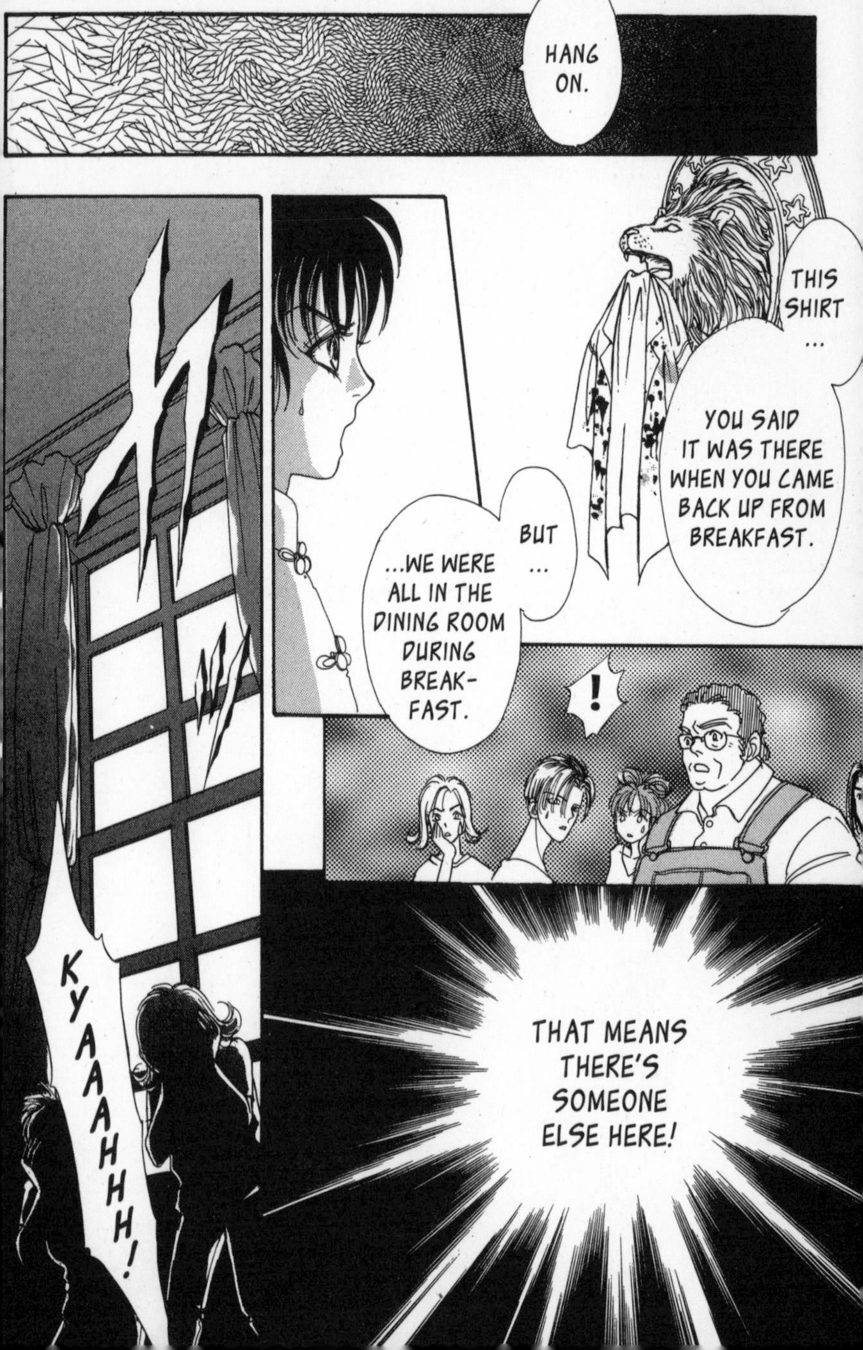
HANG ON.
THIS SHIRT ...
YOU SAID IT WAS THERE WHEN YOU CAME BACK UP FROM BREAKFAST.
BUT ...
...WE WERE ALL IN THE DINING ROOM DURING BREAK-FAST.
!
THAT MEANS THERE'S SOMEONE ELSE HERE!
KYAAAAHHH!

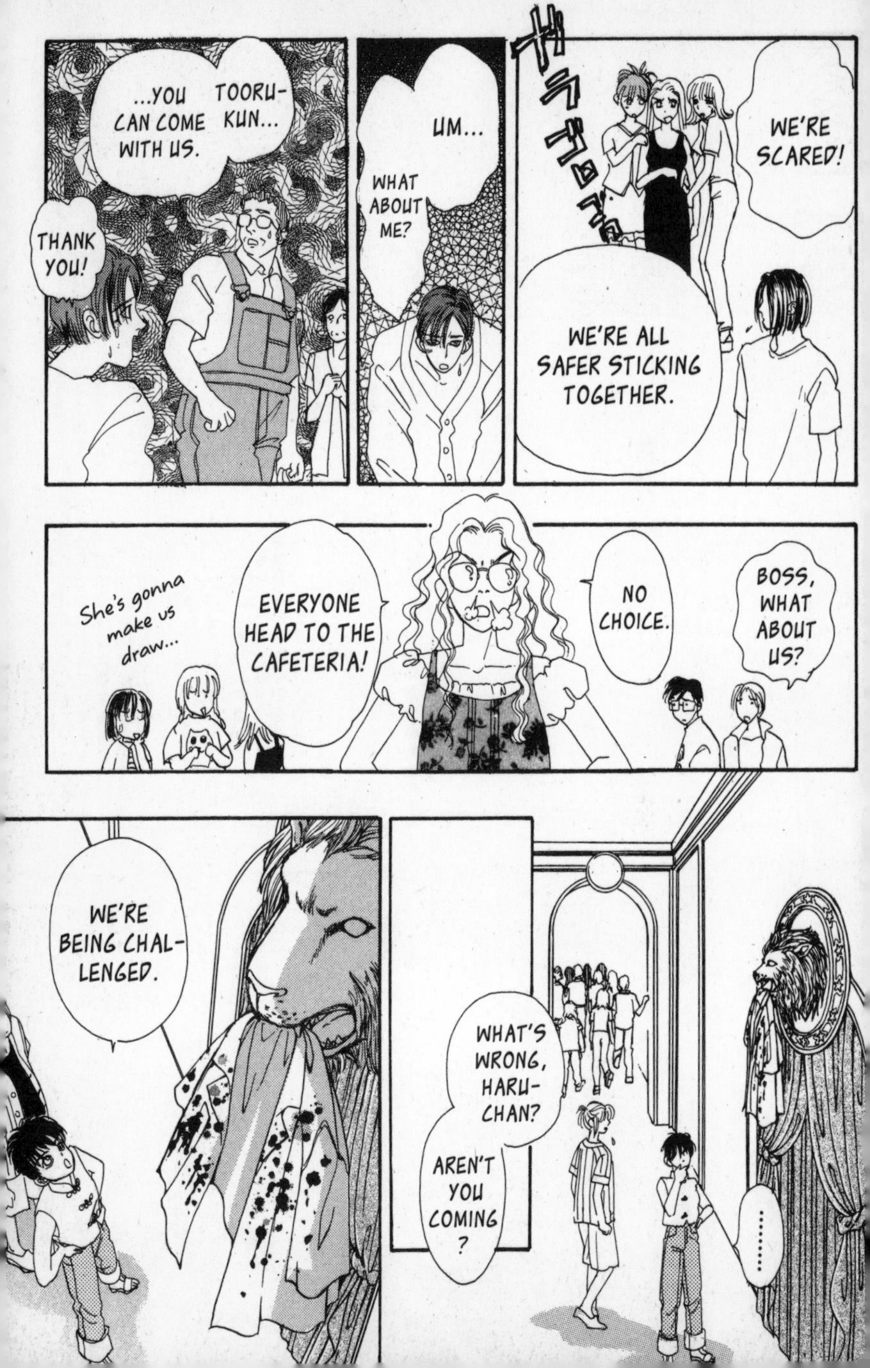
WE'RE SCARED!
WE'RE ALL SAFER STICKING TOGETHER.
UM...
WHAT ABOUT ME?
TOORU-KUN...
...YOU CAN COME WITH US.
THANK YOU!
BOSS, WHAT ABOUT US?
NO CHOICE.
EVERYONE HEAD TO THE CAFETERIA!
She's gonna make us draw...
WHAT'S WRONG, HARU-CHAN?
AREN'T YOU COMING?
....
WE'RE BEING CHAL-LENGED.

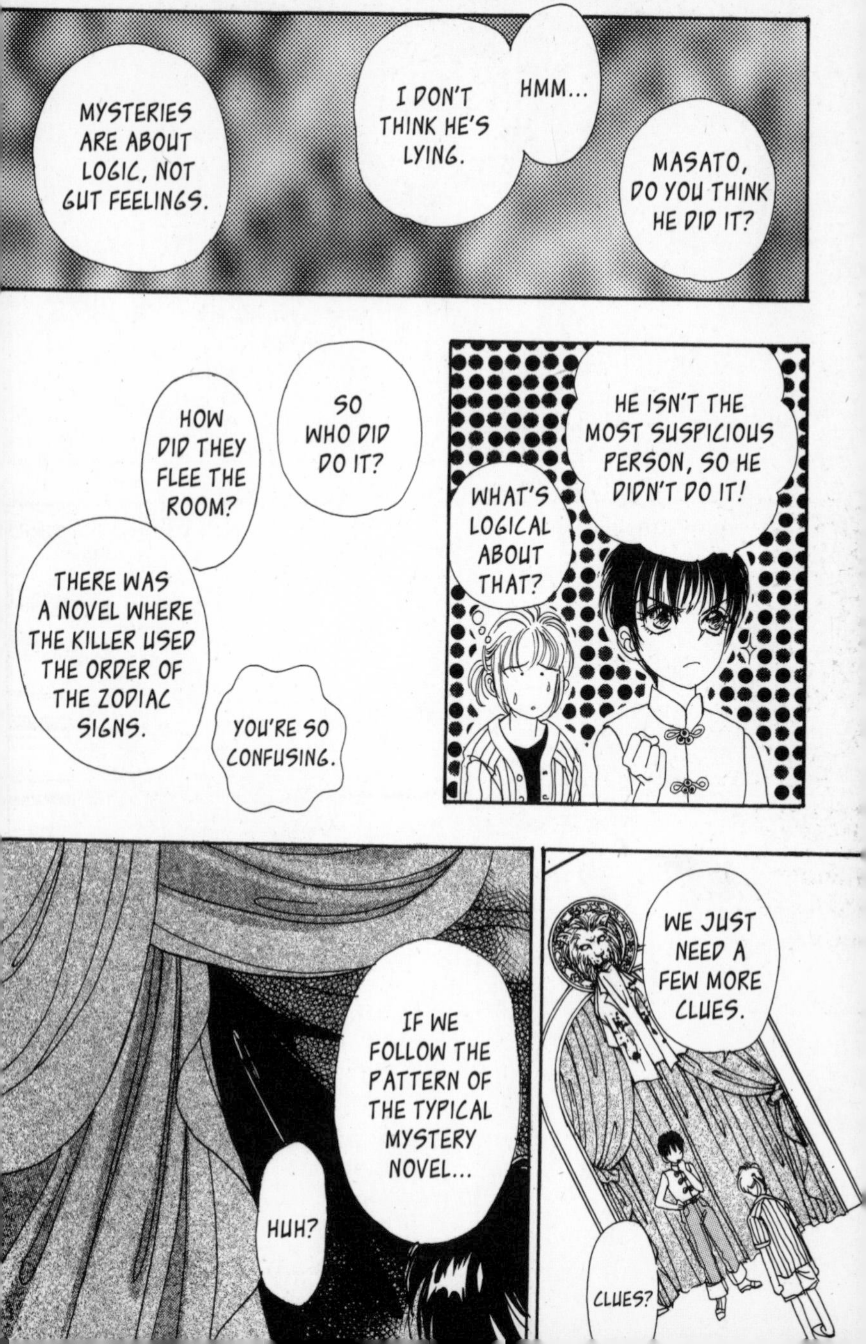
MASATO, DO YOU THINK HE DID IT?
HMM...
I DON'T THINK HE'S LYING.
MYSTERIES ARE ABOUT LOGIC, NOT GUT FEELINGS.
HE ISN'T THE MOST SUSPICIOUS PERSON, SO HE DIDN'T DO IT!
WHAT'S LOGICAL ABOUT THAT?
SO WHO DID DO IT?
HOW DID THEY FLEE THE ROOM?
THERE WAS A NOVEL WHERE THE KILLER USED THE ORDER OF THE ZODIAC SIGNS.
YOU'RE SO CONFUSING.
WE JUST NEED A FEW MORE CLUES.
CLUES?
IF WE FOLLOW THE PATTERN OF THE TYPICAL MYSTERY NOVEL...
HUH?

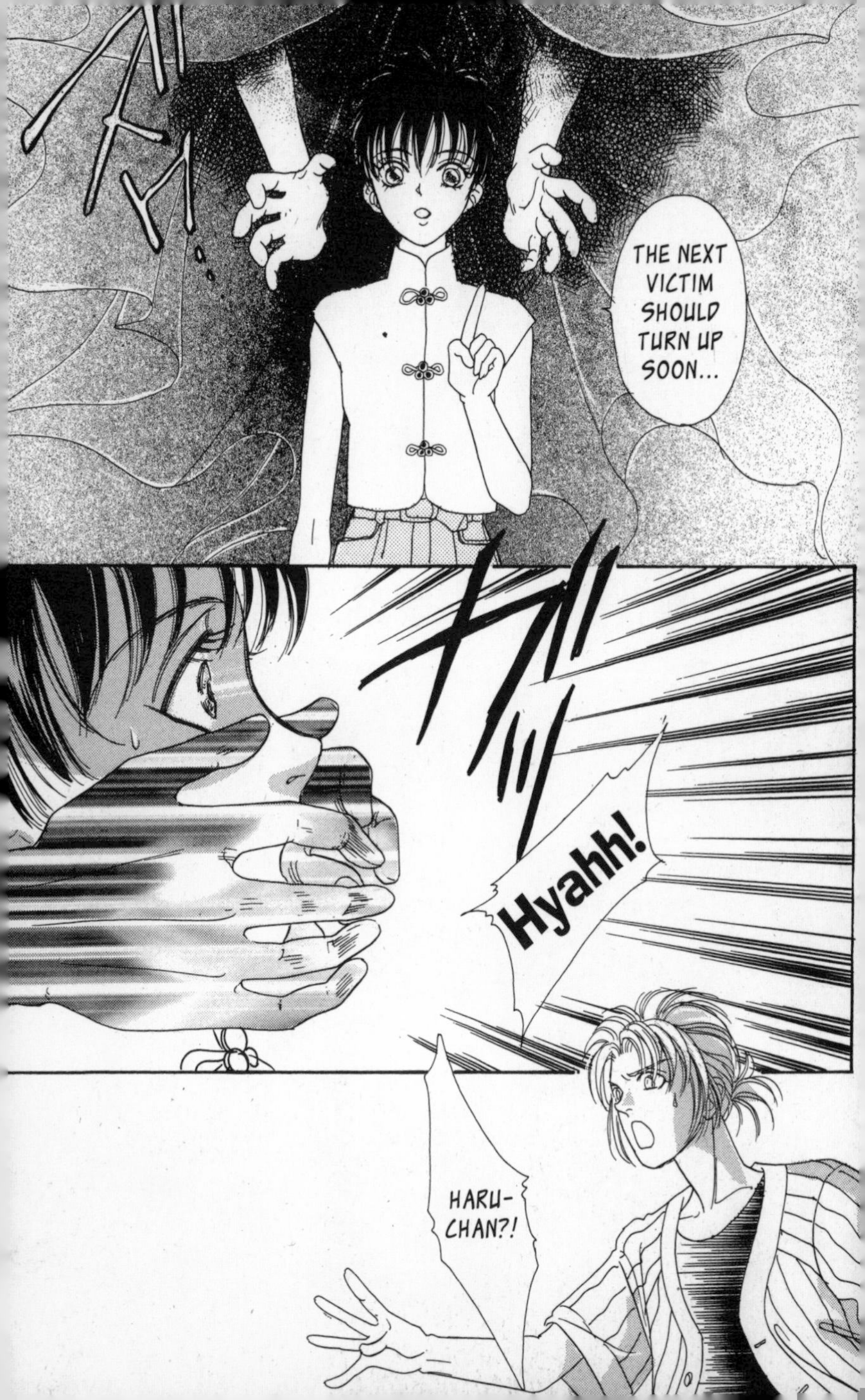
THE NEXT VICTIM SHOULD TURN UP SOON...
Hyahh!
HARU-CHAN?!

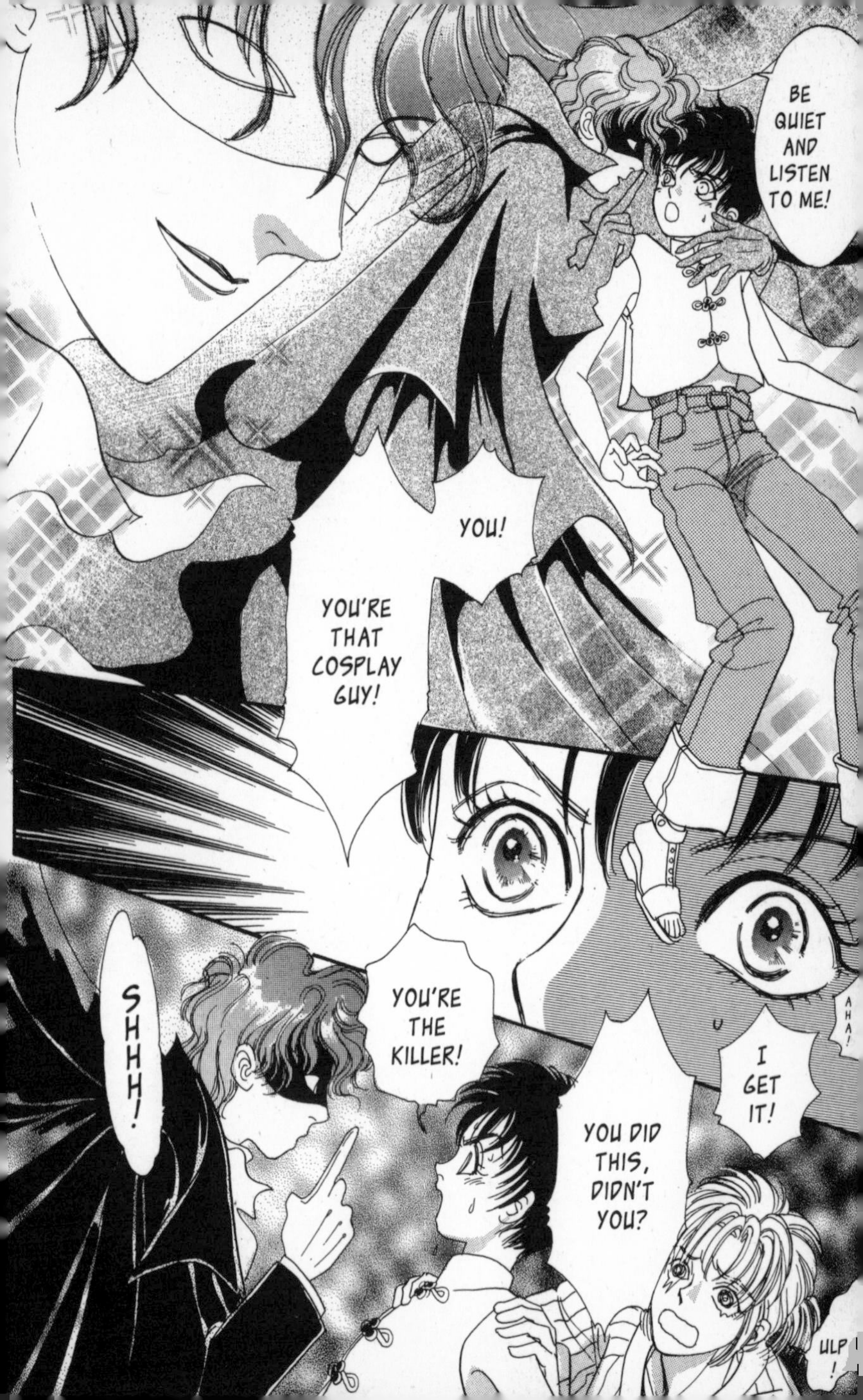
BE QUIET AND LISTEN TO ME!
YOU!
YOU'RE THAT COSPLAY GUY!
AHA!
I GET IT!
YOU DID THIS, DIDN'T YOU?
YOU'RE THE KILLER!
ULP!
SHHH!

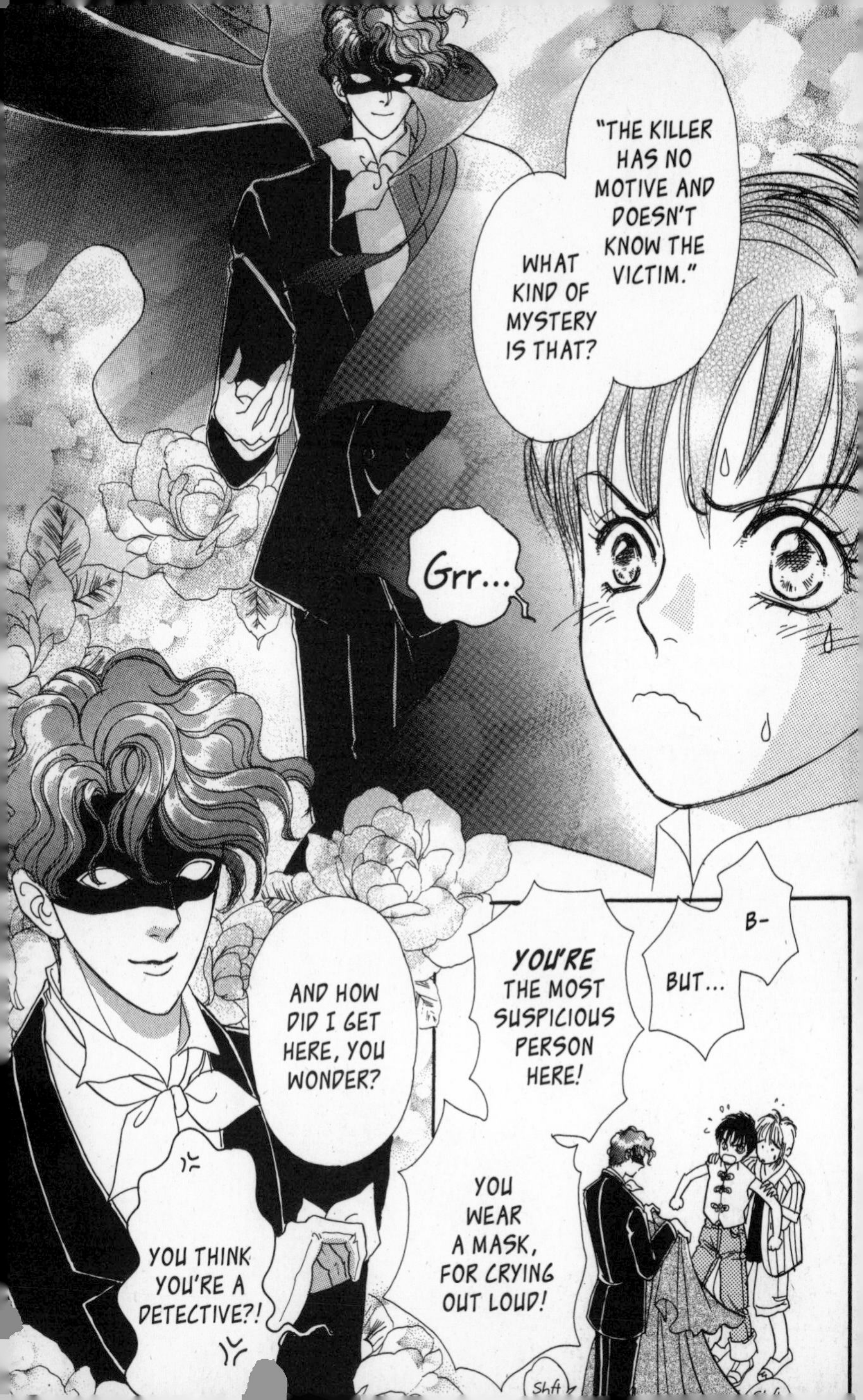
"THE KILLER HAS NO MOTIVE AND DOESN'T KNOW THE VICTIM."
WHAT KIND OF MYSTERY IS THAT?
Grr...
B- BUT...
YOU'RE THE MOST SUSPICIOUS PERSON HERE!
AND HOW DID I GET HERE, YOU WONDER?
YOU WEAR A MASK, FOR CRYING OUT LOUD!
YOU THINK YOU'RE A DETECTIVE?!
Shft

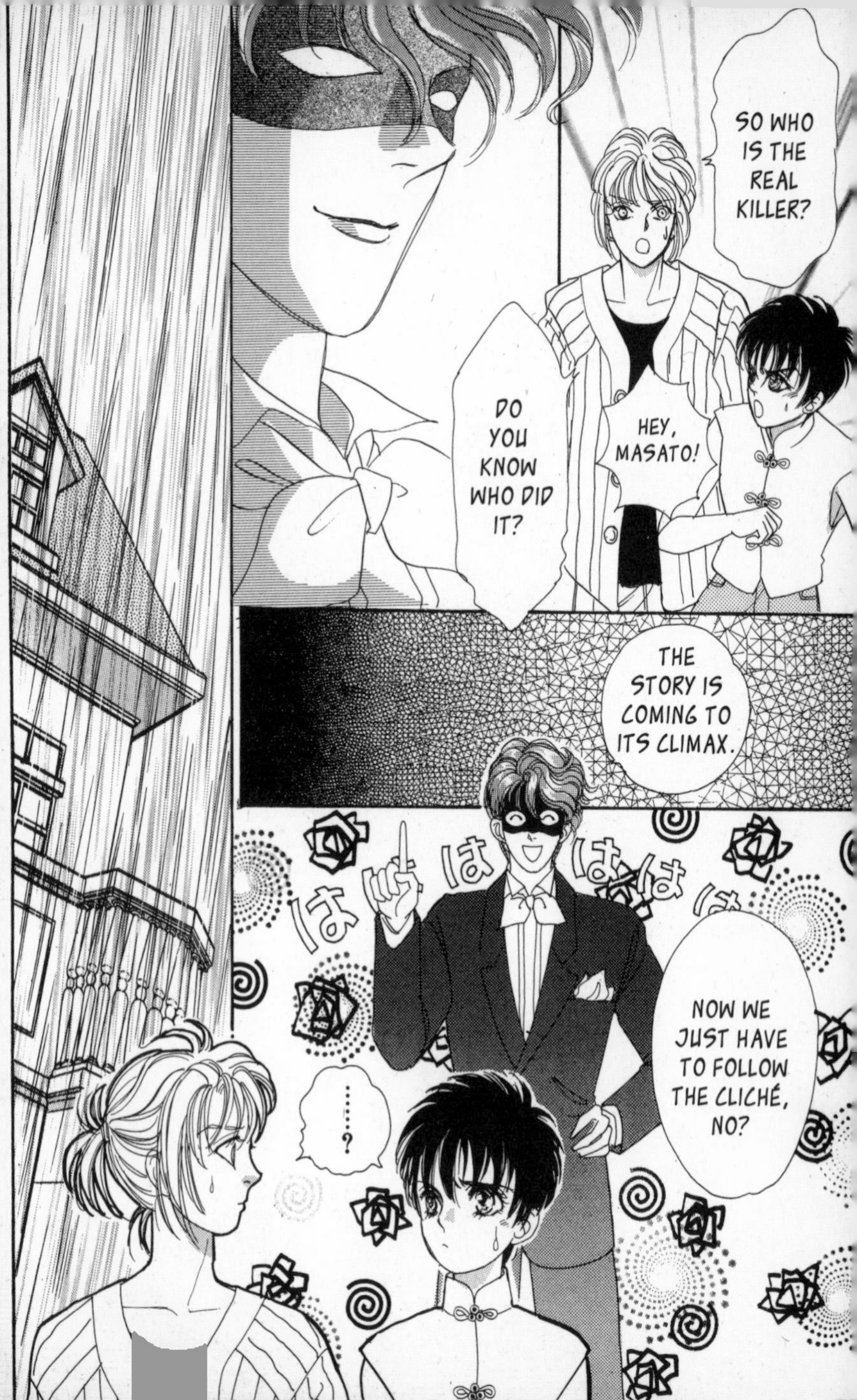
SO WHO IS THE REAL KILLER?
HEY, MASATO!
DO YOU KNOW WHO DID IT?
THE STORY IS COMING TO ITS CLIMAX.
NOW WE JUST HAVE TO FOLLOW THE CLICHÉ, NO?
はははははは
......?

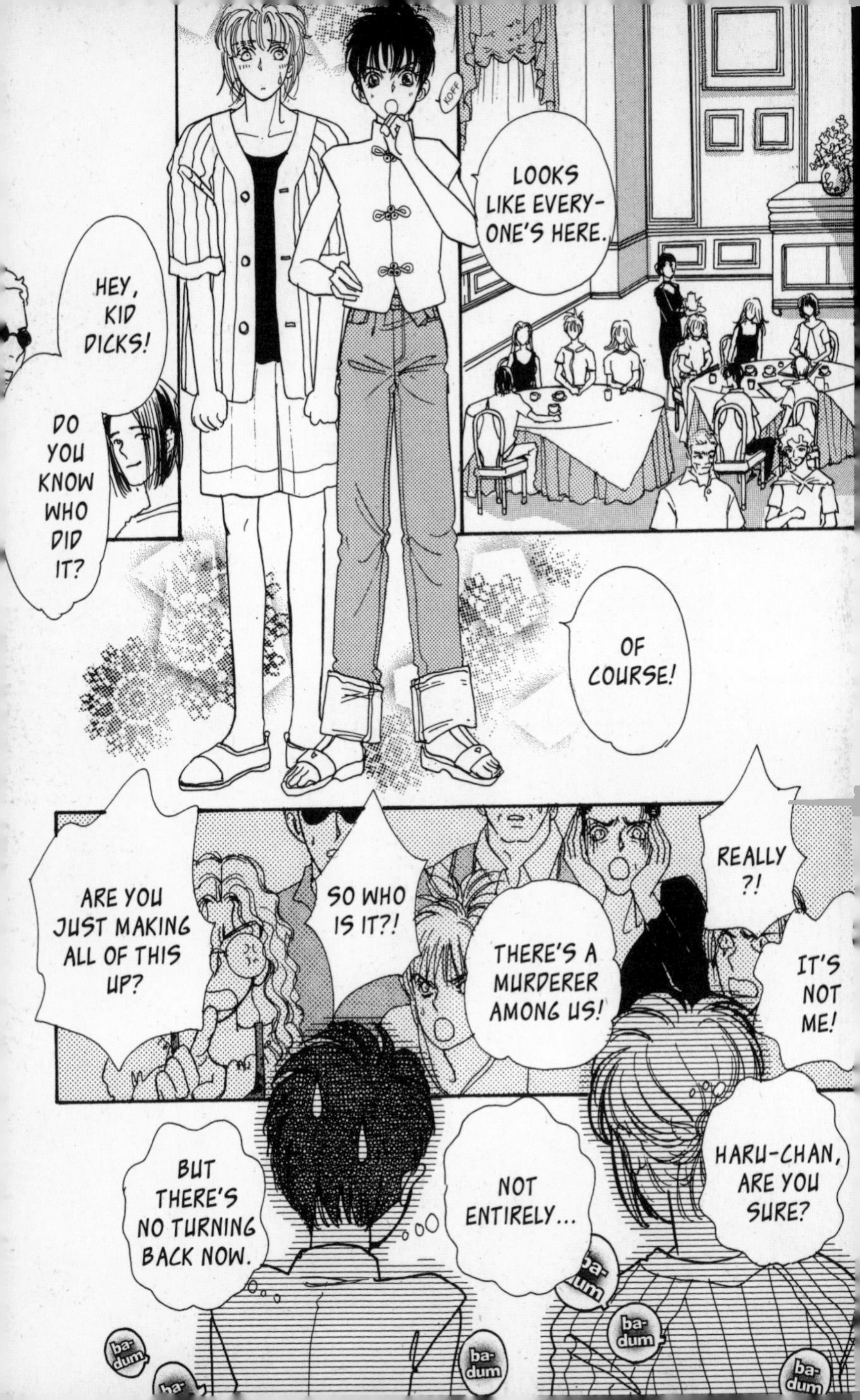
KOFF
LOOKS LIKE EVERY-ONE'S HERE.
HEY, KID DICKS!
DO YOU KNOW WHO DID IT?
OF COURSE!
REALLY?!
IT'S NOT ME!
THERE'S A MURDERER AMONG US!
SO WHO IS IT?!
ARE YOU JUST MAKING ALL OF THIS UP?
HARU-CHAN, ARE YOU SURE?
NOT ENTIRELY...
BUT THERE'S NO TURNING BACK NOW.
ba-dum
ba-dum
ba-dum
ba-dum
ba-dum

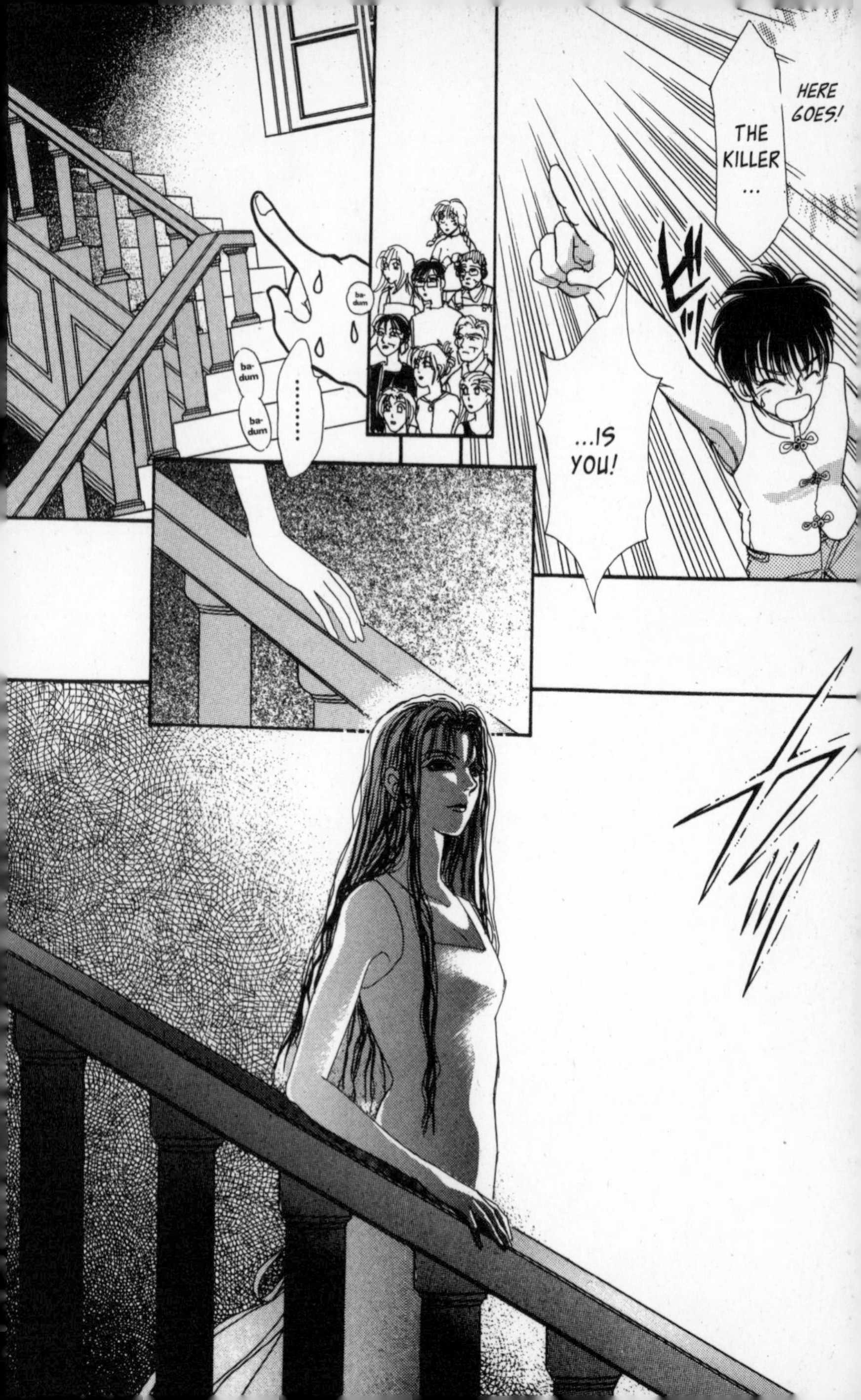
HERE GOES!
THE KILLER ...
...IS YOU!
ba-dum
....
ba-dum
ba-dum

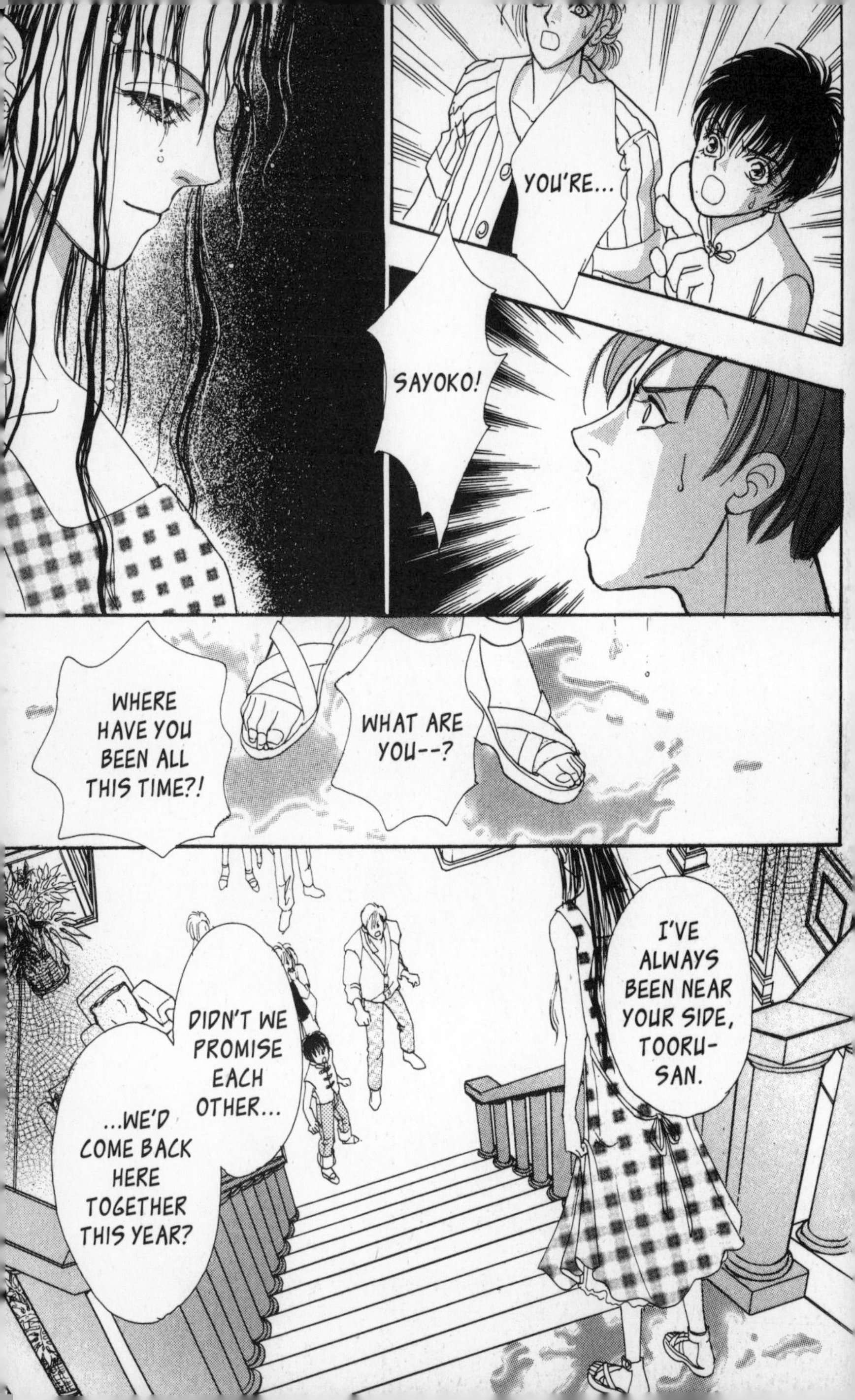
YOU'RE...
SAYOKO!
WHAT ARE YOU--?
WHERE HAVE YOU BEEN ALL THIS TIME?!
I'VE ALWAYS BEEN NEAR YOUR SIDE, TOORU-SAN.
DIDN'T WE PROMISE EACH OTHER...
...WE'D COME BACK HERE TOGETHER THIS YEAR?

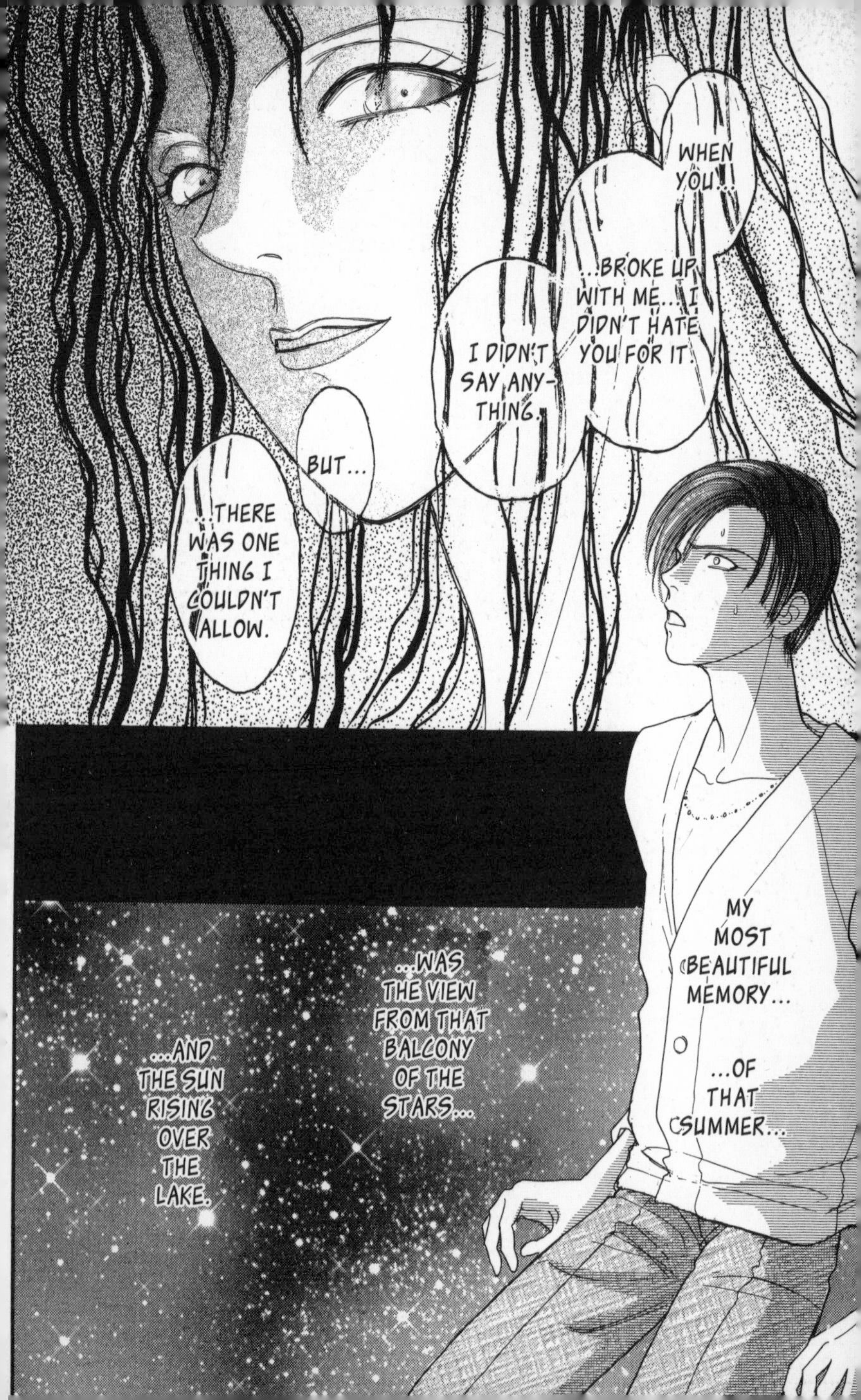
WHEN YOU...
...BROKE UP WITH ME... I DIDN'T HATE YOU FOR IT.
I DIDN'T SAY ANY-THING.
BUT...
...THERE WAS ONE THING I COULDN'T ALLOW.
MY MOST BEAUTIFUL MEMORY...
...OF THAT SUMMER...
...WAS THE VIEW FROM THAT BALCONY OF THE STARS...
...AND THE SUN RISING OVER THE LAKE.

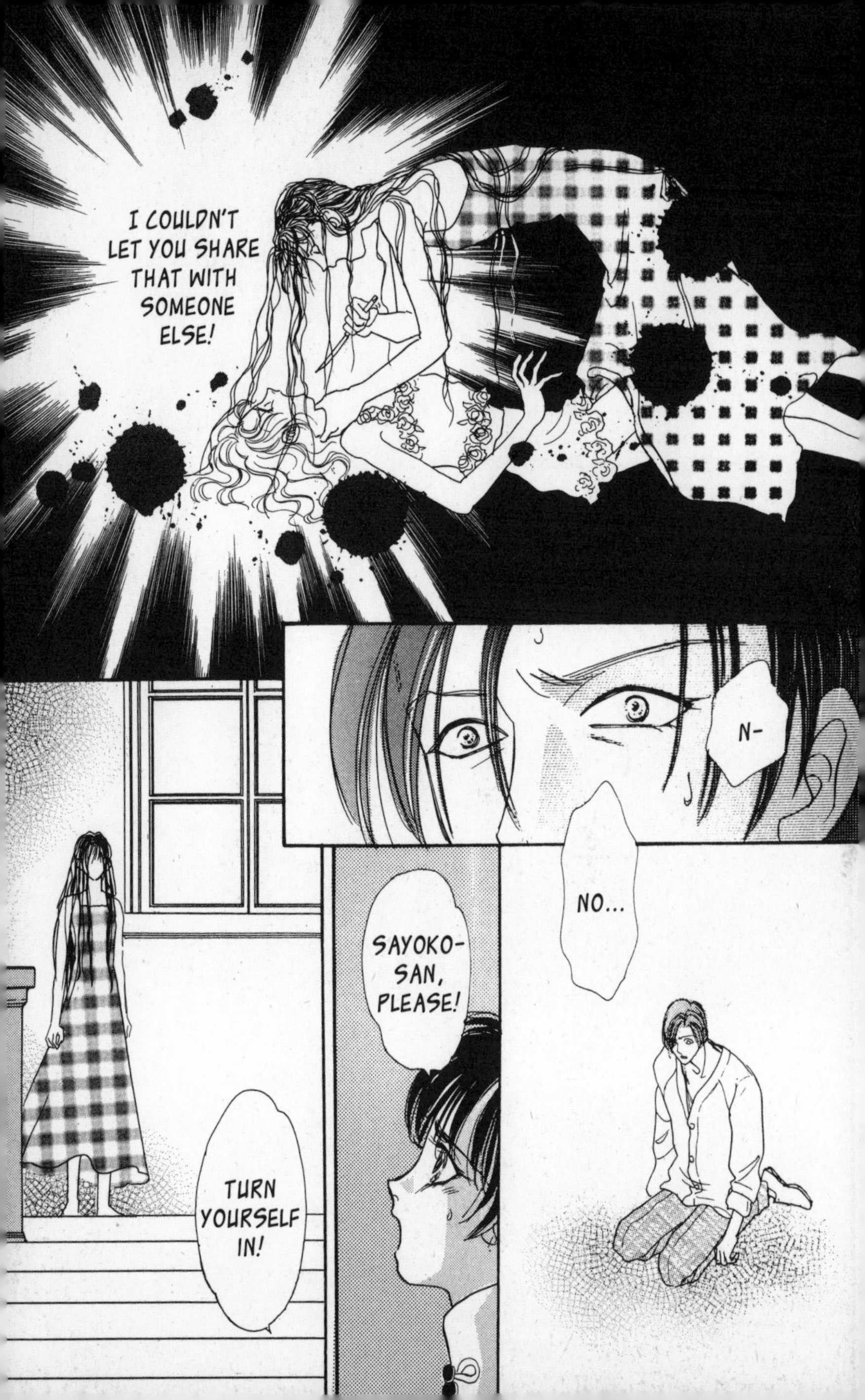
I COULDN'T LET YOU SHARE THAT WITH SOMEONE ELSE!
N-
NO...
SAYOKO-SAN, PLEASE!
TURN YOURSELF IN!

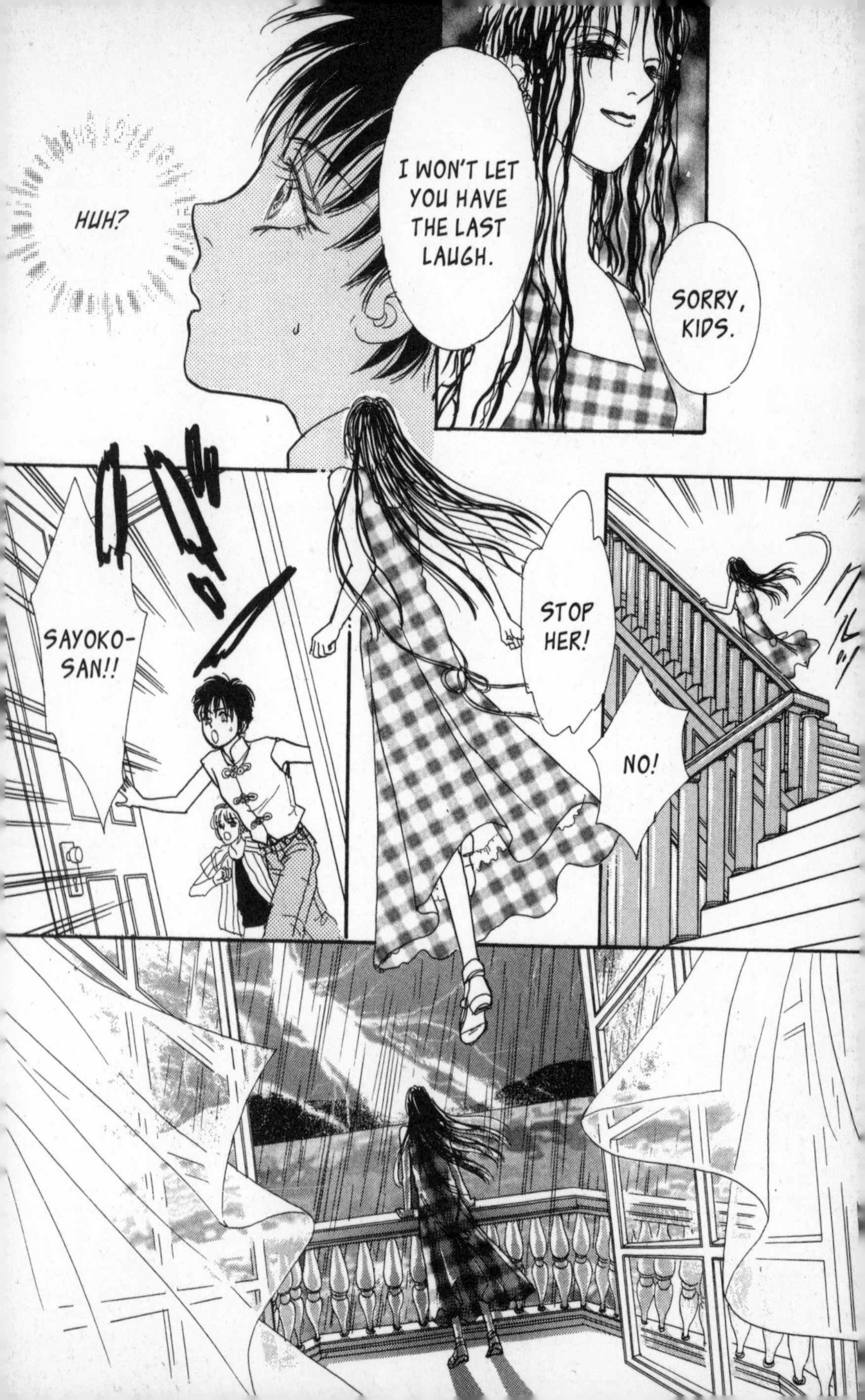
SORRY, KIDS.
I WON'T LET YOU HAVE THE LAST LAUGH.
HUH?
STOP HER!
NO!
SAYOKO-SAN!!

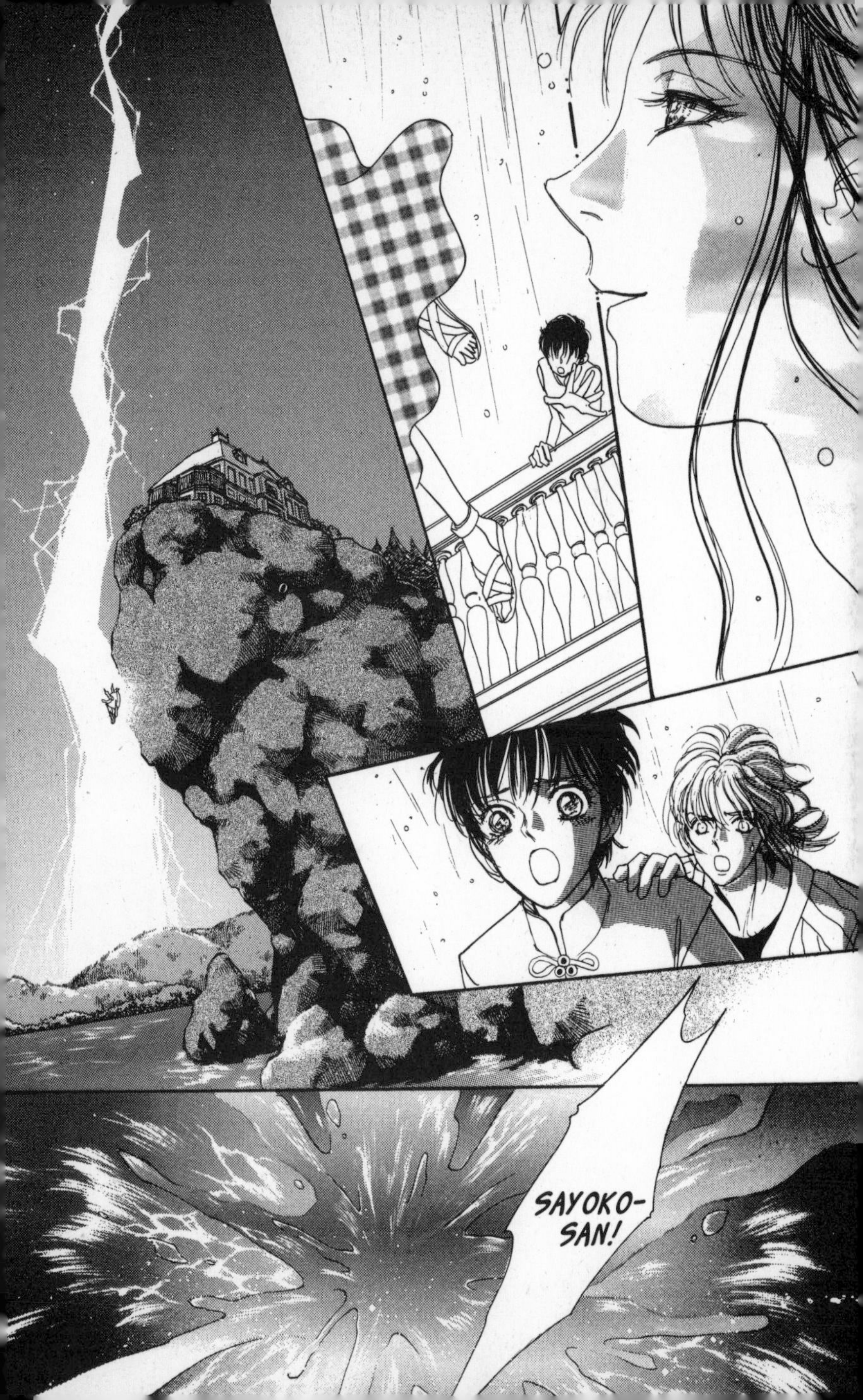
SAYOKO-SAN!

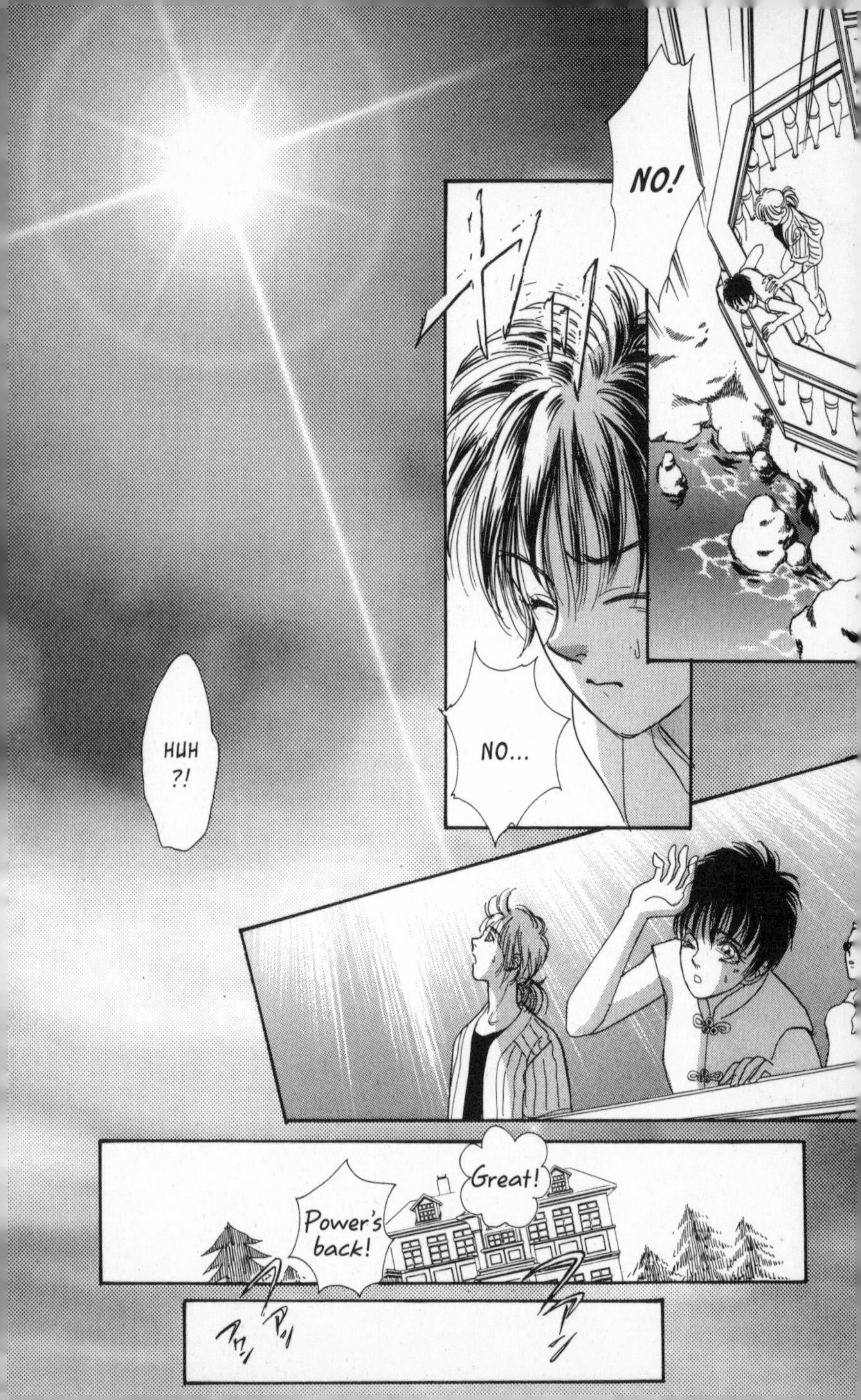
NO!
NO...
HUH ?!
Great!
Power's back!

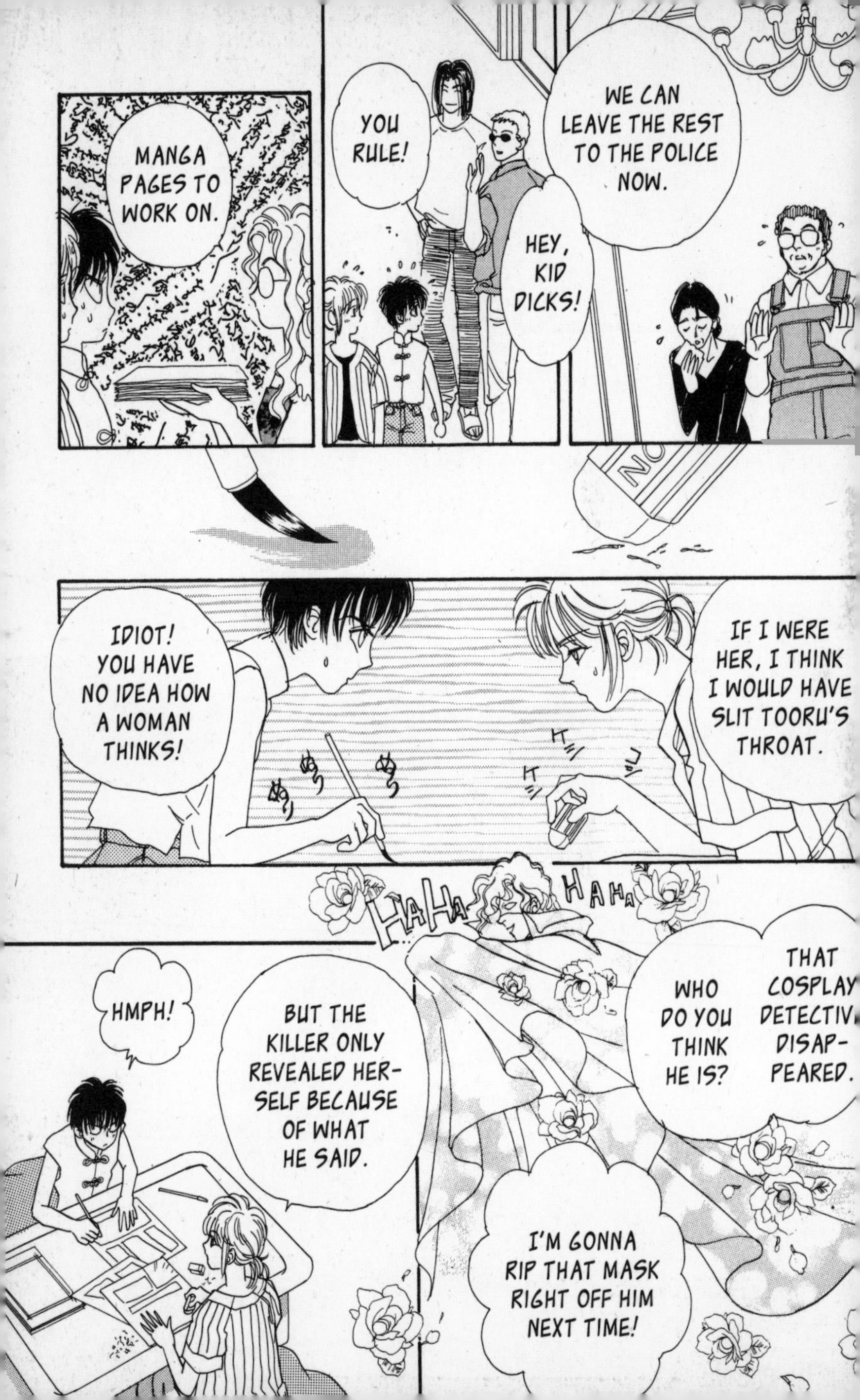
WE CAN LEAVE THE REST TO THE POLICE NOW.
HEY, KID DICKS!
YOU RULE!
MANGA PAGES TO WORK ON.
IF I WERE HER, I THINK I WOULD HAVE SLIT TOORU'S THROAT.
IDIOT! YOU HAVE NO IDEA HOW A WOMAN THINKS!
HAHAHA
HAHA
THAT COSPLAY DETECTIV DISAP-PEARED.
WHO DO YOU THINK HE IS?
I'M GONNA RIP THAT MASK RIGHT OFF HIM NEXT TIME!
BUT THE KILLER ONLY REVEALED HER-SELF BECAUSE OF WHAT HE SAID.
HMPH!

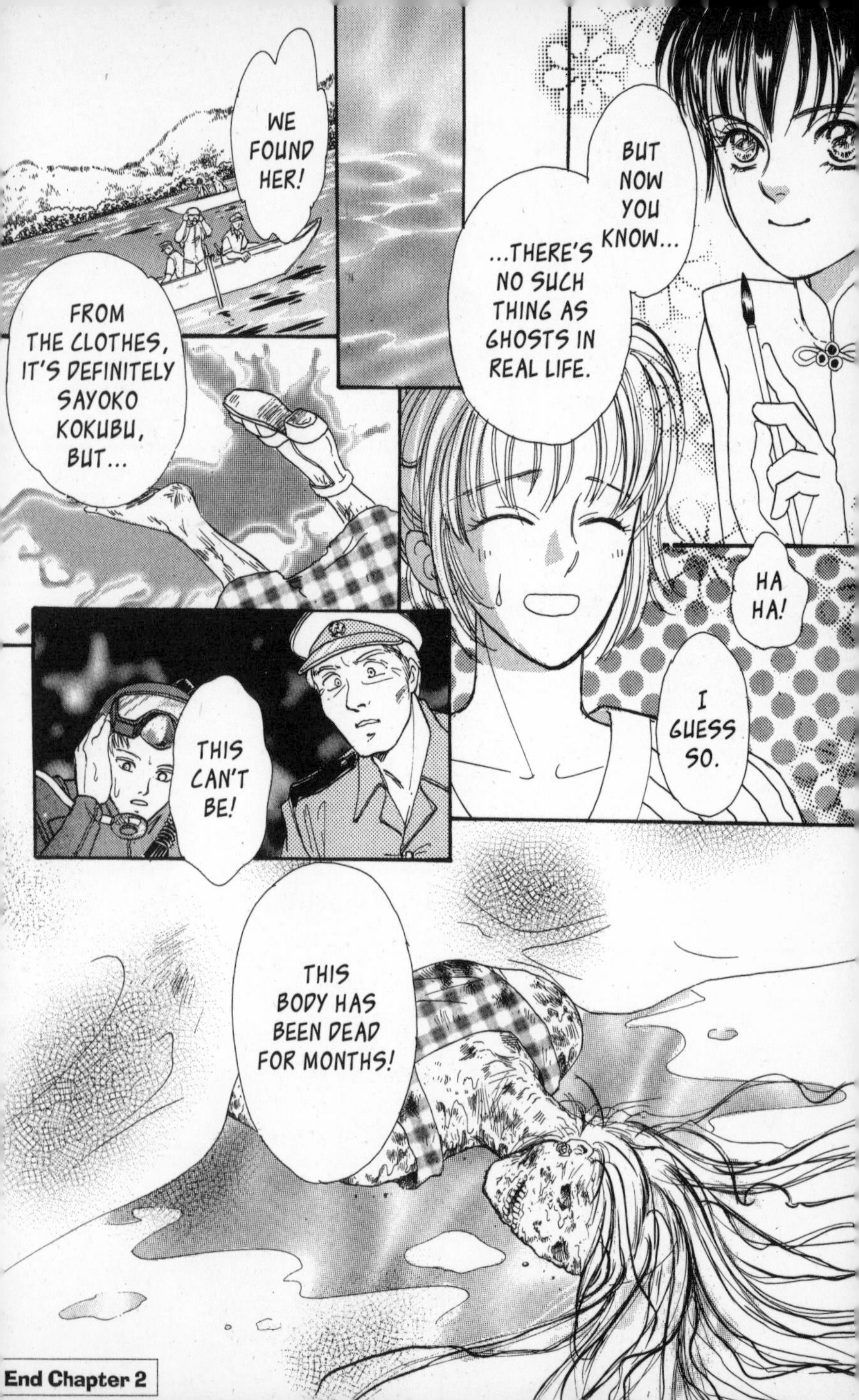

BUT NOW YOU KNOW...
...THERE'S NO SUCH THING AS GHOSTS IN REAL LIFE.
HA HA!
I GUESS SO.
WE FOUND HER!
FROM THE CLOTHES, IT'S DEFINITELY SAYOKO KOKUBU, BUT...
THIS CAN'T BE!
THIS BODY HAS BEEN DEAD FOR MONTHS!

End Chapter 2

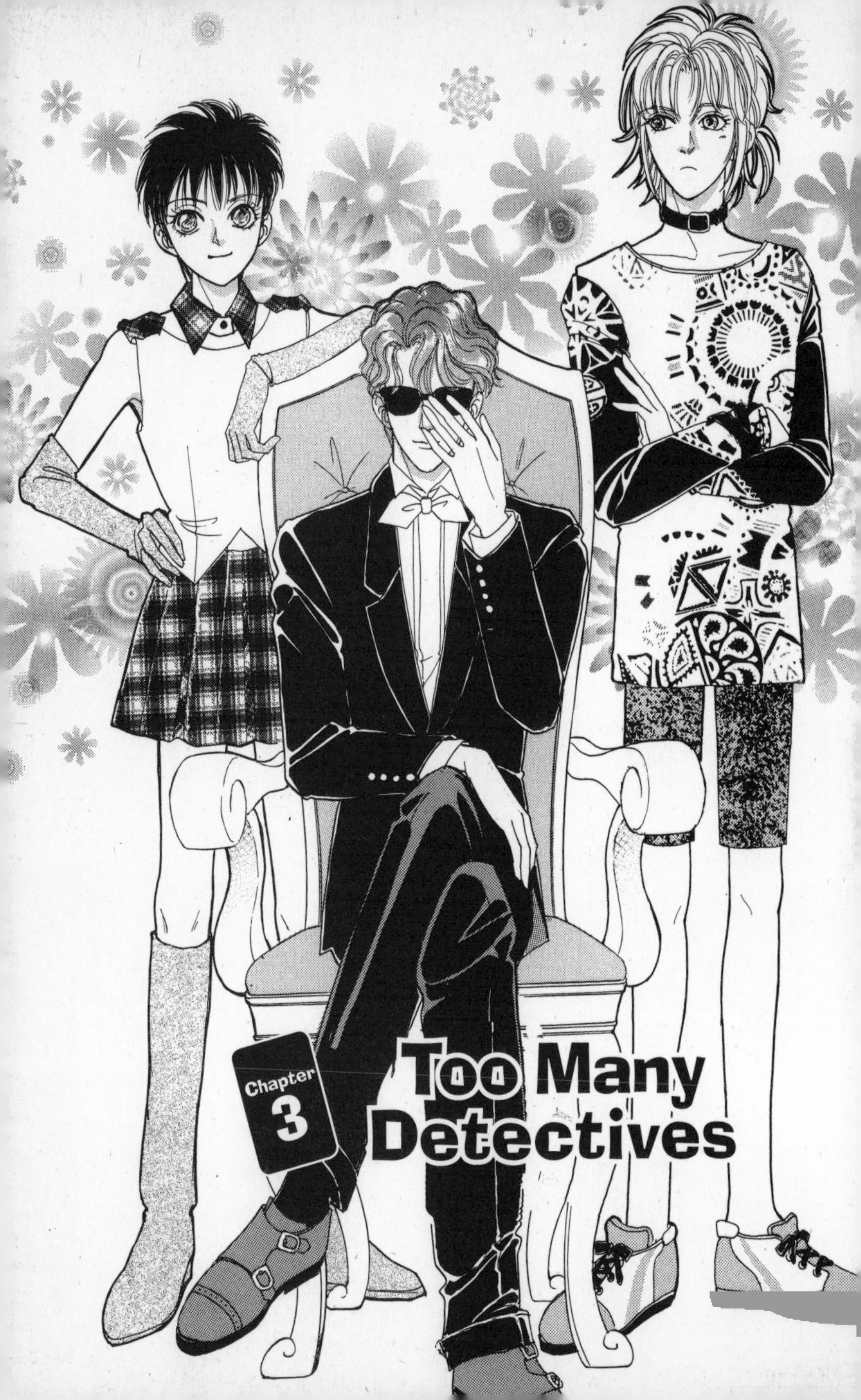
Chapter
3
Too Many
Detectives

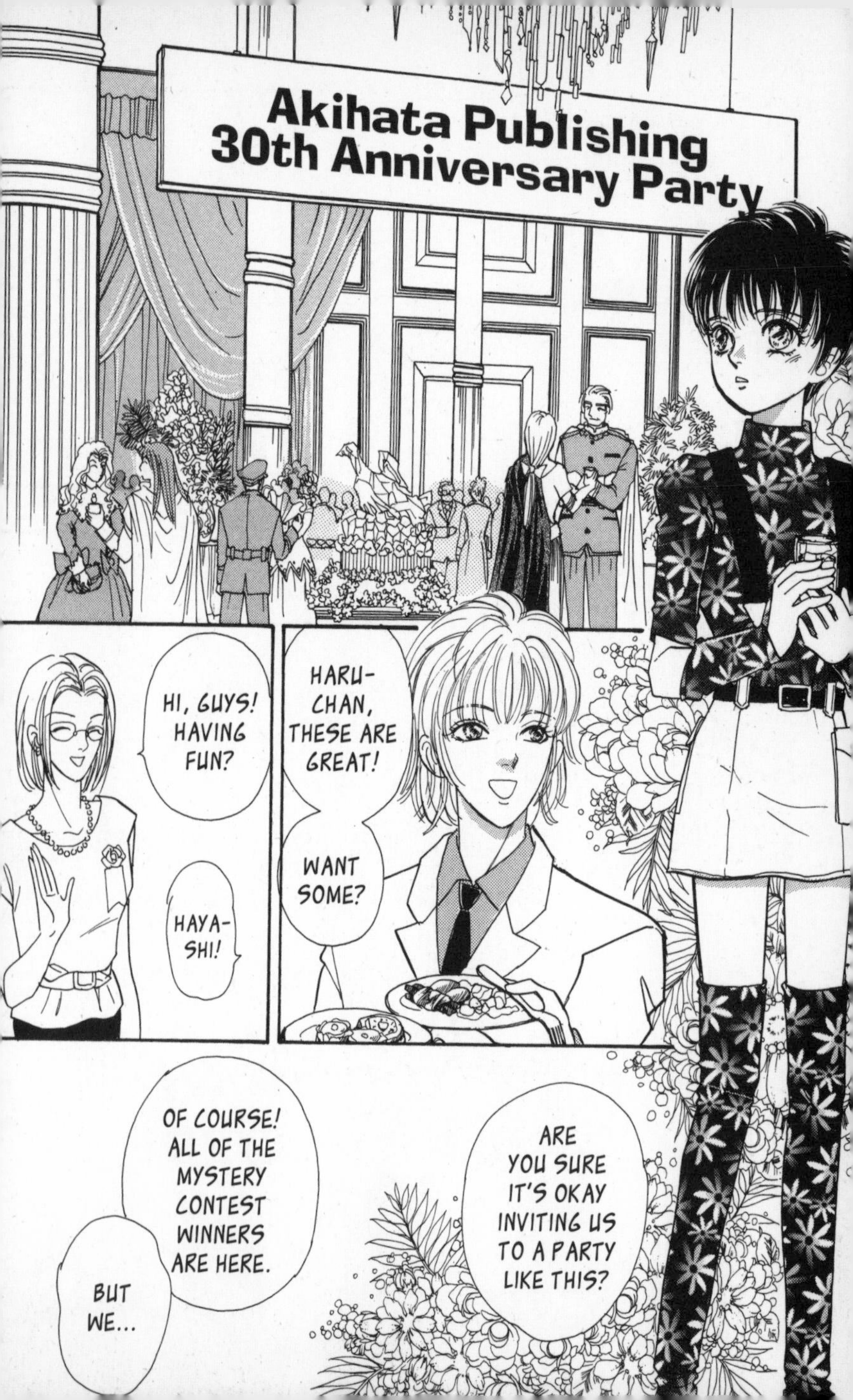
Akihata Publishing 30th Anniversary Party
HARU-CHAN, THESE ARE GREAT!
WANT SOME?
HI, GUYS! HAVING FUN?
HAYA-SHI!
ARE YOU SURE IT'S OKAY INVITING US TO A PARTY LIKE THIS?
OF COURSE! ALL OF THE MYSTERY CONTEST WINNERS ARE HERE.
BUT WE...

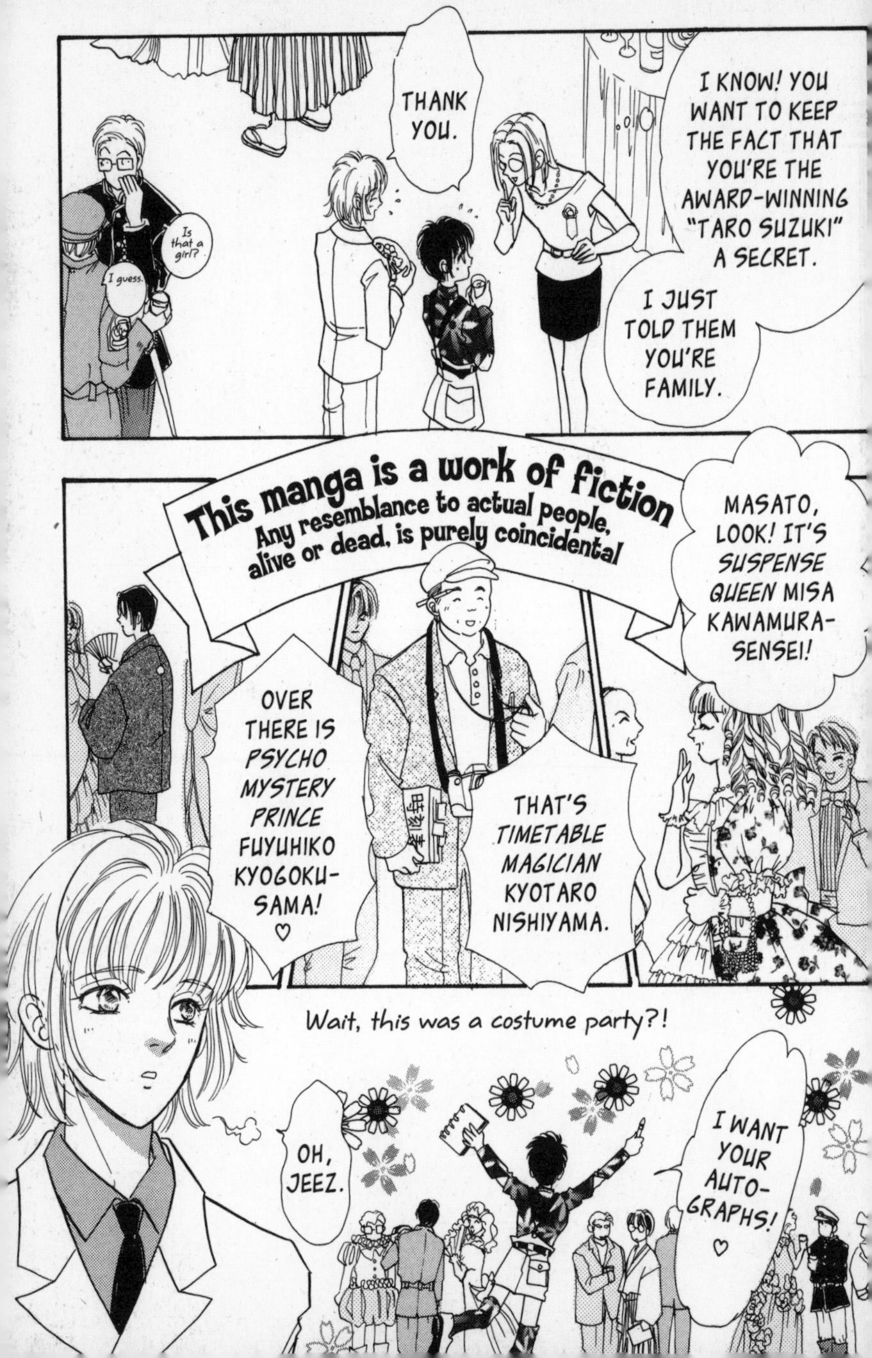
I KNOW! YOU WANT TO KEEP THE FACT THAT YOU'RE THE AWARD-WINNING "TARO SUZUKI" A SECRET.
I JUST TOLD THEM YOU'RE FAMILY.
THANK YOU.
Is that a girl?
I guess.
This manga is a work of fiction
Any resemblance to actual people, alive or dead, is purely coincidental
MASATO, LOOK! IT'S *SUSPENSE QUEEN* MISA KAWAMURA-SENSEI!
THAT'S *TIMETABLE MAGICIAN* KYOTARO NISHIYAMA.
OVER THERE IS *PSYCHO MYSTERY PRINCE* FUYUHIKO KYOGOKU-SAMA! ♡
Wait, this was a costume party?!
I WANT YOUR AUTO-GRAPHS! ♡
OH, JEEZ.

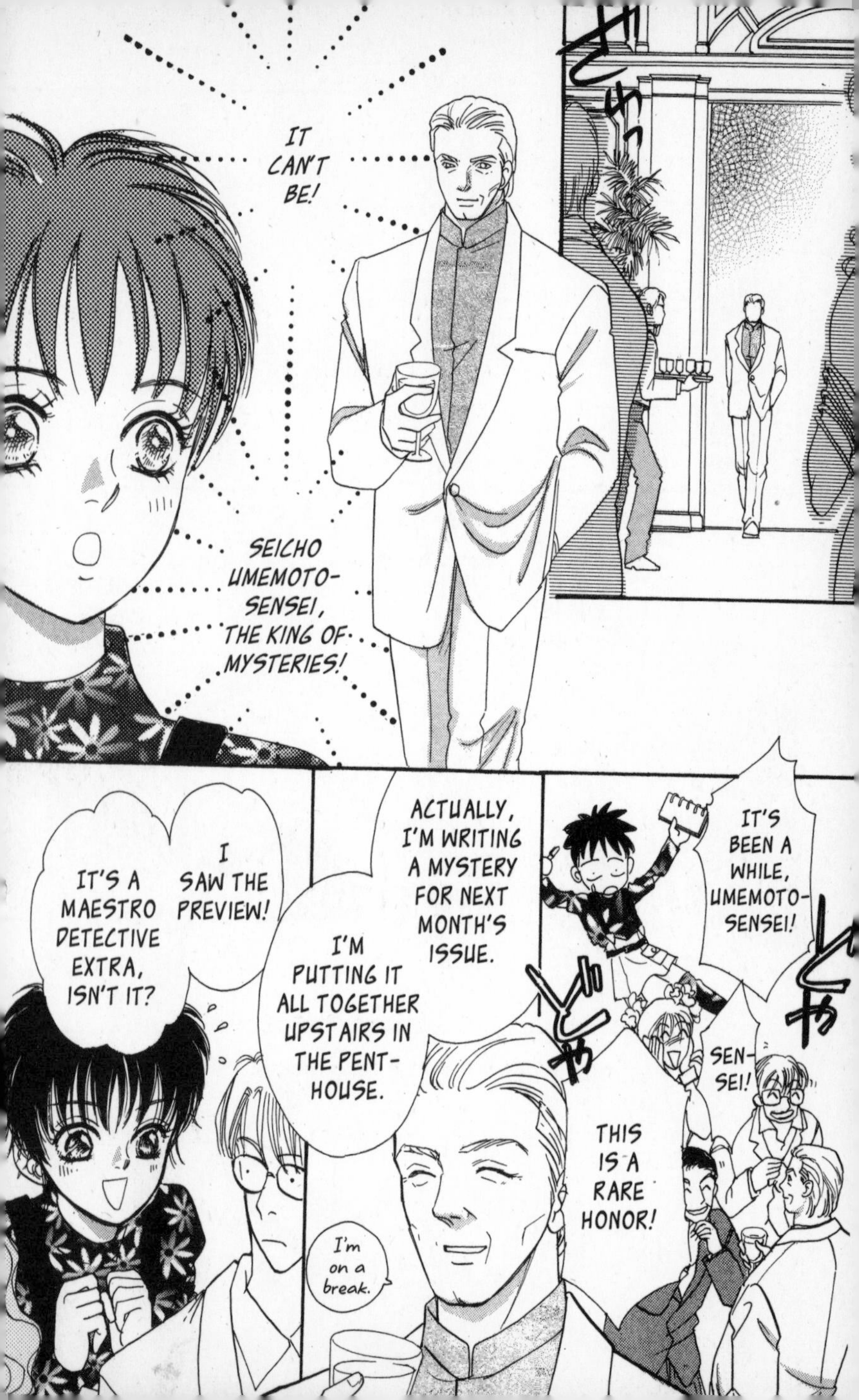
IT CAN'T BE!
SEICHO UMEMOTO-SENSEI, THE KING OF MYSTERIES!
IT'S BEEN A WHILE, UMEMOTO-SENSEI!
SEN-SEI!
THIS IS A RARE HONOR!
ACTUALLY, I'M WRITING A MYSTERY FOR NEXT MONTH'S ISSUE.
I'M PUTTING IT ALL TOGETHER UPSTAIRS IN THE PENT-HOUSE.
I SAW THE PREVIEW!
IT'S A MAESTRO DETECTIVE EXTRA, ISN'T IT?
I'm on a break.

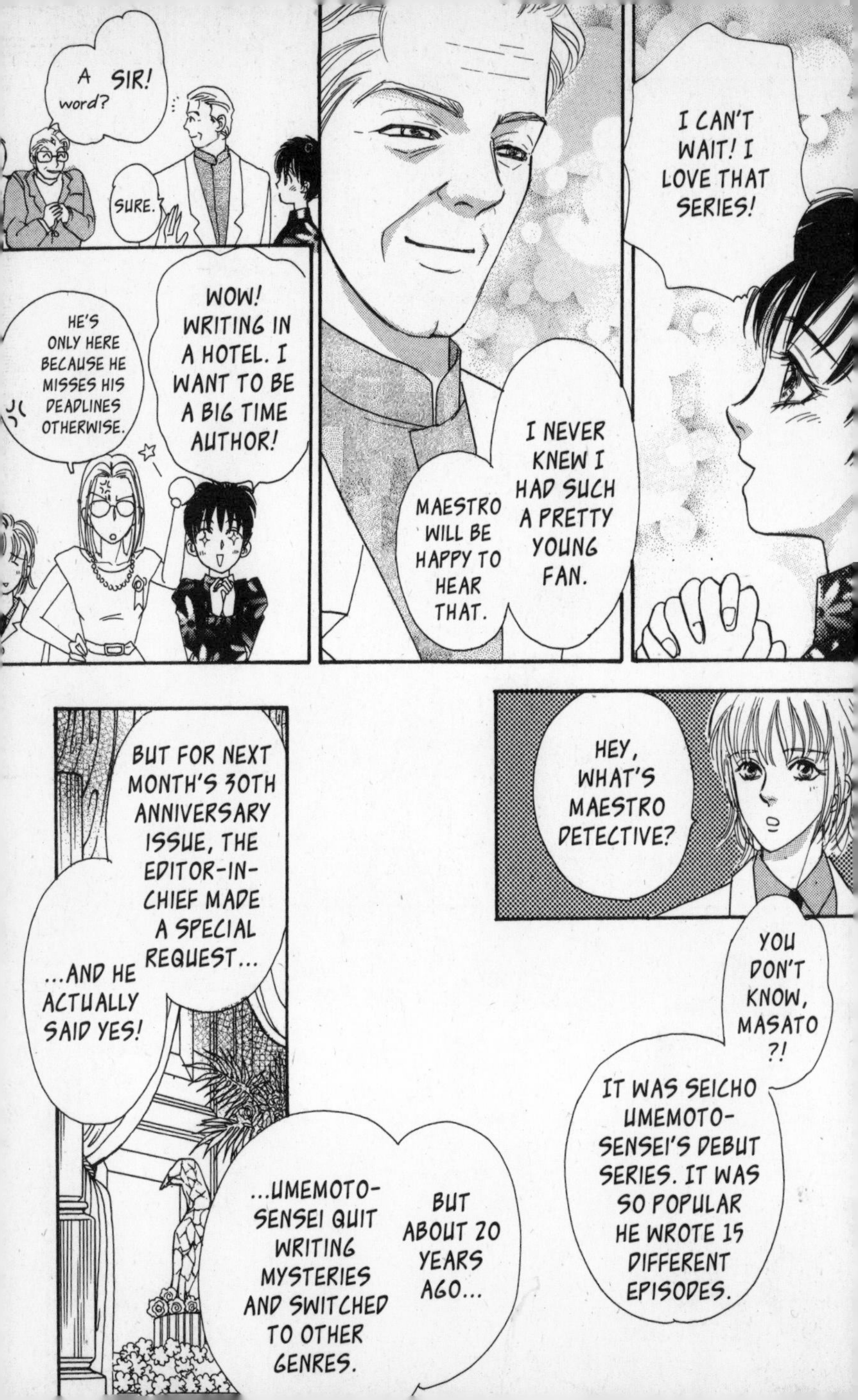

I CAN'T WAIT! I LOVE THAT SERIES!
I NEVER KNEW I HAD SUCH A PRETTY YOUNG FAN.
MAESTRO WILL BE HAPPY TO HEAR THAT.
A word? SIR!
SURE.
WOW! WRITING IN A HOTEL. I WANT TO BE A BIG TIME AUTHOR!
HE'S ONLY HERE BECAUSE HE MISSES HIS DEADLINES OTHERWISE.
HEY, WHAT'S MAESTRO DETECTIVE?
YOU DON'T KNOW, MASATO ?!
IT WAS SEICHO UMEMOTO-SENSEI'S DEBUT SERIES. IT WAS SO POPULAR HE WROTE 15 DIFFERENT EPISODES.
BUT ABOUT 20 YEARS AGO...
...UMEMOTO-SENSEI QUIT WRITING MYSTERIES AND SWITCHED TO OTHER GENRES.
BUT FOR NEXT MONTH'S 30TH ANNIVERSARY ISSUE, THE EDITOR-IN-CHIEF MADE A SPECIAL REQUEST...
...AND HE ACTUALLY SAID YES!

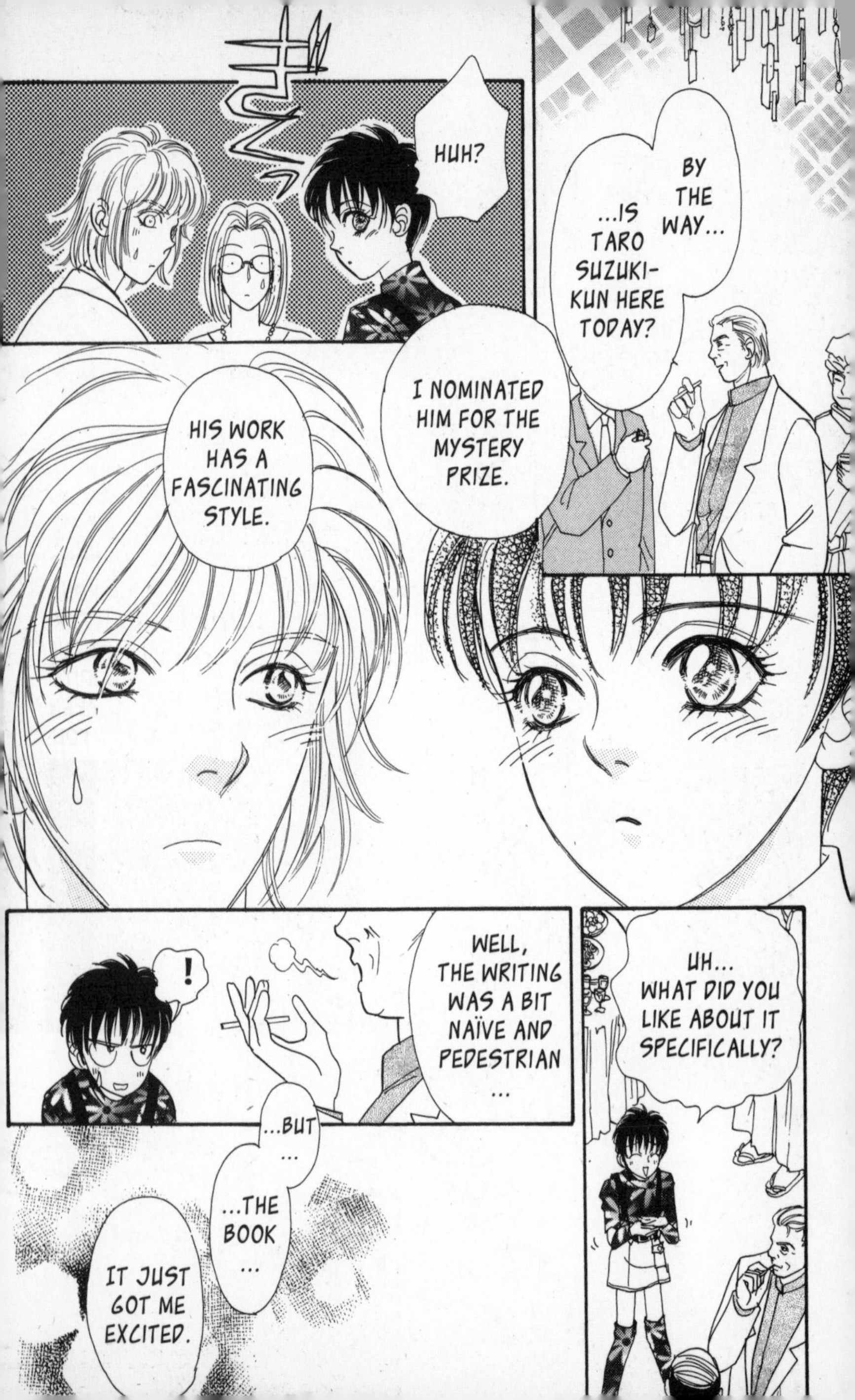
BY THE WAY...
...IS TARO SUZUKI-KUN HERE TODAY?
HUH?
I NOMINATED HIM FOR THE MYSTERY PRIZE.
HIS WORK HAS A FASCINATING STYLE.
UH... WHAT DID YOU LIKE ABOUT IT SPECIFICALLY?
!
WELL, THE WRITING WAS A BIT NAÏVE AND PEDESTRIAN ...
...BUT ...
...THE BOOK ...
IT JUST GOT ME EXCITED.

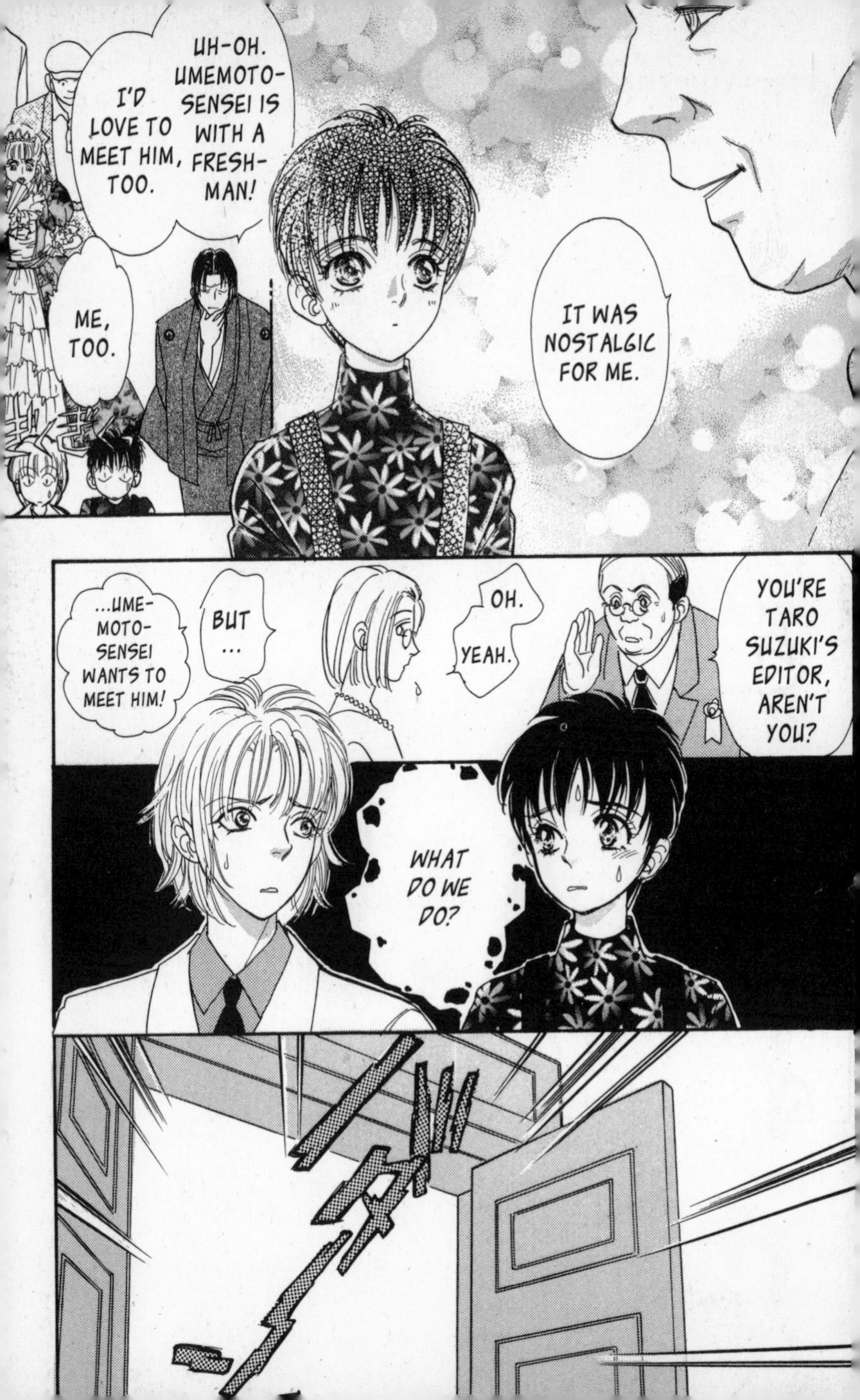
IT WAS NOSTALGIC FOR ME.
UH-OH. UMEMOTO-SENSEI IS WITH A FRESH-MAN!
I'D LOVE TO MEET HIM, TOO.
ME, TOO.
YOU'RE TARO SUZUKI'S EDITOR, AREN'T YOU?
OH.
YEAH.
BUT ...
...UME-MOTO-SENSEI WANTS TO MEET HIM!
WHAT DO WE DO?

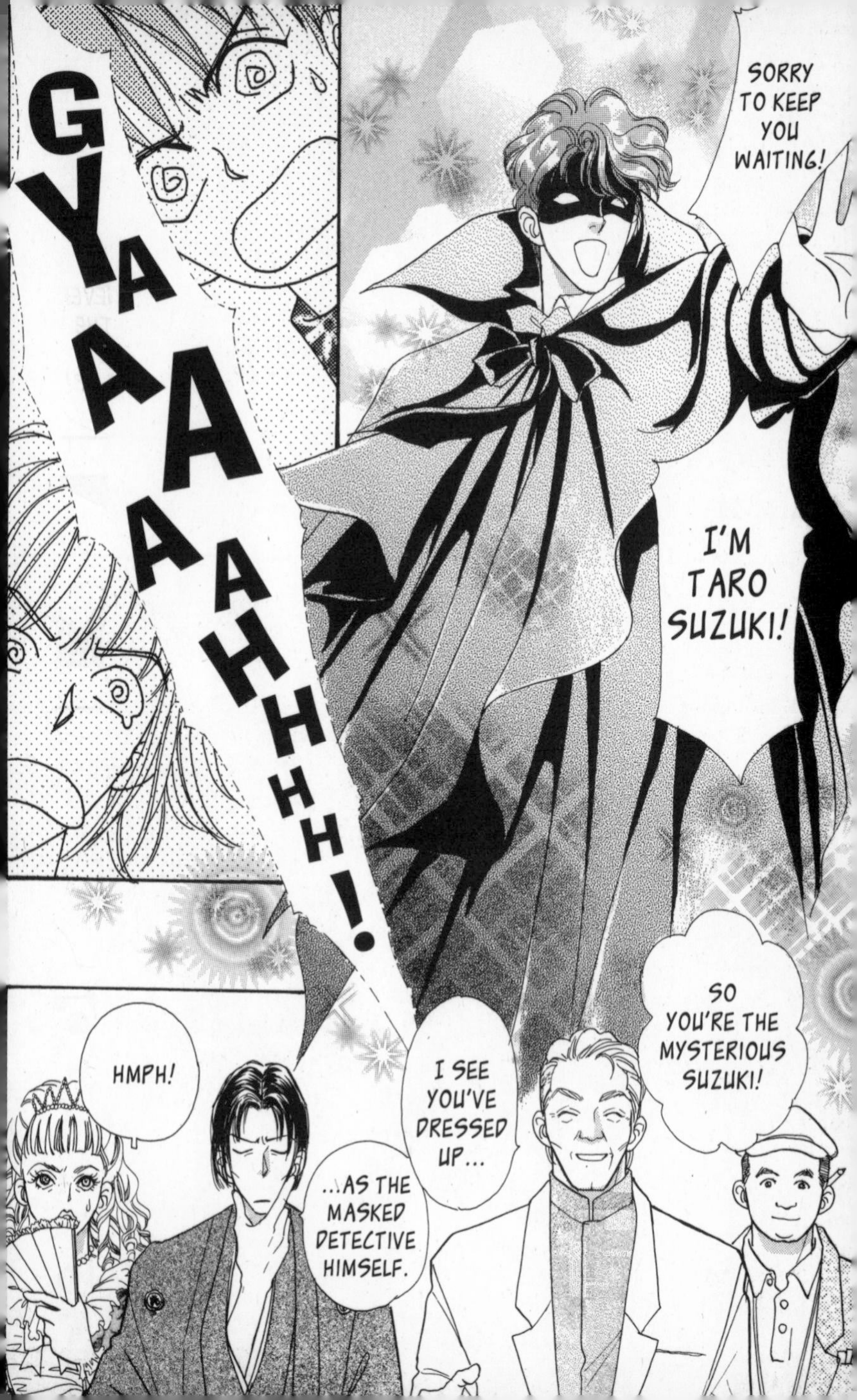
SORRY TO KEEP YOU WAITING!
I'M TARO SUZUKI!
GYAAAAAHHHH!
SO YOU'RE THE MYSTERIOUS SUZUKI!
I SEE YOU'VE DRESSED UP...
...AS THE MASKED DETECTIVE HIMSELF.
HMPH!

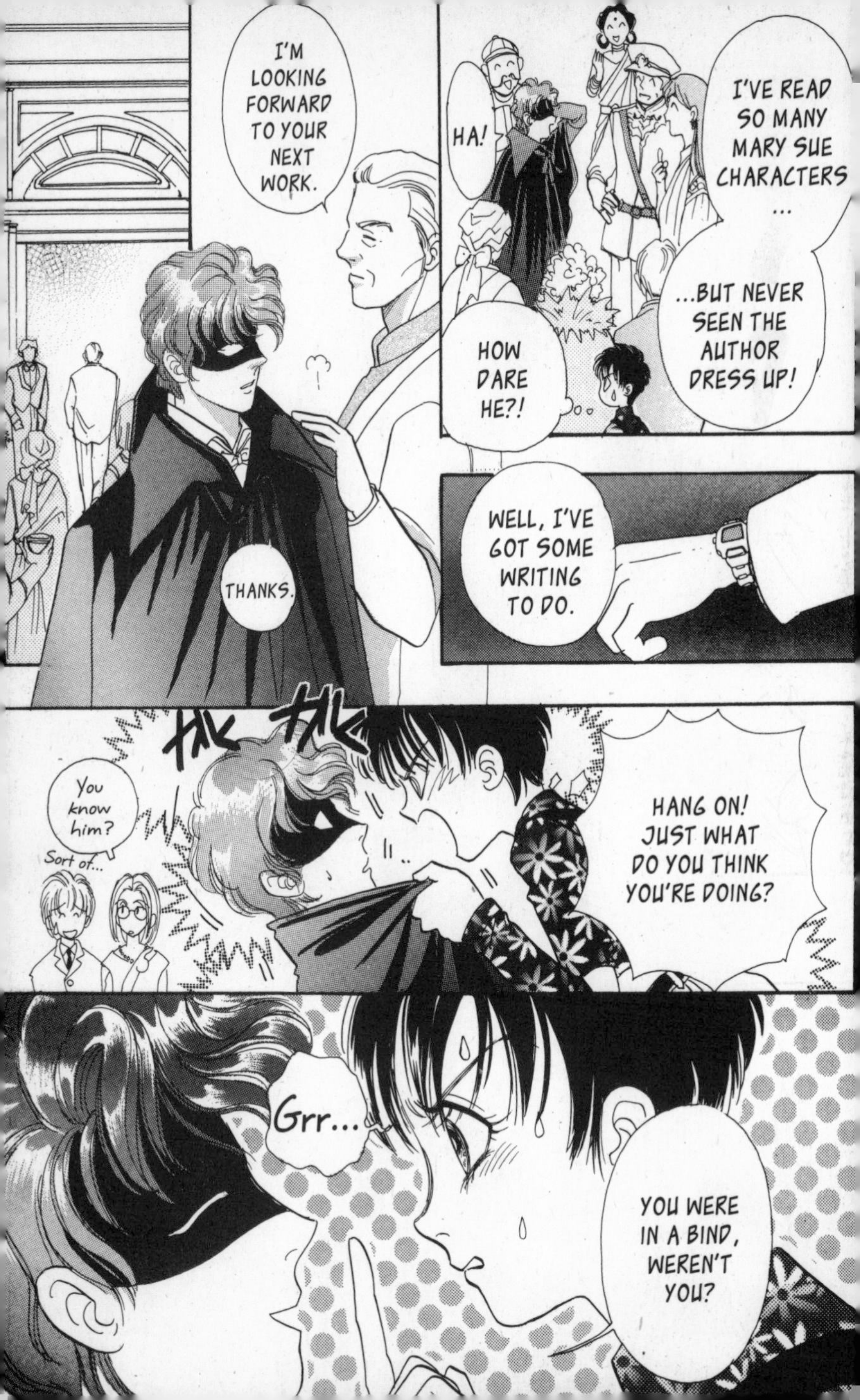
I'VE READ SO MANY MARY SUE CHARACTERS...
HA!
...BUT NEVER SEEN THE AUTHOR DRESS UP!
HOW DARE HE?!
WELL, I'VE GOT SOME WRITING TO DO.
I'M LOOKING FORWARD TO YOUR NEXT WORK.
THANKS.
HANG ON! JUST WHAT DO YOU THINK YOU'RE DOING?
You know him?
Sort of...
YOU WERE IN A BIND, WEREN'T YOU?
Grr...

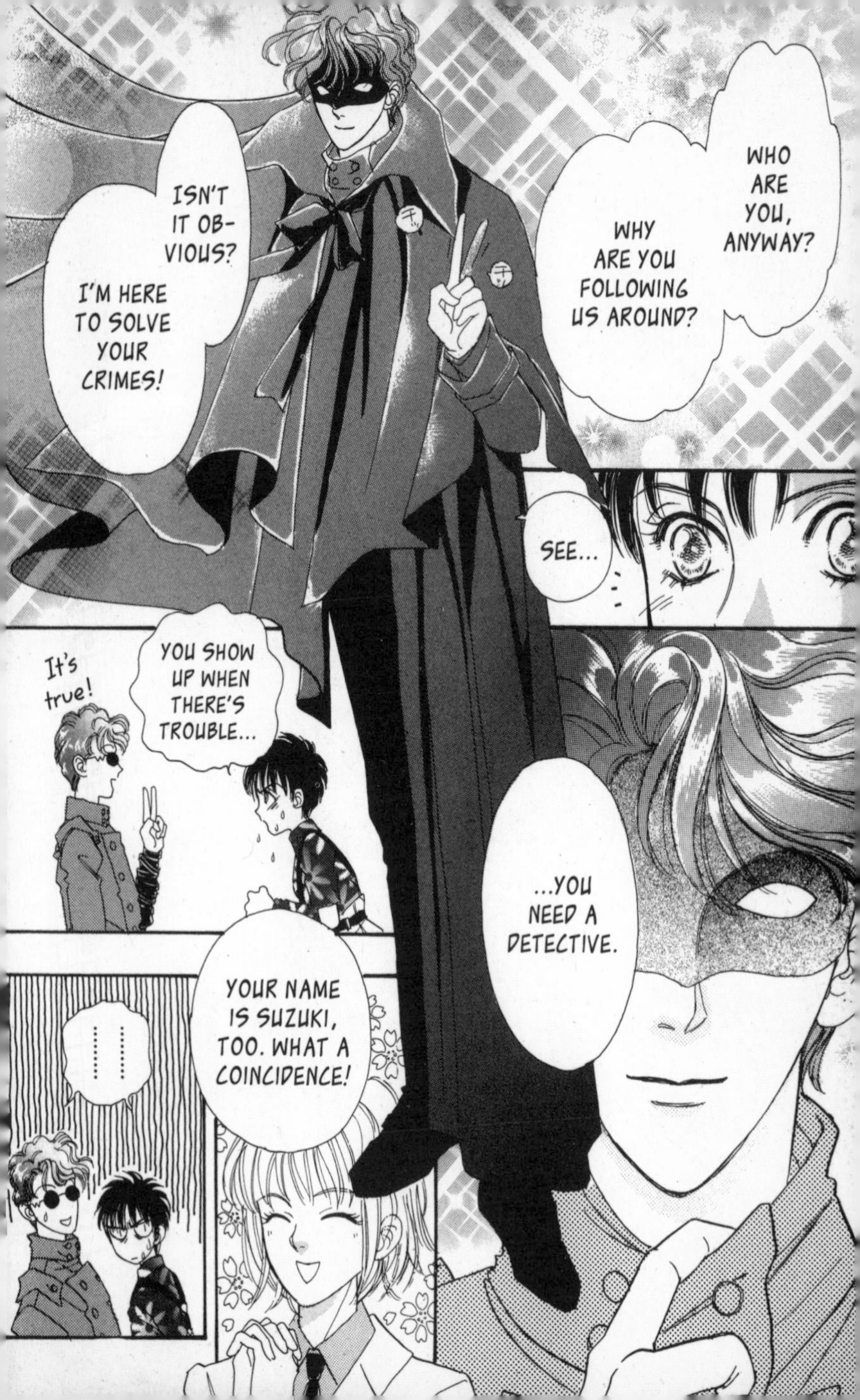
WHO ARE YOU, ANYWAY?
WHY ARE YOU FOLLOWING US AROUND?
ISN'T IT OB-VIOUS?
I'M HERE TO SOLVE YOUR CRIMES!
SEE...
...YOU NEED A DETECTIVE.
YOU SHOW UP WHEN THERE'S TROUBLE...
It's true!
YOUR NAME IS SUZUKI, TOO. WHAT A COINCIDENCE!
......

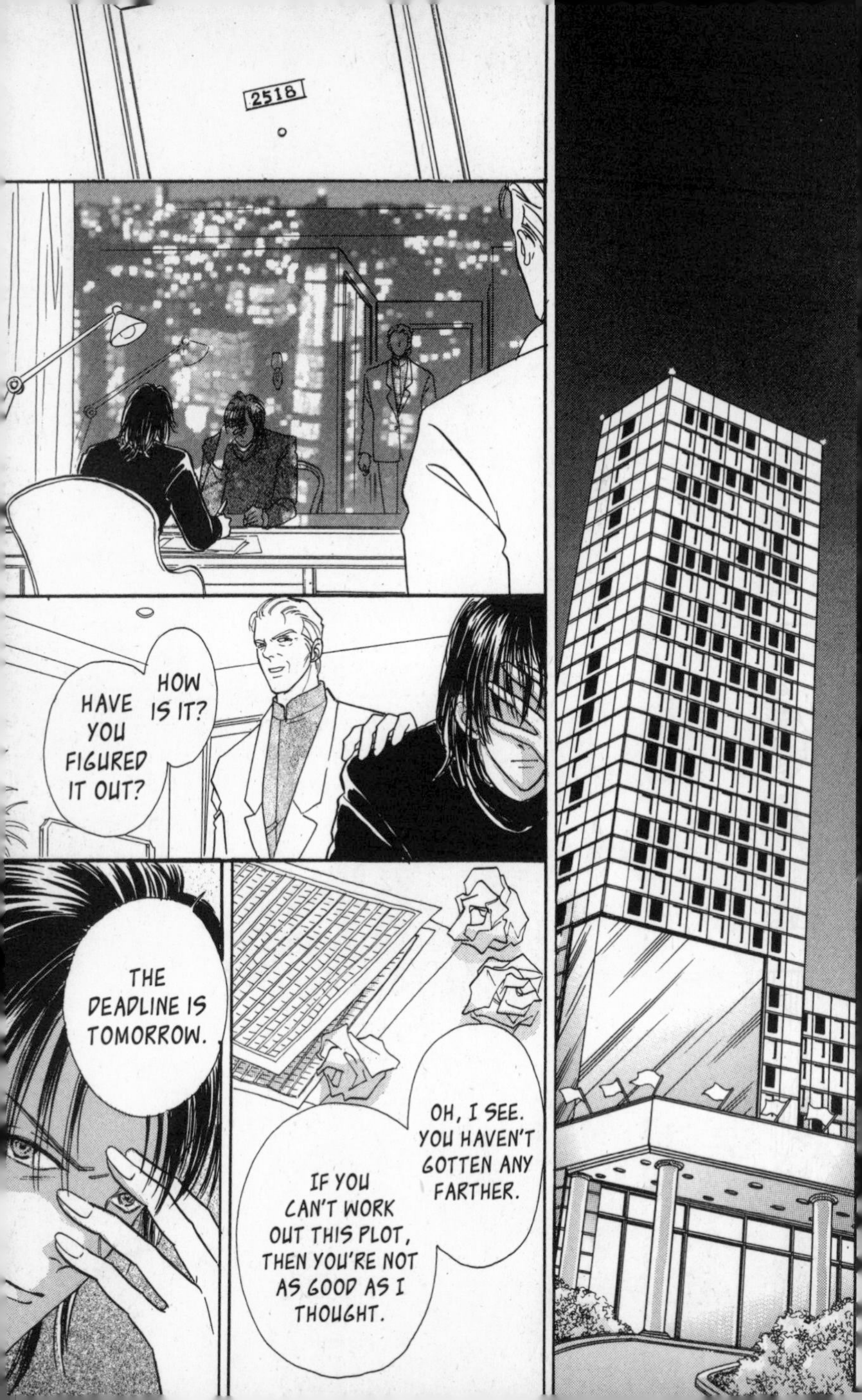
2518
HOW IS IT? HAVE YOU FIGURED IT OUT?
OH, I SEE. YOU HAVEN'T GOTTEN ANY FARTHER.
IF YOU CAN'T WORK OUT THIS PLOT, THEN YOU'RE NOT AS GOOD AS I THOUGHT.
THE DEADLINE IS TOMORROW.

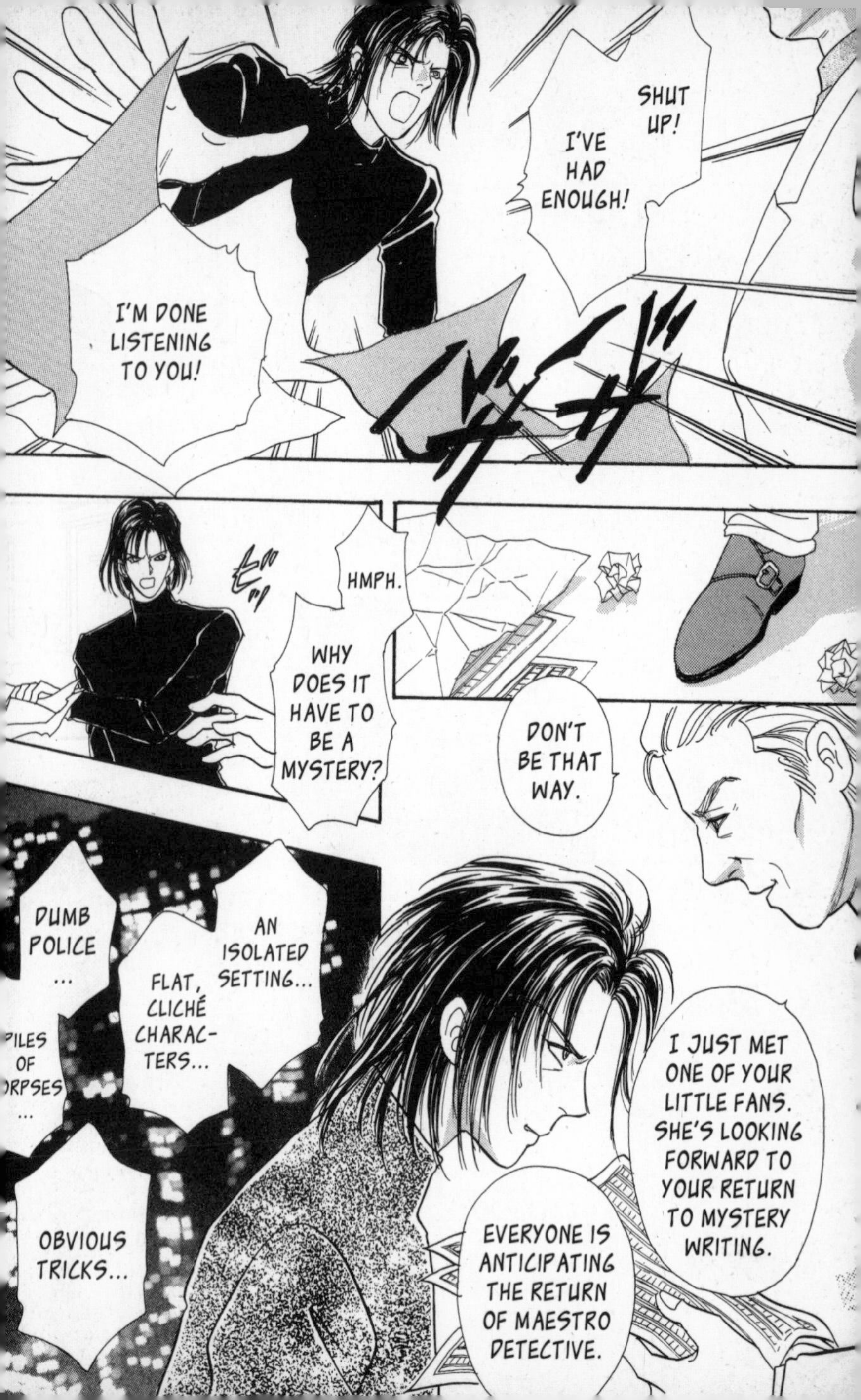
SHUT UP!
I'VE HAD ENOUGH!
I'M DONE LISTENING TO YOU!
HMPH.
WHY DOES IT HAVE TO BE A MYSTERY?
DON'T BE THAT WAY.
I JUST MET ONE OF YOUR LITTLE FANS. SHE'S LOOKING FORWARD TO YOUR RETURN TO MYSTERY WRITING.
EVERYONE IS ANTICIPATING THE RETURN OF MAESTRO DETECTIVE.
AN ISOLATED SETTING...
DUMB POLICE ...
FLAT, CLICHÉ CHARACTERS...
PILES OF ORPSES ...
OBVIOUS TRICKS...

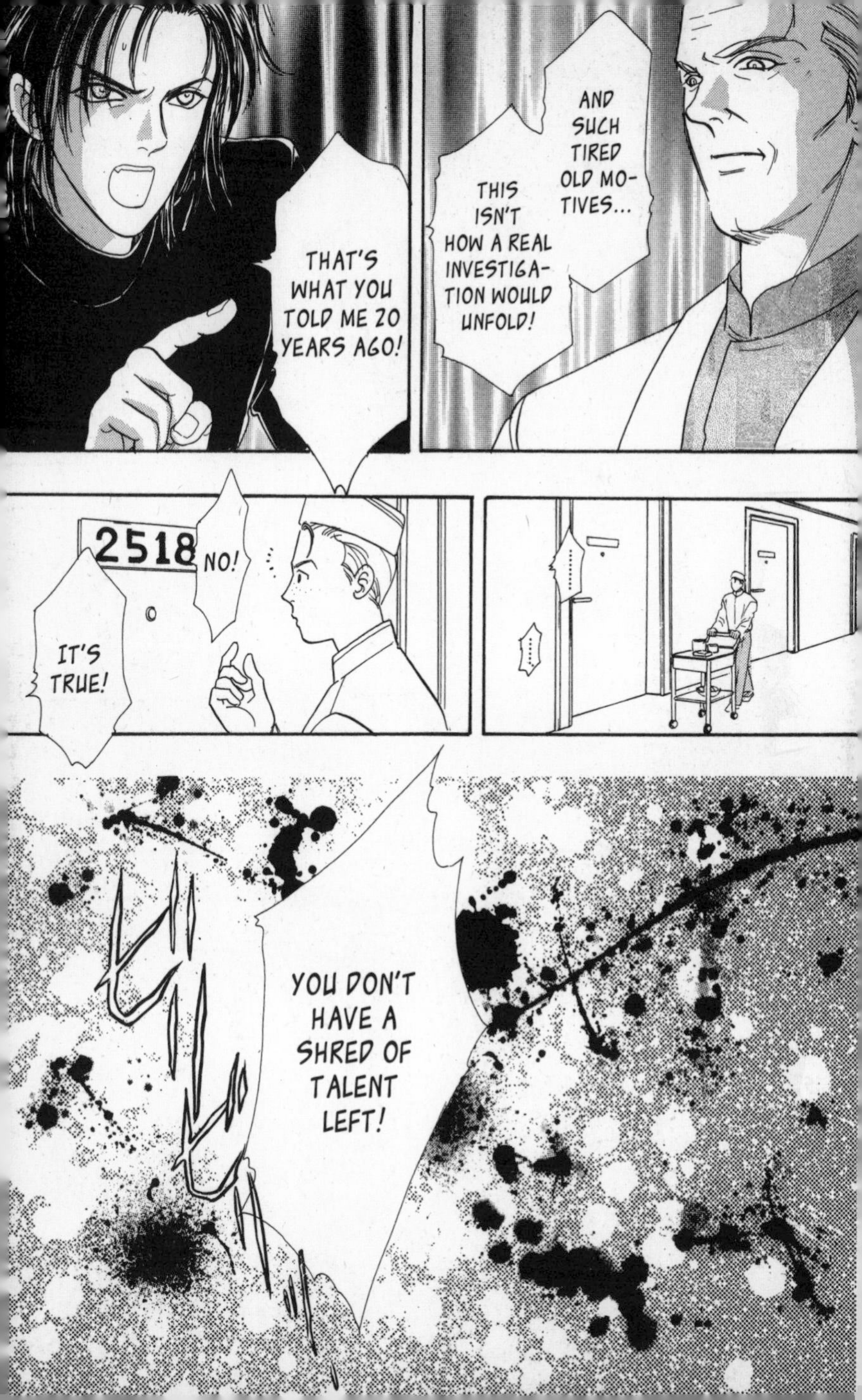

AND SUCH TIRED OLD MO-TIVES...
THIS ISN'T HOW A REAL INVESTIGA-TION WOULD UNFOLD!
THAT'S WHAT YOU TOLD ME 20 YEARS AGO!
......
......
2518
NO!
IT'S TRUE!
YOU DON'T HAVE A SHRED OF TALENT LEFT!

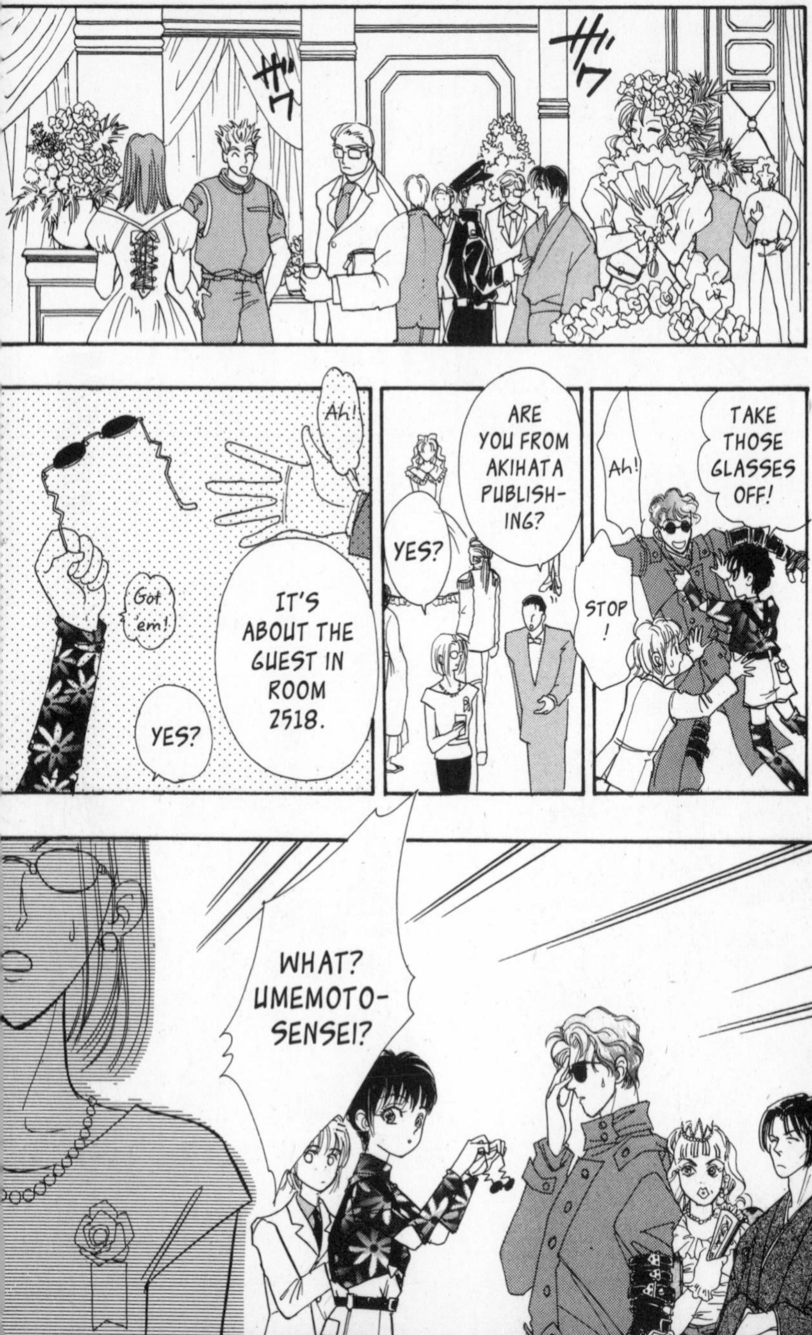
ザワ
ザワ
TAKE THOSE GLASSES OFF!
Ah!
STOP!
ARE YOU FROM AKIHATA PUBLISH-ING?
YES?
Ah!
IT'S ABOUT THE GUEST IN ROOM 2518.
Got 'em!
YES?
WHAT? UMEMOTO-SENSEI?

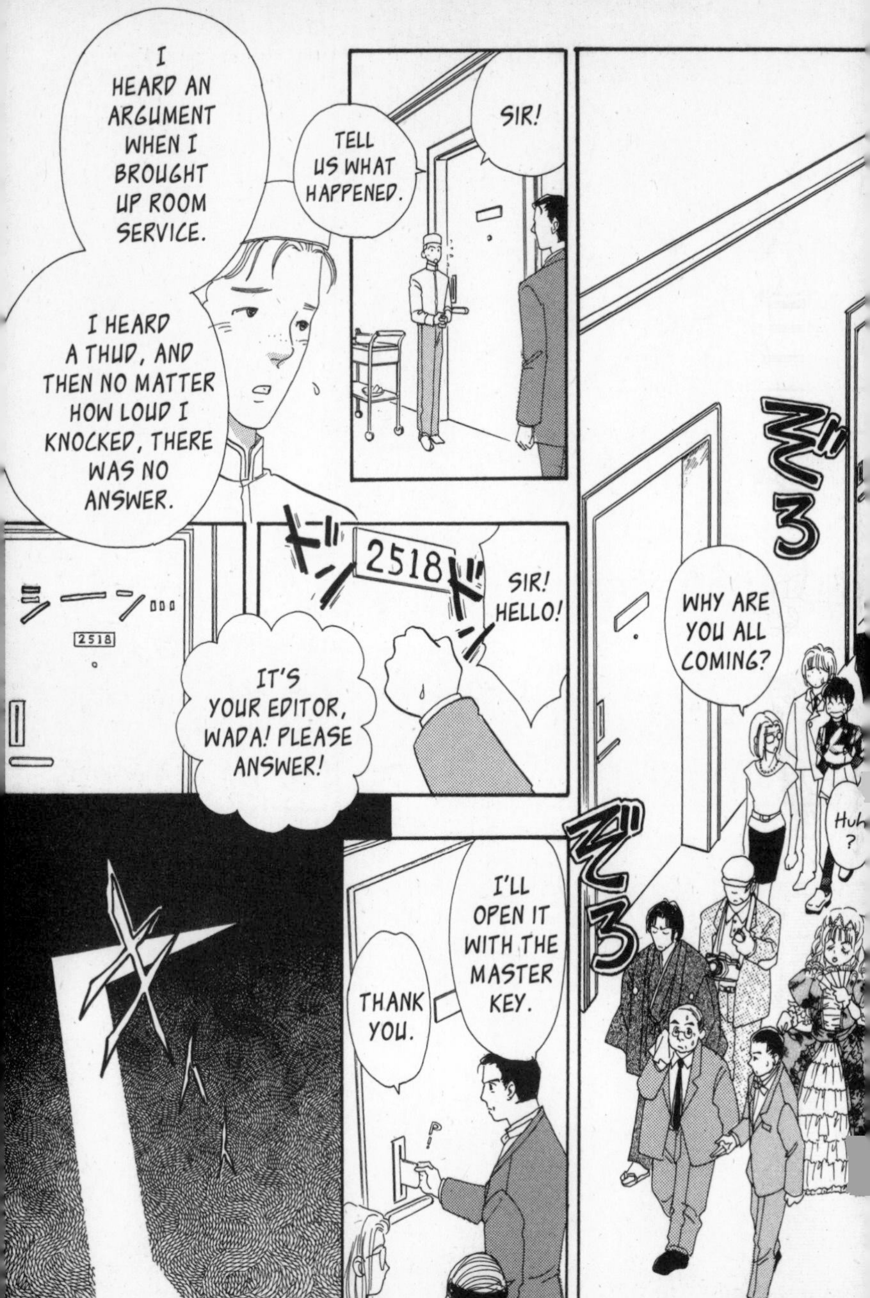
ぞろ
WHY ARE YOU ALL COMING?
Huh?
ぞろ
SIR!
TELL US WHAT HAPPENED.
I HEARD AN ARGUMENT WHEN I BROUGHT UP ROOM SERVICE.
I HEARD A THUD, AND THEN NO MATTER HOW LOUD I KNOCKED, THERE WAS NO ANSWER.
2518
ドンドン
SIR! HELLO!
IT'S YOUR EDITOR, WADA! PLEASE ANSWER!
シーン...
2518
I'LL OPEN IT WITH THE MASTER KEY.
THANK YOU.

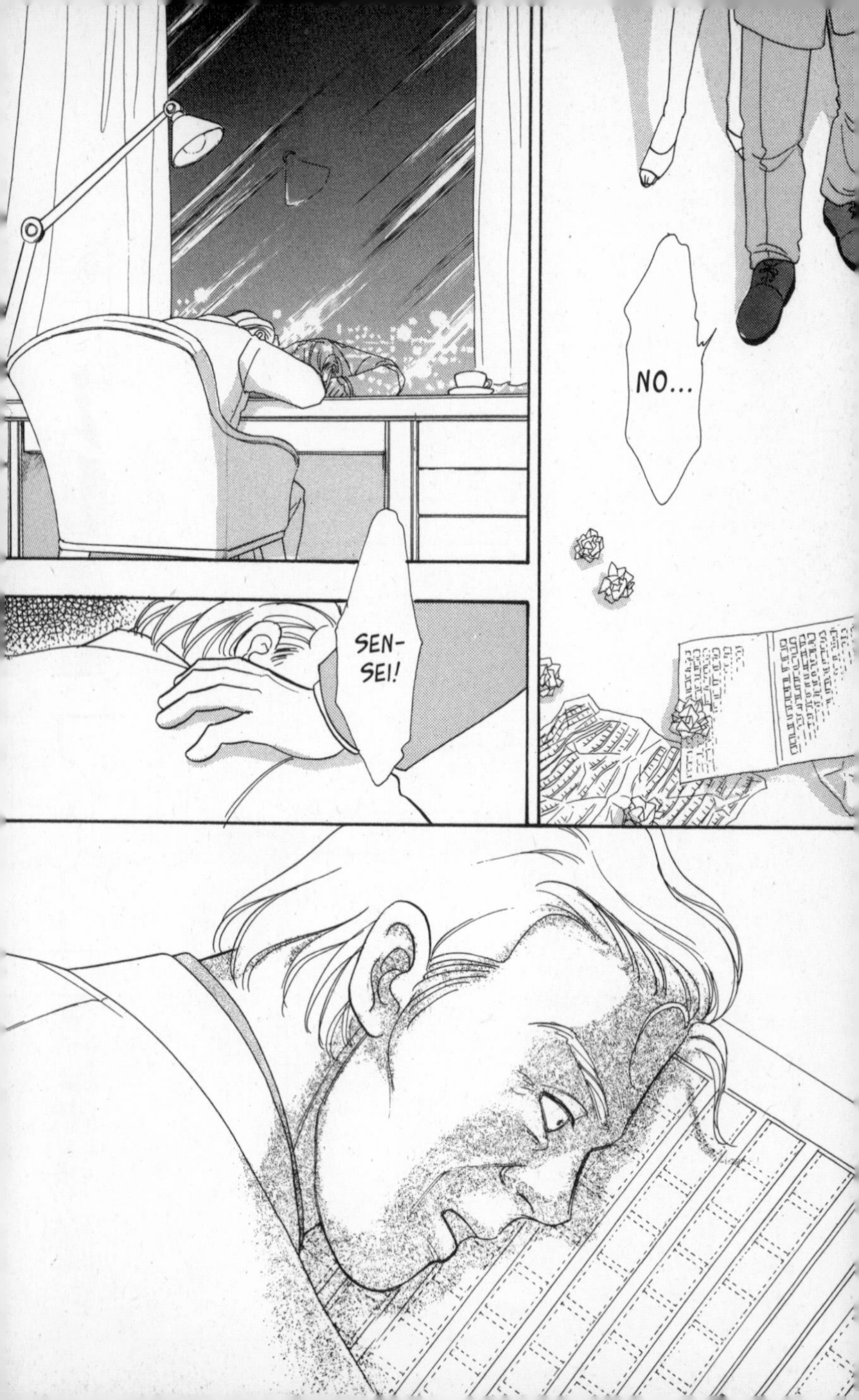
NO...
SEN-SEI!

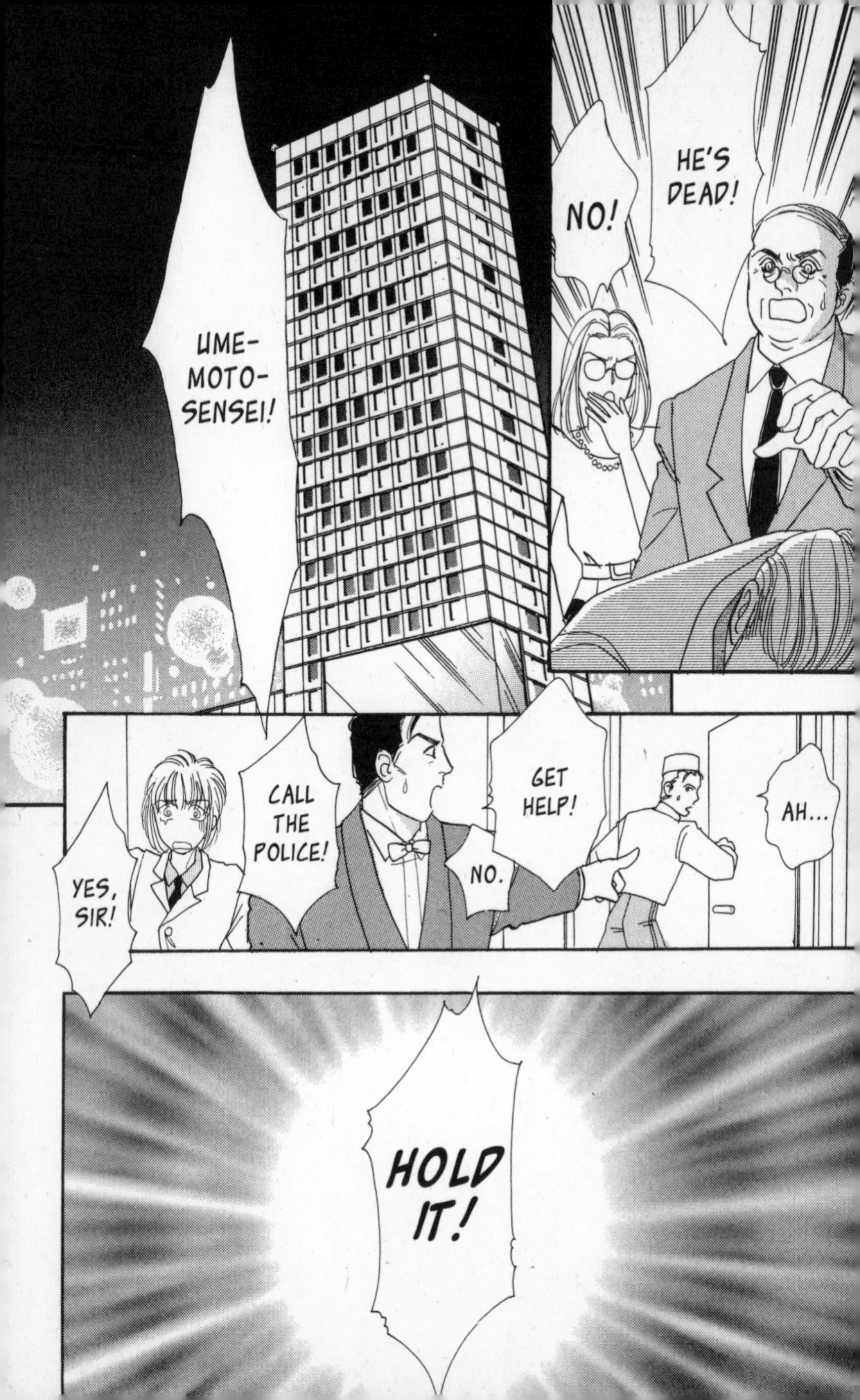
HE'S DEAD!
NO!
UME-MOTO-SENSEI!
AH...
GET HELP!
NO.
CALL THE POLICE!
YES, SIR!
HOLD IT!

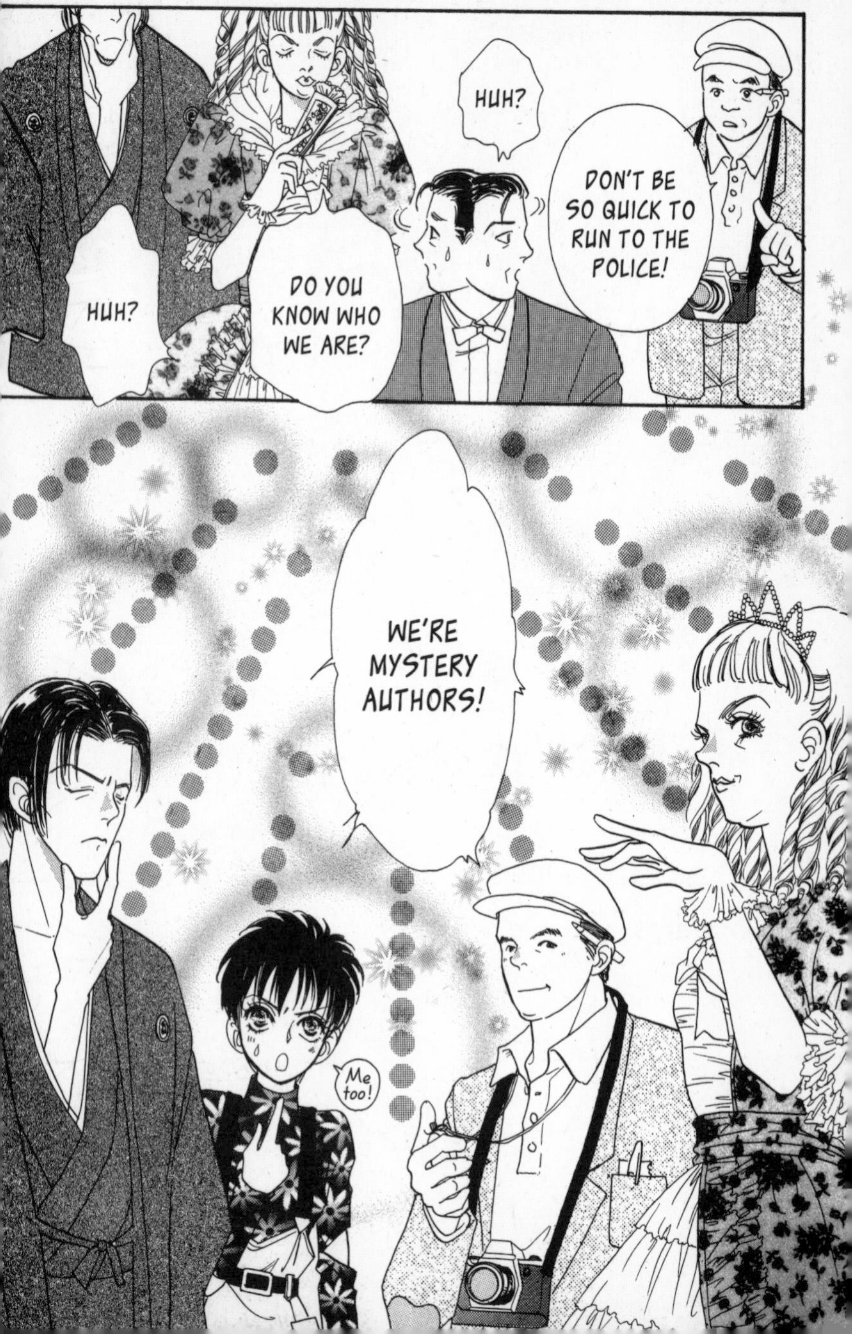
DON'T BE SO QUICK TO RUN TO THE POLICE!
HUH?
DO YOU KNOW WHO WE ARE?
HUH?
WE'RE MYSTERY AUTHORS!
Me too!

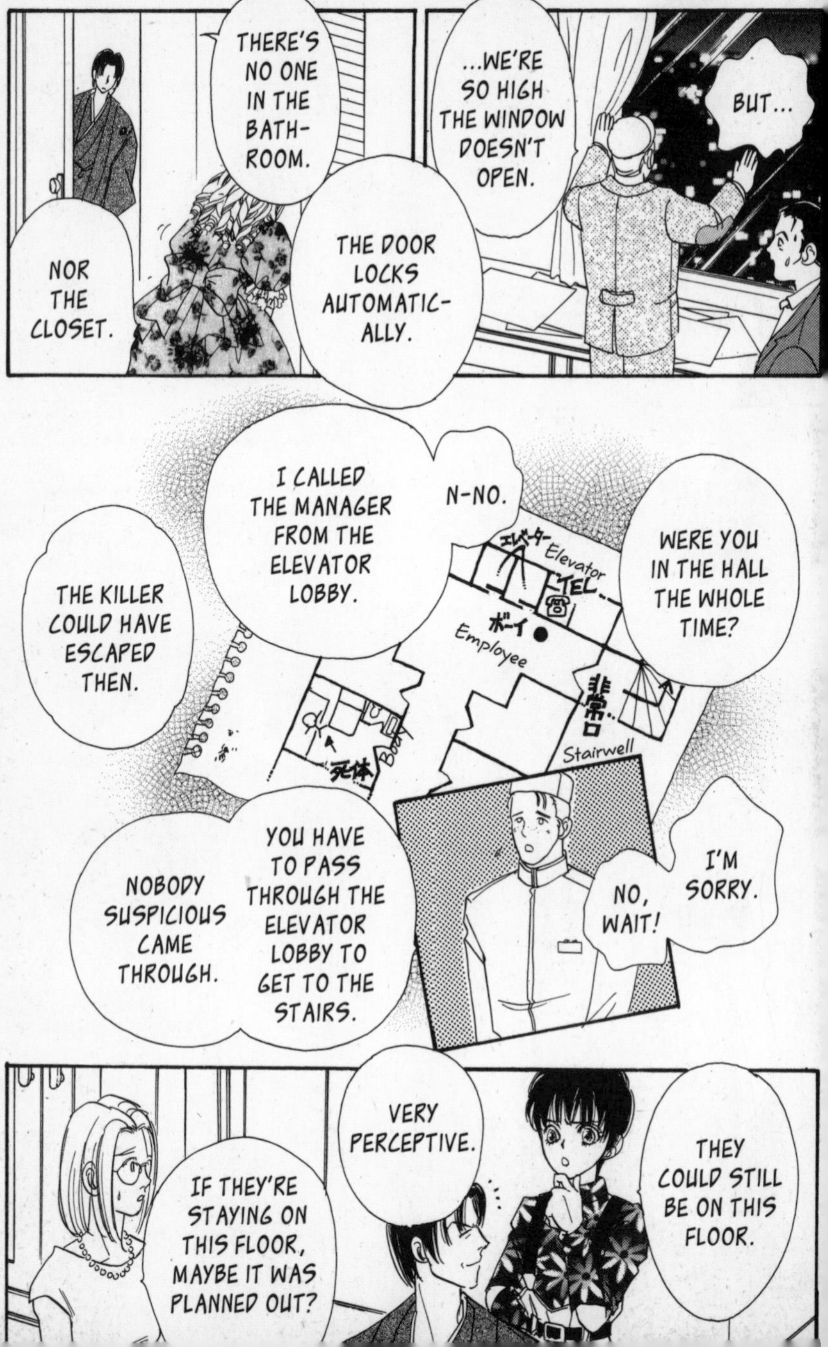
BUT...
...WE'RE SO HIGH THE WINDOW DOESN'T OPEN.
THERE'S NO ONE IN THE BATH-ROOM.
THE DOOR LOCKS AUTOMATIC-ALLY.
NOR THE CLOSET.
WERE YOU IN THE HALL THE WHOLE TIME?
N-NO.
I CALLED THE MANAGER FROM THE ELEVATOR LOBBY.
THE KILLER COULD HAVE ESCAPED THEN.
エレベーター Elevator
TEL
ボーイ Employee
非常口 Stairwell
死体 Body
I'M SORRY.
NO, WAIT!
YOU HAVE TO PASS THROUGH THE ELEVATOR LOBBY TO GET TO THE STAIRS.
NOBODY SUSPICIOUS CAME THROUGH.
THEY COULD STILL BE ON THIS FLOOR.
VERY PERCEPTIVE.
IF THEY'RE STAYING ON THIS FLOOR, MAYBE IT WAS PLANNED OUT?

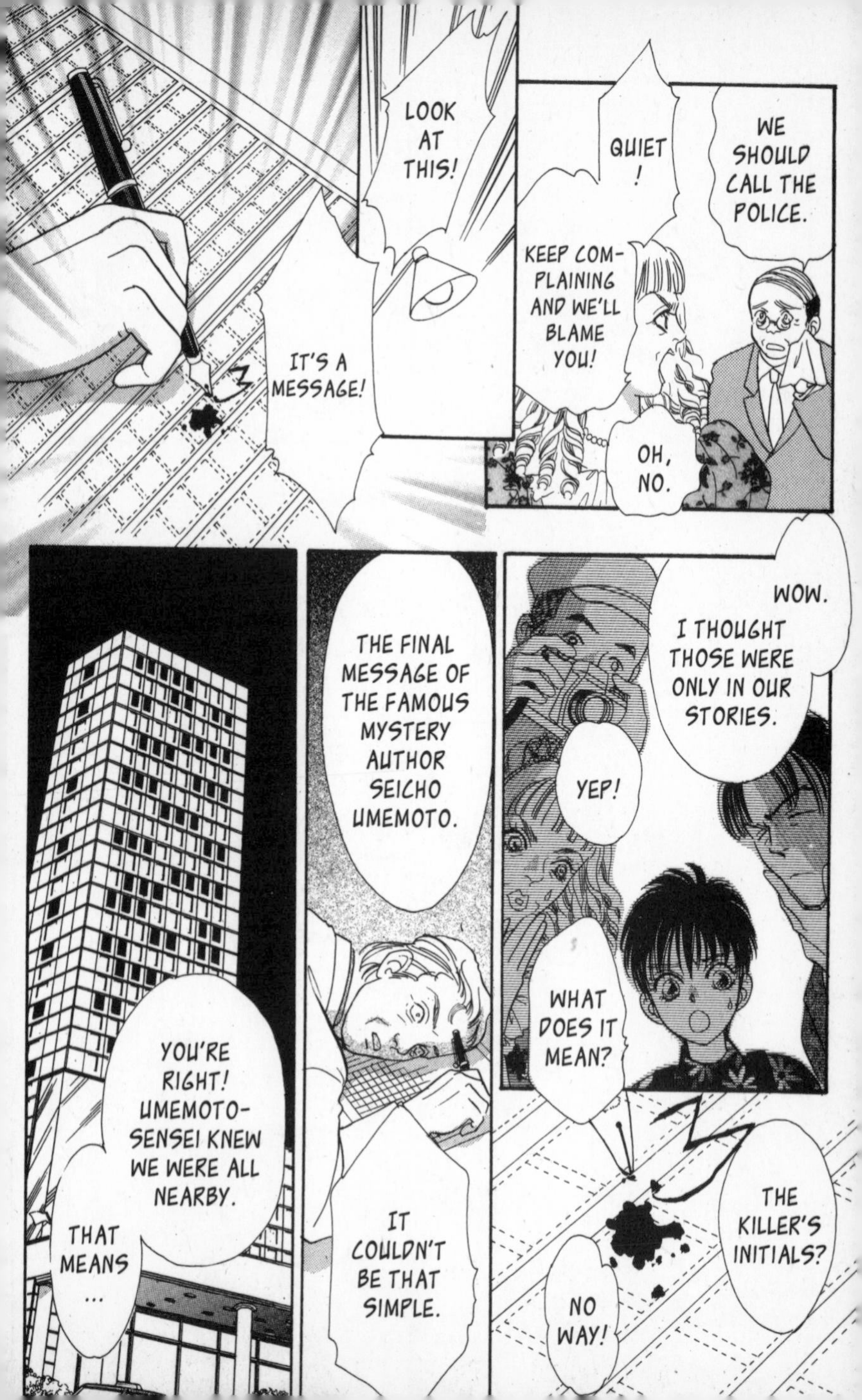
WE SHOULD CALL THE POLICE.
QUIET!
KEEP COMPLAINING AND WE'LL BLAME YOU!
OH, NO.
LOOK AT THIS!
IT'S A MESSAGE!
WOW. I THOUGHT THOSE WERE ONLY IN OUR STORIES.
YEP!
WHAT DOES IT MEAN?
THE KILLER'S INITIALS?
NO WAY!
THE FINAL MESSAGE OF THE FAMOUS MYSTERY AUTHOR SEICHO UMEMOTO.
IT COULDN'T BE THAT SIMPLE.
YOU'RE RIGHT! UMEMOTO-SENSEI KNEW WE WERE ALL NEARBY.
THAT MEANS ...

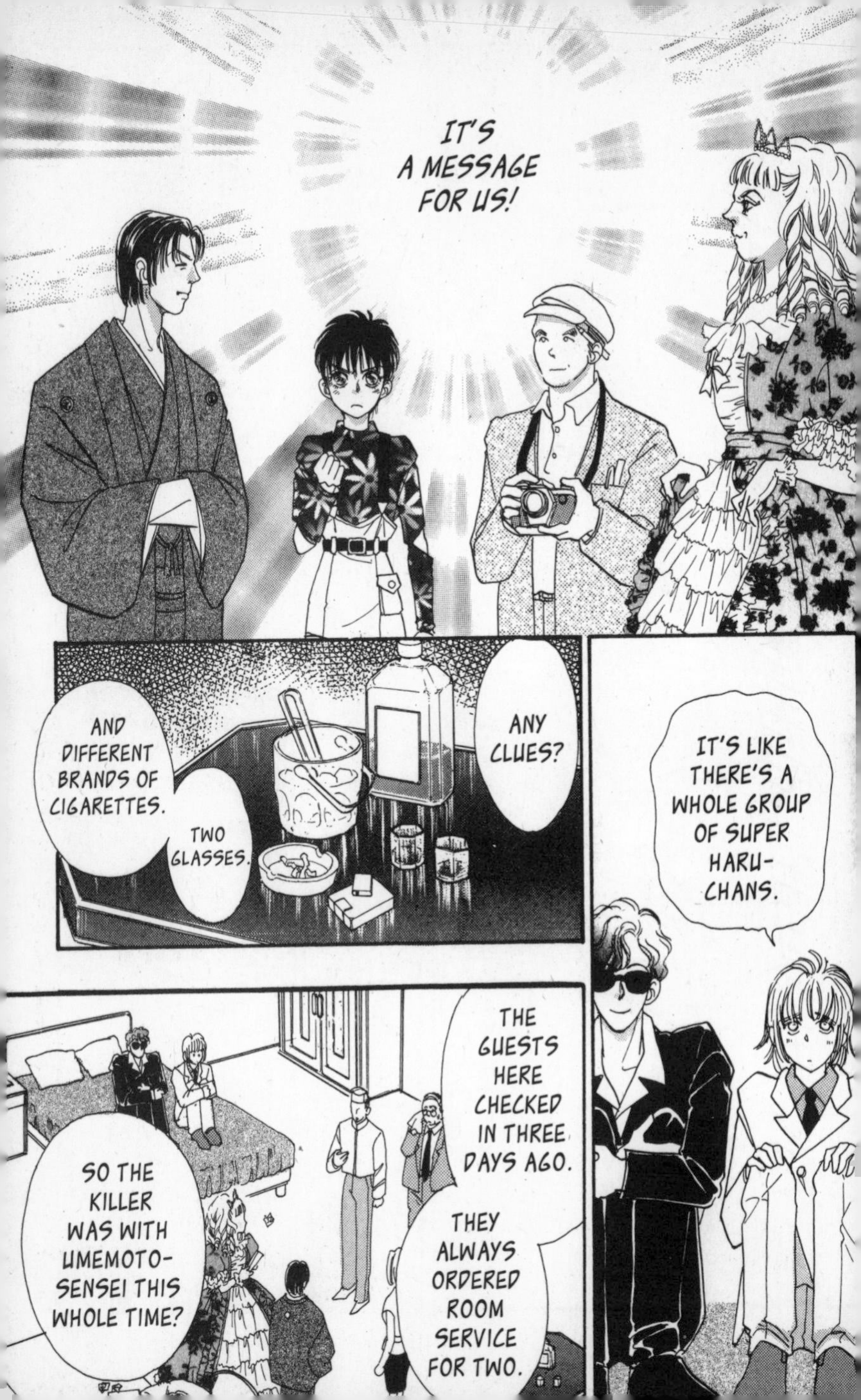
IT'S A MESSAGE FOR US!
IT'S LIKE THERE'S A WHOLE GROUP OF SUPER HARU-CHANS.
ANY CLUES?
TWO GLASSES.
AND DIFFERENT BRANDS OF CIGARETTES.
THE GUESTS HERE CHECKED IN THREE DAYS AGO.
THEY ALWAYS ORDERED ROOM SERVICE FOR TWO.
SO THE KILLER WAS WITH UMEMOTO-SENSEI THIS WHOLE TIME?

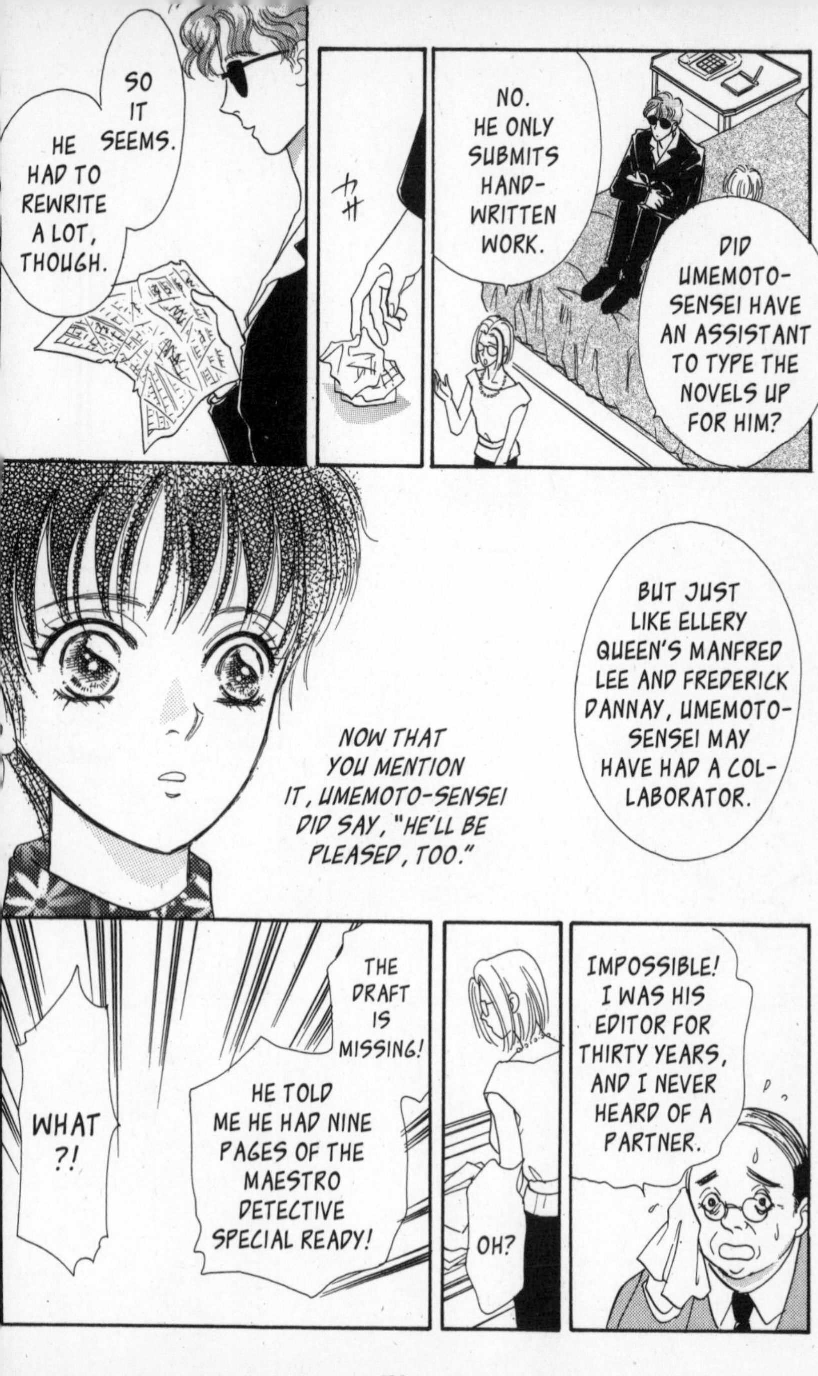

DID UMEMOTO-SENSEI HAVE AN ASSISTANT TO TYPE THE NOVELS UP FOR HIM?
NO. HE ONLY SUBMITS HAND-WRITTEN WORK.
SO IT SEEMS.
HE HAD TO REWRITE A LOT, THOUGH.
BUT JUST LIKE ELLERY QUEEN'S MANFRED LEE AND FREDERICK DANNAY, UMEMOTO-SENSEI MAY HAVE HAD A COL-LABORATOR.
NOW THAT YOU MENTION IT, UMEMOTO-SENSEI DID SAY, "HE'LL BE PLEASED, TOO."
IMPOSSIBLE! I WAS HIS EDITOR FOR THIRTY YEARS, AND I NEVER HEARD OF A PARTNER.
OH?
THE DRAFT IS MISSING!
HE TOLD ME HE HAD NINE PAGES OF THE MAESTRO DETECTIVE SPECIAL READY!
WHAT ?!

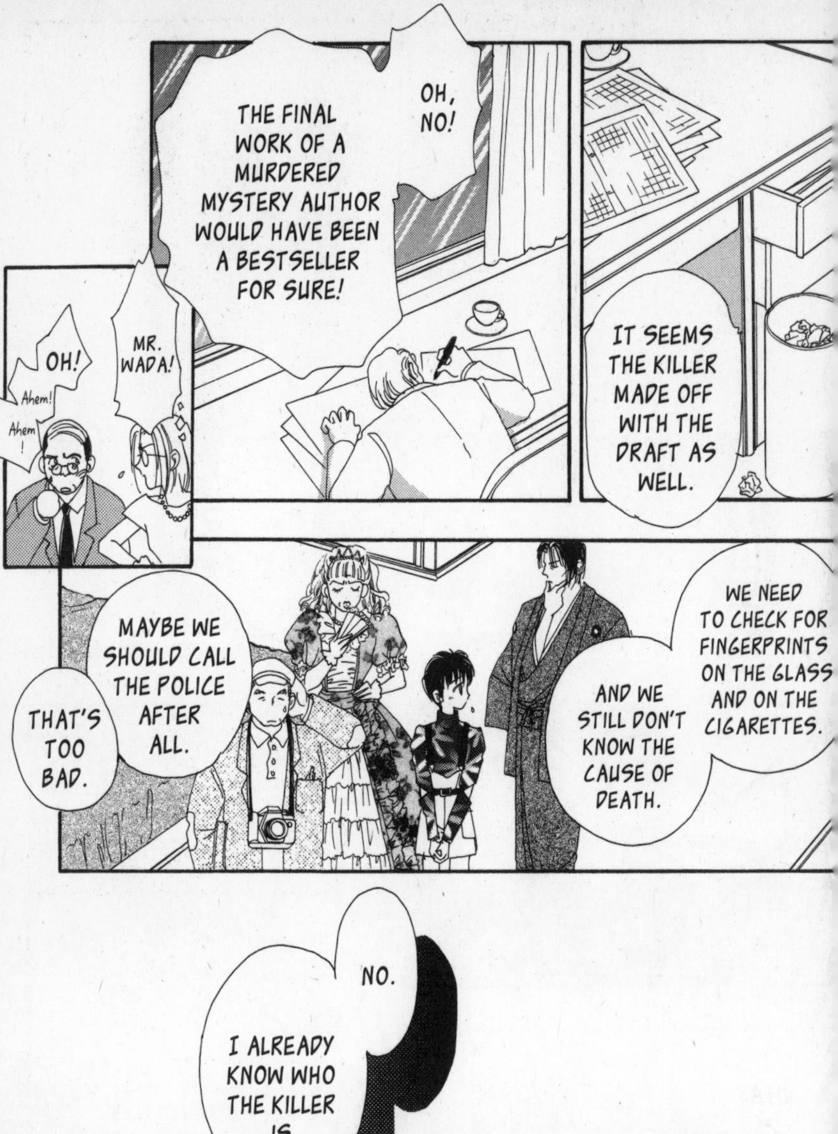
IT SEEMS THE KILLER MADE OFF WITH THE DRAFT AS WELL.
OH, NO!
THE FINAL WORK OF A MURDERED MYSTERY AUTHOR WOULD HAVE BEEN A BESTSELLER FOR SURE!
MR. WADA!
OH!
Ahem!
Ahem!
WE NEED TO CHECK FOR FINGERPRINTS ON THE GLASS AND ON THE CIGARETTES.
AND WE STILL DON'T KNOW THE CAUSE OF DEATH.
MAYBE WE SHOULD CALL THE POLICE AFTER ALL.
THAT'S TOO BAD.
NO.
I ALREADY KNOW WHO THE KILLER IS.

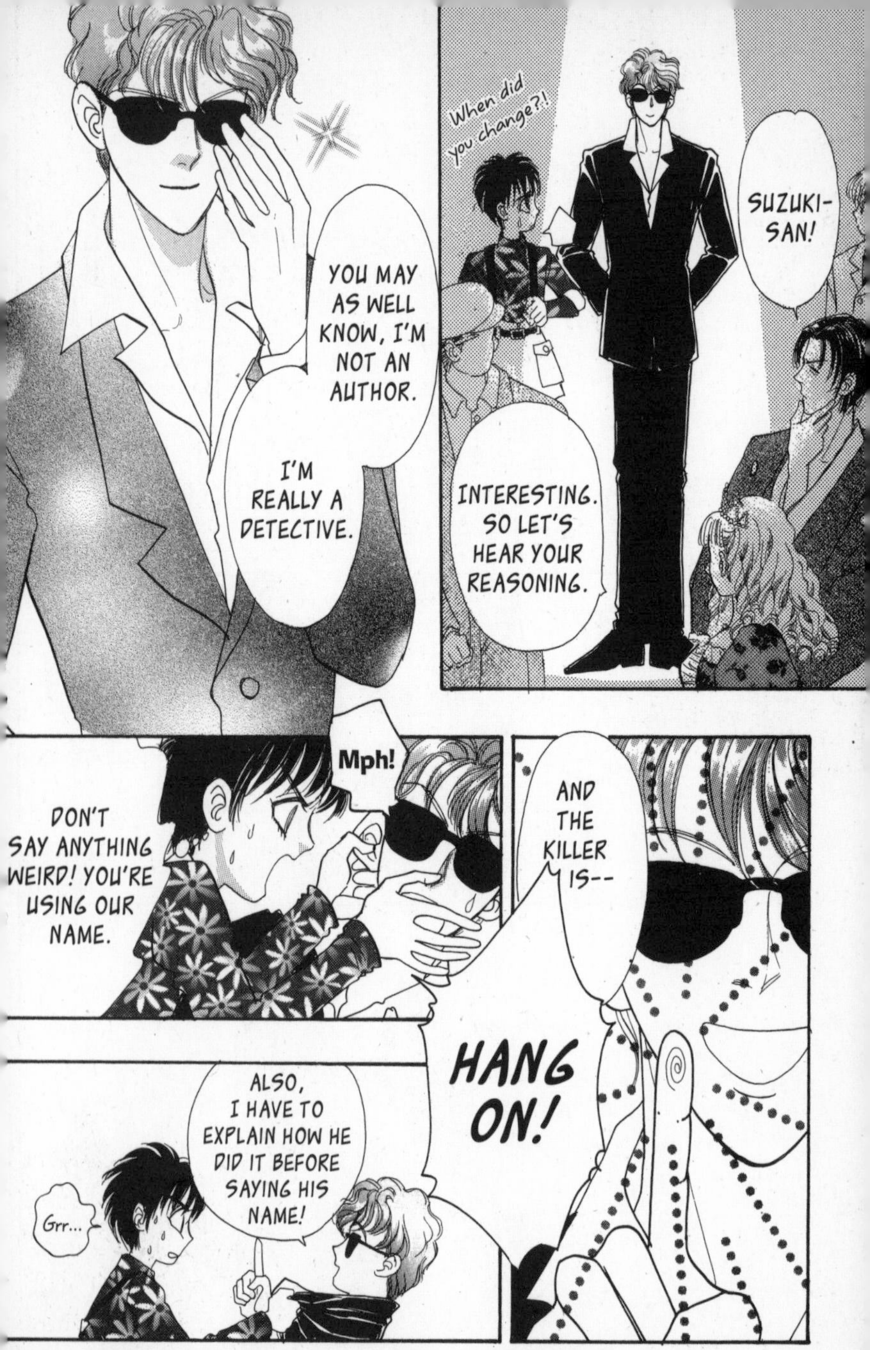
SUZUKI-SAN!
When did you change?!
INTERESTING. SO LET'S HEAR YOUR REASONING.
YOU MAY AS WELL KNOW, I'M NOT AN AUTHOR.
I'M REALLY A DETECTIVE.
AND THE KILLER IS--
HANG ON!
Mph!
DON'T SAY ANYTHING WEIRD! YOU'RE USING OUR NAME.
ALSO, I HAVE TO EXPLAIN HOW HE DID IT BEFORE SAYING HIS NAME!
Grr...

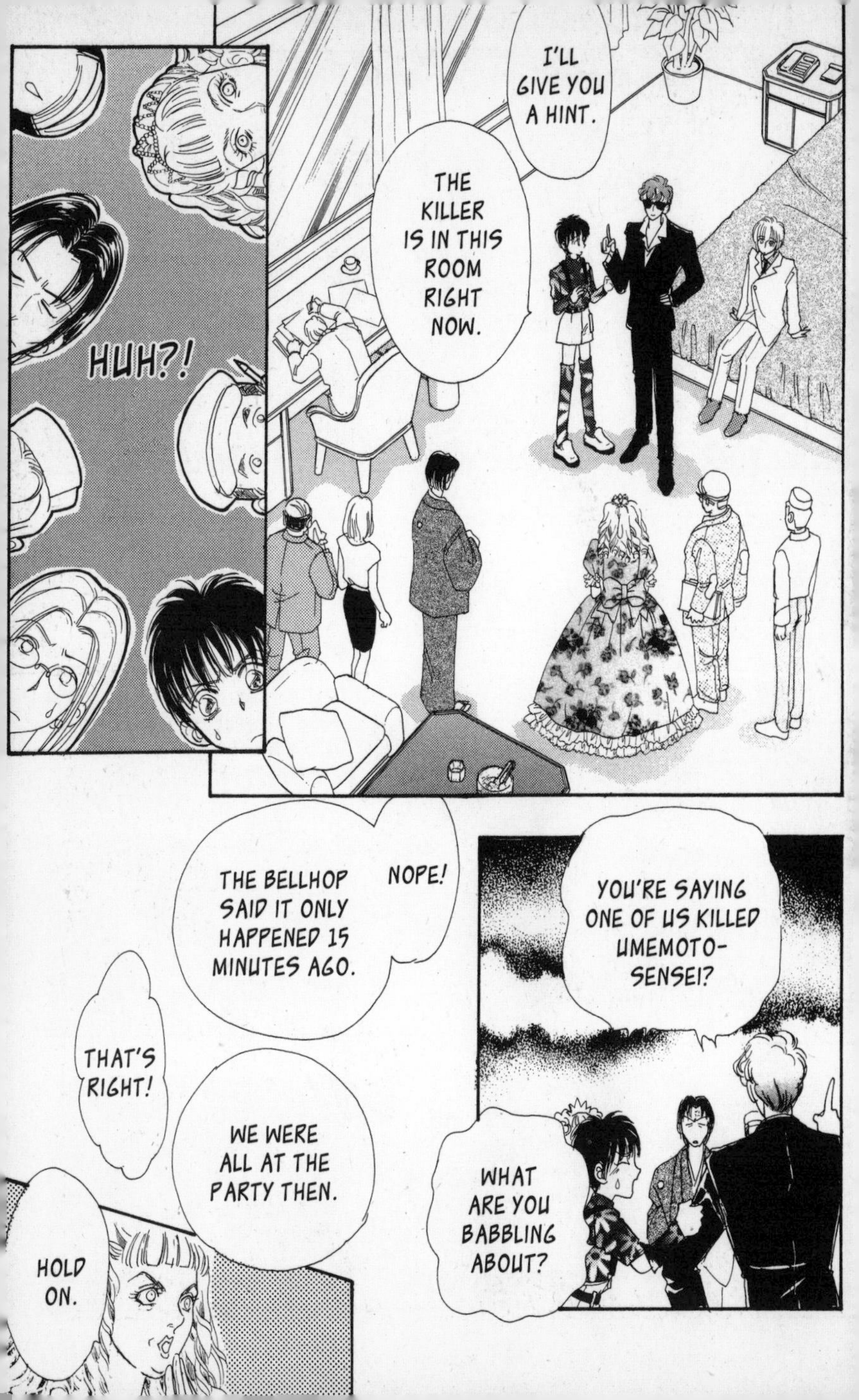
I'LL GIVE YOU A HINT.
THE KILLER IS IN THIS ROOM RIGHT NOW.
HUH?!
YOU'RE SAYING ONE OF US KILLED UMEMOTO-SENSEI?
WHAT ARE YOU BABBLING ABOUT?
NOPE!
THE BELLHOP SAID IT ONLY HAPPENED 15 MINUTES AGO.
THAT'S RIGHT!
WE WERE ALL AT THE PARTY THEN.
HOLD ON.

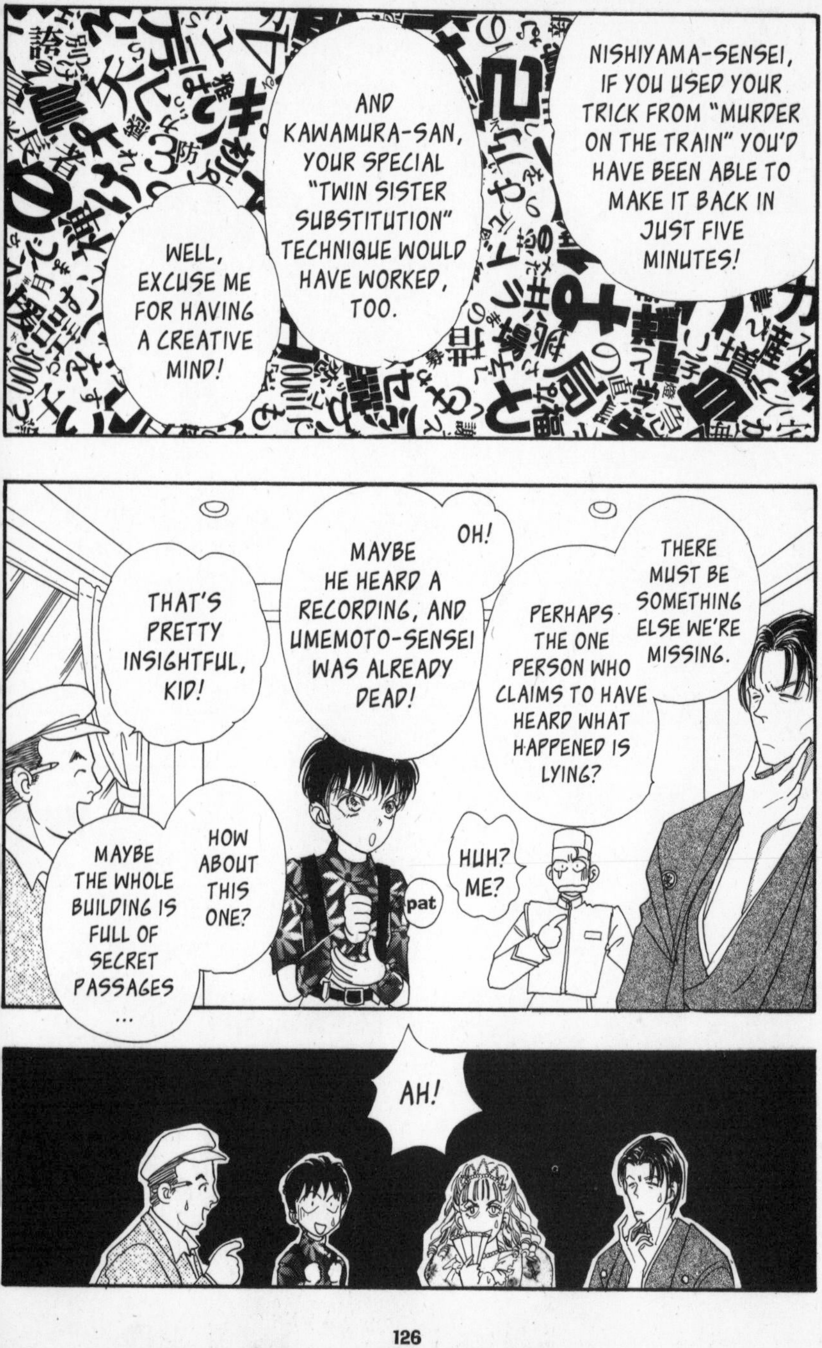

NISHIYAMA-SENSEI, IF YOU USED YOUR TRICK FROM "MURDER ON THE TRAIN" YOU'D HAVE BEEN ABLE TO MAKE IT BACK IN JUST FIVE MINUTES!
AND KAWAMURA-SAN, YOUR SPECIAL "TWIN SISTER SUBSTITUTION" TECHNIQUE WOULD HAVE WORKED, TOO.
WELL, EXCUSE ME FOR HAVING A CREATIVE MIND!
THERE MUST BE SOMETHING ELSE WE'RE MISSING.
PERHAPS THE ONE PERSON WHO CLAIMS TO HAVE HEARD WHAT HAPPENED IS LYING?
HUH? ME?
OH!
MAYBE HE HEARD A RECORDING, AND UMEMOTO-SENSEI WAS ALREADY DEAD!
THAT'S PRETTY INSIGHTFUL, KID!
HOW ABOUT THIS ONE?
MAYBE THE WHOLE BUILDING IS FULL OF SECRET PASSAGES ...
pat
AH!

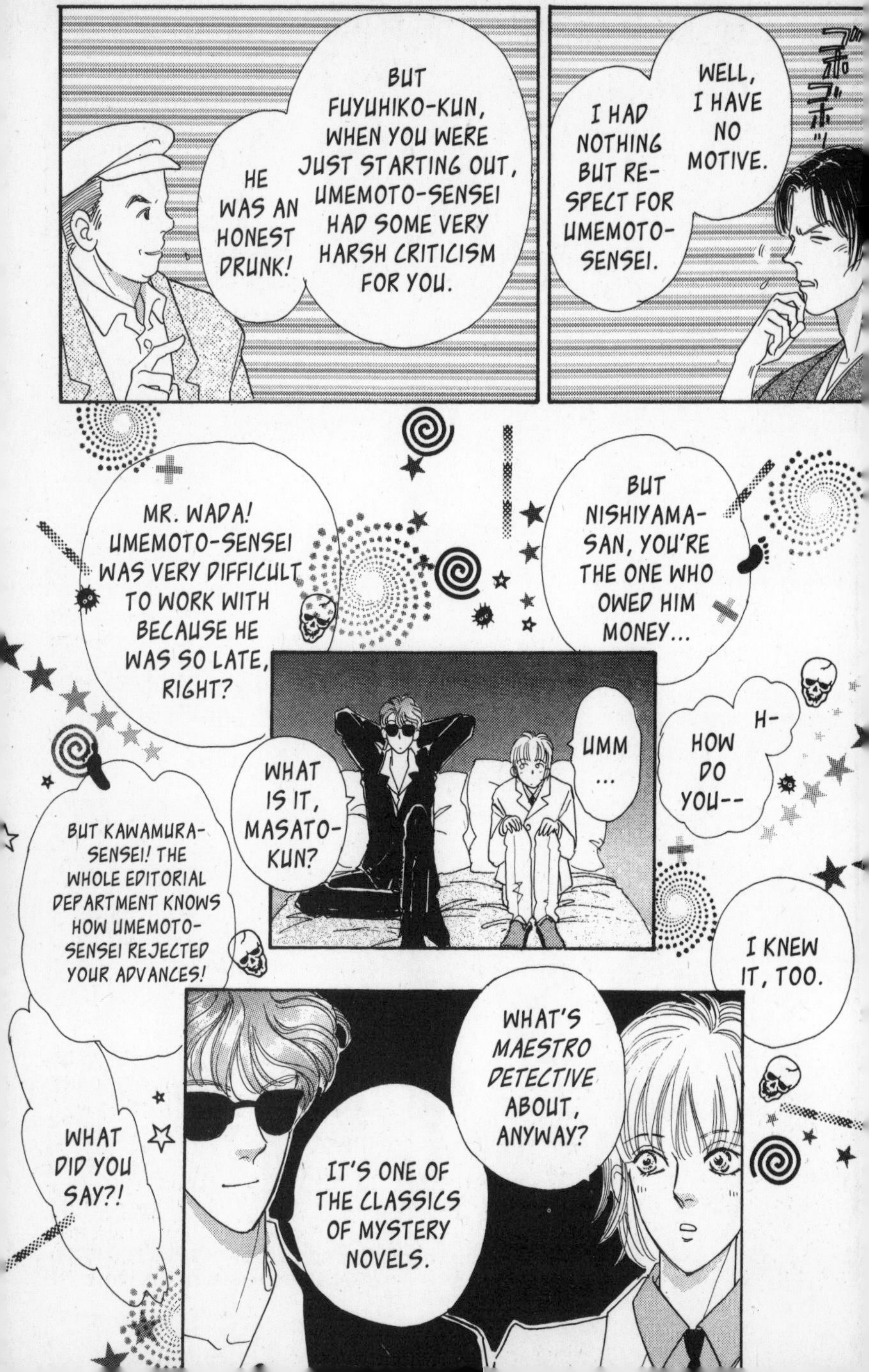
ゴボゴボッ
WELL, I HAVE NO MOTIVE.
I HAD NOTHING BUT RE-SPECT FOR UMEMOTO-SENSEI.
BUT FUYUHIKO-KUN, WHEN YOU WERE JUST STARTING OUT, UMEMOTO-SENSEI HAD SOME VERY HARSH CRITICISM FOR YOU.
HE WAS AN HONEST DRUNK!
BUT NISHIYAMA-SAN, YOU'RE THE ONE WHO OWED HIM MONEY...
MR. WADA! UMEMOTO-SENSEI WAS VERY DIFFICULT TO WORK WITH BECAUSE HE WAS SO LATE, RIGHT?
H- HOW DO YOU--
UMM ...
WHAT IS IT, MASATO-KUN?
BUT KAWAMURA-SENSEI! THE WHOLE EDITORIAL DEPARTMENT KNOWS HOW UMEMOTO-SENSEI REJECTED YOUR ADVANCES!
I KNEW IT, TOO.
WHAT'S MAESTRO DETECTIVE ABOUT, ANYWAY?
IT'S ONE OF THE CLASSICS OF MYSTERY NOVELS.
WHAT DID YOU SAY?!

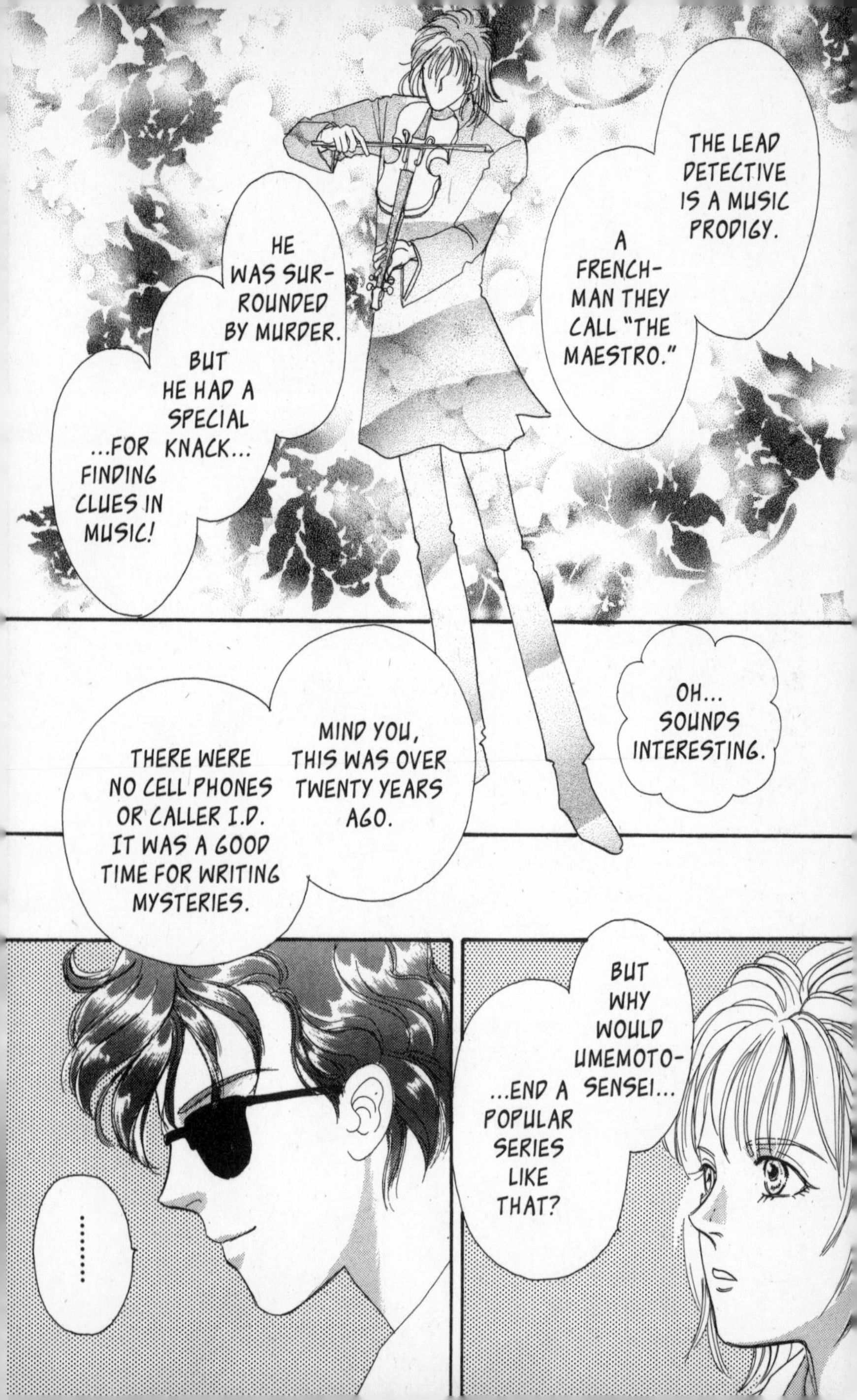
THE LEAD DETECTIVE IS A MUSIC PRODIGY.
A FRENCHMAN THEY CALL "THE MAESTRO."
HE WAS SURROUNDED BY MURDER.
BUT HE HAD A SPECIAL KNACK...
...FOR FINDING CLUES IN MUSIC!
OH... SOUNDS INTERESTING.
MIND YOU, THIS WAS OVER TWENTY YEARS AGO.
THERE WERE NO CELL PHONES OR CALLER I.D. IT WAS A GOOD TIME FOR WRITING MYSTERIES.
BUT WHY WOULD UMEMOTO-SENSEI...
...END A POPULAR SERIES LIKE THAT?
......

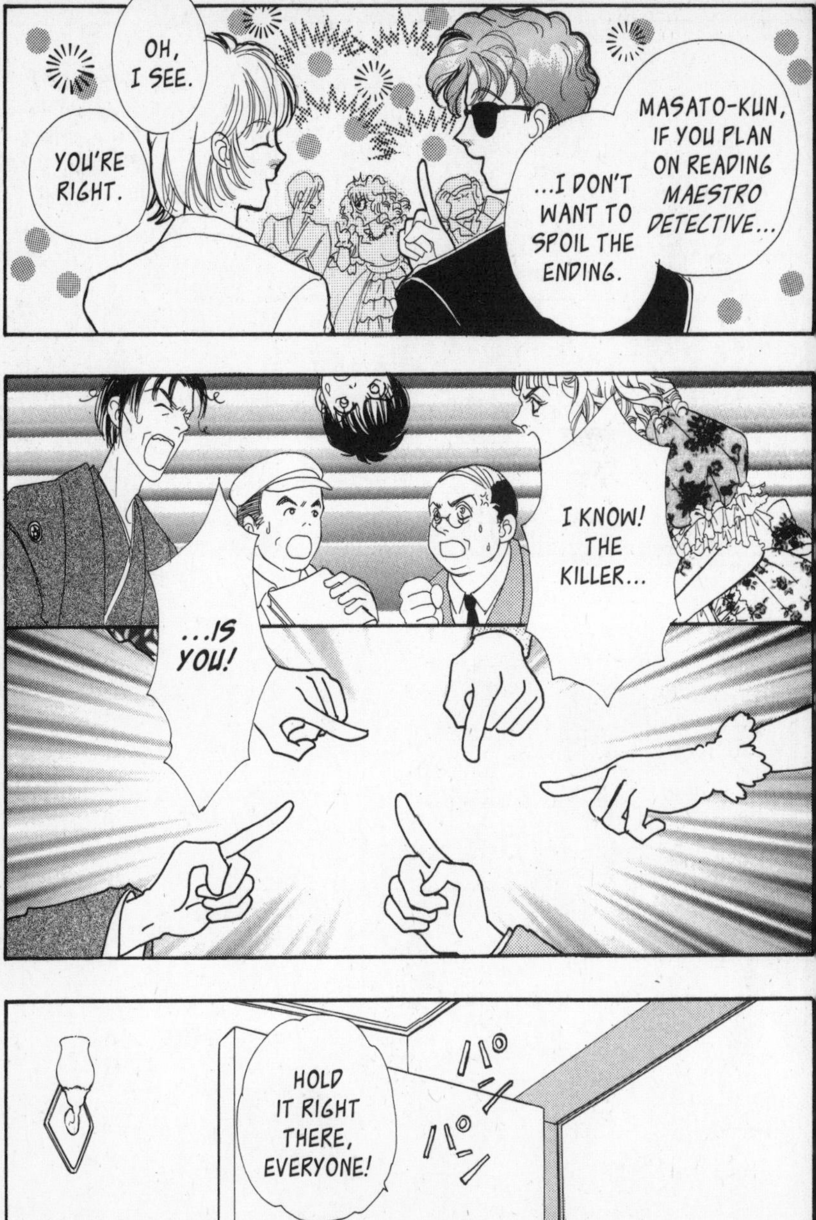
MASATO-KUN, IF YOU PLAN ON READING MAESTRO DETECTIVE...
...I DON'T WANT TO SPOIL THE ENDING.
OH, I SEE.
YOU'RE RIGHT.
I KNOW! THE KILLER...
...IS YOU!
HOLD IT RIGHT THERE, EVERYONE!
2518

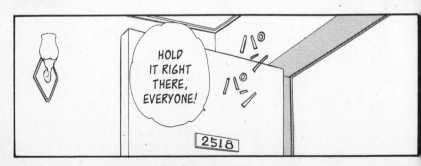

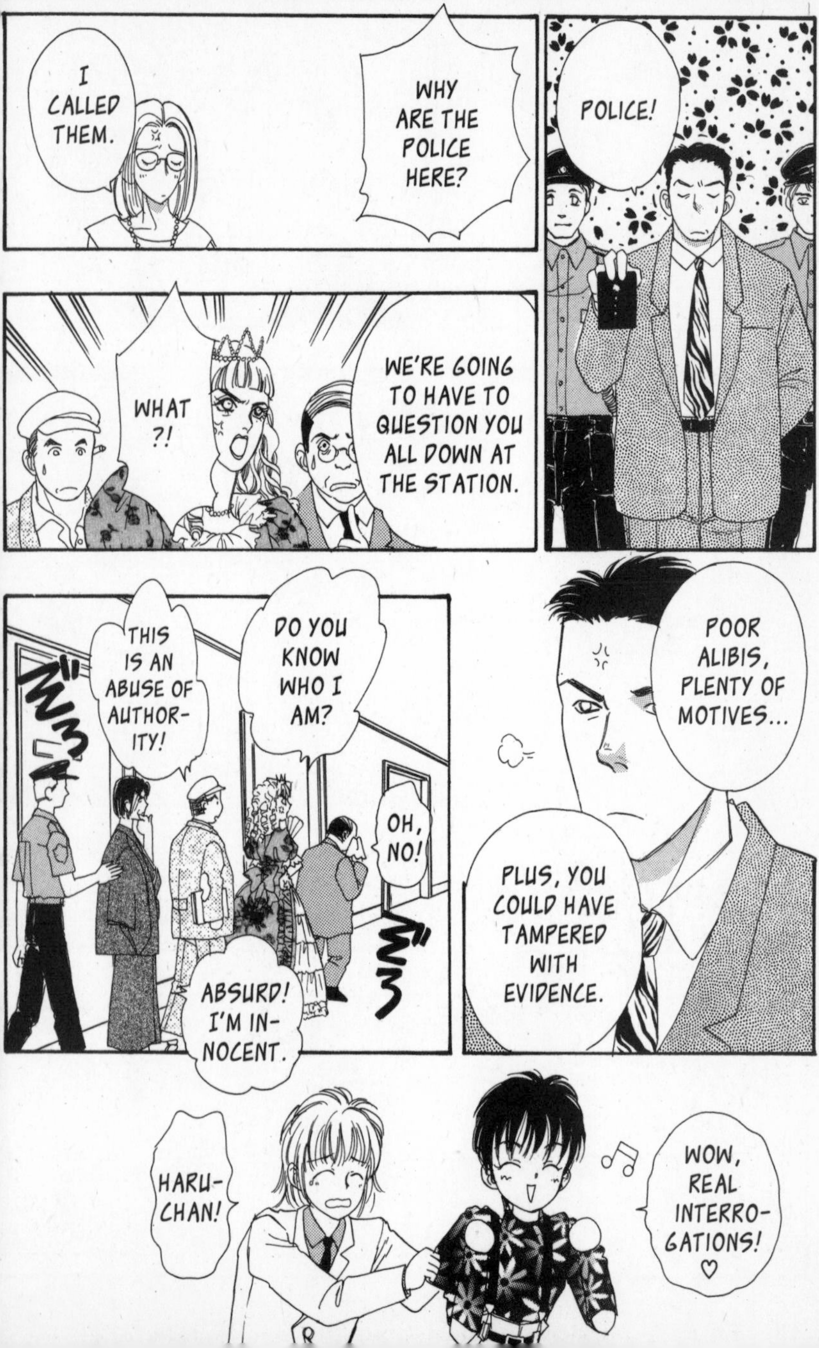
POLICE!
WHY ARE THE POLICE HERE?
I CALLED THEM.
WE'RE GOING TO HAVE TO QUESTION YOU ALL DOWN AT THE STATION.
WHAT?!
POOR ALIBIS, PLENTY OF MOTIVES...
PLUS, YOU COULD HAVE TAMPERED WITH EVIDENCE.
DO YOU KNOW WHO I AM?
THIS IS AN ABUSE OF AUTHOR-ITY!
OH, NO!
ABSURD! I'M IN-NOCENT.
WOW, REAL INTERRO-GATIONS! ♡
HARU-CHAN!

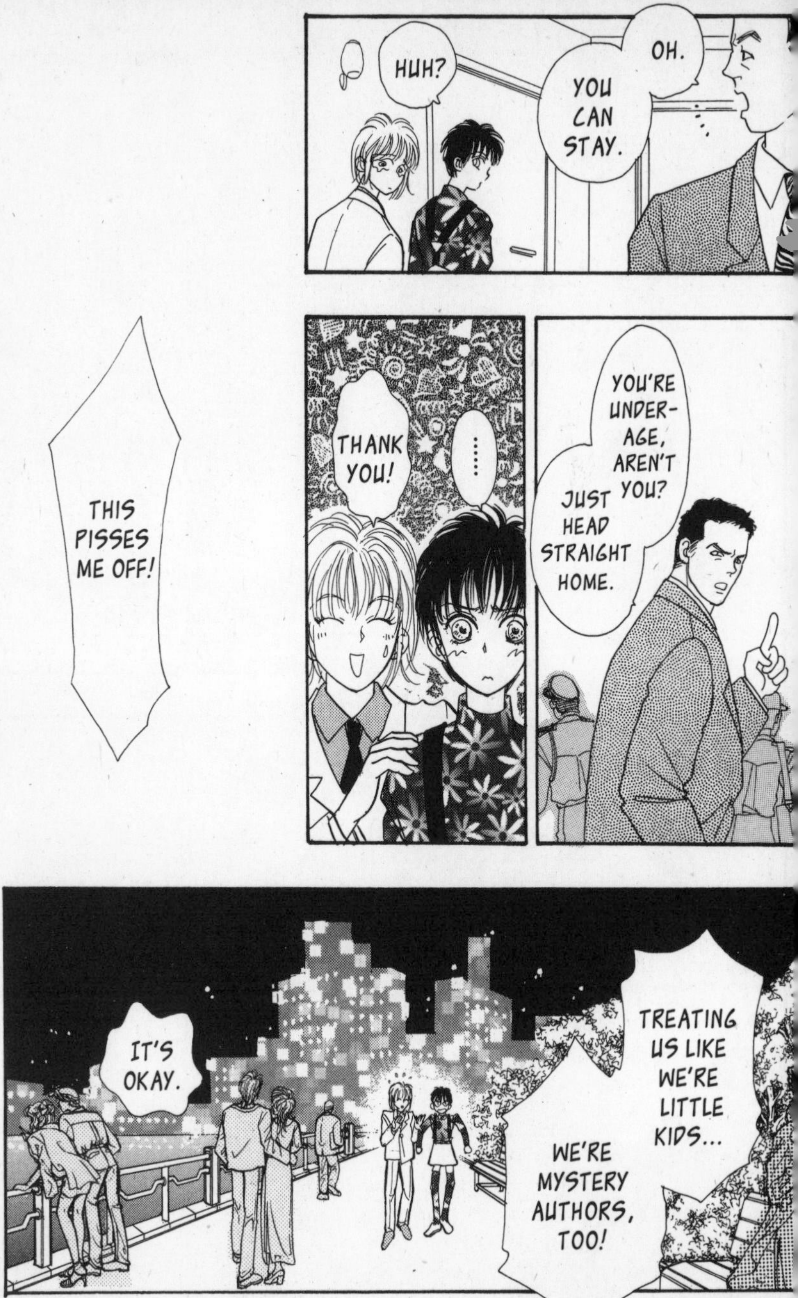
OH.
YOU CAN STAY.
HUH?
YOU'RE UNDER-AGE, AREN'T YOU?
JUST HEAD STRAIGHT HOME.
......
THANK YOU!
THIS PISSES ME OFF!
TREATING US LIKE WE'RE LITTLE KIDS...
WE'RE MYSTERY AUTHORS, TOO!
IT'S OKAY.

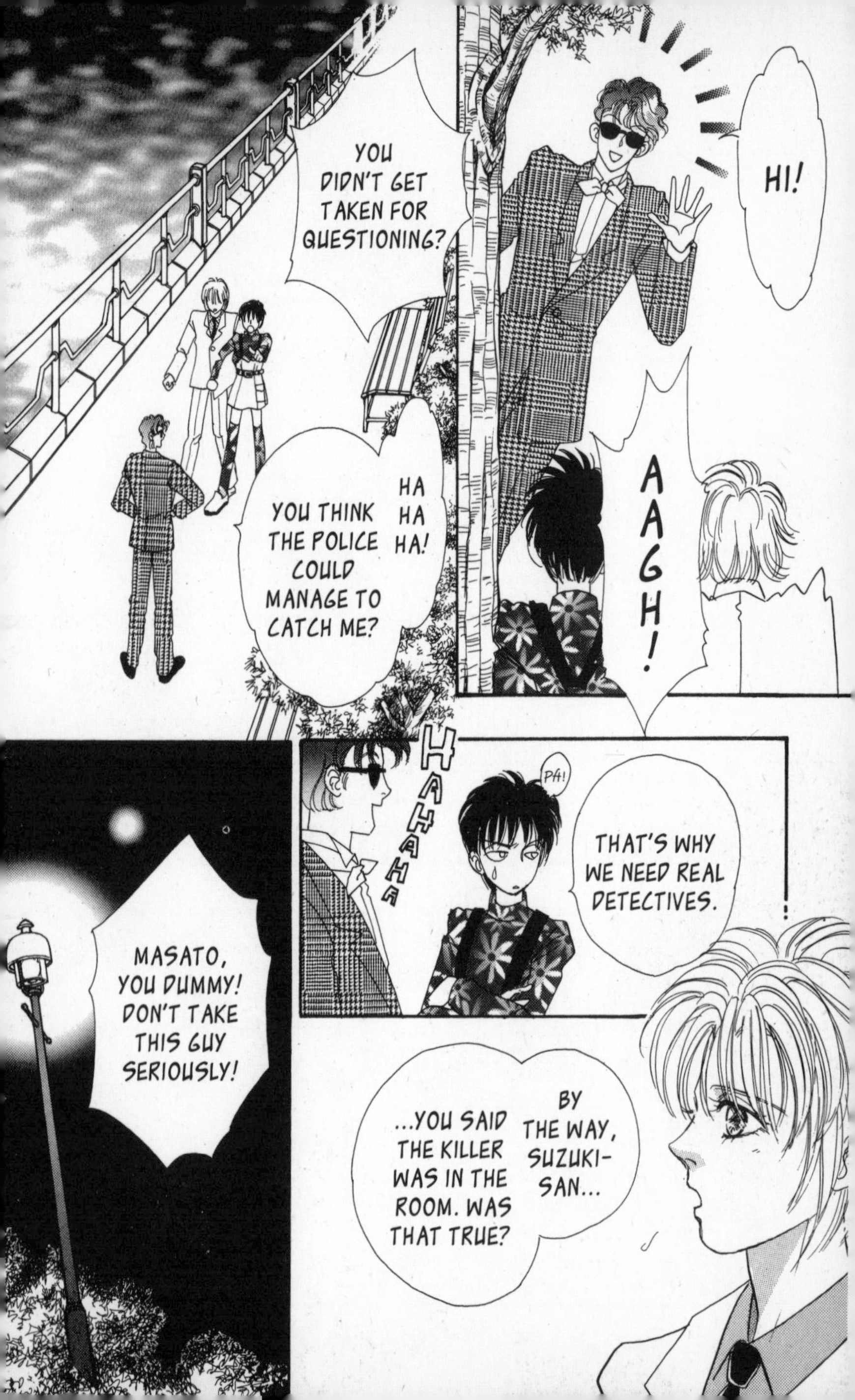
HI!
AAGH!
YOU DIDN'T GET TAKEN FOR QUESTIONING?
HA HA HA!
YOU THINK THE POLICE COULD MANAGE TO CATCH ME?
THAT'S WHY WE NEED REAL DETECTIVES.
PA!
HAHAHAHA
BY THE WAY, SUZUKI-SAN...
...YOU SAID THE KILLER WAS IN THE ROOM. WAS THAT TRUE?
MASATO, YOU DUMMY! DON'T TAKE THIS GUY SERIOUSLY!

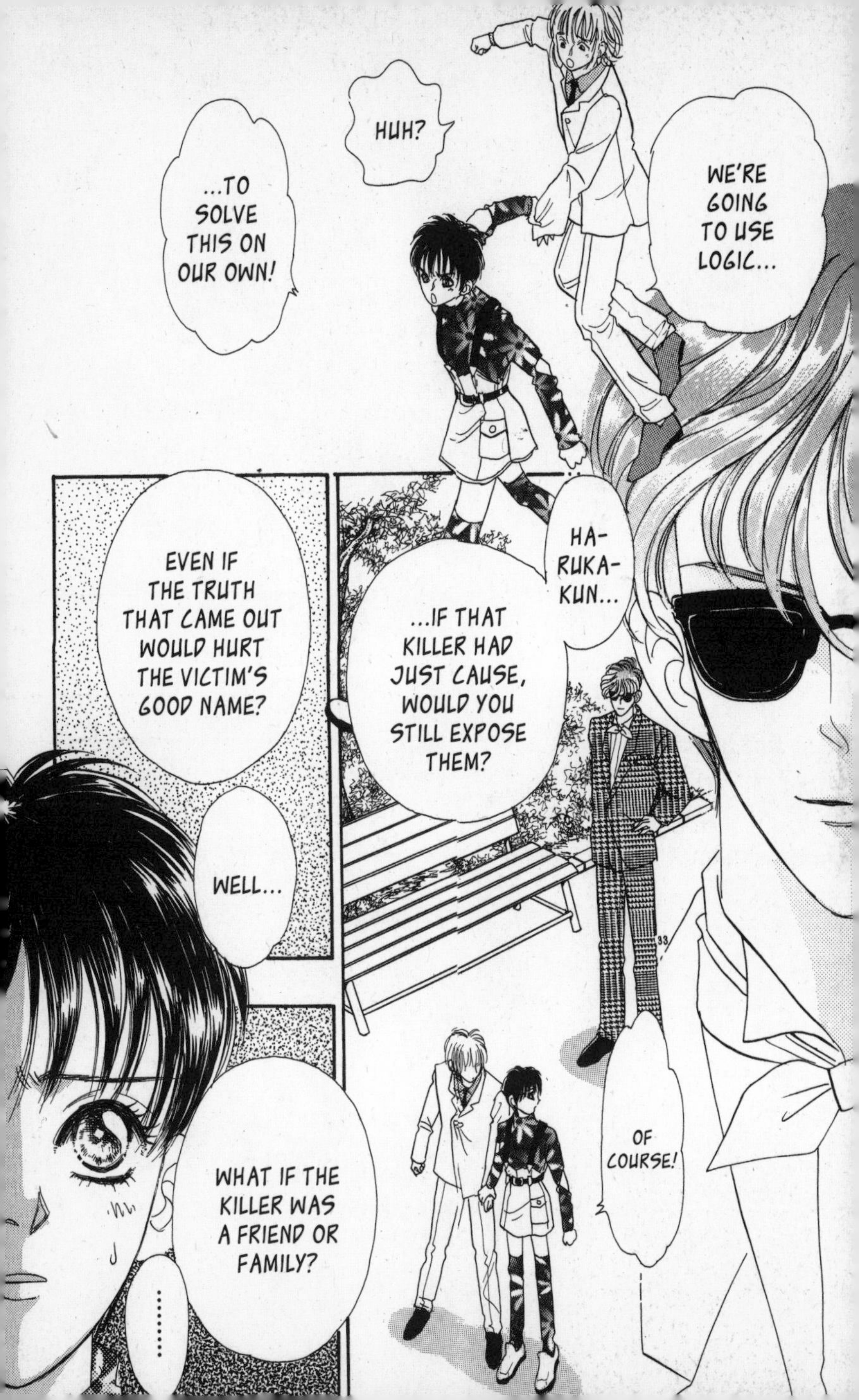
WE'RE GOING TO USE LOGIC...
HUH?
...TO SOLVE THIS ON OUR OWN!
HA-RUKA-KUN...
...IF THAT KILLER HAD JUST CAUSE, WOULD YOU STILL EXPOSE THEM?
EVEN IF THE TRUTH THAT CAME OUT WOULD HURT THE VICTIM'S GOOD NAME?
WELL...
OF COURSE!
WHAT IF THE KILLER WAS A FRIEND OR FAMILY?
......

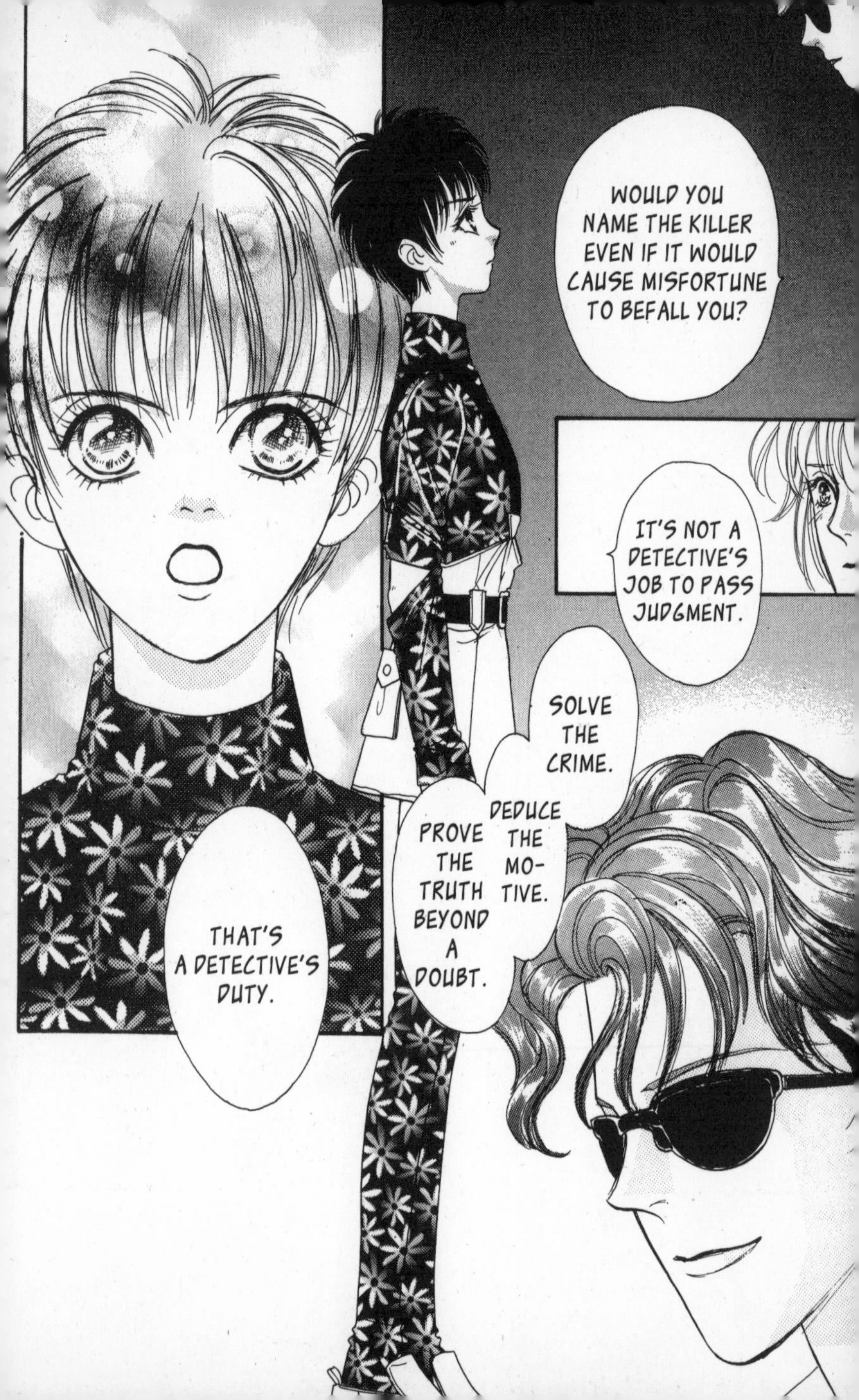
WOULD YOU NAME THE KILLER EVEN IF IT WOULD CAUSE MISFORTUNE TO BEFALL YOU?
IT'S NOT A DETECTIVE'S JOB TO PASS JUDGMENT.
SOLVE THE CRIME.
DEDUCE THE MO-TIVE.
PROVE THE TRUTH BEYOND A DOUBT.
THAT'S A DETECTIVE'S DUTY.

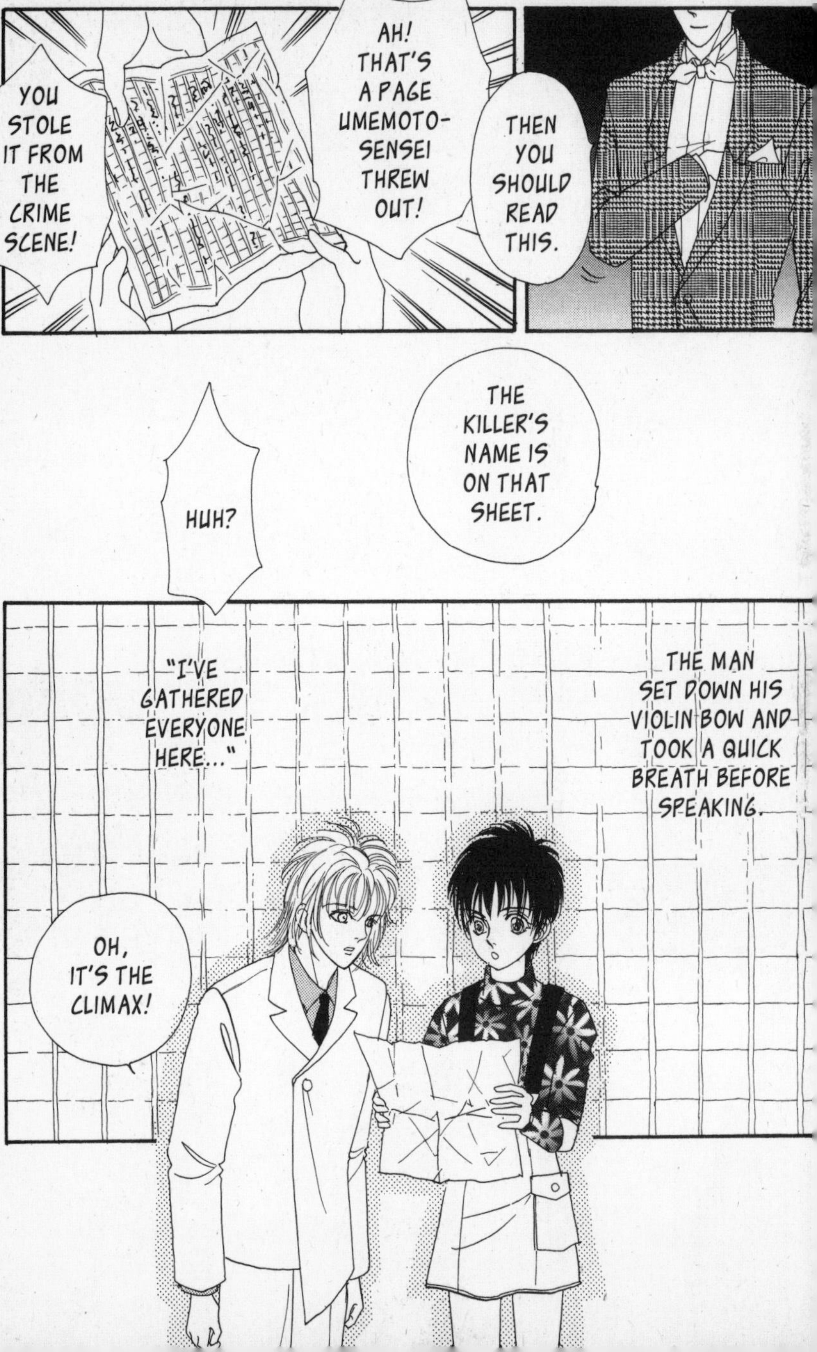
THEN YOU SHOULD READ THIS.
AH! THAT'S A PAGE UMEMOTO-SENSEI THREW OUT!
YOU STOLE IT FROM THE CRIME SCENE!
THE KILLER'S NAME IS ON THAT SHEET.
HUH?
THE MAN SET DOWN HIS VIOLIN BOW AND TOOK A QUICK BREATH BEFORE SPEAKING.
"I'VE GATHERED EVERYONE HERE..."
OH, IT'S THE CLIMAX!

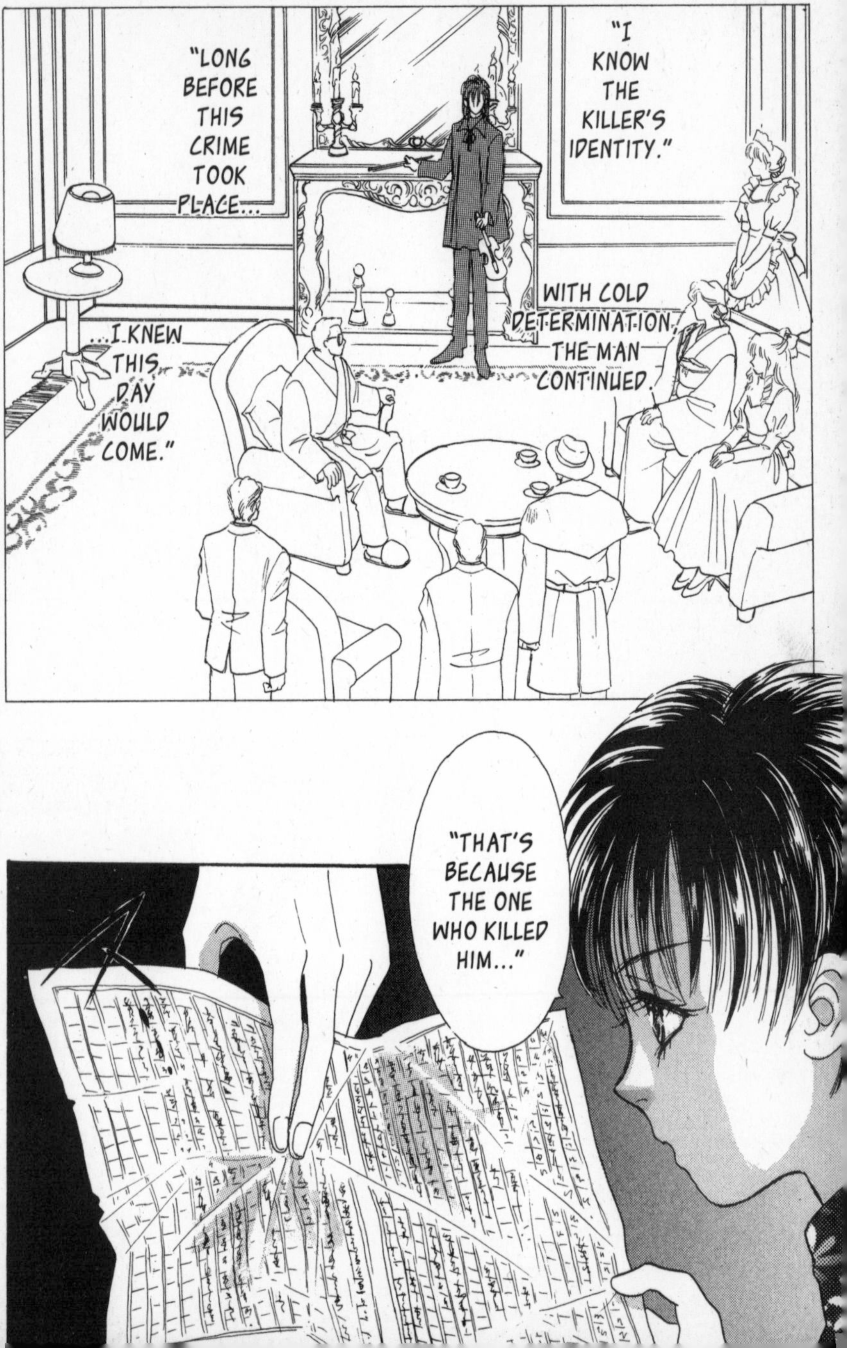
"I KNOW THE KILLER'S IDENTITY."
WITH COLD DETERMINATION, THE MAN CONTINUED.
"LONG BEFORE THIS CRIME TOOK PLACE...
...I KNEW THIS DAY WOULD COME."
"THAT'S BECAUSE THE ONE WHO KILLED HIM..."

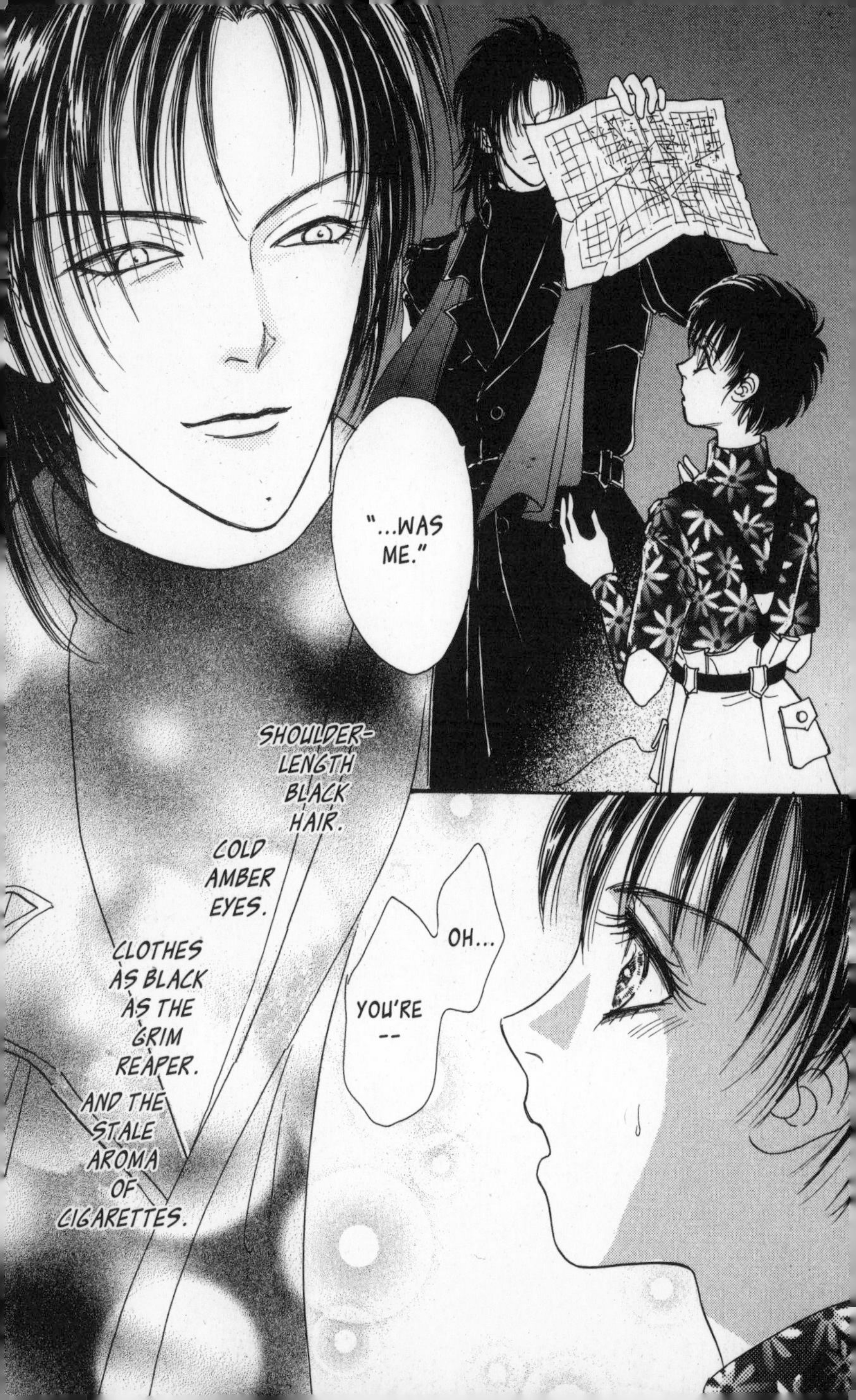
"...WAS ME."
OH...
YOU'RE --
SHOULDER-LENGTH BLACK HAIR.
COLD AMBER EYES.
CLOTHES AS BLACK AS THE GRIM REAPER.
AND THE STALE AROMA OF CIGARETTES.

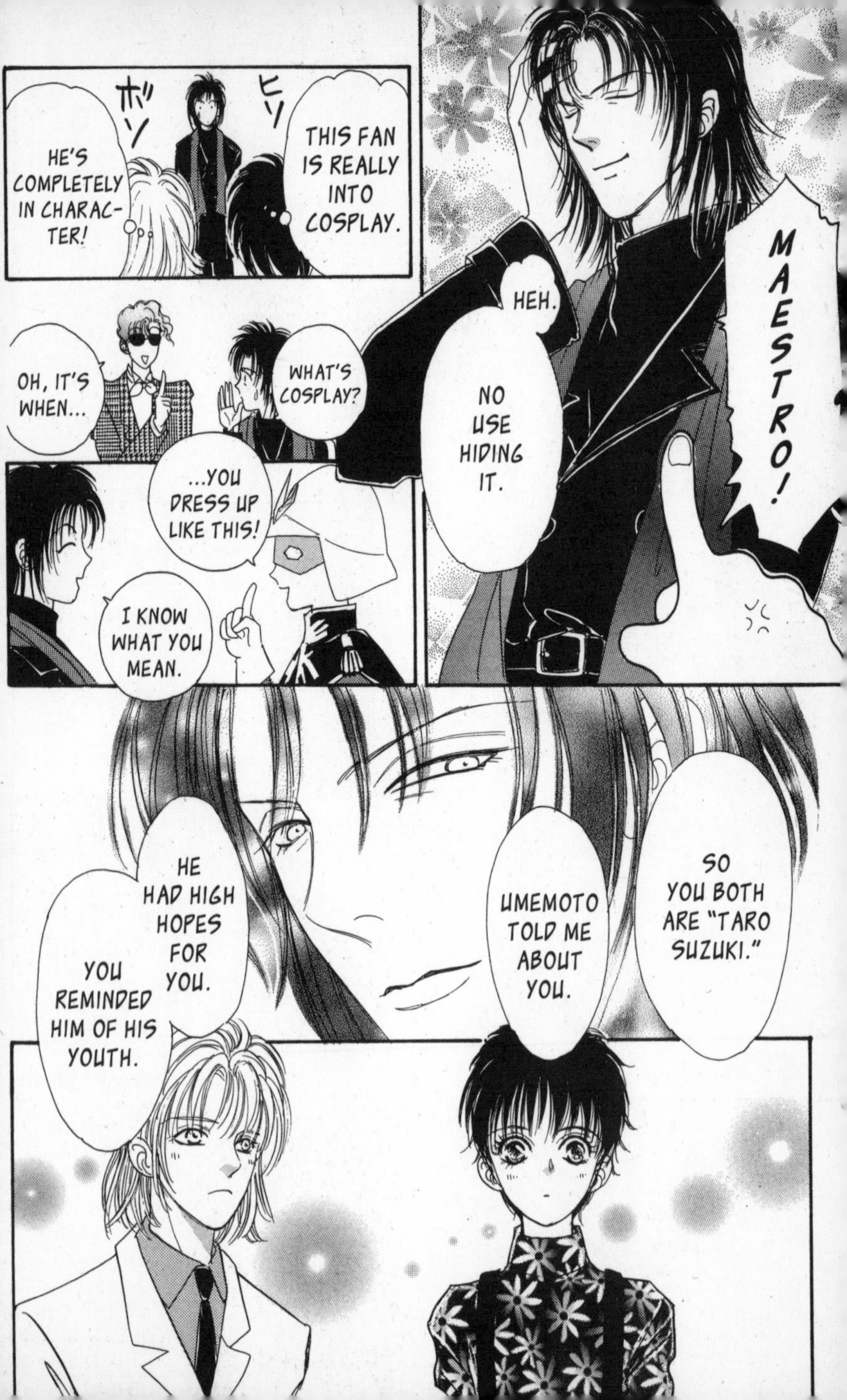
MAESTRO!
HEH.
NO USE HIDING IT.
ヒソ
THIS FAN IS REALLY INTO COSPLAY.
ボソ
HE'S COMPLETELY IN CHARACTER!
WHAT'S COSPLAY?
OH, IT'S WHEN...
...YOU DRESS UP LIKE THIS!
I KNOW WHAT YOU MEAN.
SO YOU BOTH ARE "TARO SUZUKI."
UMEMOTO TOLD ME ABOUT YOU.
HE HAD HIGH HOPES FOR YOU.
YOU REMINDED HIM OF HIS YOUTH.

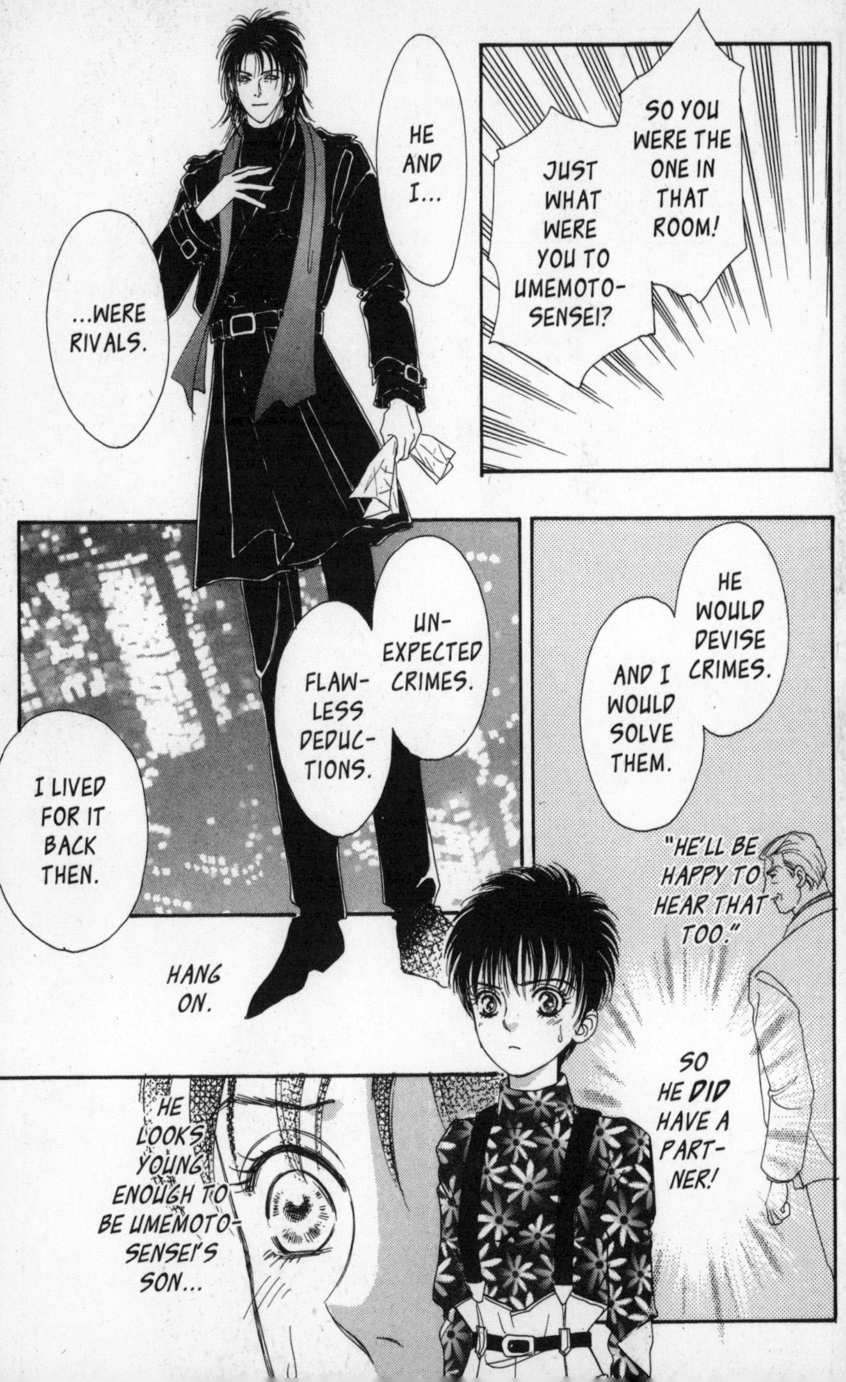
SO YOU WERE THE ONE IN THAT ROOM!
JUST WHAT WERE YOU TO UMEMOTO-SENSEI?
HE AND I...
...WERE RIVALS.
HE WOULD DEVISE CRIMES.
AND I WOULD SOLVE THEM.
"HE'LL BE HAPPY TO HEAR THAT TOO."
UN-EXPECTED CRIMES.
FLAW-LESS DEDUC-TIONS.
I LIVED FOR IT BACK THEN.
HANG ON.
SO HE **DID** HAVE A PART-NER!
HE LOOKS YOUNG ENOUGH TO BE UMEMOTO-SENSEI'S SON...

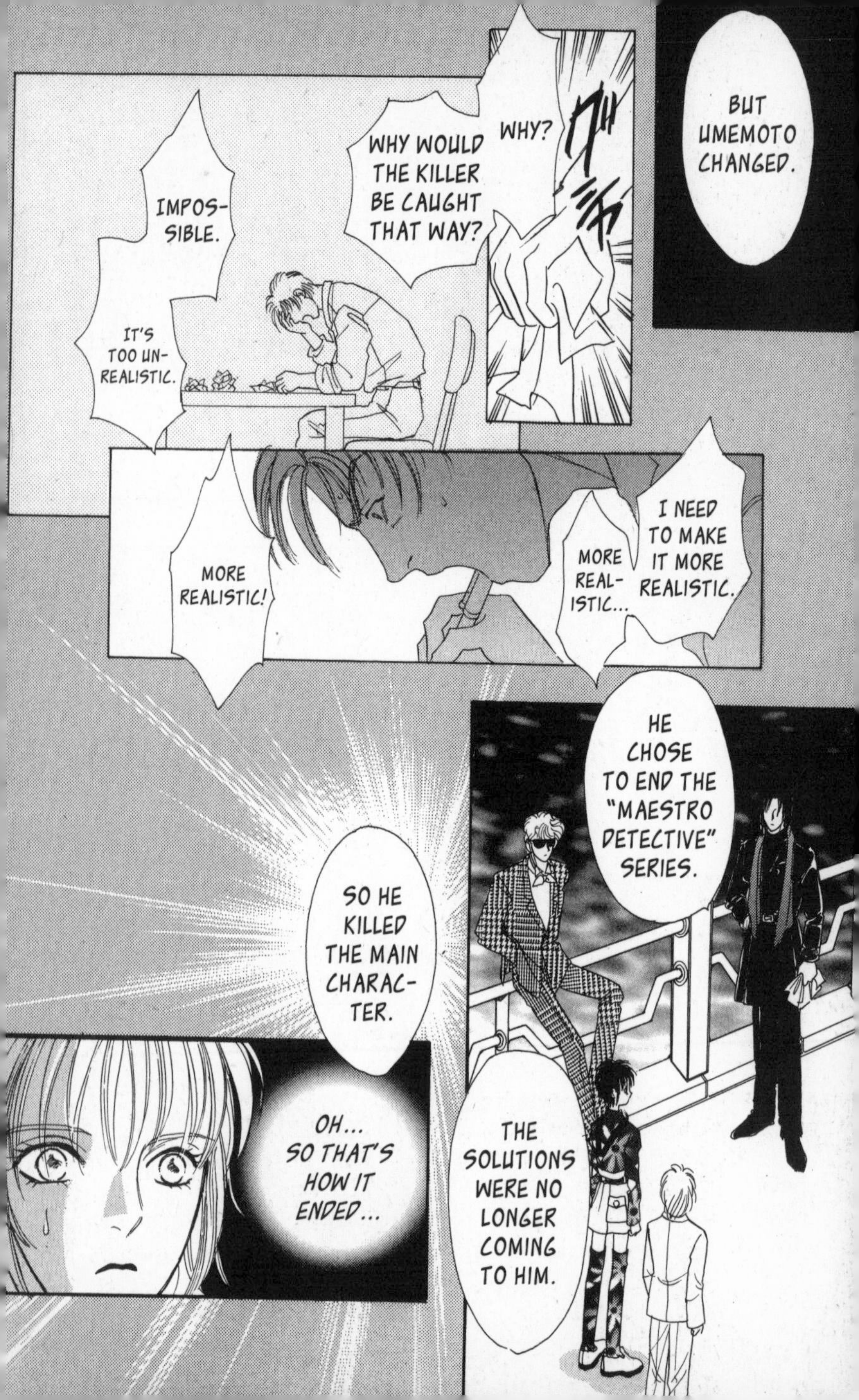
BUT UMEMOTO CHANGED.
WHY?
WHY WOULD THE KILLER BE CAUGHT THAT WAY?
IMPOS-SIBLE.
IT'S TOO UN-REALISTIC.
I NEED TO MAKE IT MORE REALISTIC.
MORE REAL-ISTIC...
MORE REALISTIC!
HE CHOSE TO END THE "MAESTRO DETECTIVE" SERIES.
SO HE KILLED THE MAIN CHARAC-TER.
THE SOLUTIONS WERE NO LONGER COMING TO HIM.
OH... SO THAT'S HOW IT ENDED...

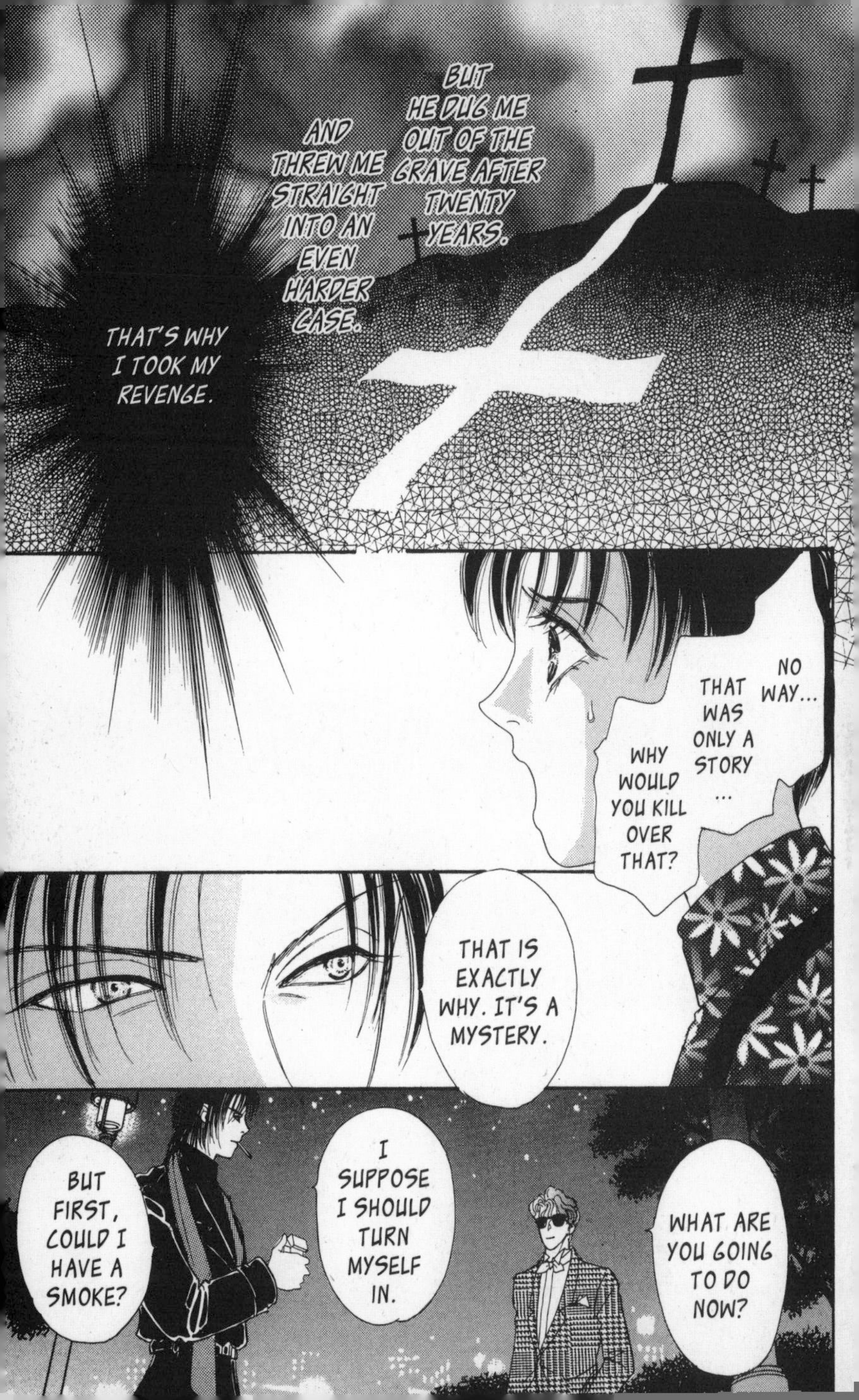
BUT HE DUG ME OUT OF THE GRAVE AFTER TWENTY YEARS.
AND THREW ME STRAIGHT INTO AN EVEN HARDER CASE.
THAT'S WHY I TOOK MY REVENGE.
NO WAY...
THAT WAS ONLY A STORY...
WHY WOULD YOU KILL OVER THAT?
THAT IS EXACTLY WHY. IT'S A MYSTERY.
WHAT ARE YOU GOING TO DO NOW?
I SUPPOSE I SHOULD TURN MYSELF IN.
BUT FIRST, COULD I HAVE A SMOKE?

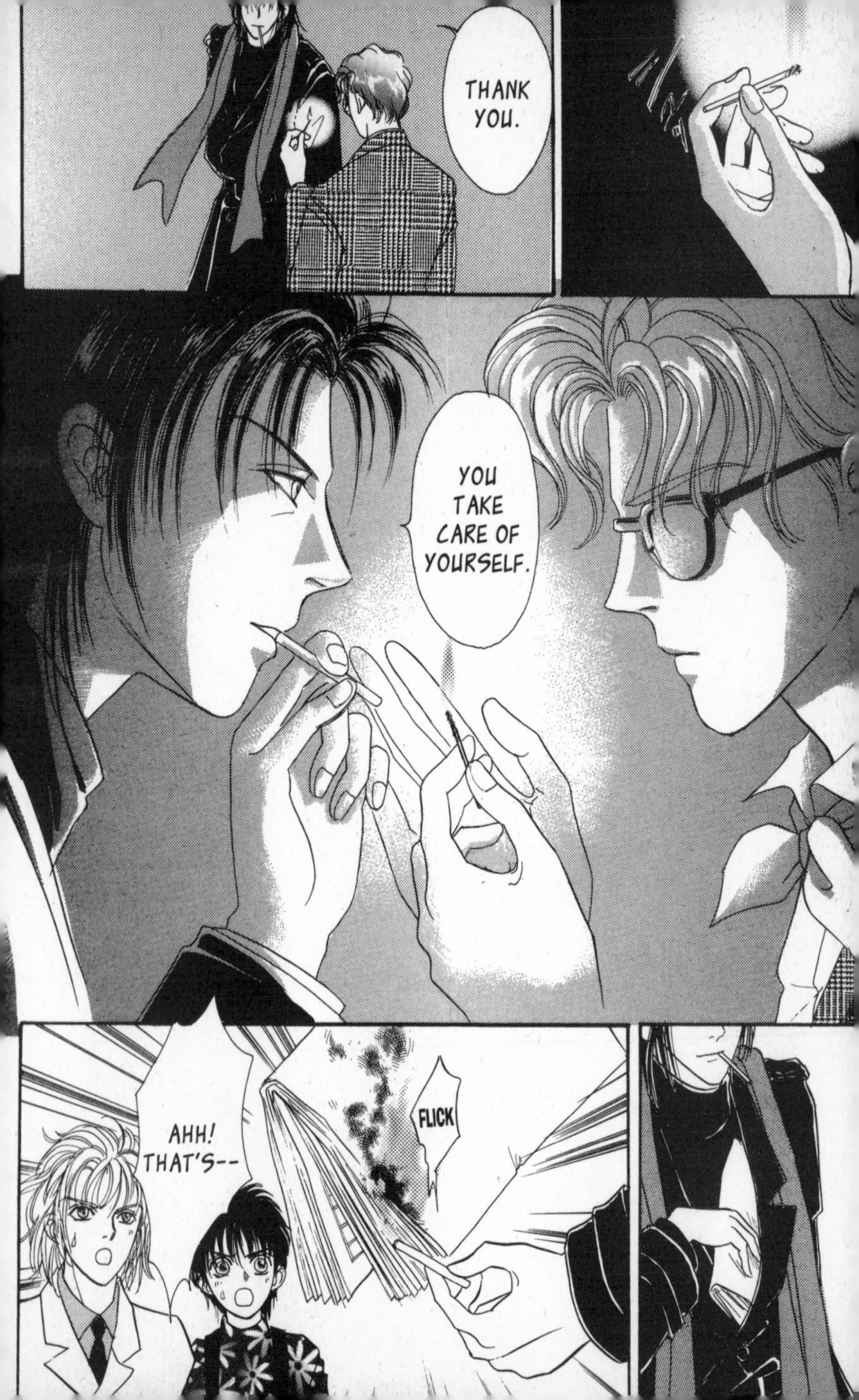
THANK YOU.
YOU TAKE CARE OF YOURSELF.
FLICK
AHH! THAT'S--

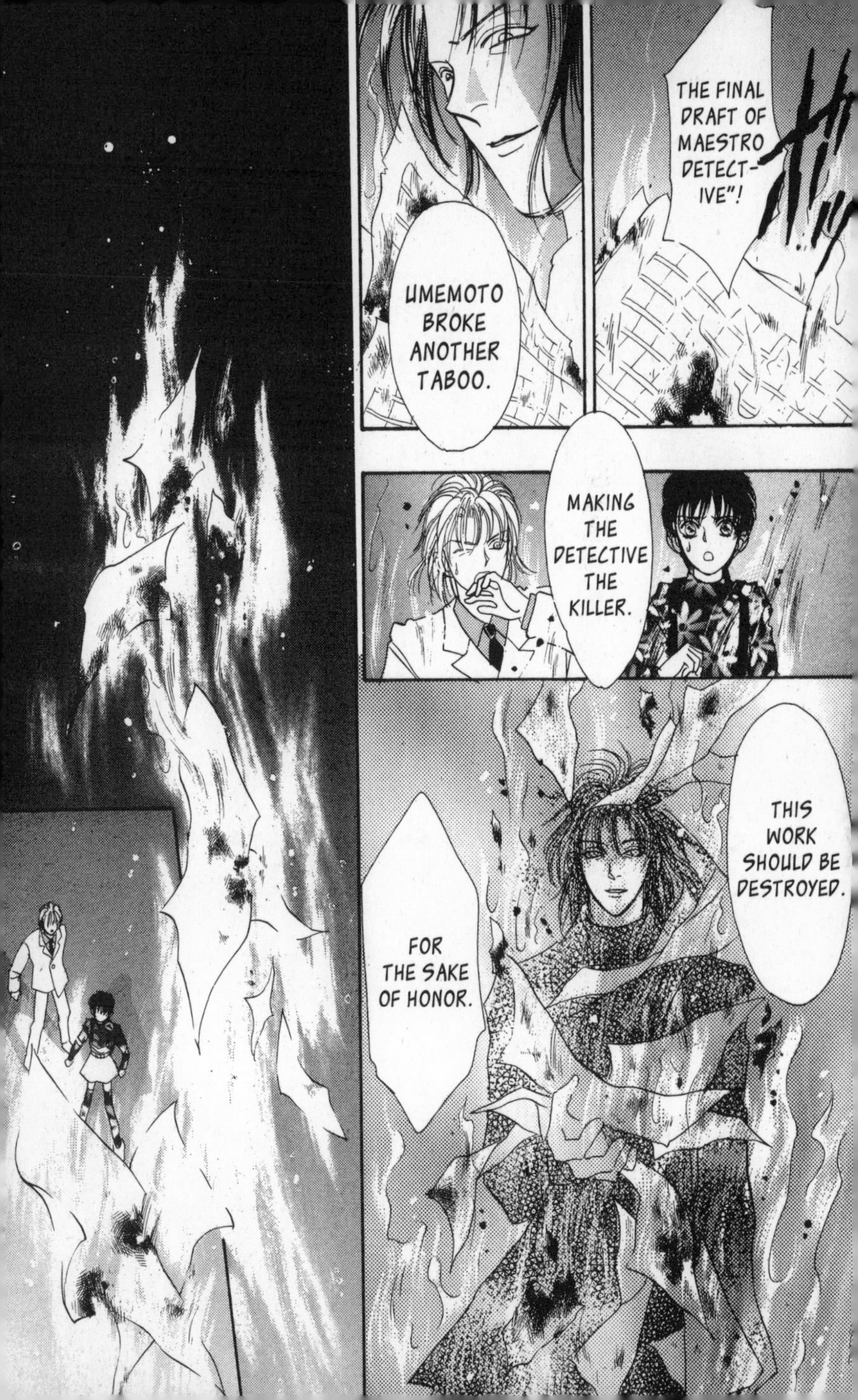
THE FINAL DRAFT OF MAESTRO DETECTIVE"!
UMEMOTO BROKE ANOTHER TABOO.
MAKING THE DETECTIVE THE KILLER.
THIS WORK SHOULD BE DESTROYED.
FOR THE SAKE OF HONOR.

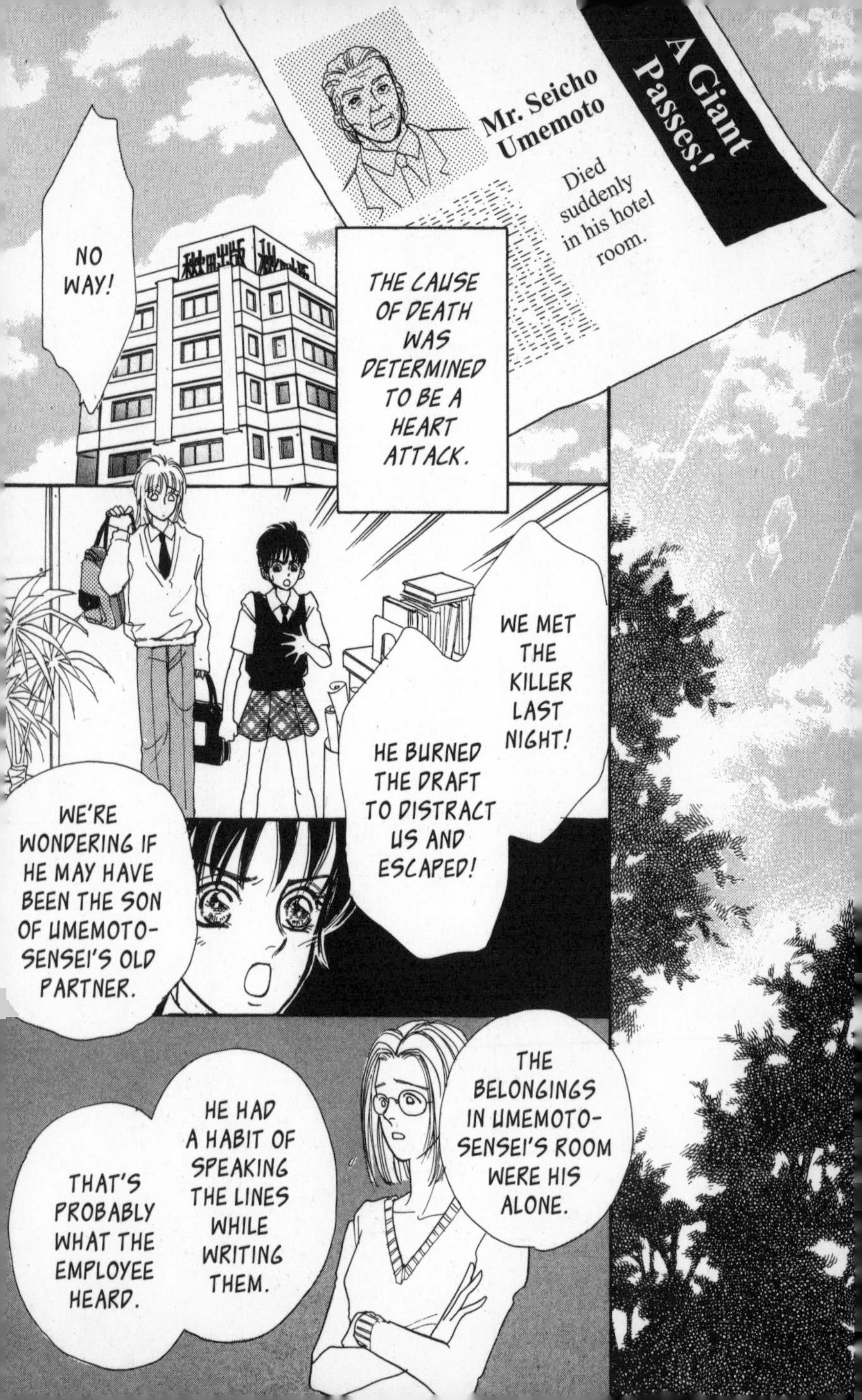
A Giant Passes!
Mr. Seicho Umemoto
Died suddenly in his hotel room.
THE CAUSE OF DEATH WAS DETERMINED TO BE A HEART ATTACK.
NO WAY!
WE MET THE KILLER LAST NIGHT!
HE BURNED THE DRAFT TO DISTRACT US AND ESCAPED!
WE'RE WONDERING IF HE MAY HAVE BEEN THE SON OF UMEMOTO-SENSEI'S OLD PARTNER.
THE BELONGINGS IN UMEMOTO-SENSEI'S ROOM WERE HIS ALONE.
HE HAD A HABIT OF SPEAKING THE LINES WHILE WRITING THEM.
THAT'S PROBABLY WHAT THE EMPLOYEE HEARD.

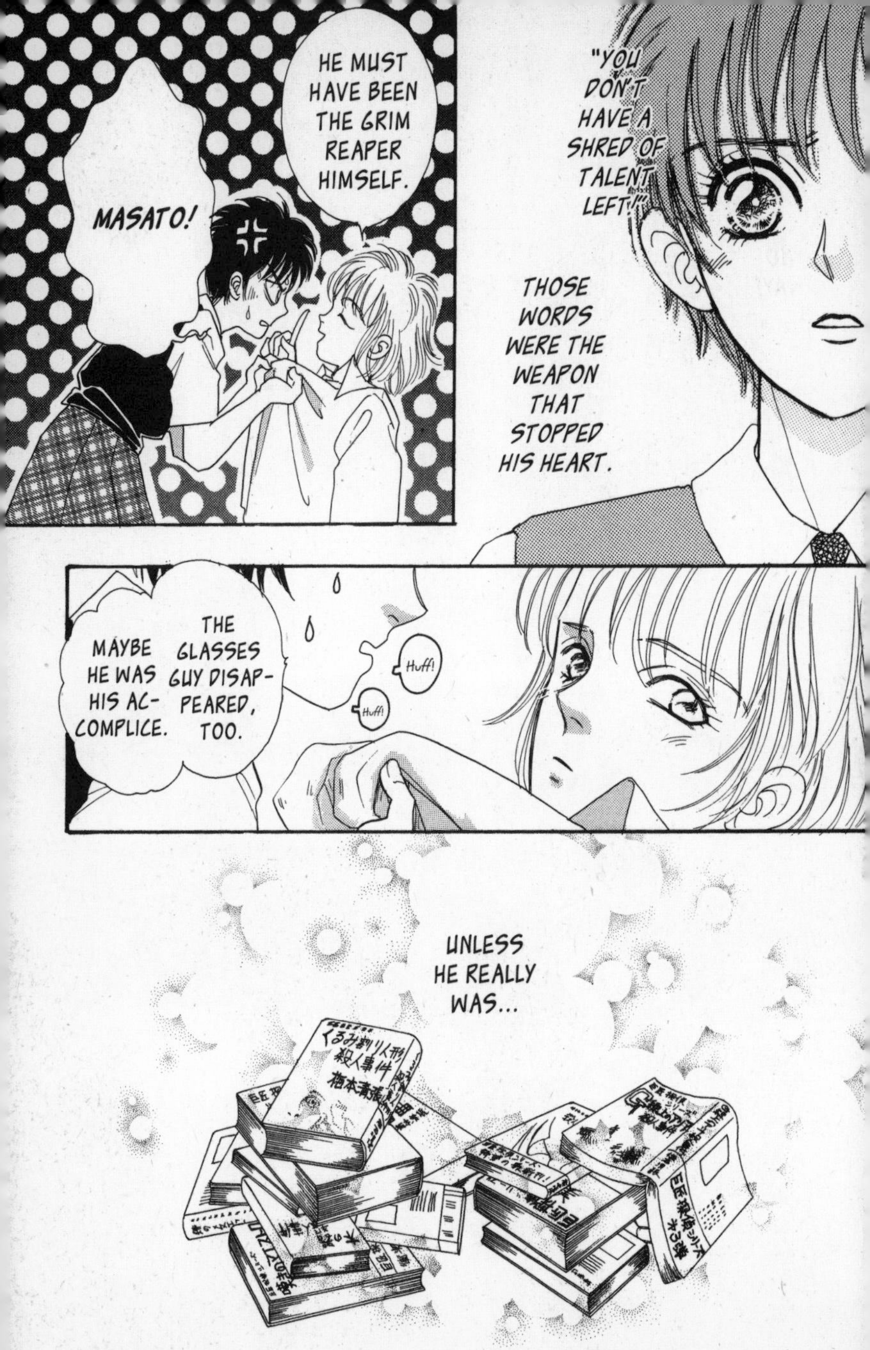
"YOU DON'T HAVE A SHRED OF TALENT LEFT!"
THOSE WORDS WERE THE WEAPON THAT STOPPED HIS HEART.
HE MUST HAVE BEEN THE GRIM REAPER HIMSELF.
MASATO!
Huff!
Huff!
THE GLASSES GUY DISAPPEARED, TOO.
MAYBE HE WAS HIS ACCOMPLICE.
UNLESS HE REALLY WAS...
くるみ割り人形
殺人事件

End Chapter 3

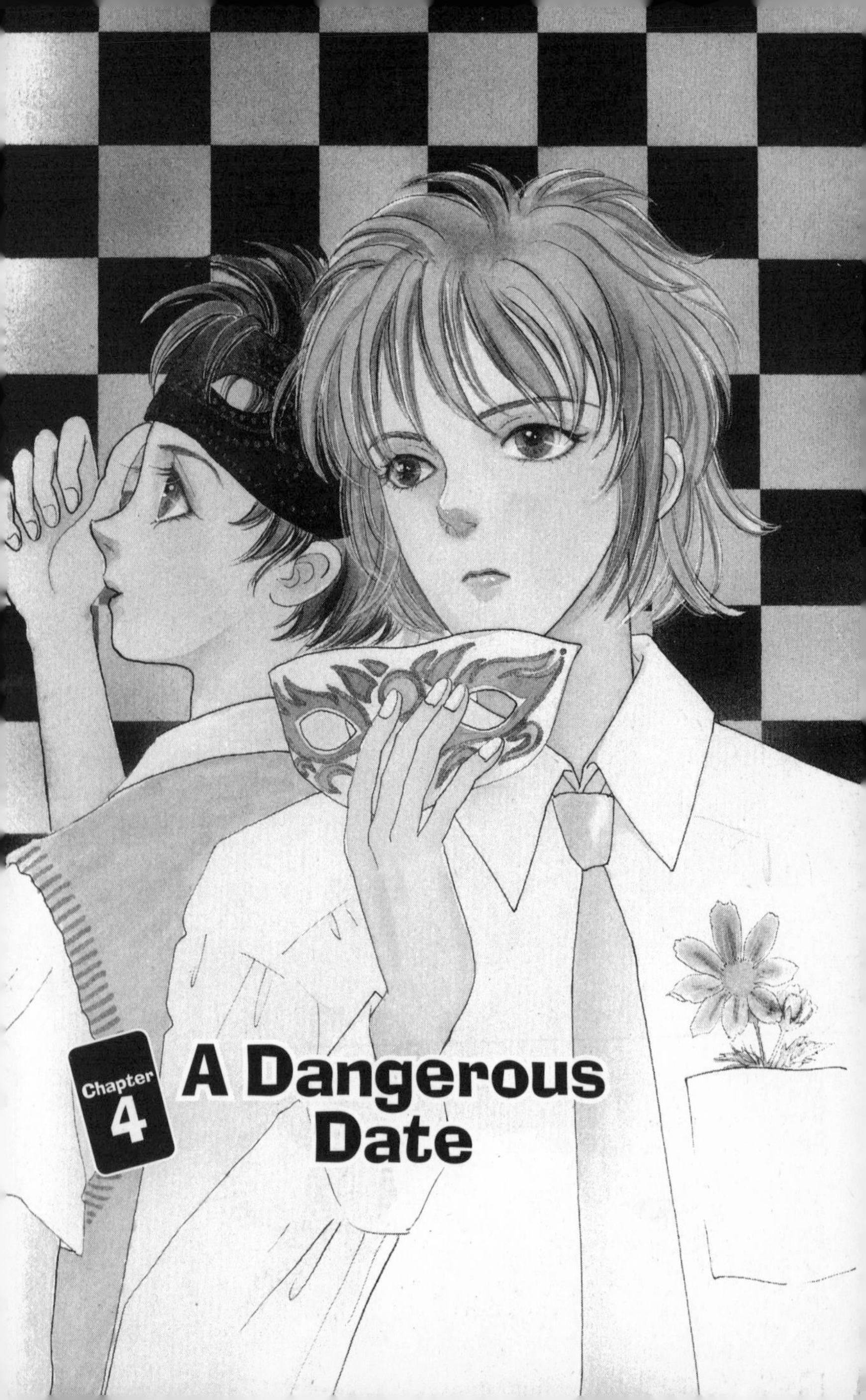
Chapter 4
A Dangerous Date

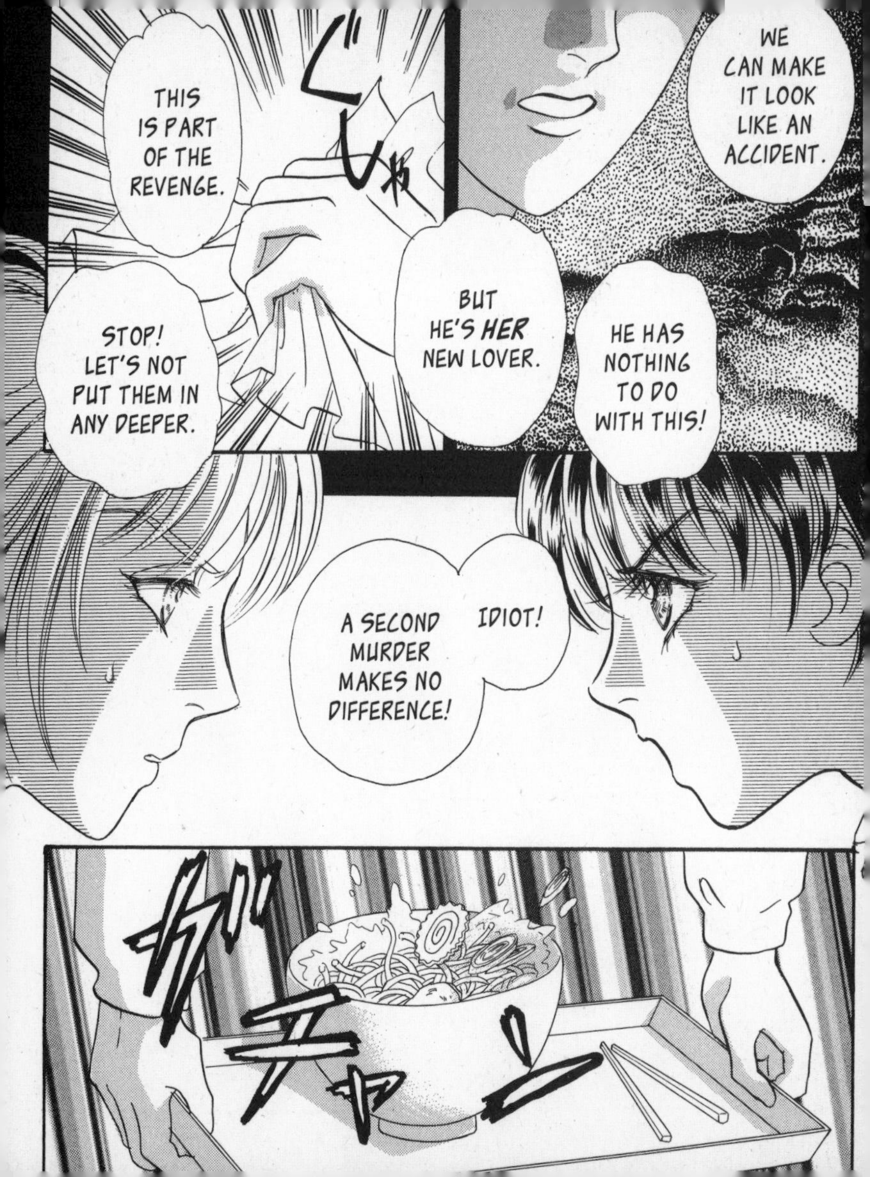

WE CAN MAKE IT LOOK LIKE AN ACCIDENT.
ぐしゃ
THIS IS PART OF THE REVENGE.
HE HAS NOTHING TO DO WITH THIS!
BUT HE'S **HER** NEW LOVER.
STOP! LET'S NOT PUT THEM IN ANY DEEPER.
IDIOT!
A SECOND MURDER MAKES NO DIFFERENCE!

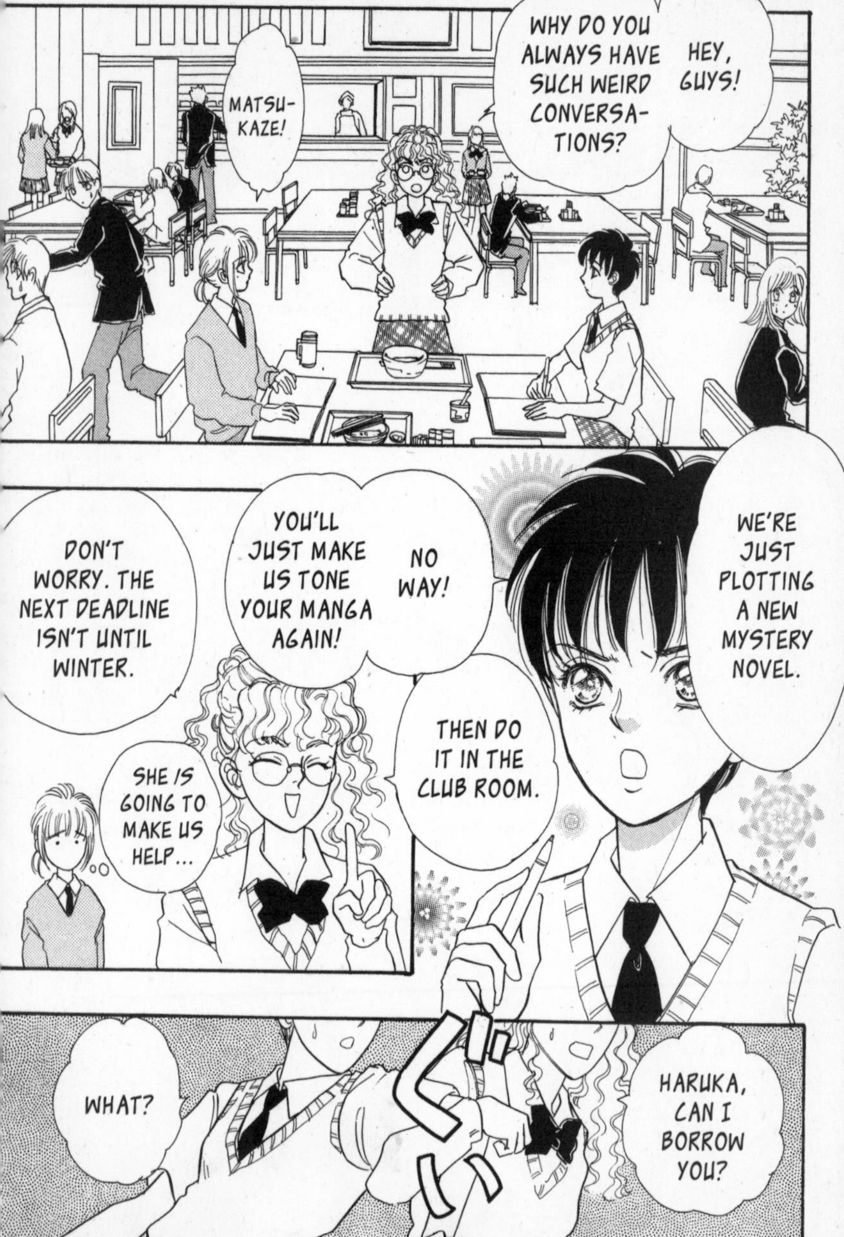
HEY, GUYS!
WHY DO YOU ALWAYS HAVE SUCH WEIRD CONVERSATIONS?
MATSU-KAZE!
WE'RE JUST PLOTTING A NEW MYSTERY NOVEL.
THEN DO IT IN THE CLUB ROOM.
NO WAY!
YOU'LL JUST MAKE US TONE YOUR MANGA AGAIN!
DON'T WORRY. THE NEXT DEADLINE ISN'T UNTIL WINTER.
SHE IS GOING TO MAKE US HELP...
HARUKA, CAN I BORROW YOU?
WHAT?

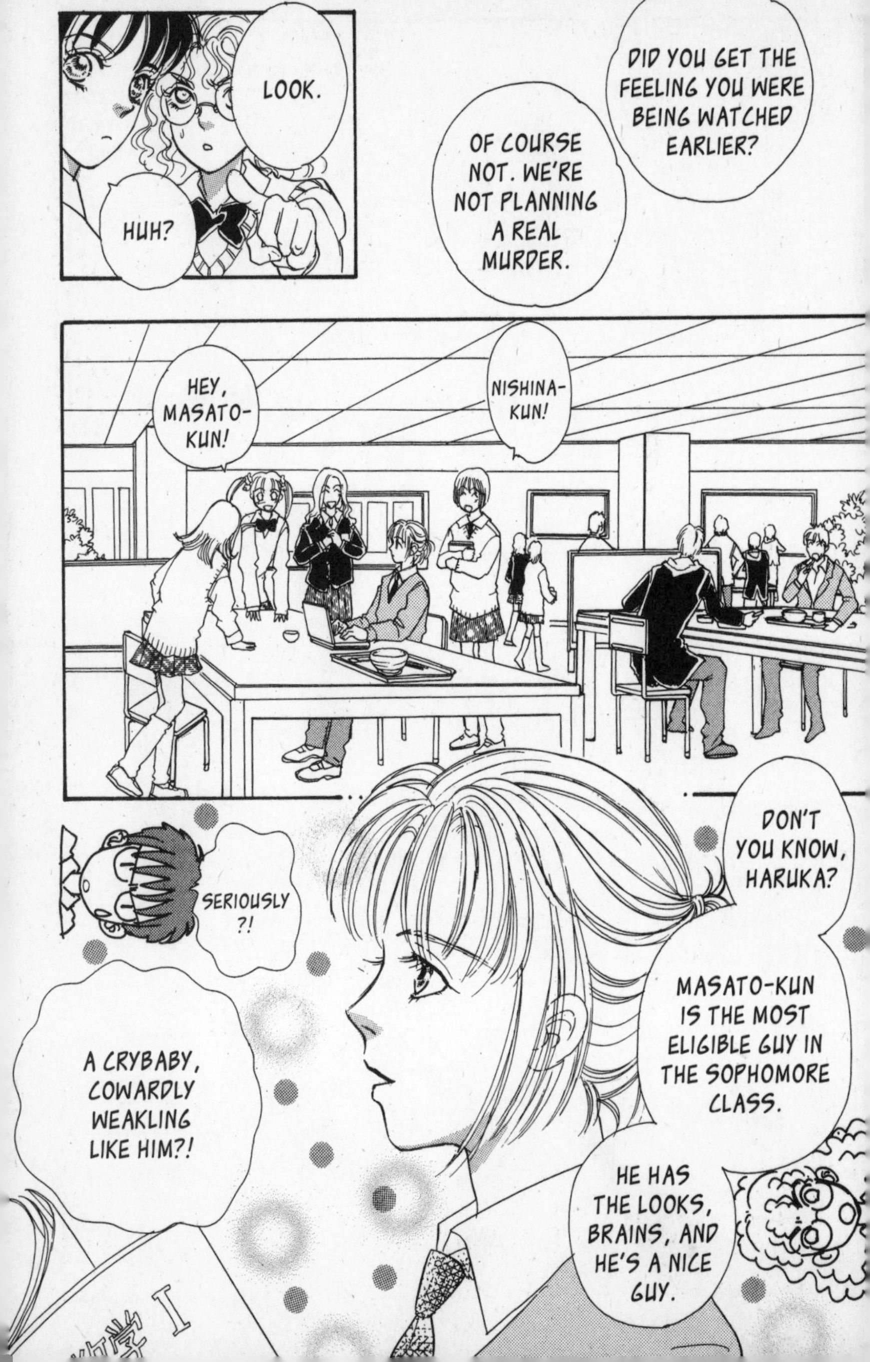
DID YOU GET THE FEELING YOU WERE BEING WATCHED EARLIER?
OF COURSE NOT. WE'RE NOT PLANNING A REAL MURDER.
LOOK.
HUH?
NISHINA-KUN!
HEY, MASATO-KUN!
DON'T YOU KNOW, HARUKA?
MASATO-KUN IS THE MOST ELIGIBLE GUY IN THE SOPHOMORE CLASS.
HE HAS THE LOOKS, BRAINS, AND HE'S A NICE GUY.
SERIOUSLY?!
A CRYBABY, COWARDLY WEAKLING LIKE HIM?!

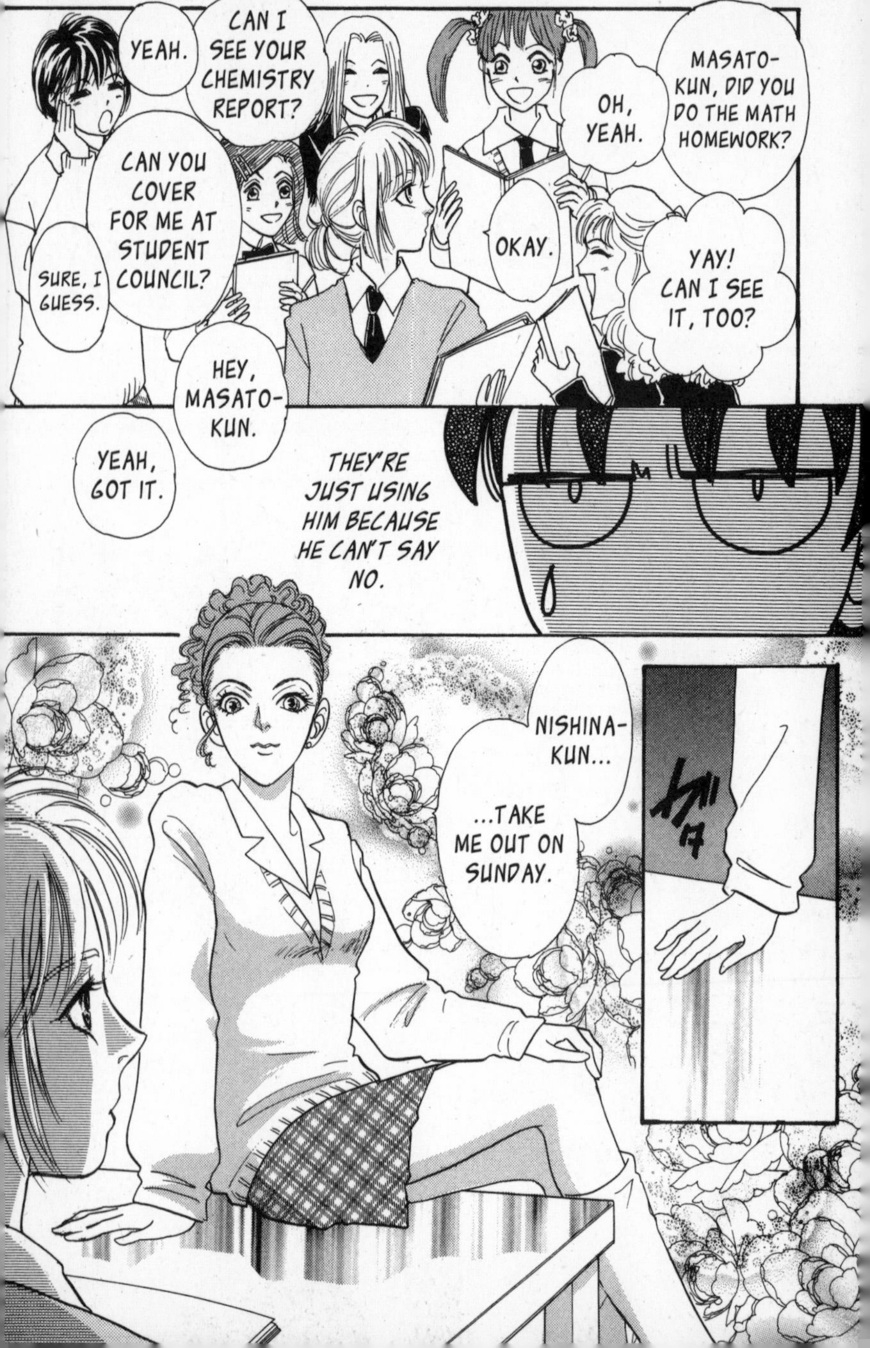
MASATO-KUN, DID YOU DO THE MATH HOMEWORK?
OH, YEAH.
YAY! CAN I SEE IT, TOO?
OKAY.
CAN I SEE YOUR CHEMISTRY REPORT?
YEAH.
CAN YOU COVER FOR ME AT STUDENT COUNCIL?
SURE, I GUESS.
HEY, MASATO-KUN.
YEAH, GOT IT.
THEY'RE JUST USING HIM BECAUSE HE CAN'T SAY NO.
NISHINA-KUN...
...TAKE ME OUT ON SUNDAY.

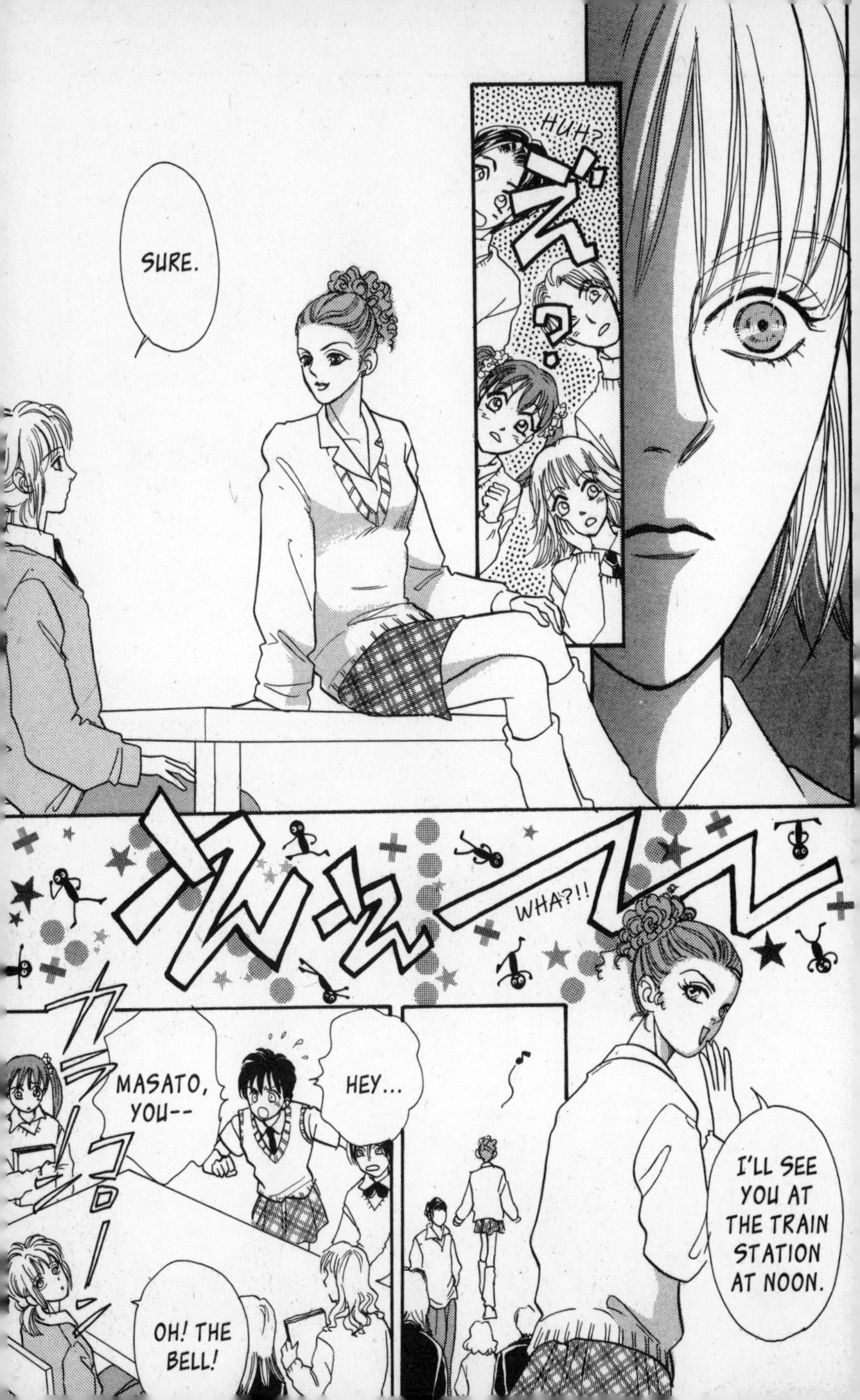
HUH?
SURE.
WHA?!!
I'LL SEE YOU AT THE TRAIN STATION AT NOON.
HEY...
MASATO, YOU--
OH! THE BELL!

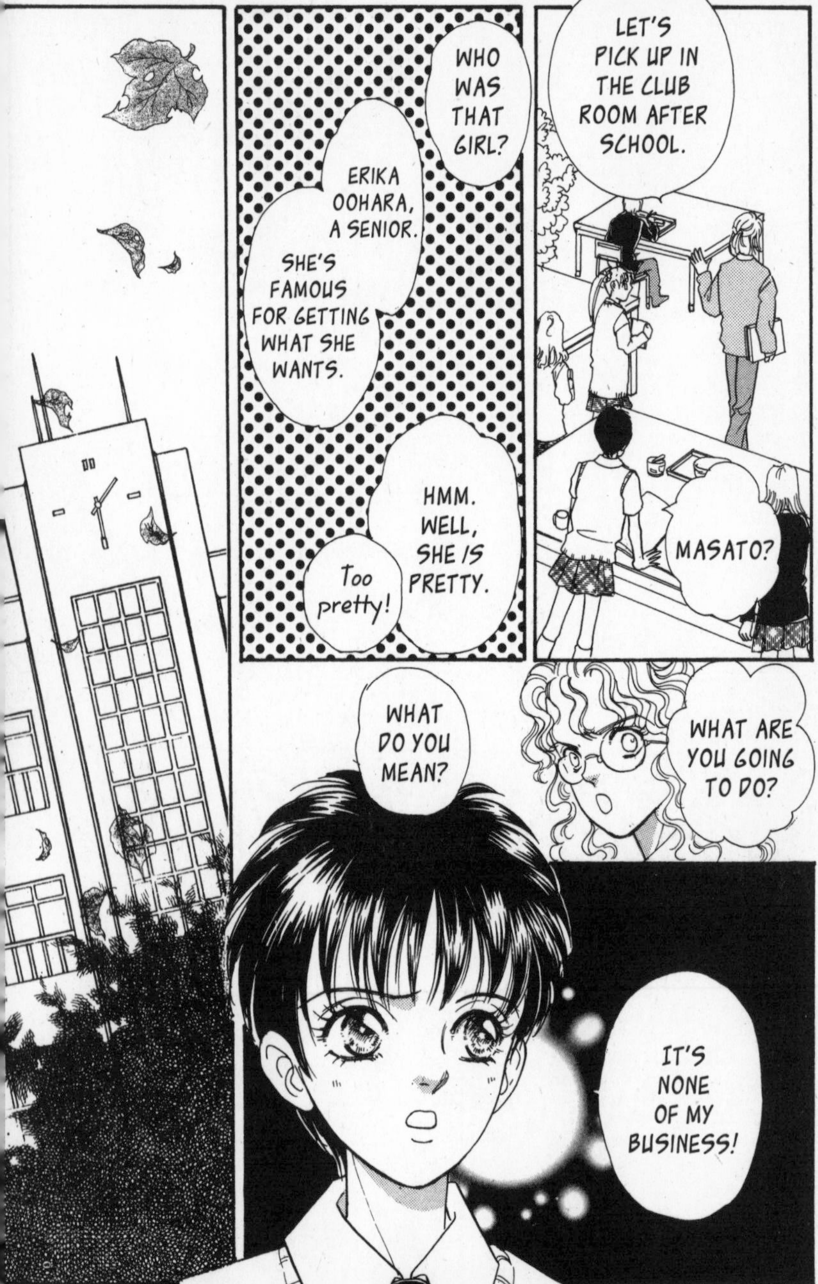
LET'S PICK UP IN THE CLUB ROOM AFTER SCHOOL.
MASATO?
WHO WAS THAT GIRL?
ERIKA OOHARA, A SENIOR.
SHE'S FAMOUS FOR GETTING WHAT SHE WANTS.
HMM. WELL, SHE IS PRETTY.
Too pretty!
WHAT ARE YOU GOING TO DO?
WHAT DO YOU MEAN?
IT'S NONE OF MY BUSINESS!

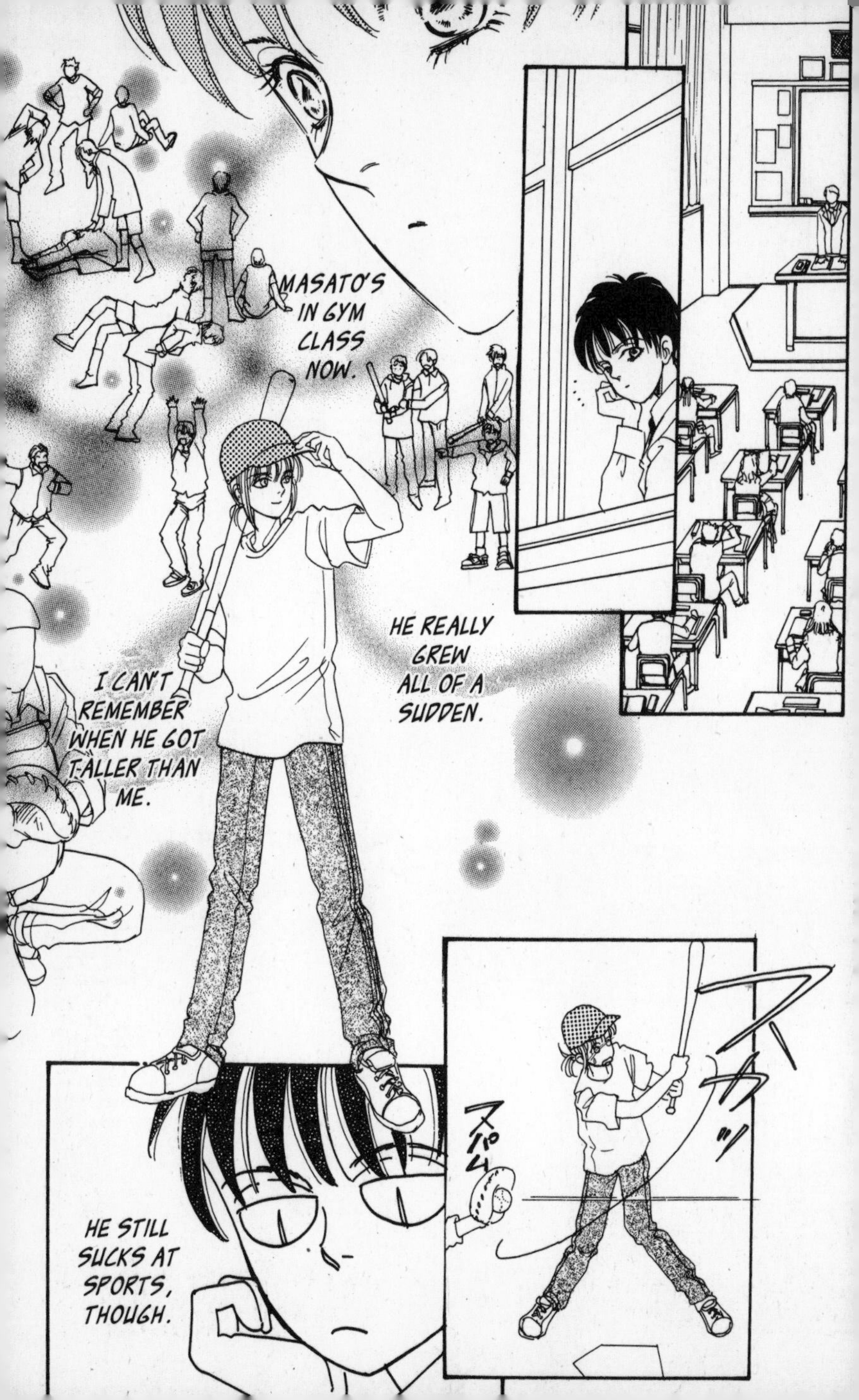
MASATO'S IN GYM CLASS NOW.
HE REALLY GREW ALL OF A SUDDEN.
I CAN'T REMEMBER WHEN HE GOT TALLER THAN ME.
HE STILL SUCKS AT SPORTS, THOUGH.

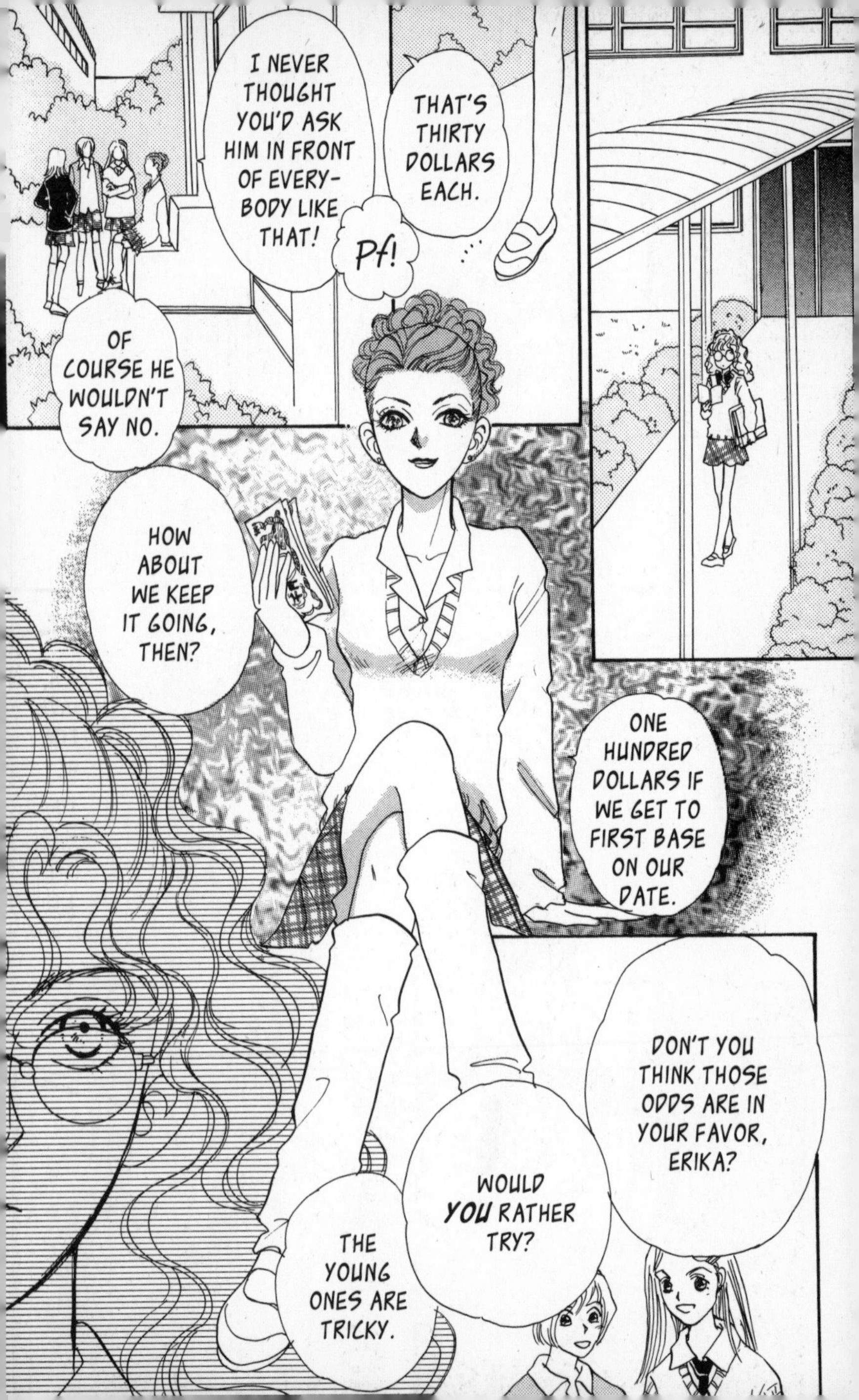
THAT'S THIRTY DOLLARS EACH.
I NEVER THOUGHT YOU'D ASK HIM IN FRONT OF EVERY-BODY LIKE THAT!
Pf!
OF COURSE HE WOULDN'T SAY NO.
HOW ABOUT WE KEEP IT GOING, THEN?
ONE HUNDRED DOLLARS IF WE GET TO FIRST BASE ON OUR DATE.
DON'T YOU THINK THOSE ODDS ARE IN YOUR FAVOR, ERIKA?
WOULD *YOU* RATHER TRY?
THE YOUNG ONES ARE TRICKY.

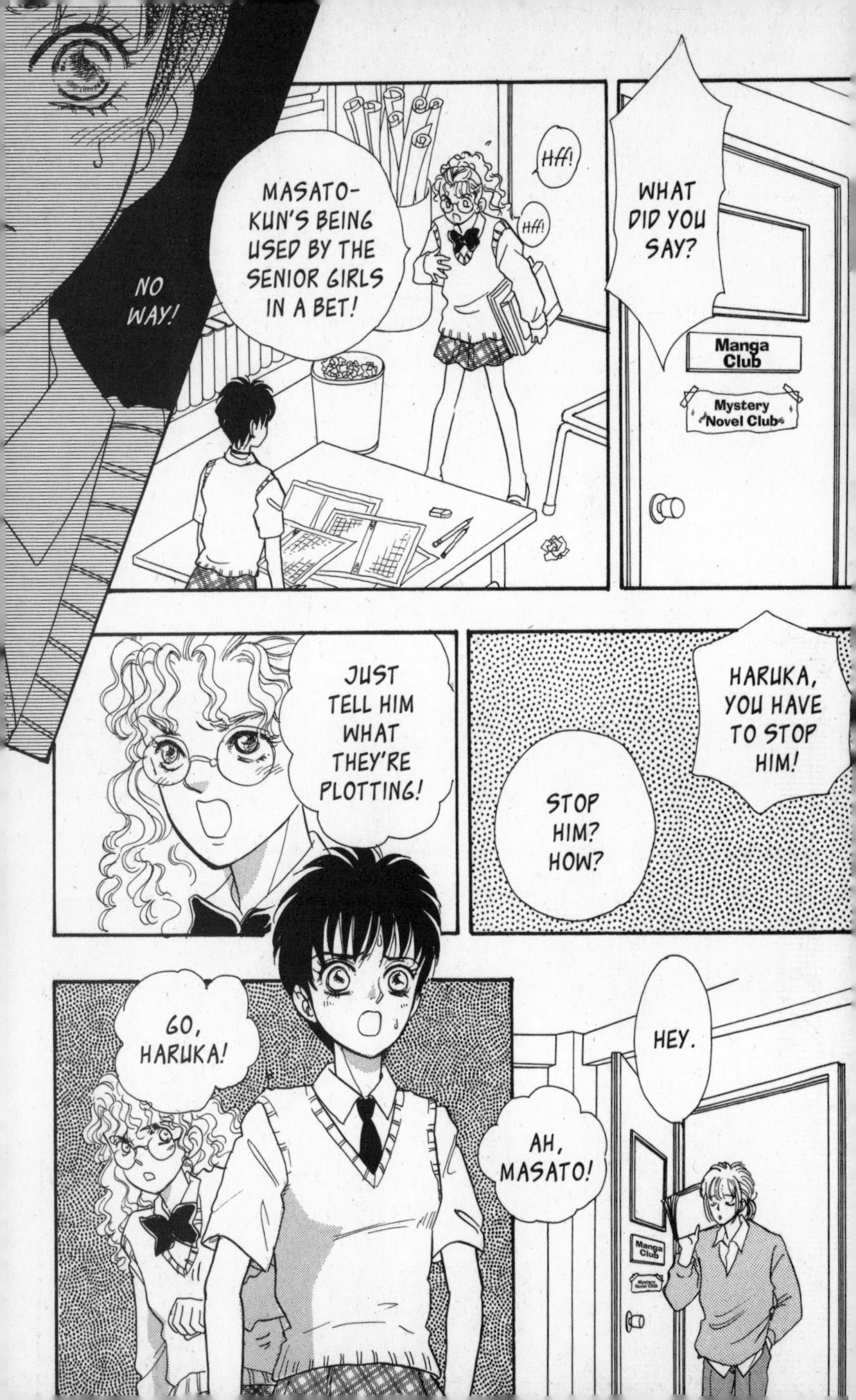
WHAT DID YOU SAY?
Manga Club
Mystery Novel Club
Hff!
Hff!
MASATO-KUN'S BEING USED BY THE SENIOR GIRLS IN A BET!
NO WAY!
HARUKA, YOU HAVE TO STOP HIM!
STOP HIM? HOW?
JUST TELL HIM WHAT THEY'RE PLOTTING!
HEY.
Manga Club
Mystery Novel Club
AH, MASATO!
GO, HARUKA!

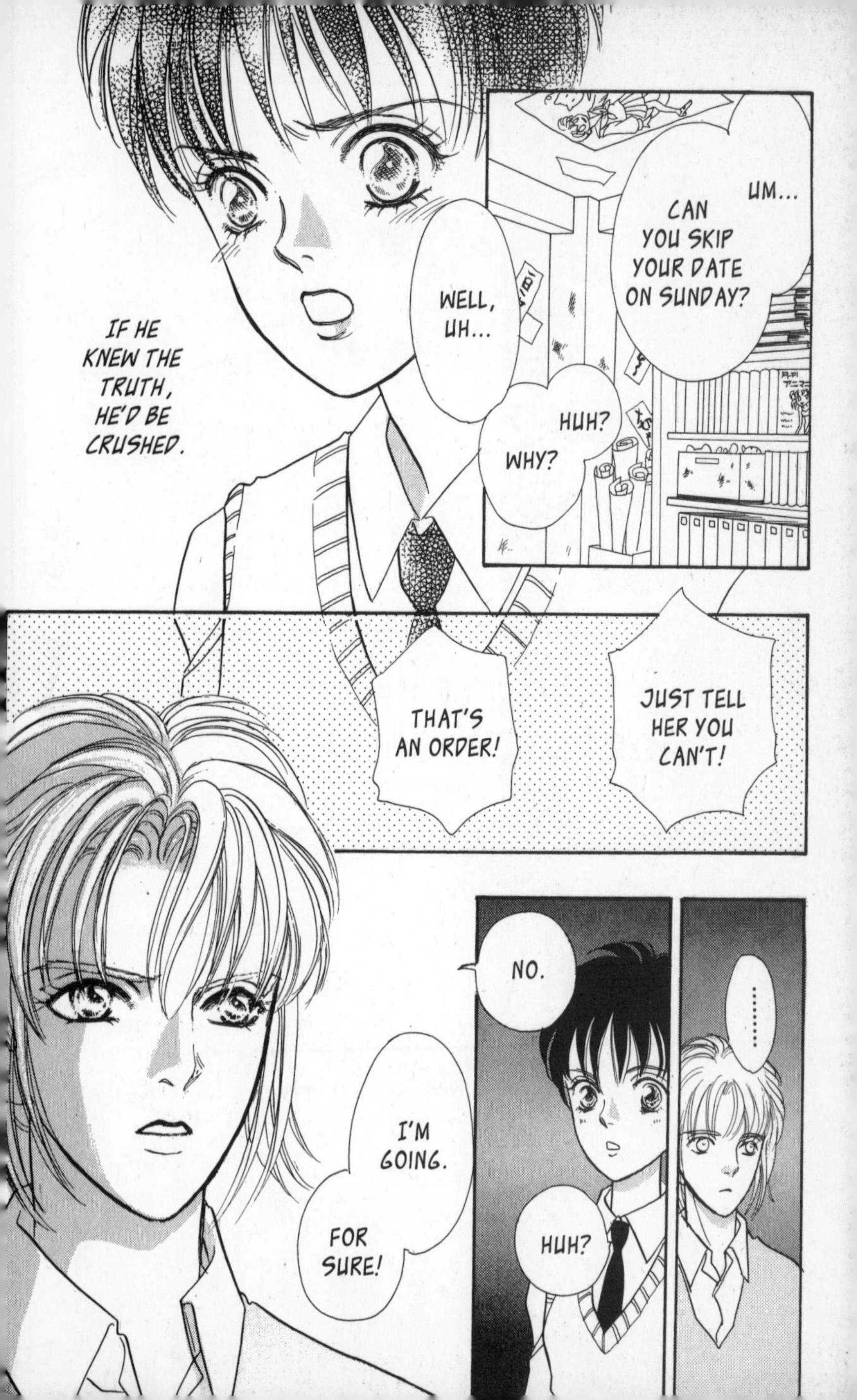
UM...
CAN YOU SKIP YOUR DATE ON SUNDAY?
HUH?
WHY?
WELL, UH...
IF HE KNEW THE TRUTH, HE'D BE CRUSHED.
JUST TELL HER YOU CAN'T!
THAT'S AN ORDER!
......
NO.
HUH?
I'M GOING.
FOR SURE!

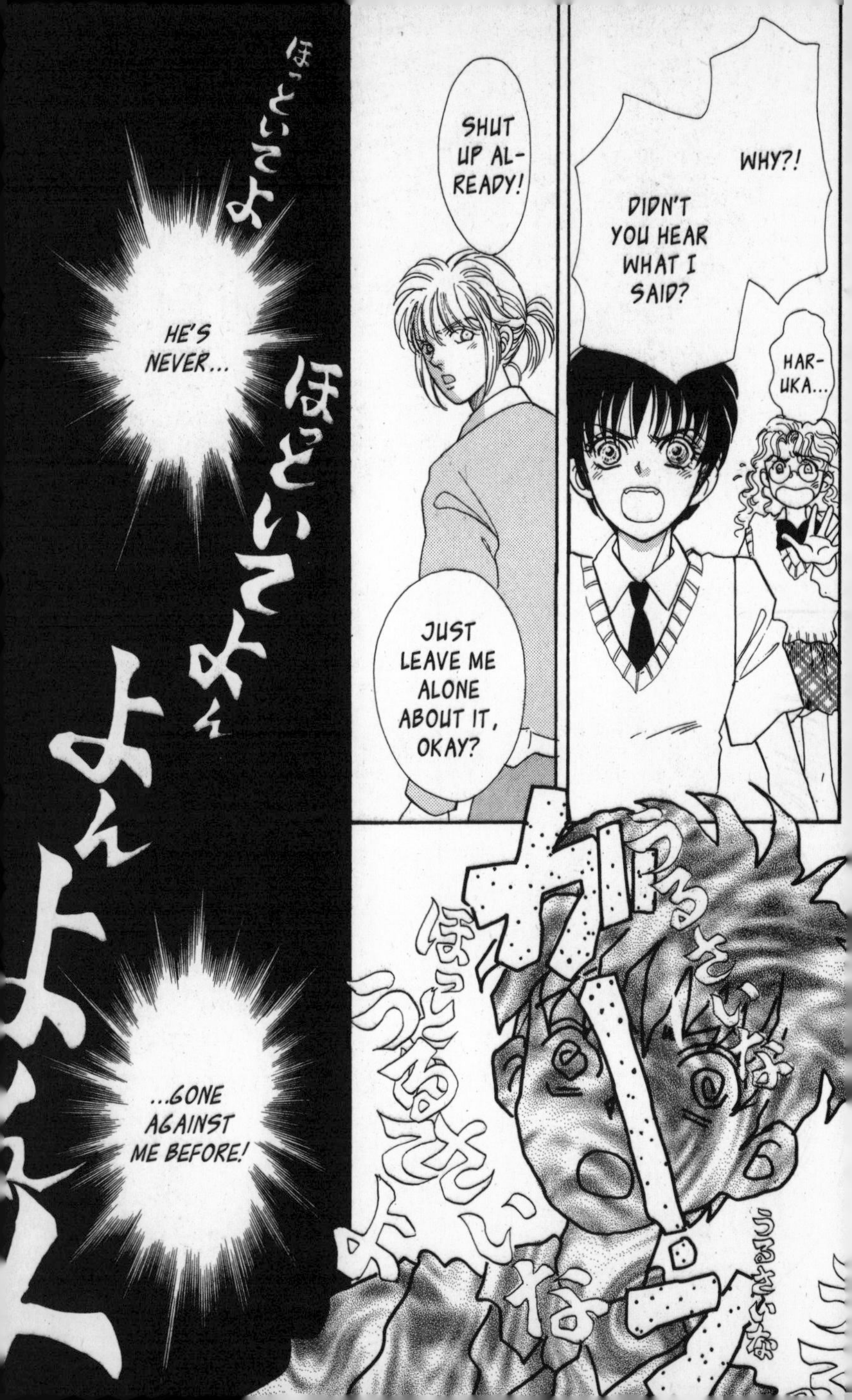
WHY?!
DIDN'T YOU HEAR WHAT I SAID?
HAR-UKA...
SHUT UP AL-READY!
JUST LEAVE ME ALONE ABOUT IT, OKAY?
うるさいな
うるさいな
ほっといてよ
HE'S NEVER...
...GONE AGAINST ME BEFORE!

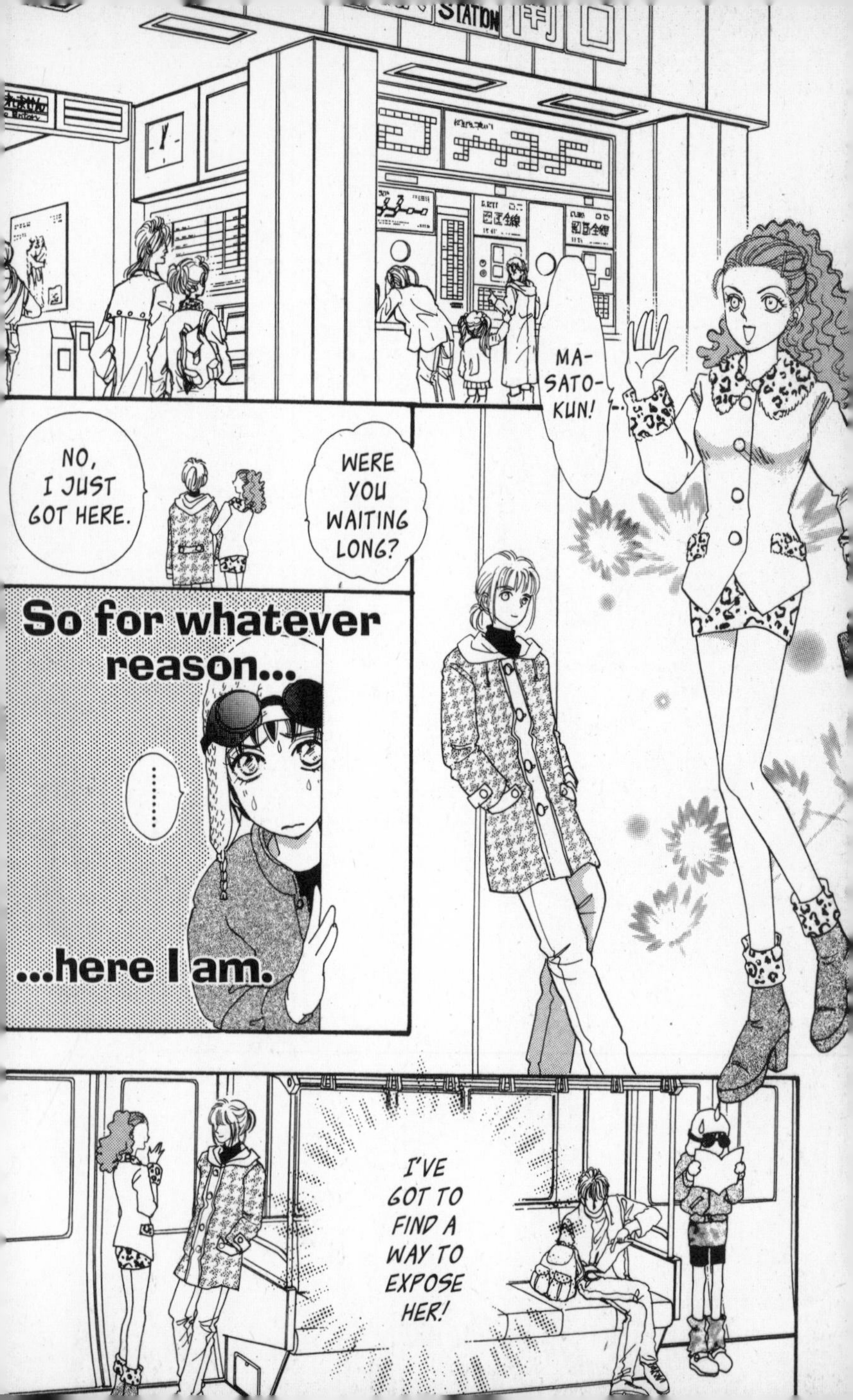
STATION
MA-SATO-KUN!
WERE YOU WAITING LONG?
NO, I JUST GOT HERE.
So for whatever reason...
......
...here I am.
I'VE GOT TO FIND A WAY TO EXPOSE HER!

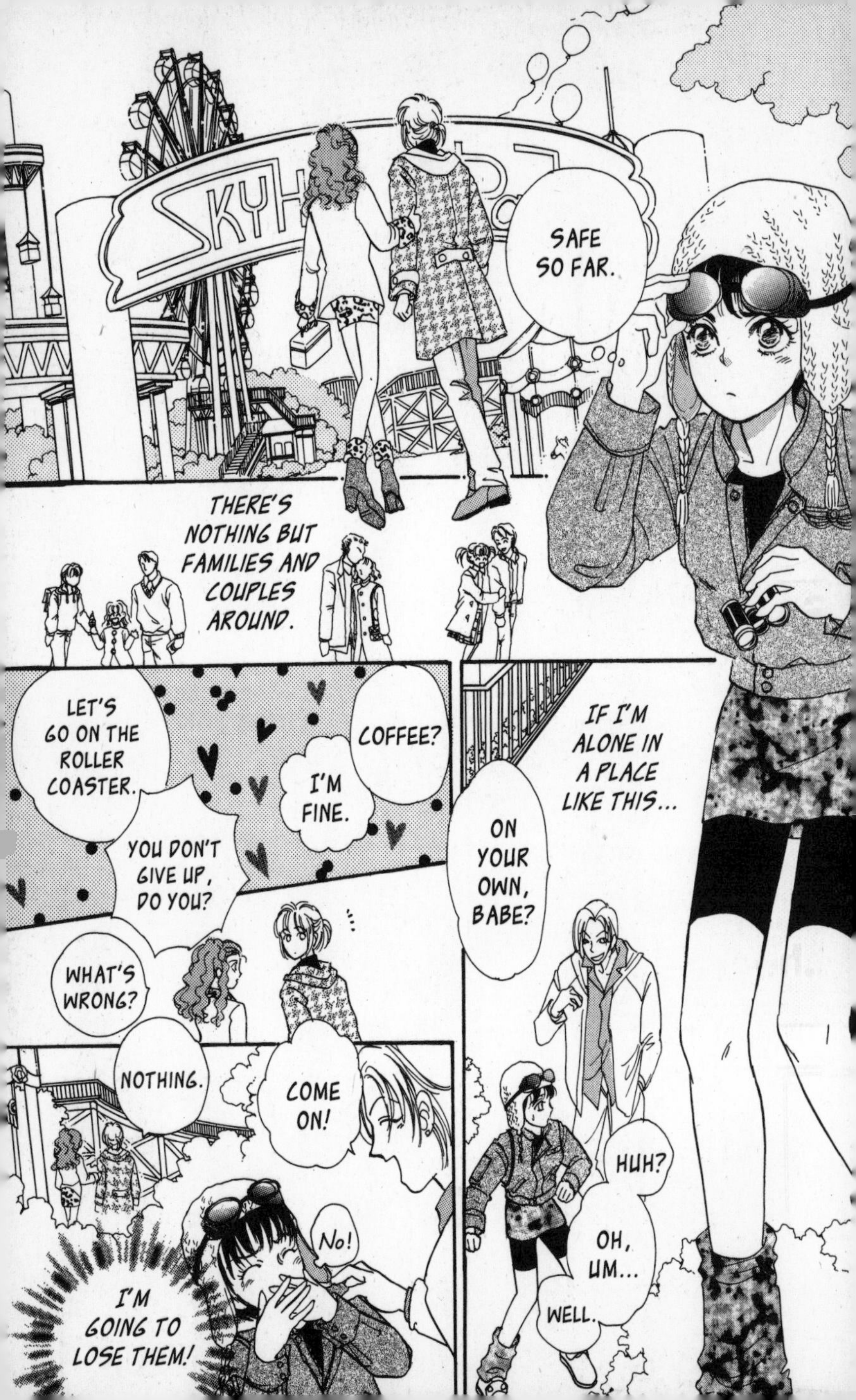
SKYH
SAFE SO FAR.
THERE'S NOTHING BUT FAMILIES AND COUPLES AROUND.
IF I'M ALONE IN A PLACE LIKE THIS...
ON YOUR OWN, BABE?
HUH?
OH, UM...
WELL.
COFFEE?
LET'S GO ON THE ROLLER COASTER.
I'M FINE.
YOU DON'T GIVE UP, DO YOU?
WHAT'S WRONG?
NOTHING.
COME ON!
No!
I'M GOING TO LOSE THEM!

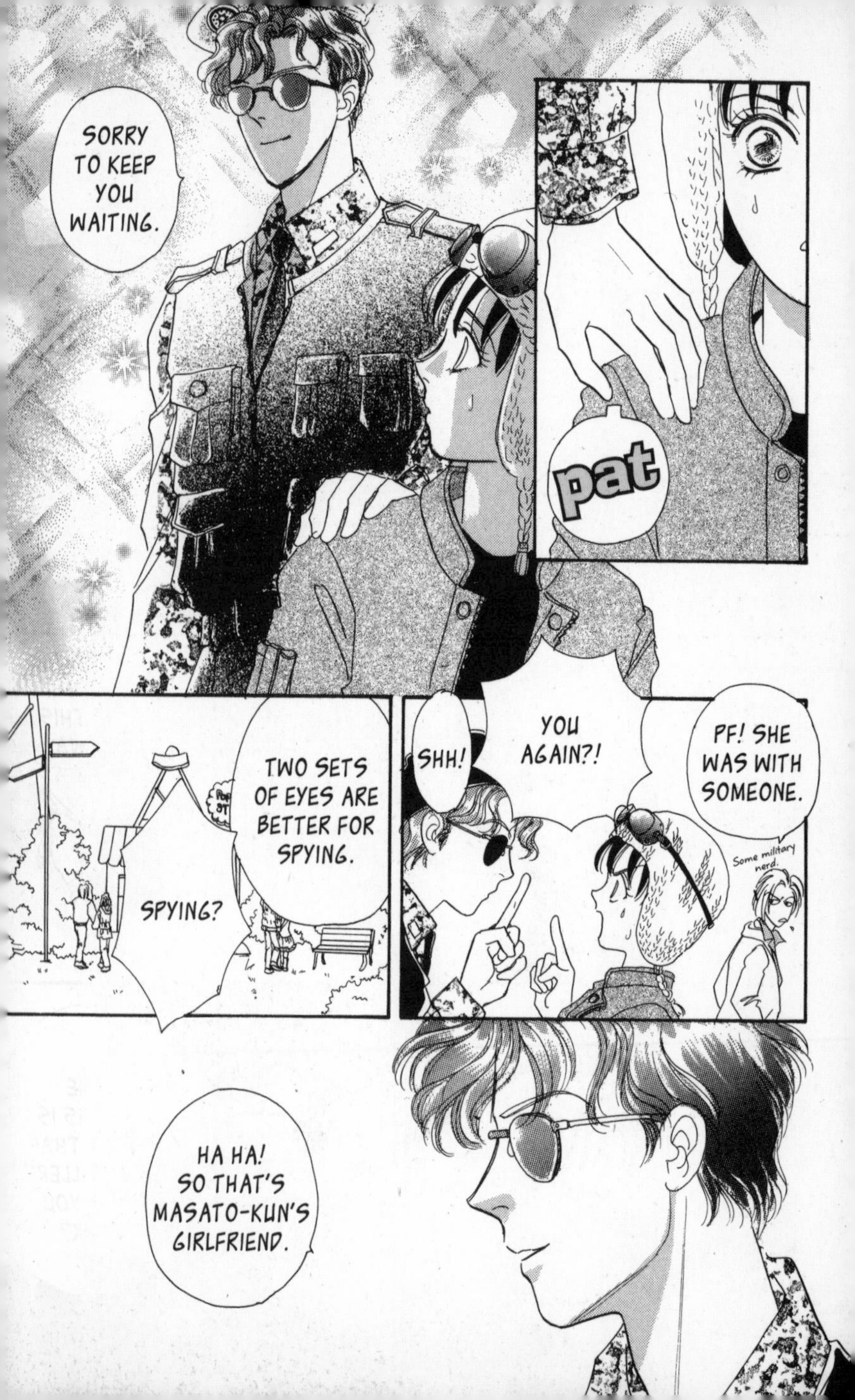

pat
SORRY TO KEEP YOU WAITING.
PF! SHE WAS WITH SOMEONE.
Some military nerd.
YOU AGAIN?!
SHH!
TWO SETS OF EYES ARE BETTER FOR SPYING.
SPYING?
HA HA! SO THAT'S MASATO-KUN'S GIRLFRIEND.

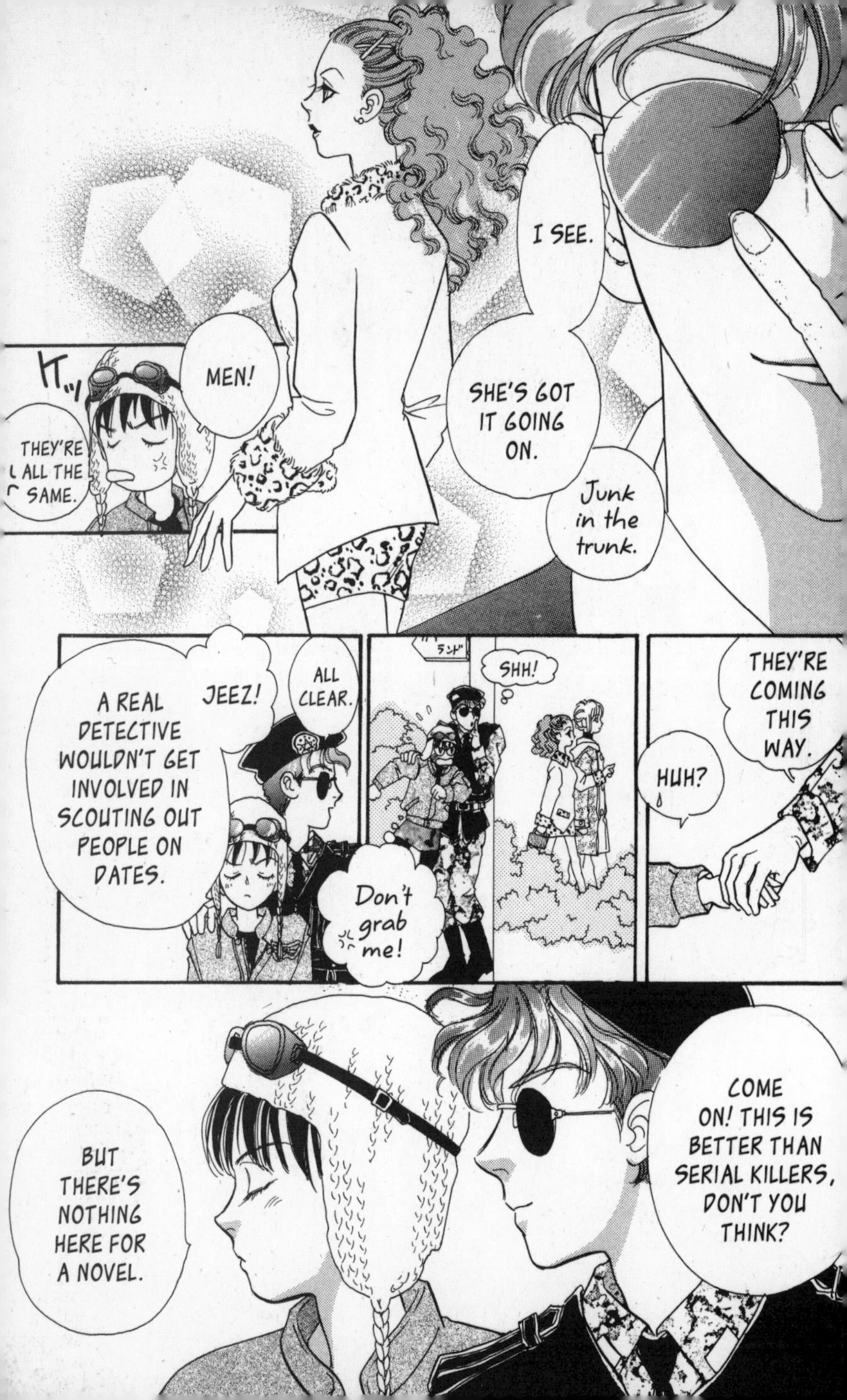
I SEE.
SHE'S GOT IT GOING ON.
Junk in the trunk.
ケッ
MEN!
THEY'RE ALL THE SAME.
THEY'RE COMING THIS WAY.
HUH?
ランド
SHH!
Don't grab me!
ALL CLEAR.
JEEZ!
A REAL DETECTIVE WOULDN'T GET INVOLVED IN SCOUTING OUT PEOPLE ON DATES.
COME ON! THIS IS BETTER THAN SERIAL KILLERS, DON'T YOU THINK?
BUT THERE'S NOTHING HERE FOR A NOVEL.

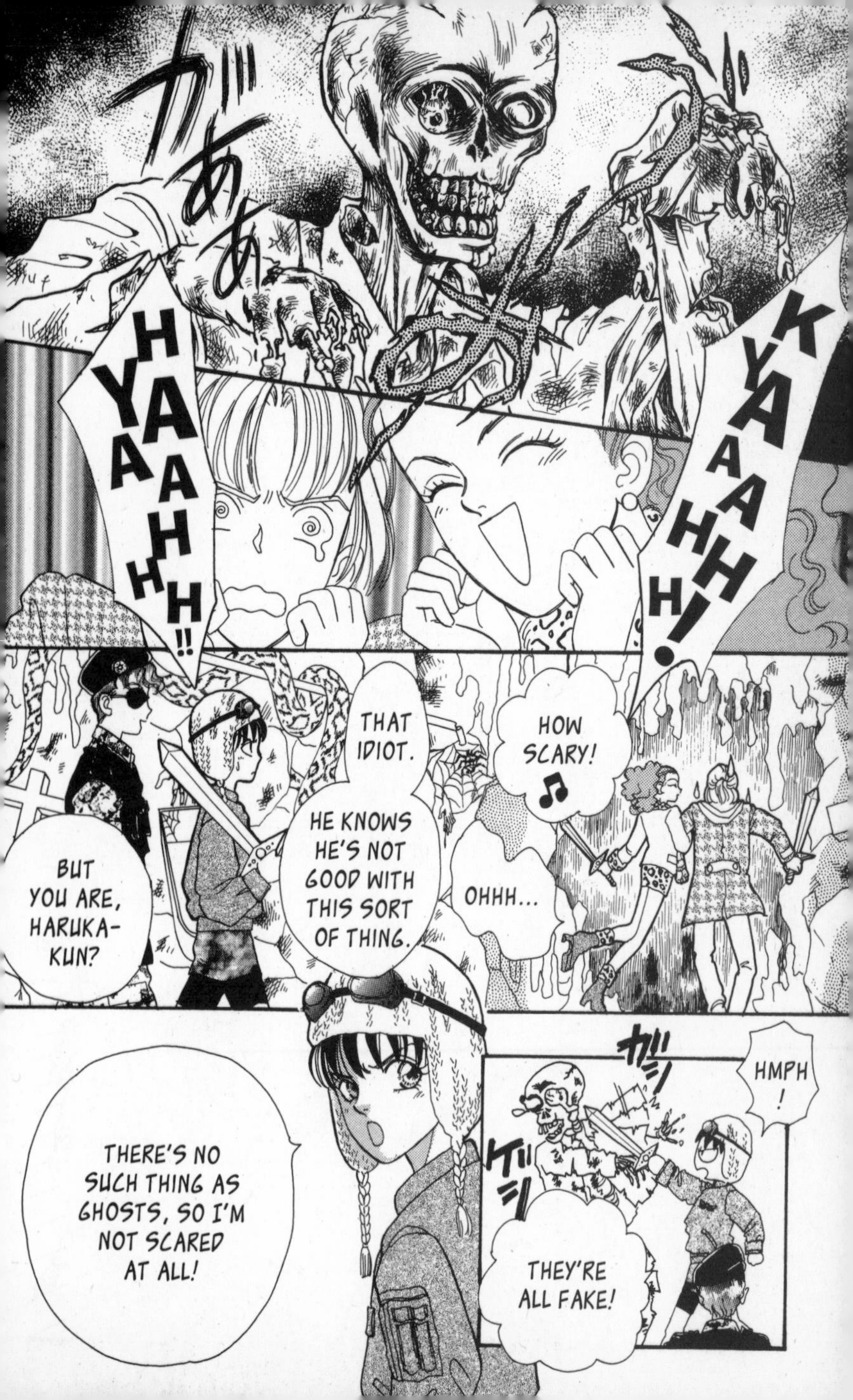
KYAAAHHHH!
HYAAAHHHH!!
HOW SCARY! ♫
THAT IDIOT.
HE KNOWS HE'S NOT GOOD WITH THIS SORT OF THING.
OHHH...
BUT YOU ARE, HARUKA-KUN?
HMPH!
THEY'RE ALL FAKE!
THERE'S NO SUCH THING AS GHOSTS, SO I'M NOT SCARED AT ALL!

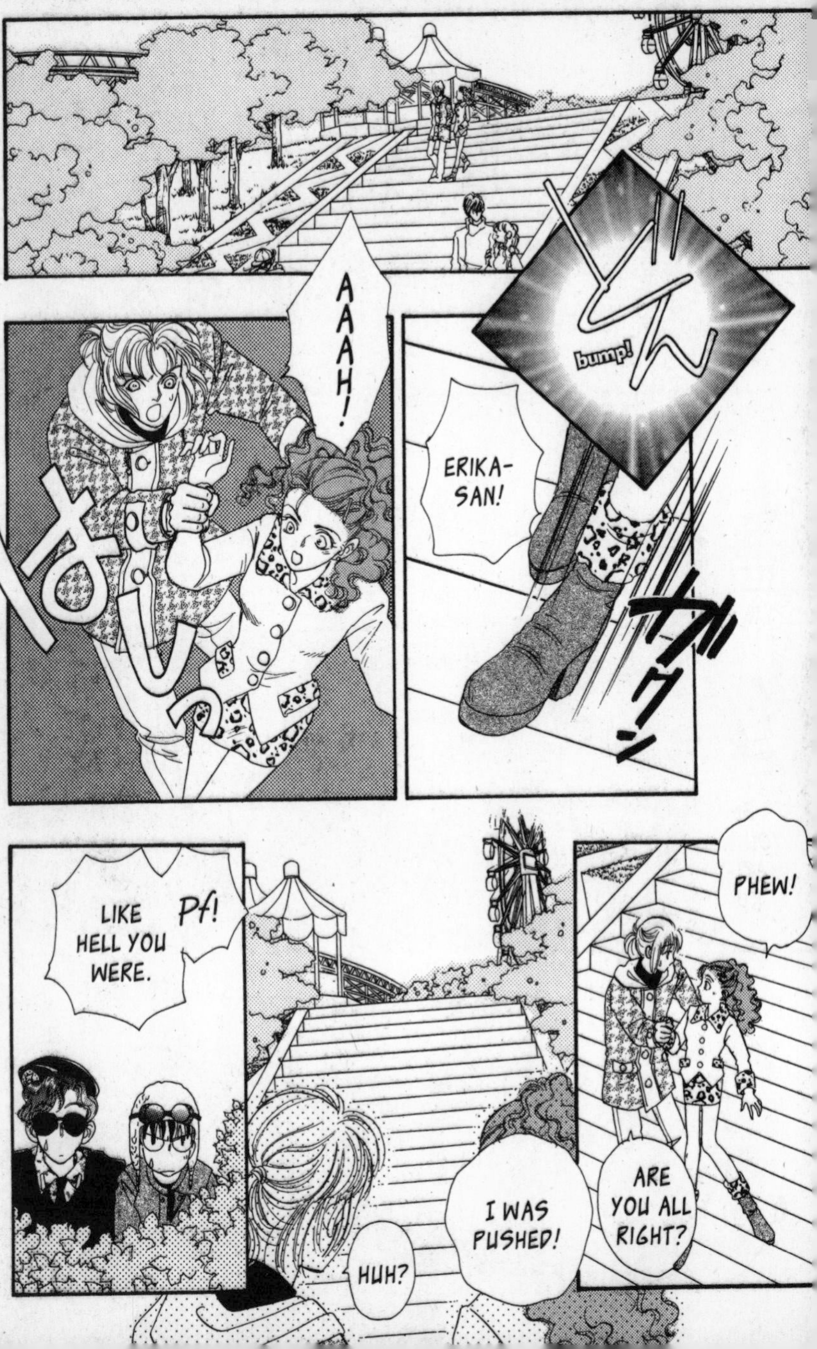
bump!
ERIKA-SAN!
AAAAH!
PHEW!
ARE YOU ALL RIGHT?
I WAS PUSHED!
HUH?
LIKE HELL YOU WERE.
Pf!

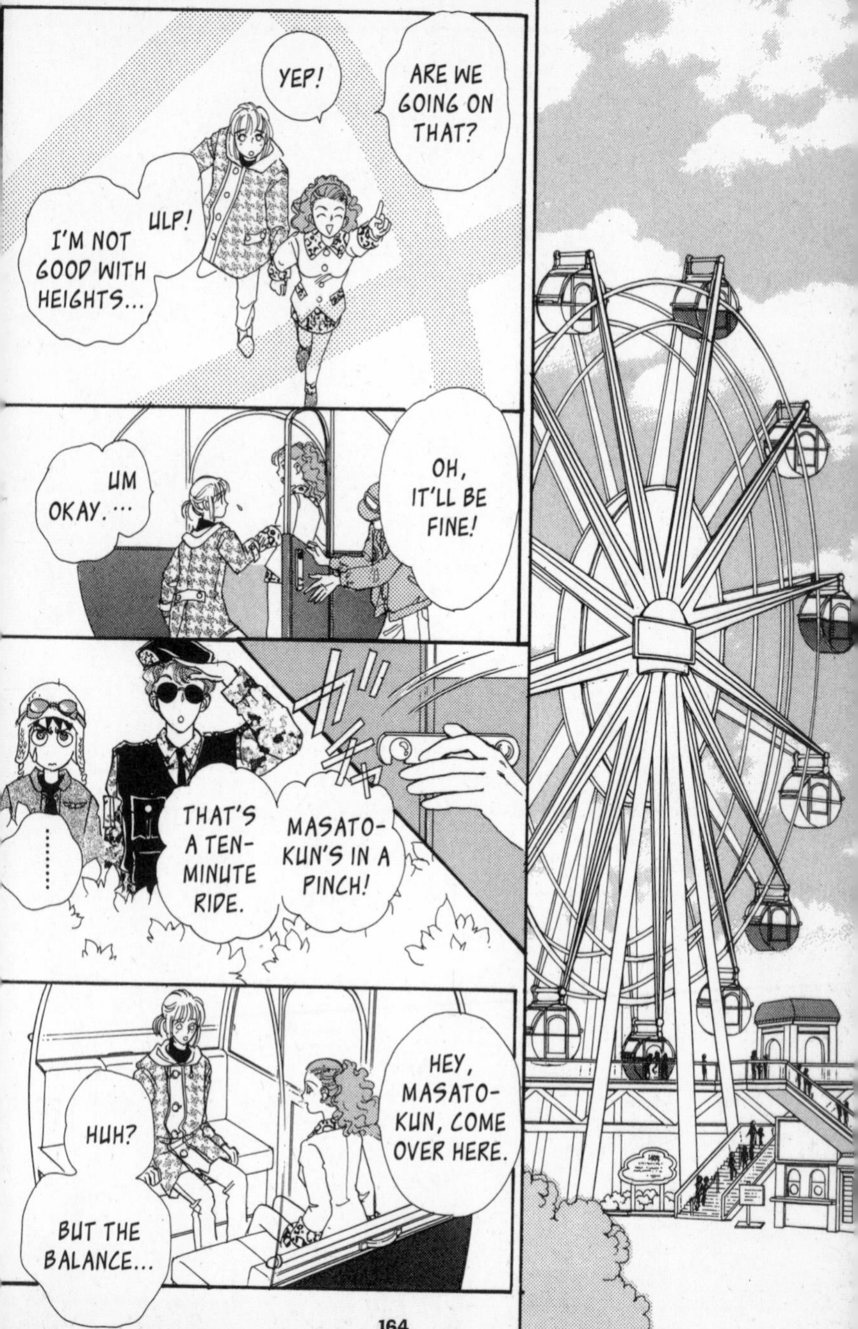
ARE WE GOING ON THAT?
YEP!
ULP!
I'M NOT GOOD WITH HEIGHTS...
OH, IT'LL BE FINE!
UM OKAY....
MASATO-KUN'S IN A PINCH!
THAT'S A TEN-MINUTE RIDE.
....
HEY, MASATO-KUN, COME OVER HERE.
HUH?
BUT THE BALANCE...

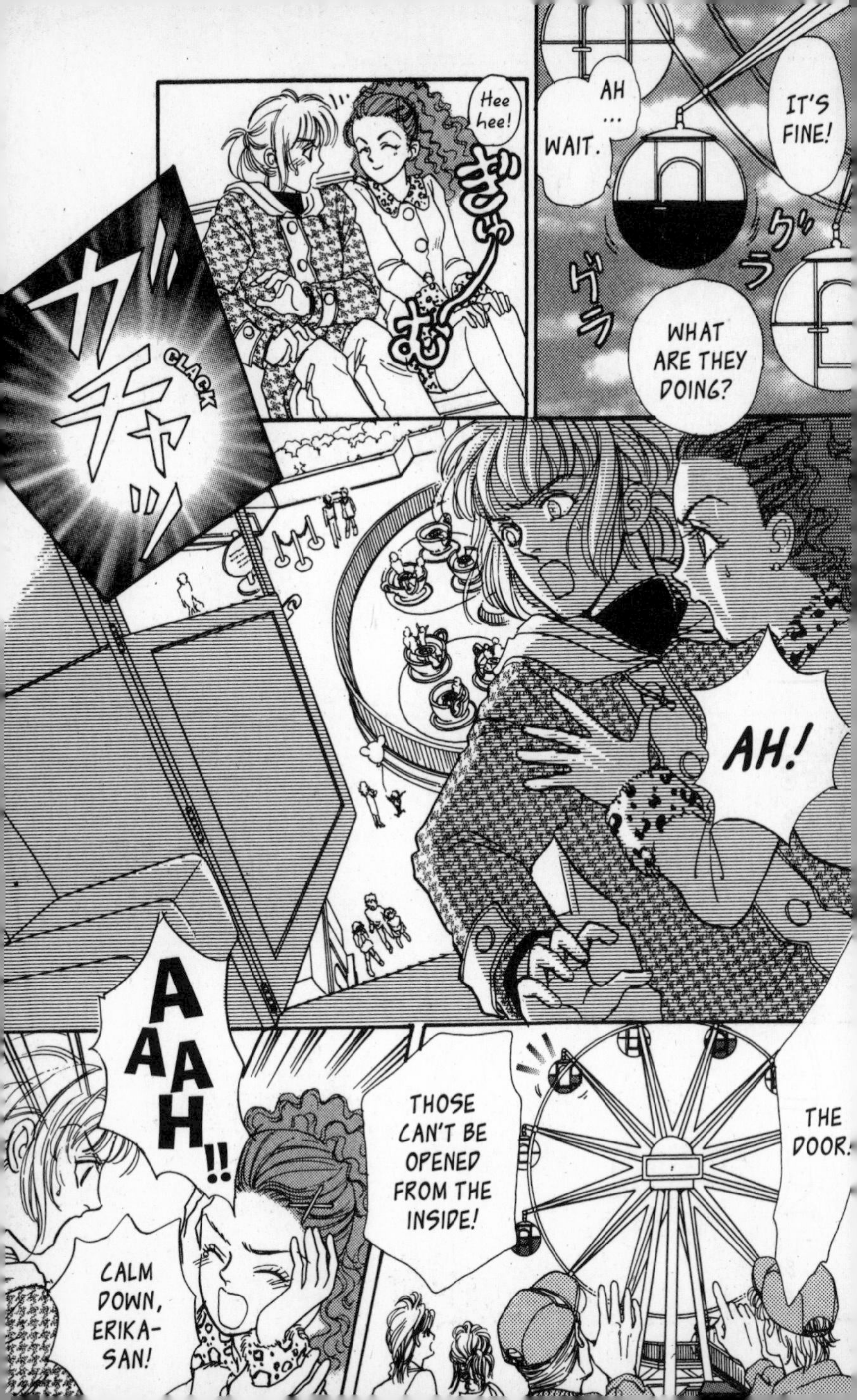
IT'S FINE!
AH ... WAIT.
WHAT ARE THEY DOING?
Hee hee!
CLACK
AH!
THE DOOR.
THOSE CAN'T BE OPENED FROM THE INSIDE!
AAAH!!
CALM DOWN, ERIKA-SAN!

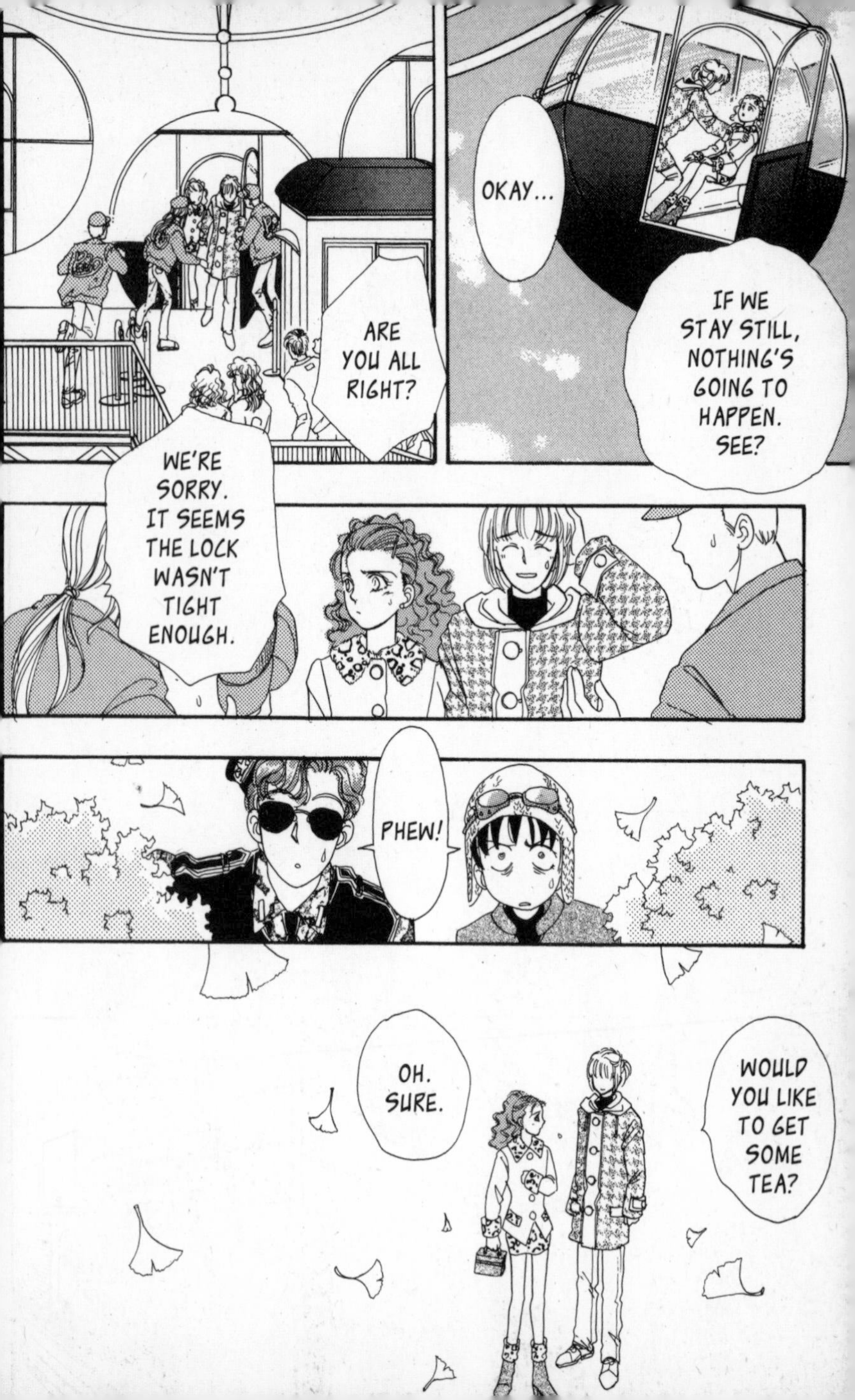
IF WE STAY STILL, NOTHING'S GOING TO HAPPEN. SEE?
OKAY...
ARE YOU ALL RIGHT?
WE'RE SORRY. IT SEEMS THE LOCK WASN'T TIGHT ENOUGH.
PHEW!
WOULD YOU LIKE TO GET SOME TEA?
OH. SURE.

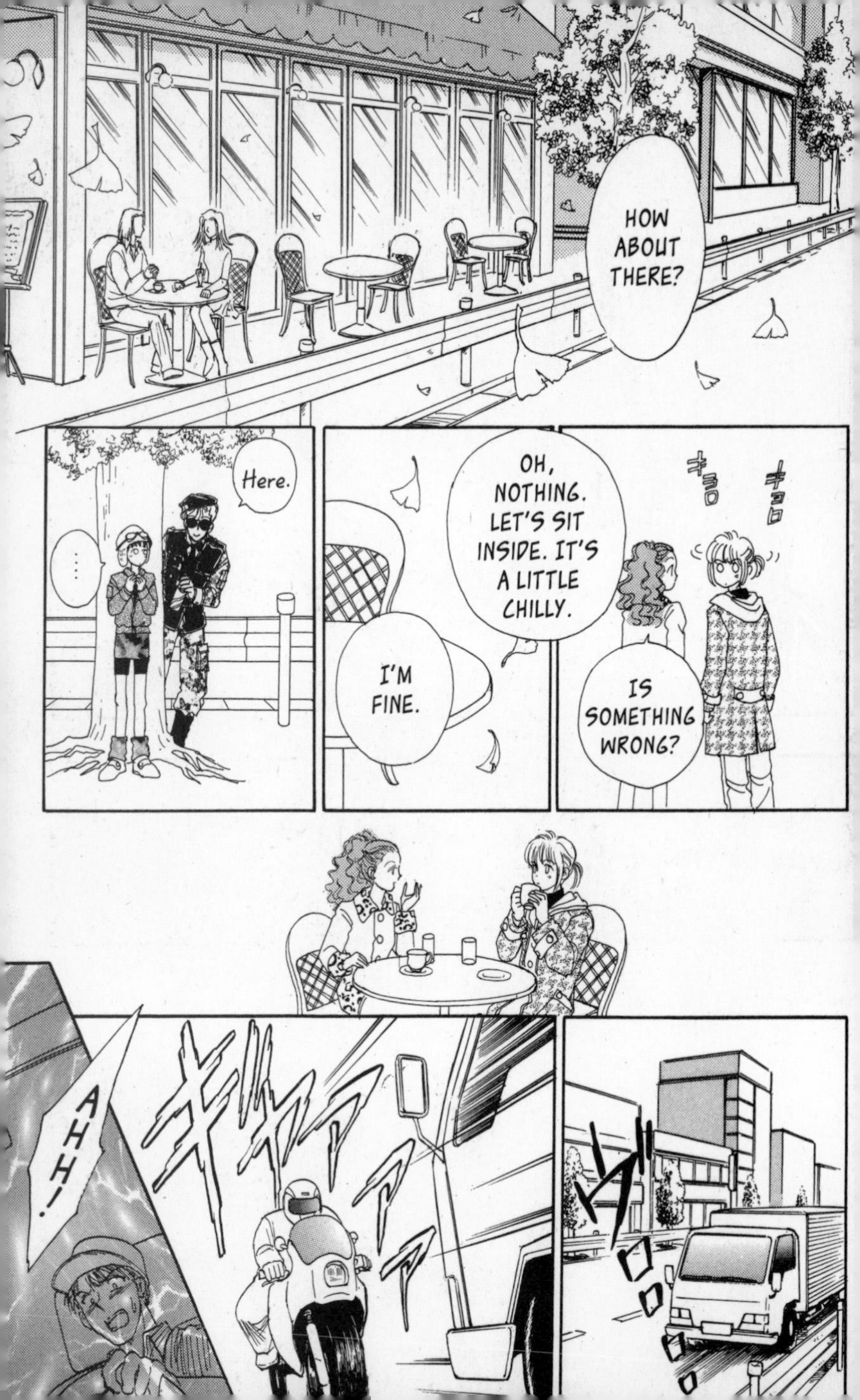
HOW ABOUT THERE?
キョロ キョロ
IS SOMETHING WRONG?
OH, NOTHING. LET'S SIT INSIDE. IT'S A LITTLE CHILLY.
I'M FINE.
Here.
.....
AHH!

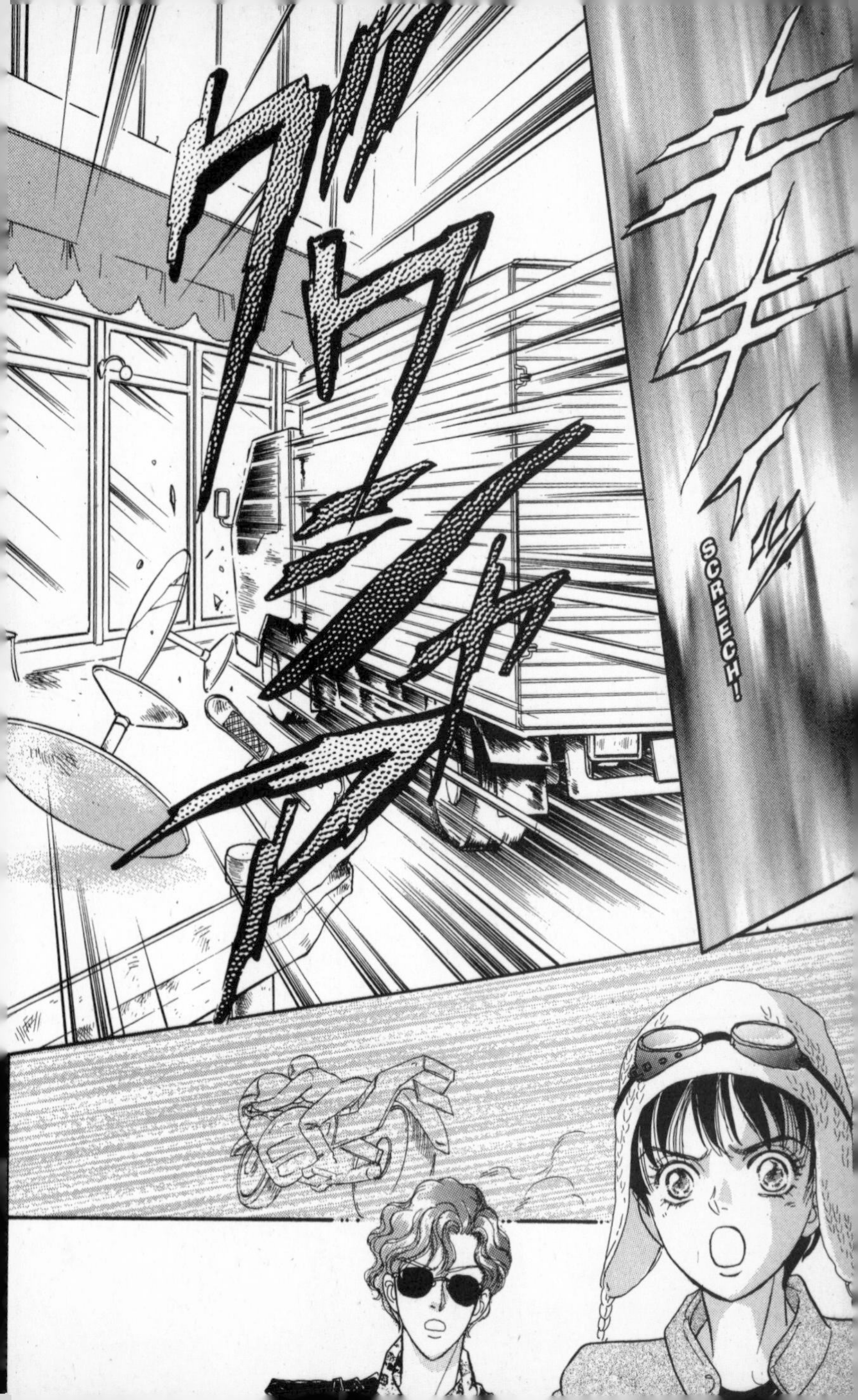
SCREECH!

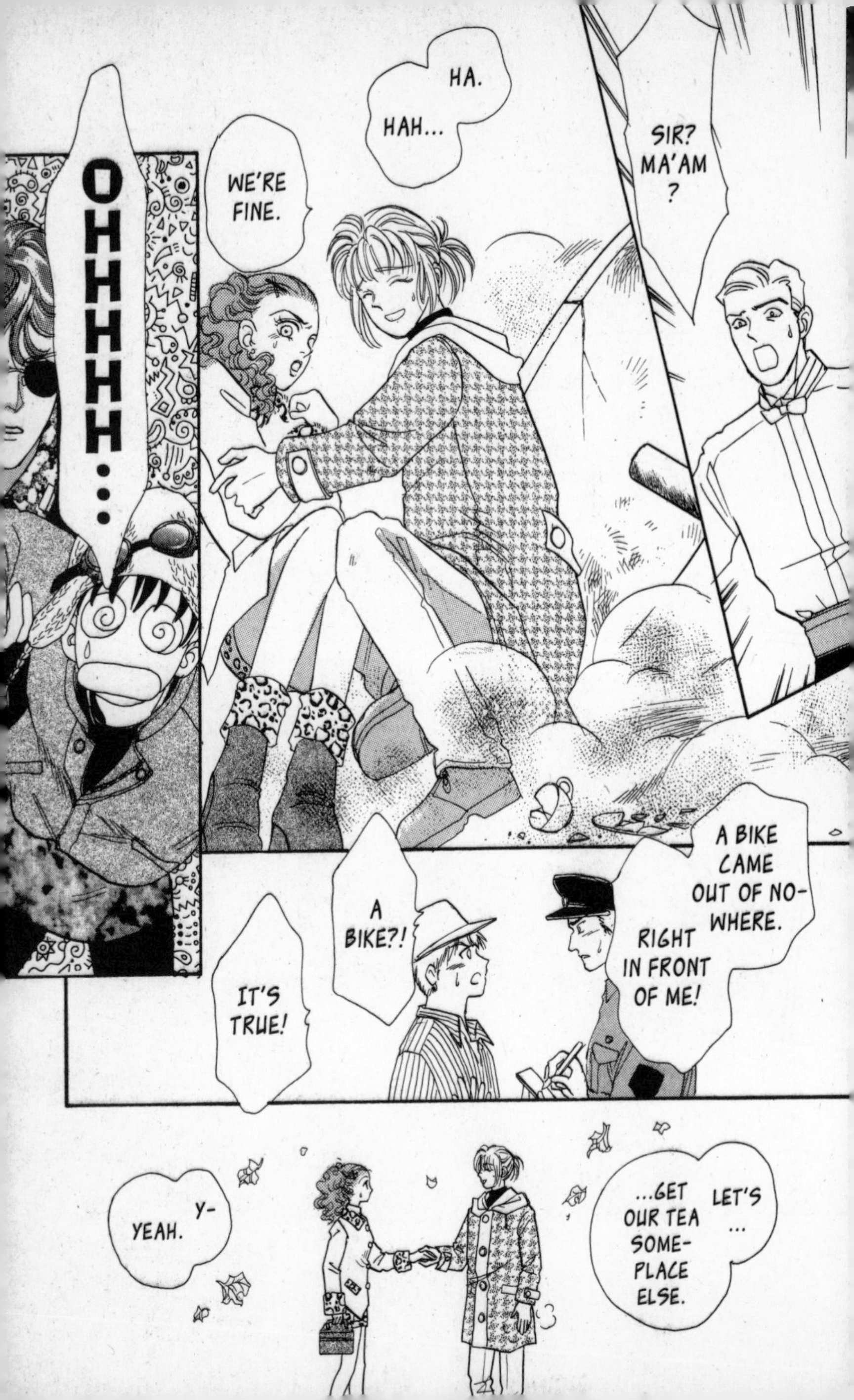
SIR? MA'AM ?
HA.
HAH...
WE'RE FINE.
OHHHHH...
A BIKE CAME OUT OF NO-WHERE.
RIGHT IN FRONT OF ME!
A BIKE?!
IT'S TRUE!
LET'S ...
...GET OUR TEA SOME-PLACE ELSE.
Y-
YEAH.

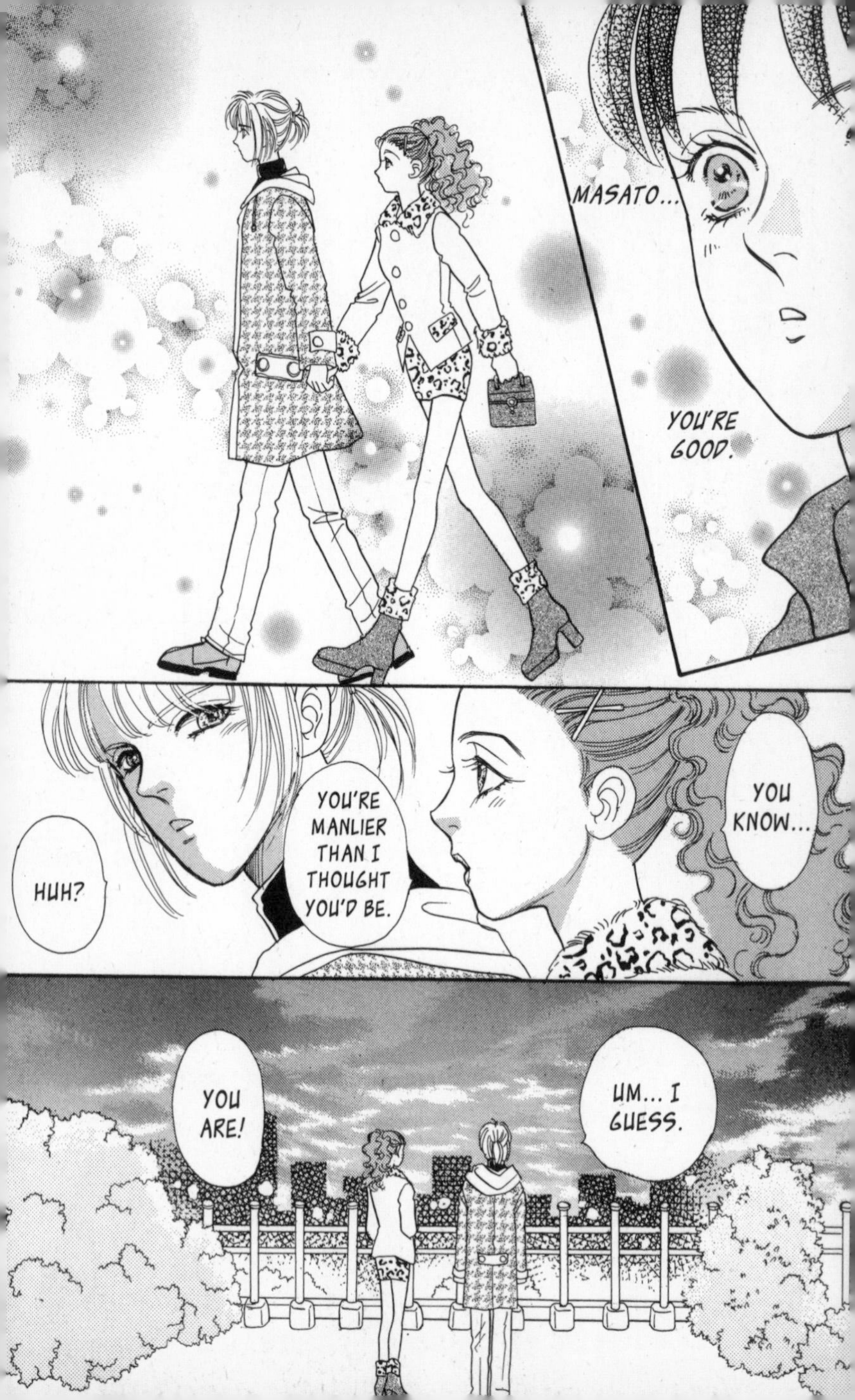
MASATO...
YOU'RE GOOD.
YOU KNOW...
YOU'RE MANLIER THAN I THOUGHT YOU'D BE.
HUH?
UM... I GUESS.
YOU ARE!

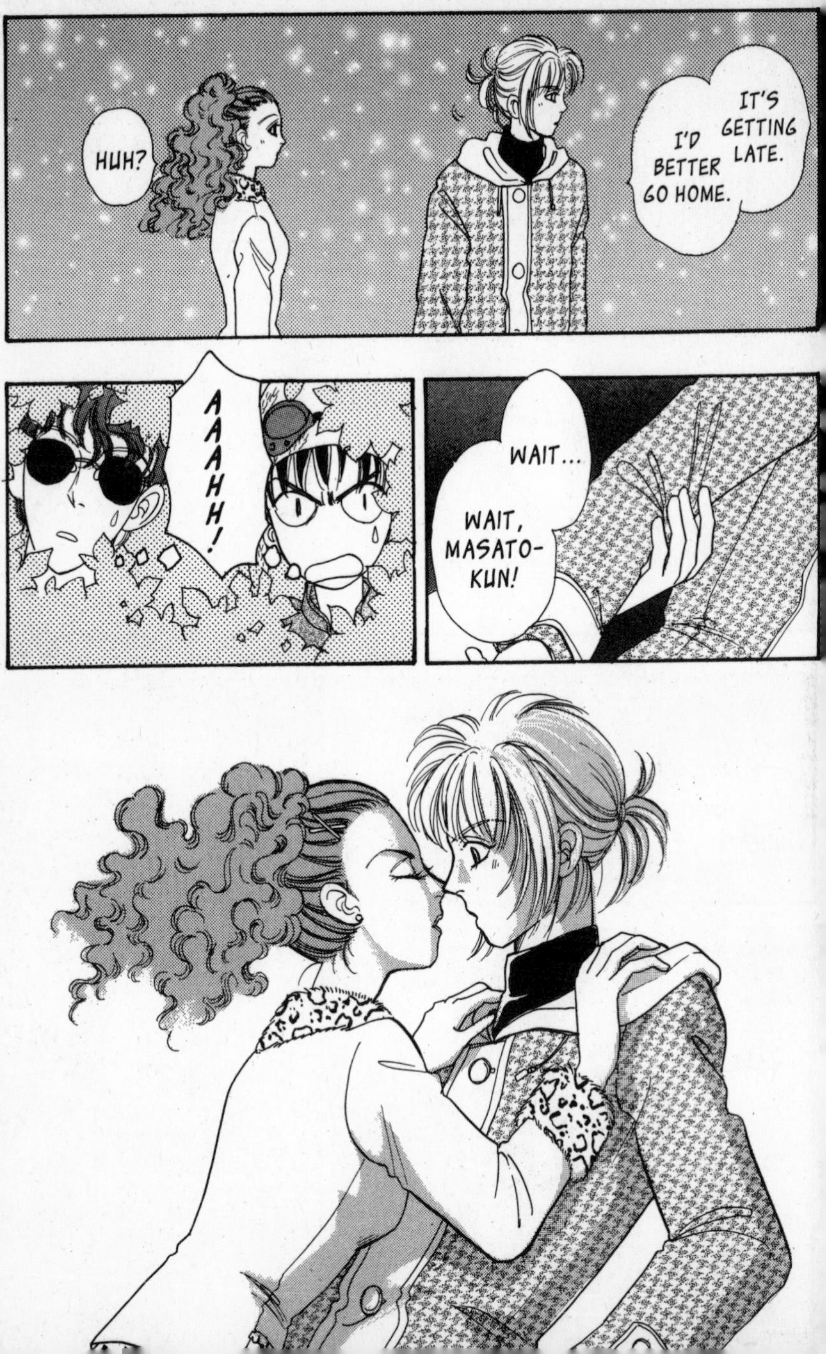
IT'S GETTING LATE.
I'D BETTER GO HOME.
HUH?
WAIT...
WAIT, MASATO-KUN!
AAAHH!

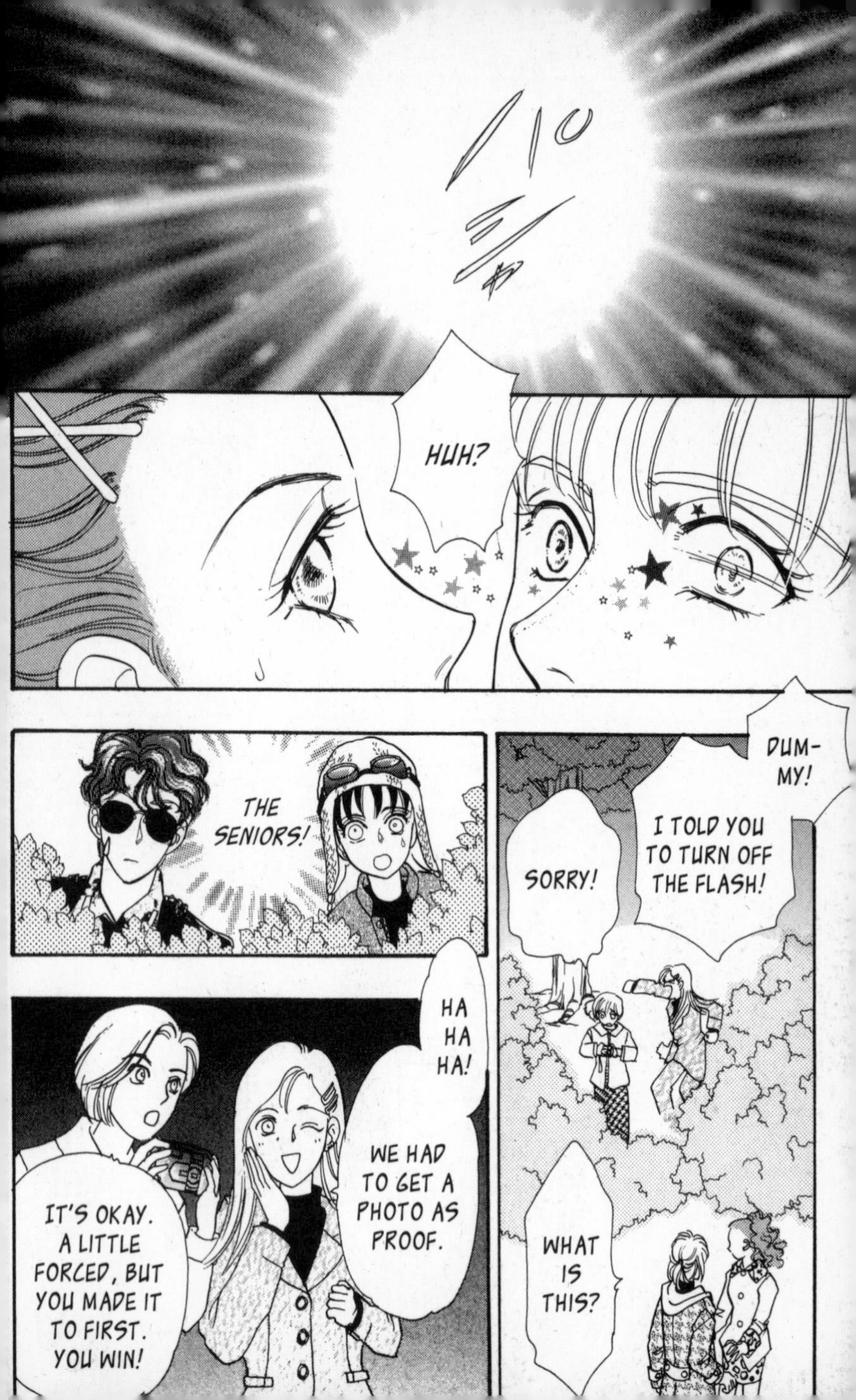
HUH?
DUM-MY!
I TOLD YOU TO TURN OFF THE FLASH!
SORRY!
WHAT IS THIS?
THE SENIORS!
HA HA HA!
WE HAD TO GET A PHOTO AS PROOF.
IT'S OKAY. A LITTLE FORCED, BUT YOU MADE IT TO FIRST. YOU WIN!

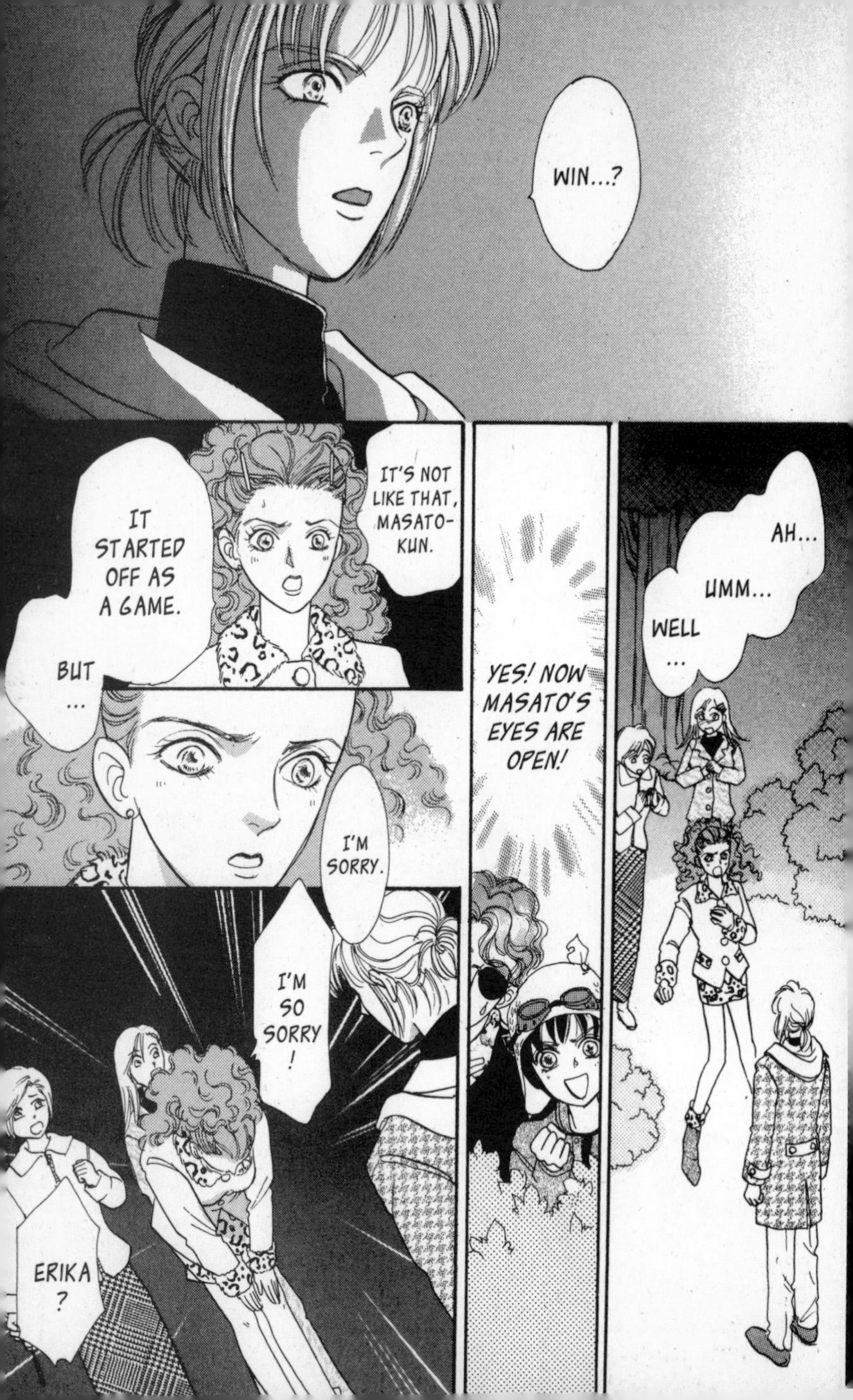
WIN...?
AH...
UMM...
WELL ...
YES! NOW MASATO'S EYES ARE OPEN!
IT'S NOT LIKE THAT, MASATO-KUN.
IT STARTED OFF AS A GAME.
BUT ...
I'M SORRY.
I'M SO SORRY!
ERIKA?

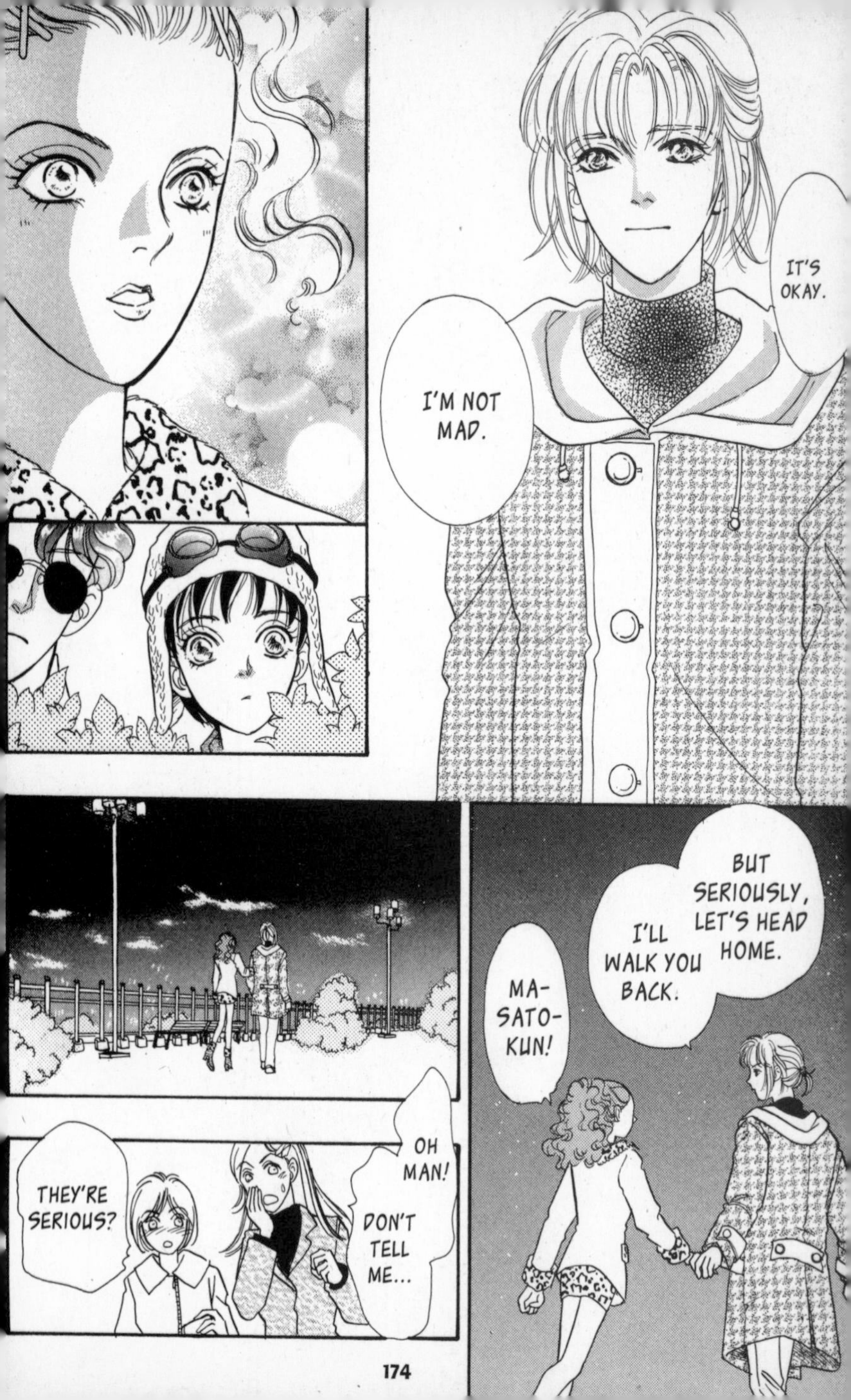
IT'S OKAY.
I'M NOT MAD.
BUT SERIOUSLY, LET'S HEAD HOME.
I'LL WALK YOU BACK.
MA-SATO-KUN!
OH MAN!
DON'T TELL ME...
THEY'RE SERIOUS?

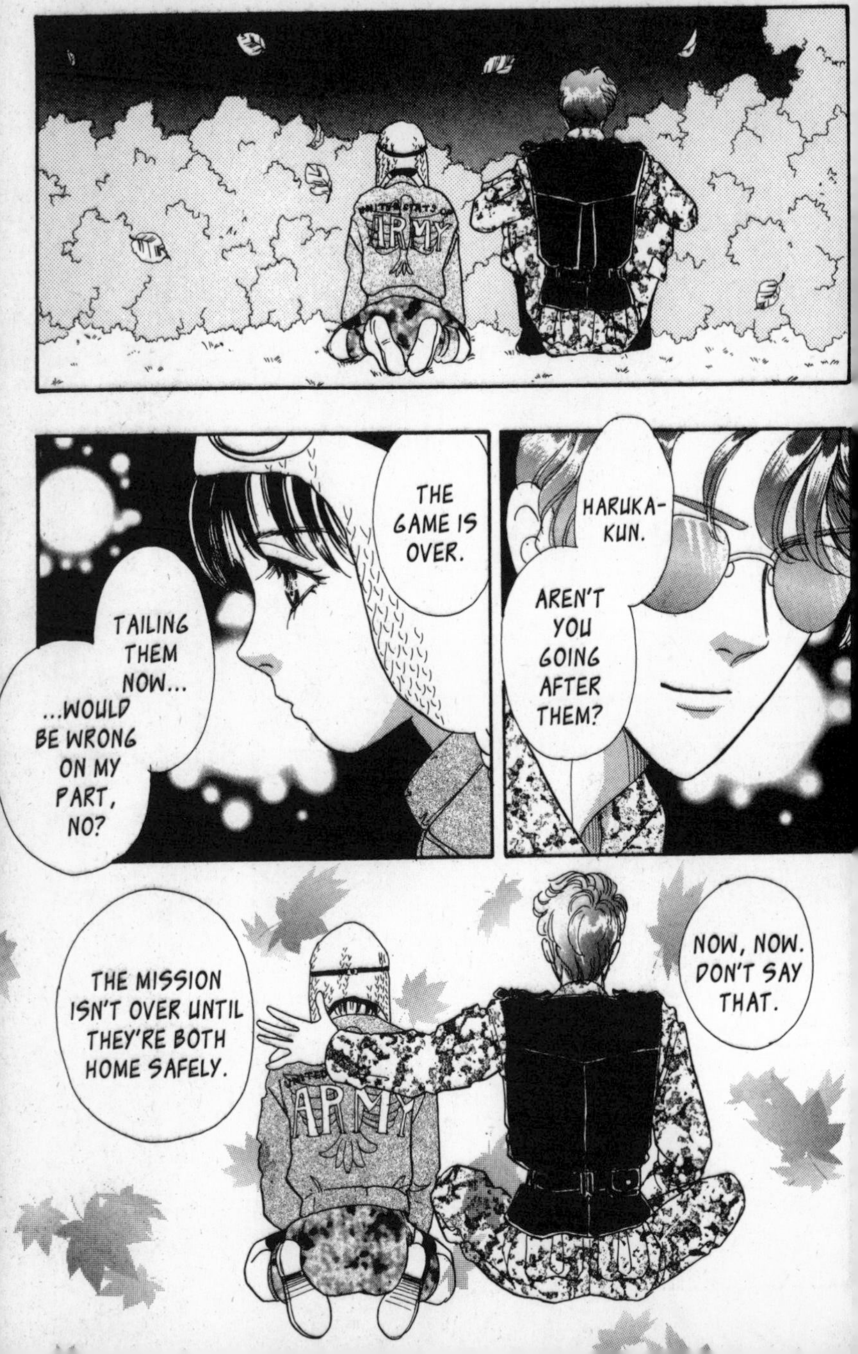
HARUKA-KUN.
AREN'T YOU GOING AFTER THEM?
THE GAME IS OVER.
TAILING THEM NOW...
...WOULD BE WRONG ON MY PART, NO?
NOW, NOW. DON'T SAY THAT.
THE MISSION ISN'T OVER UNTIL THEY'RE BOTH HOME SAFELY.

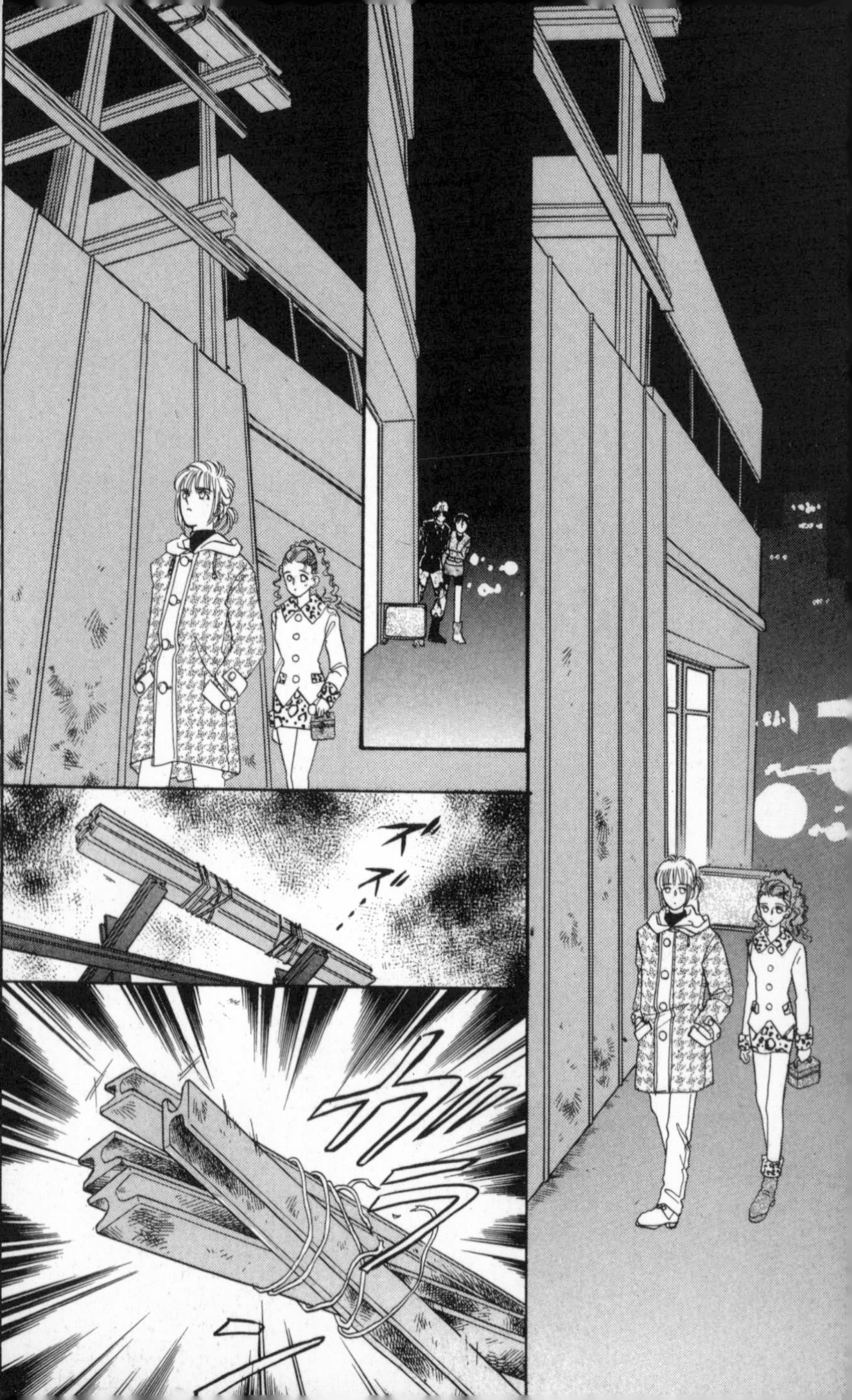
ズズ…

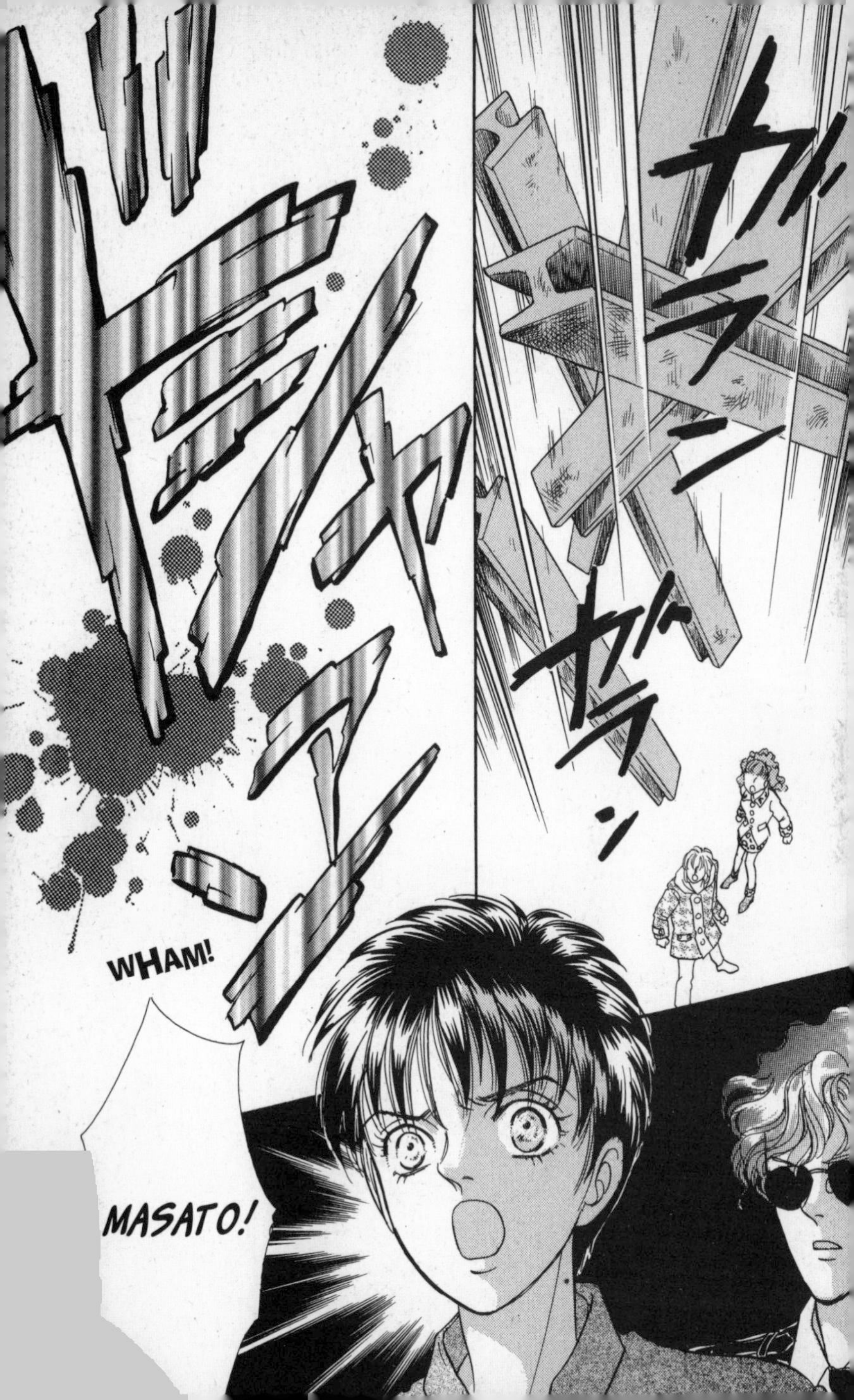
カラーン
ガラン
WHAM!
MASATO!

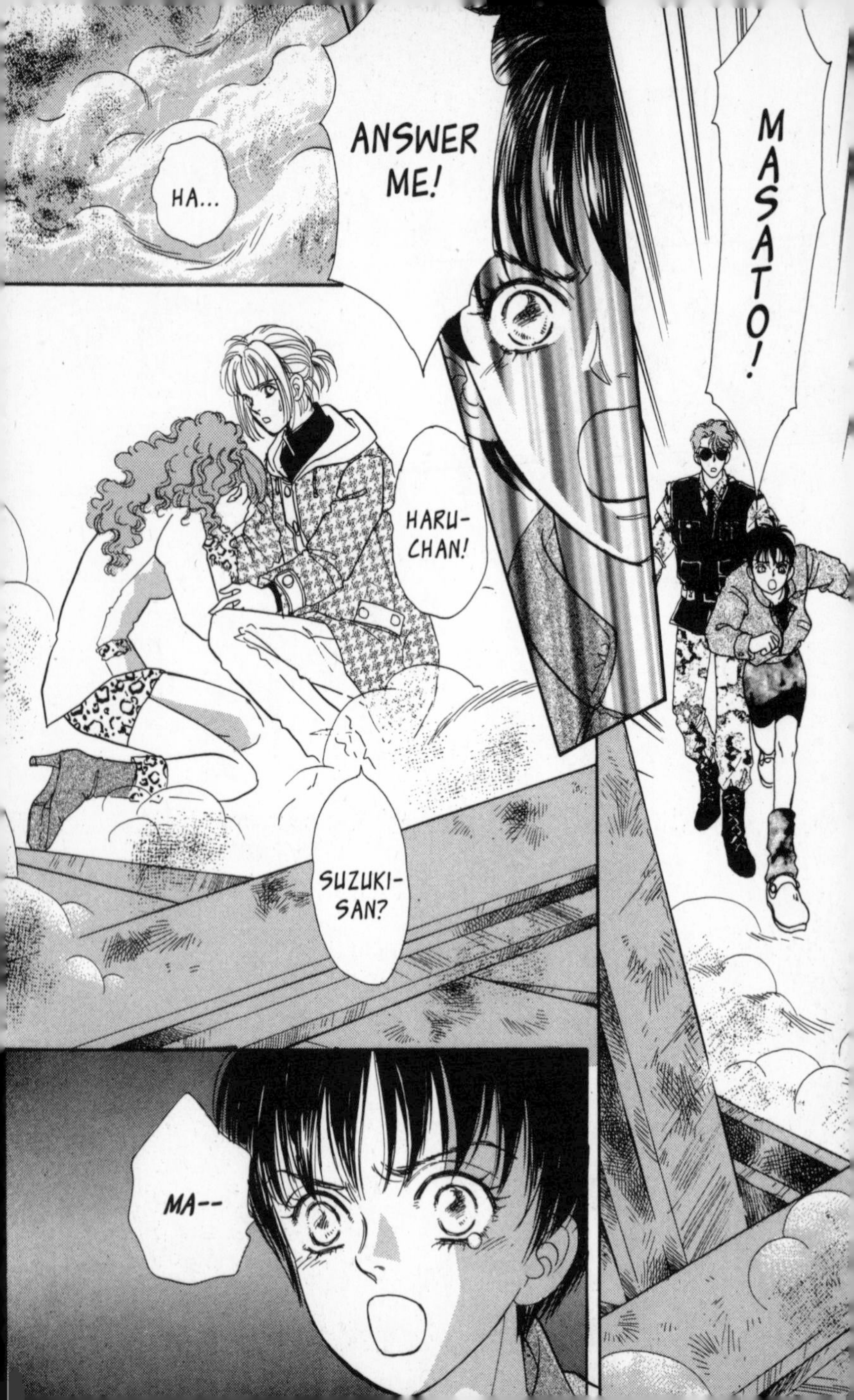
MASATO!
ANSWER ME!
HA...
HARU-CHAN!
SUZUKI-SAN?
MA--

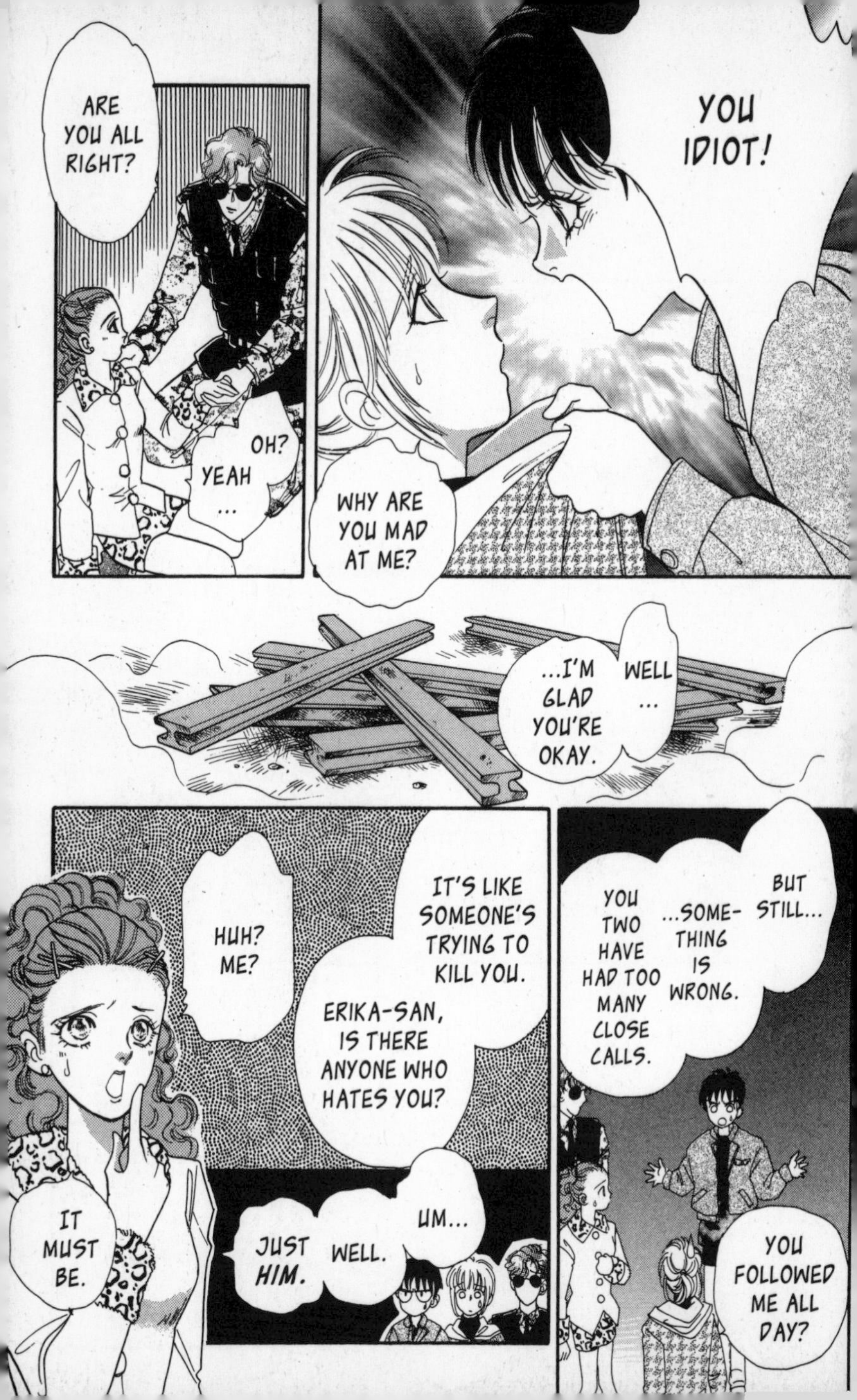
YOU IDIOT!
WHY ARE YOU MAD AT ME?
ARE YOU ALL RIGHT?
OH? YEAH ...
WELL ...
...I'M GLAD YOU'RE OKAY.
BUT STILL...
...SOME-THING IS WRONG.
YOU TWO HAVE HAD TOO MANY CLOSE CALLS.
YOU FOLLOWED ME ALL DAY?
IT'S LIKE SOMEONE'S TRYING TO KILL YOU.
HUH? ME?
ERIKA-SAN, IS THERE ANYONE WHO HATES YOU?
UM...
WELL.
JUST *HIM.*
IT MUST BE.

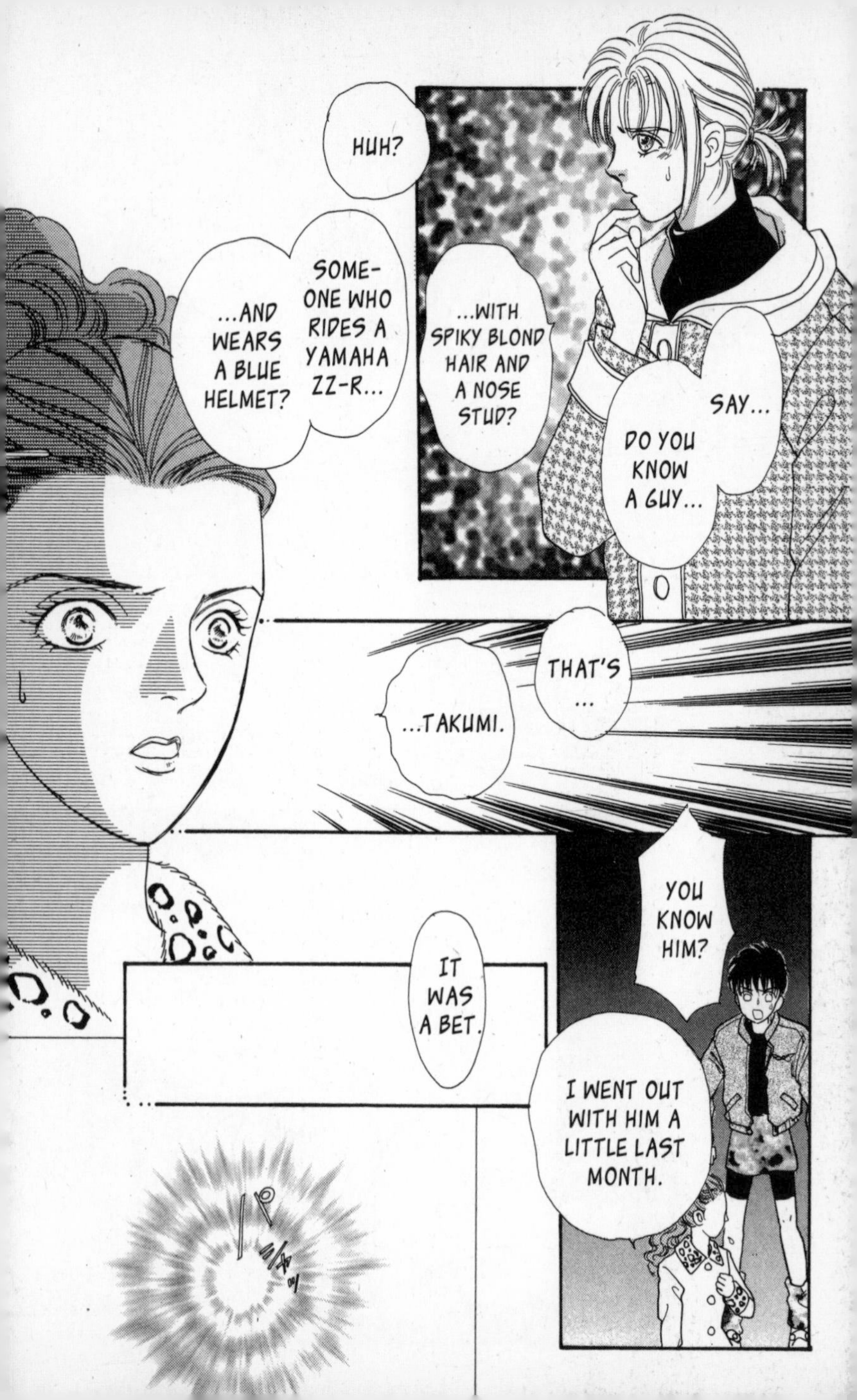

SAY...
DO YOU KNOW A GUY...
...WITH SPIKY BLOND HAIR AND A NOSE STUD?
SOME-ONE WHO RIDES A YAMAHA ZZ-R...
...AND WEARS A BLUE HELMET?
HUH?
THAT'S...
...TAKUMI.
YOU KNOW HIM?
I WENT OUT WITH HIM A LITTLE LAST MONTH.
IT WAS A BET.

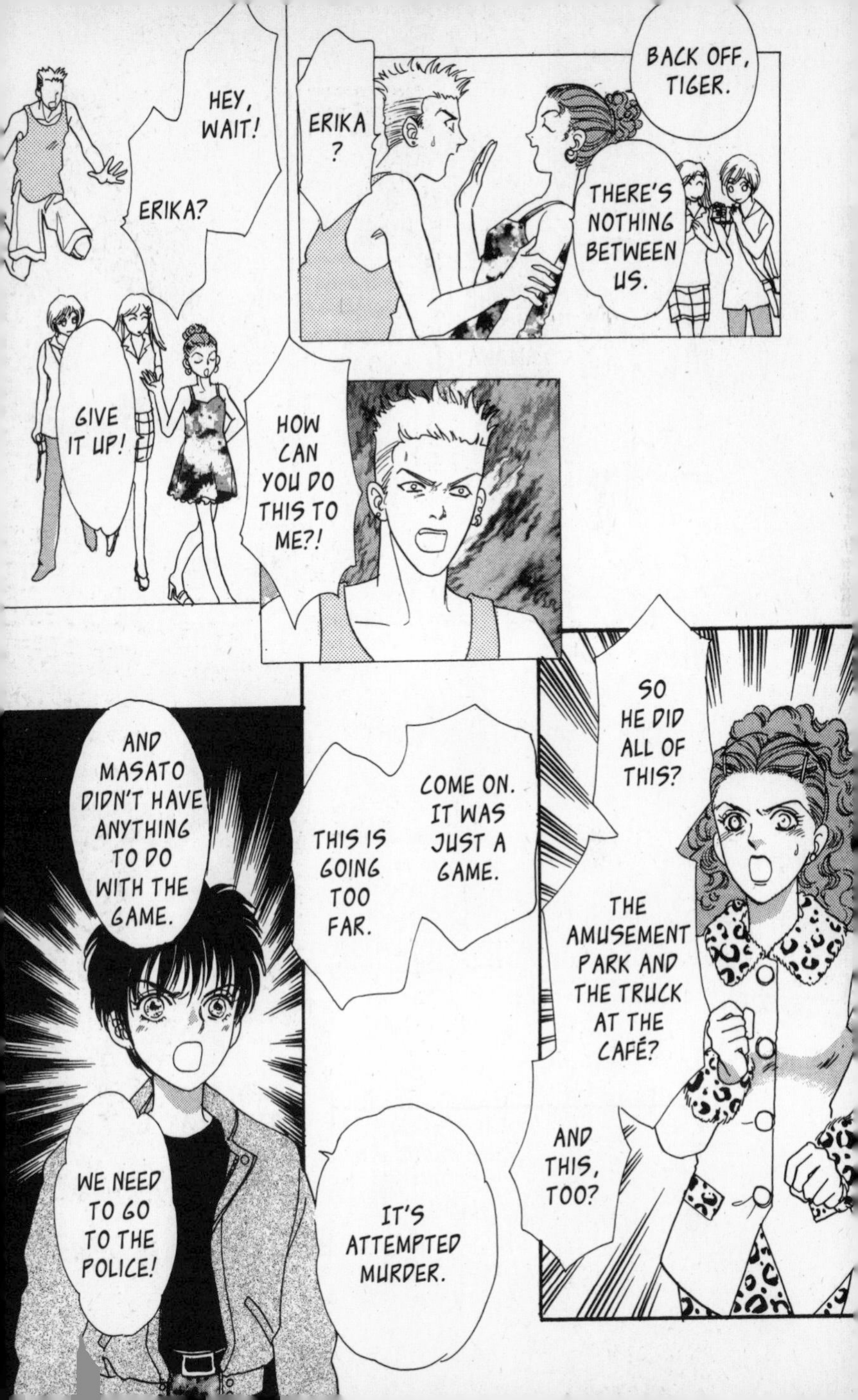
BACK OFF, TIGER.
ERIKA?
THERE'S NOTHING BETWEEN US.
HEY, WAIT!
ERIKA?
GIVE IT UP!
HOW CAN YOU DO THIS TO ME?!
SO HE DID ALL OF THIS?
THE AMUSEMENT PARK AND THE TRUCK AT THE CAFÉ?
AND THIS, TOO?
COME ON. IT WAS JUST A GAME.
THIS IS GOING TOO FAR.
IT'S ATTEMPTED MURDER.
AND MASATO DIDN'T HAVE ANYTHING TO DO WITH THE GAME.
WE NEED TO GO TO THE POLICE!

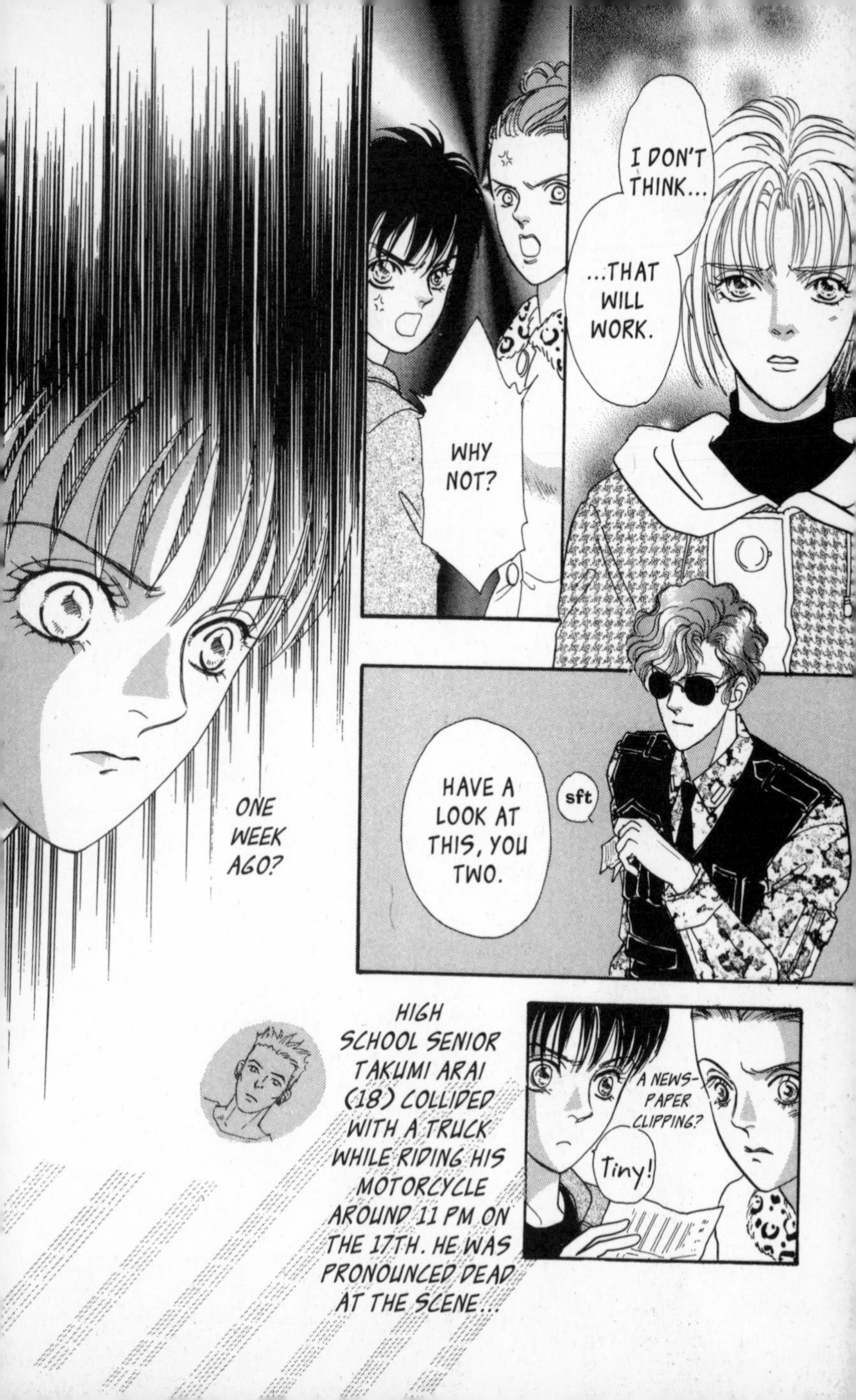
I DON'T THINK...
...THAT WILL WORK.
WHY NOT?
sft
HAVE A LOOK AT THIS, YOU TWO.
A NEWS-PAPER CLIPPING?
Tiny!
ONE WEEK AGO?
HIGH SCHOOL SENIOR TAKUMI ARAI (18) COLLIDED WITH A TRUCK WHILE RIDING HIS MOTORCYCLE AROUND 11 PM ON THE 17TH. HE WAS PRONOUNCED DEAD AT THE SCENE...

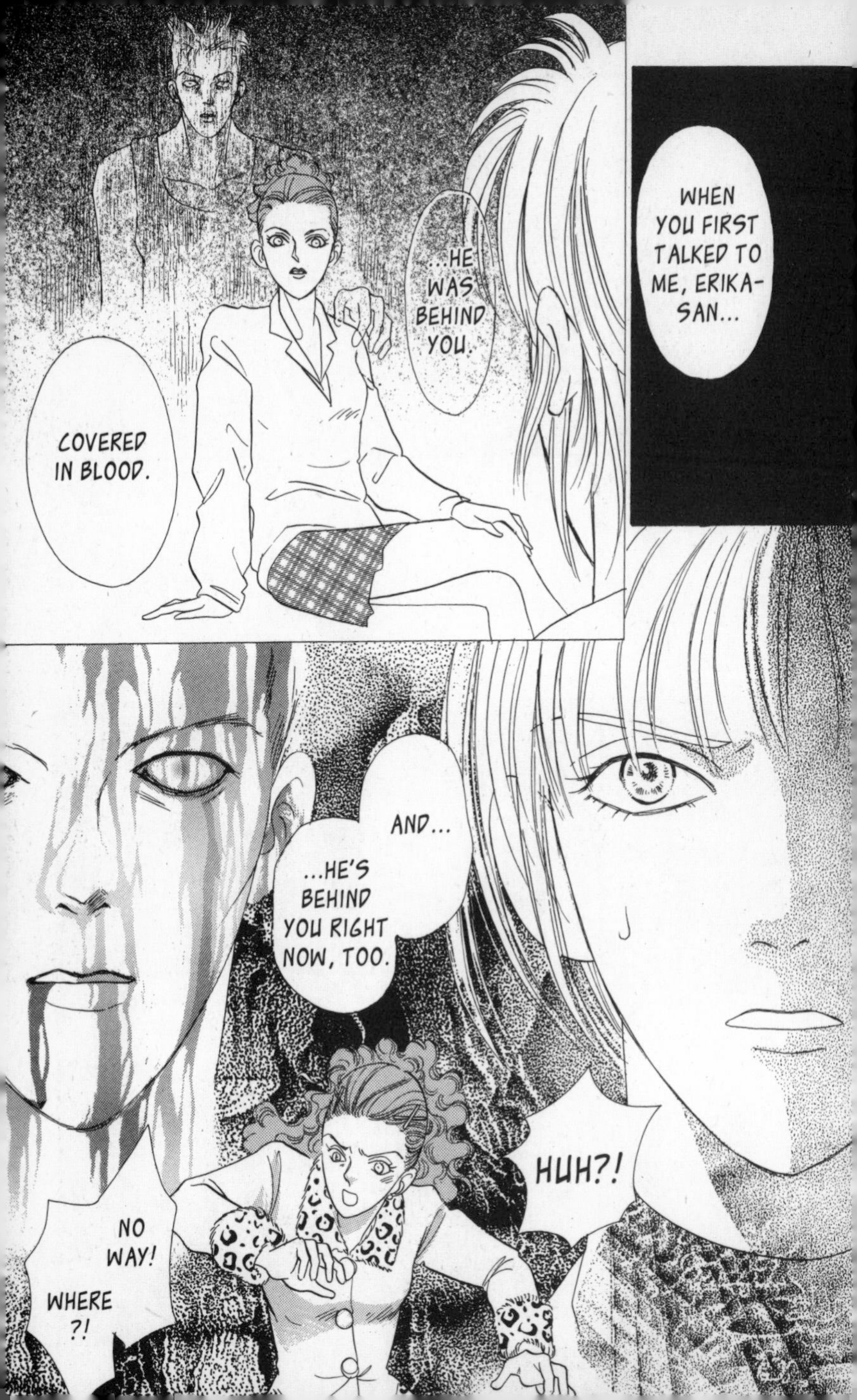
WHEN YOU FIRST TALKED TO ME, ERIKA-SAN...
...HE WAS BEHIND YOU.
COVERED IN BLOOD.
AND...
...HE'S BEHIND YOU RIGHT NOW, TOO.
HUH?!
NO WAY!
WHERE ?!

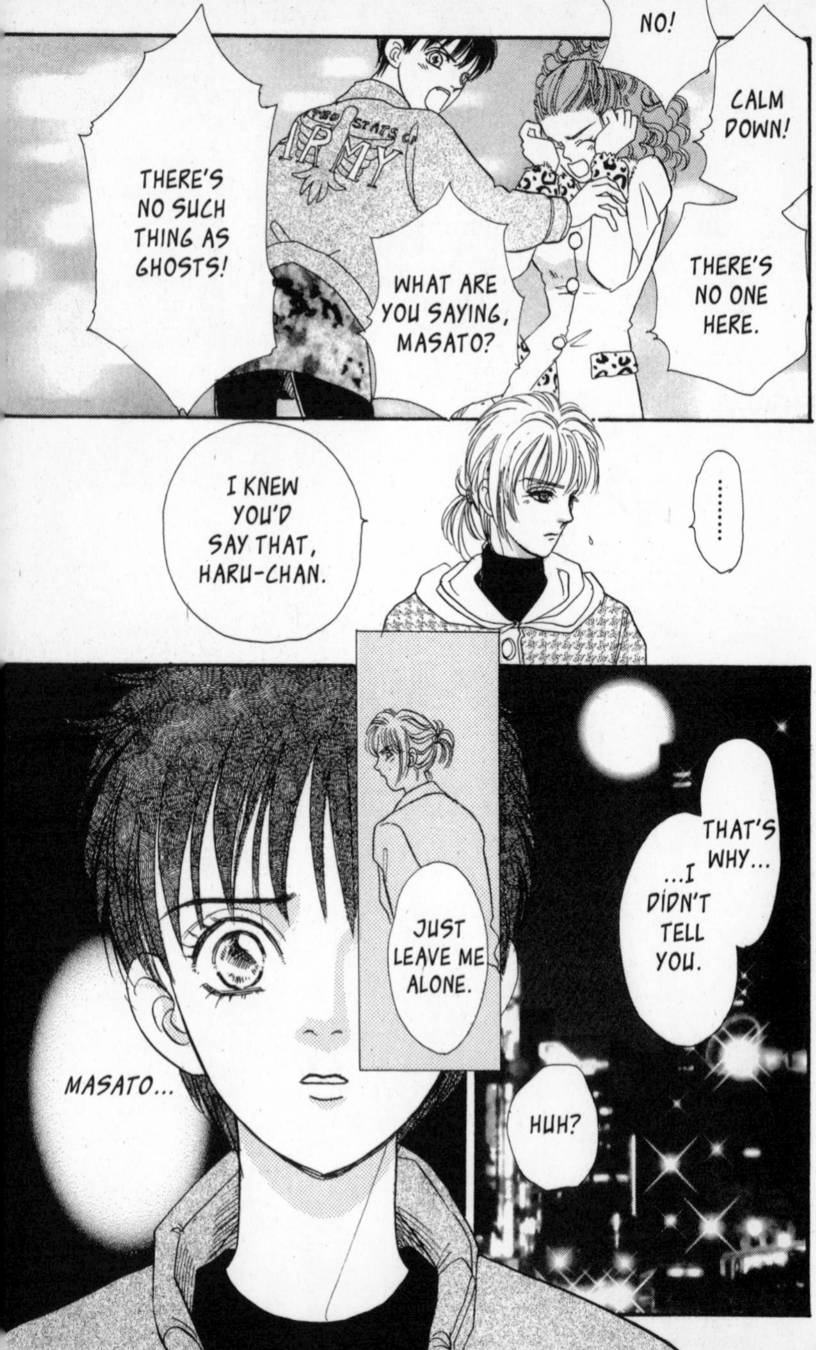
NO!
CALM DOWN!
THERE'S NO ONE HERE.
WHAT ARE YOU SAYING, MASATO?
THERE'S NO SUCH THING AS GHOSTS!
......
I KNEW YOU'D SAY THAT, HARU-CHAN.
THAT'S WHY...
...I DIDN'T TELL YOU.
HUH?
JUST LEAVE ME ALONE.
MASATO...

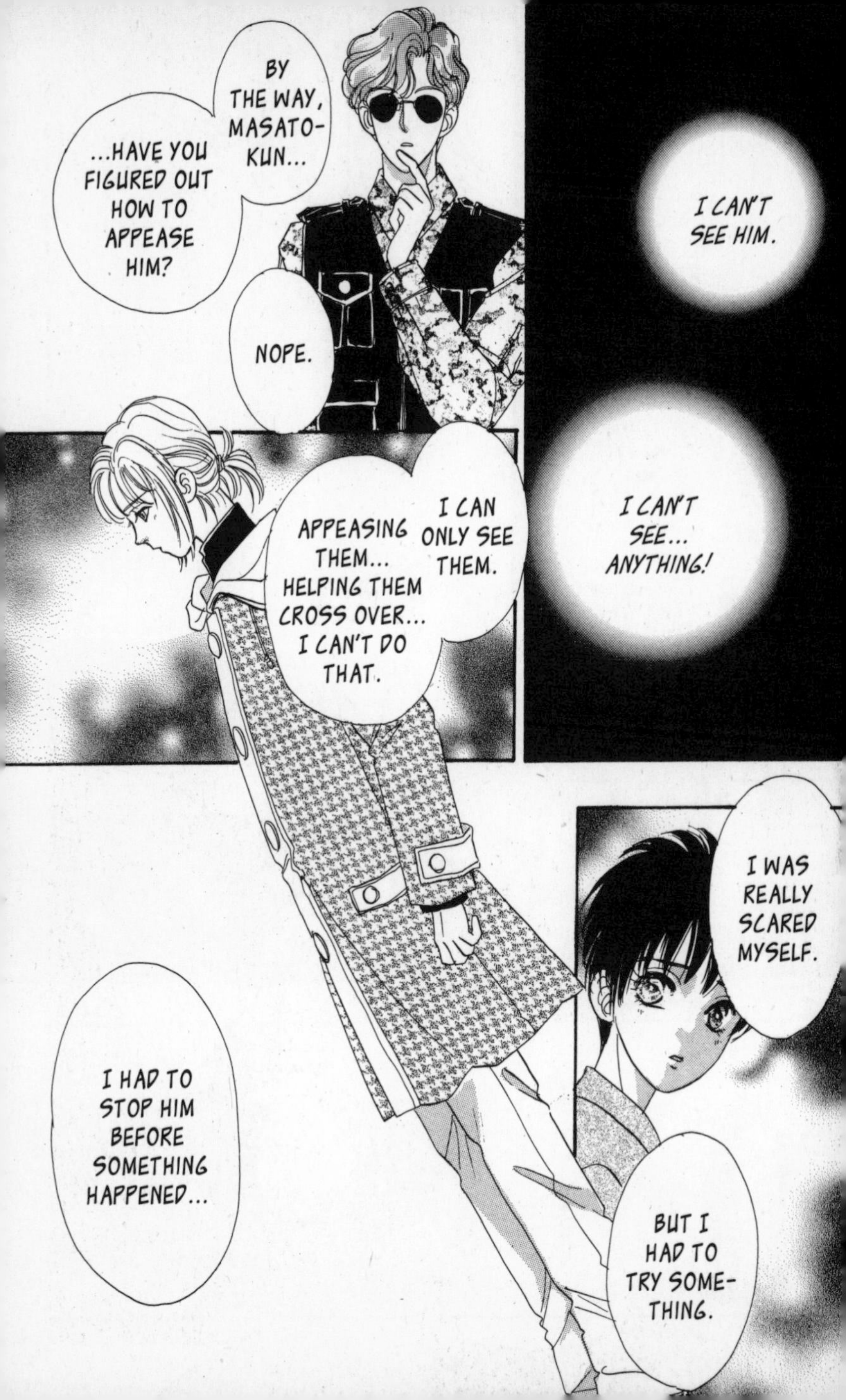
I CAN'T SEE HIM.
I CAN'T SEE... ANYTHING!
BY THE WAY, MASATO-KUN...
...HAVE YOU FIGURED OUT HOW TO APPEASE HIM?
NOPE.
I CAN ONLY SEE THEM.
APPEASING THEM... HELPING THEM CROSS OVER... I CAN'T DO THAT.
I WAS REALLY SCARED MYSELF.
BUT I HAD TO TRY SOME-THING.
I HAD TO STOP HIM BEFORE SOMETHING HAPPENED...

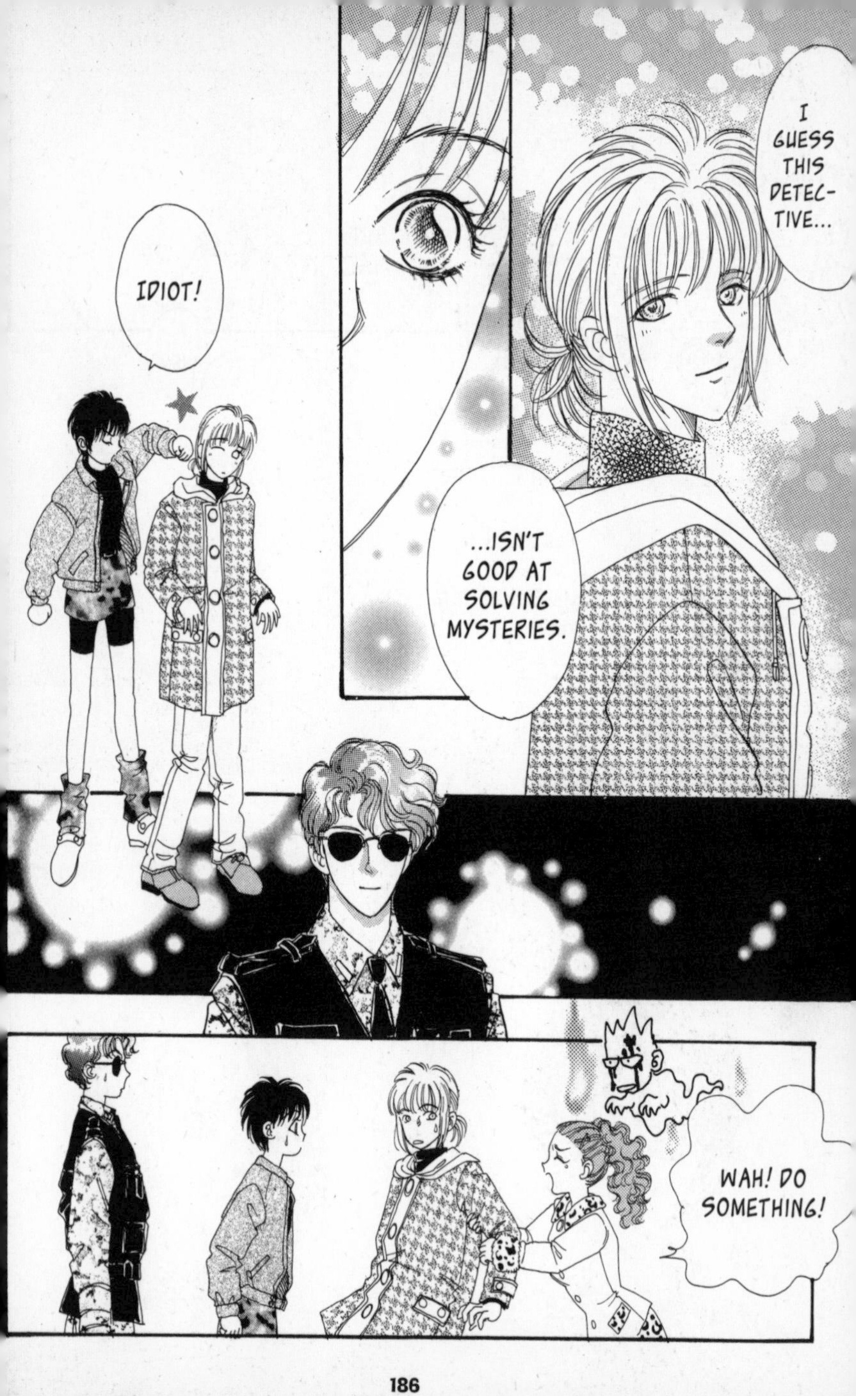
I GUESS THIS DETEC-TIVE...
...ISN'T GOOD AT SOLVING MYSTERIES.
IDIOT!
WAH! DO SOMETHING!

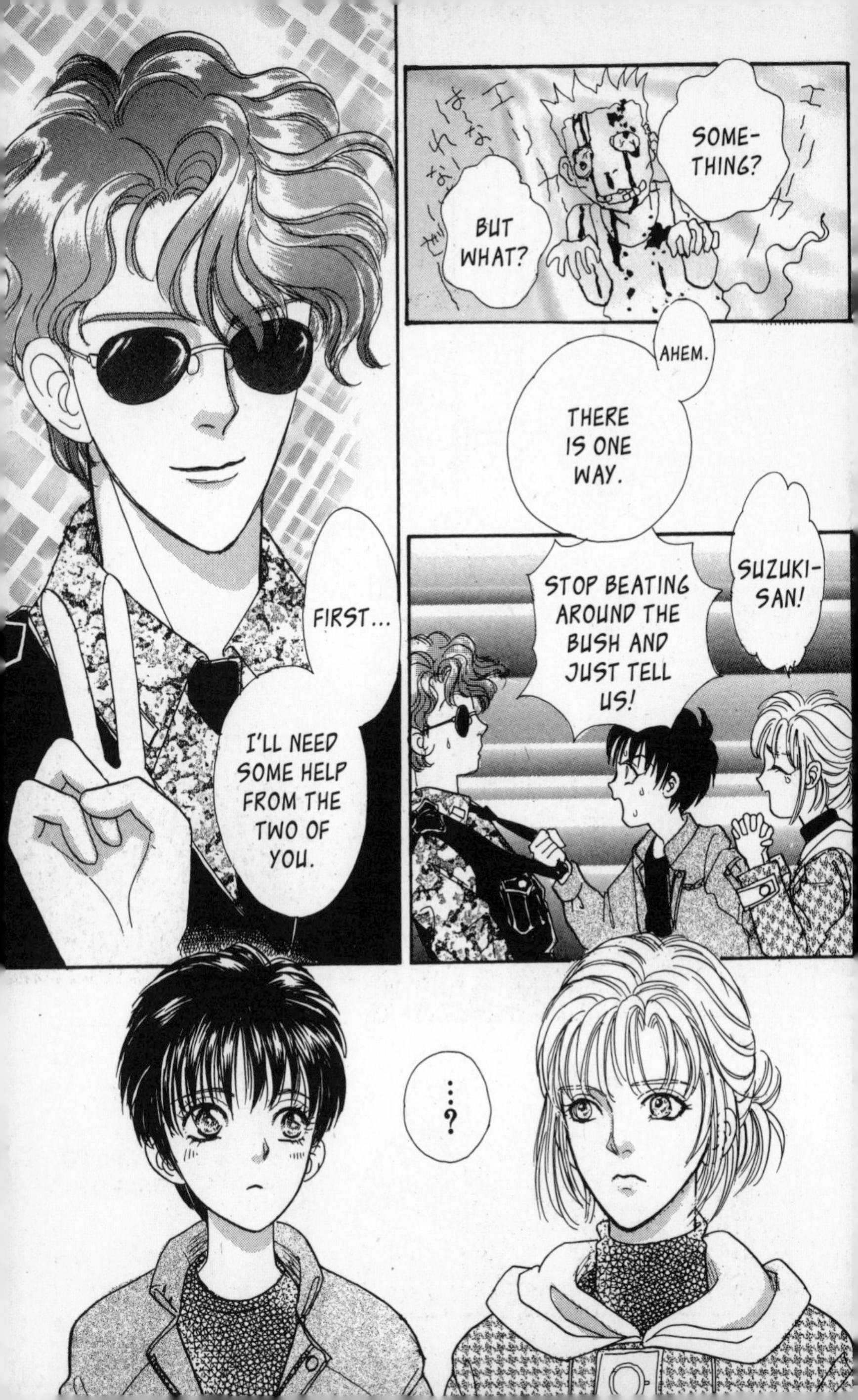
SOME-THING?
BUT WHAT?
AHEM.
THERE IS ONE WAY.
SUZUKI-SAN!
STOP BEATING AROUND THE BUSH AND JUST TELL US!
FIRST...
I'LL NEED SOME HELP FROM THE TWO OF YOU.
...?

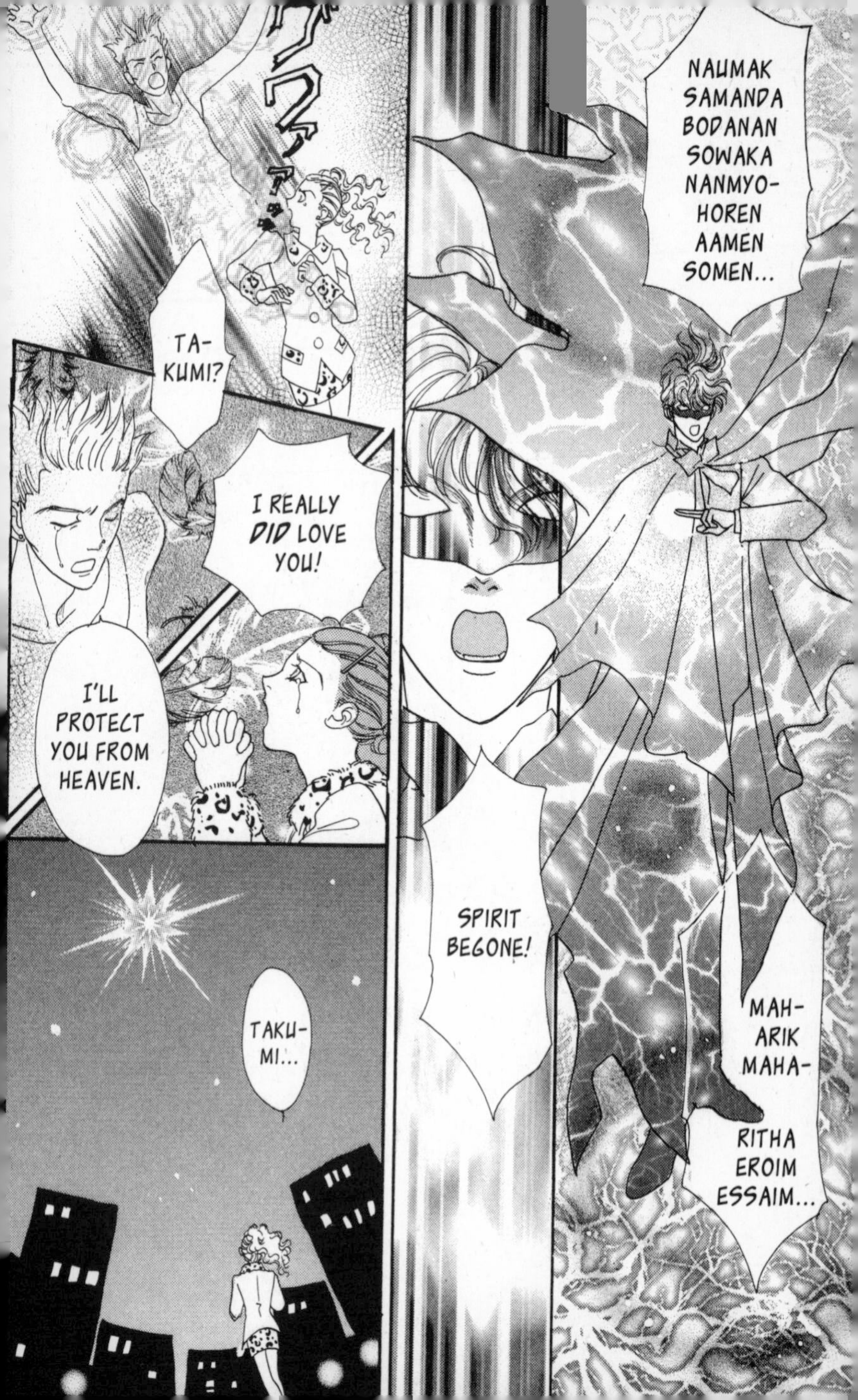
NAUMAK SAMANDA BODANAN SOWAKA NANMYO-HOREN AAMEN SOMEN...
MAH-ARIK MAHA-RITHA EROIM ESSAIM...
SPIRIT BEGONE!
TA-KUMI?
I REALLY *DID* LOVE YOU!
I'LL PROTECT YOU FROM HEAVEN.
TAKU-MI...

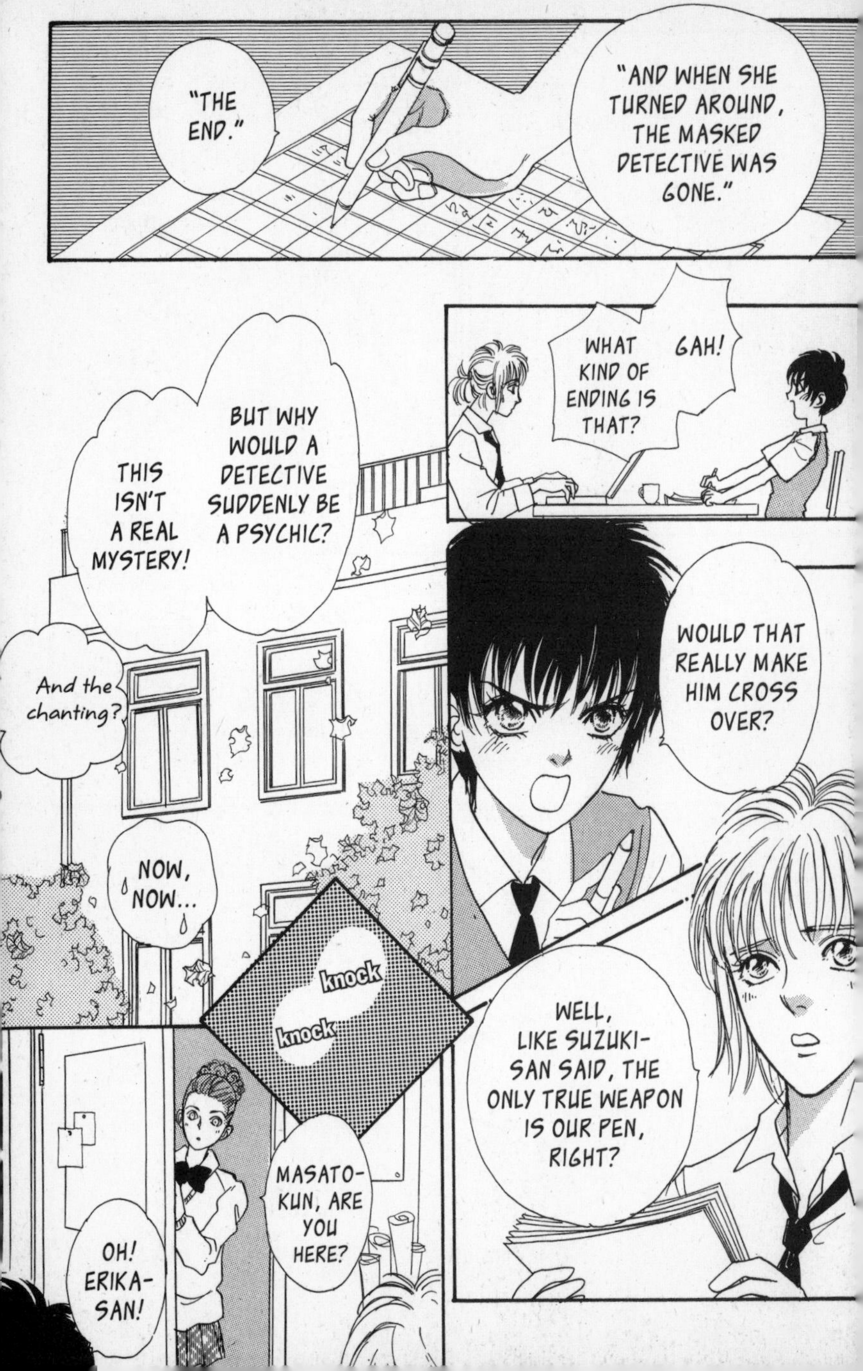
"AND WHEN SHE TURNED AROUND, THE MASKED DETECTIVE WAS GONE."
"THE END."
GAH!
WHAT KIND OF ENDING IS THAT?
WOULD THAT REALLY MAKE HIM CROSS OVER?
WELL, LIKE SUZUKI-SAN SAID, THE ONLY TRUE WEAPON IS OUR PEN, RIGHT?
BUT WHY WOULD A DETECTIVE SUDDENLY BE A PSYCHIC?
THIS ISN'T A REAL MYSTERY!
And the chanting?
NOW, NOW...
knock
knock
MASATO-KUN, ARE YOU HERE?
OH! ERIKA-SAN!

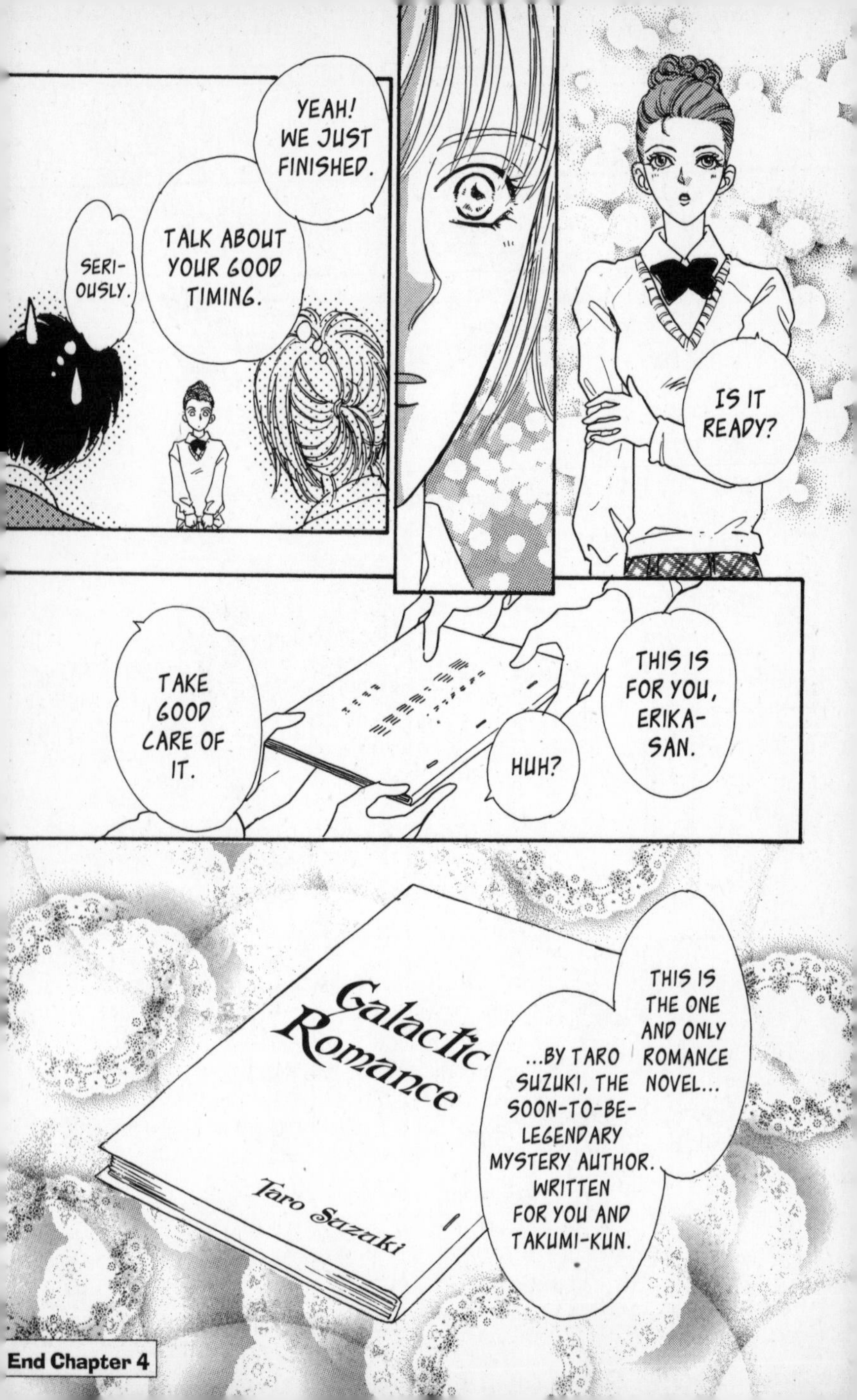
IS IT READY?
YEAH! WE JUST FINISHED.
TALK ABOUT YOUR GOOD TIMING.
SERI-OUSLY.
THIS IS FOR YOU, ERIKA-SAN.
HUH?
TAKE GOOD CARE OF IT.
THIS IS THE ONE AND ONLY ROMANCE NOVEL...
...BY TARO SUZUKI, THE SOON-TO-BE-LEGENDARY MYSTERY AUTHOR. WRITTEN FOR YOU AND TAKUMI-KUN.
Galactic Romance
Taro Suzuki
End Chapter 4

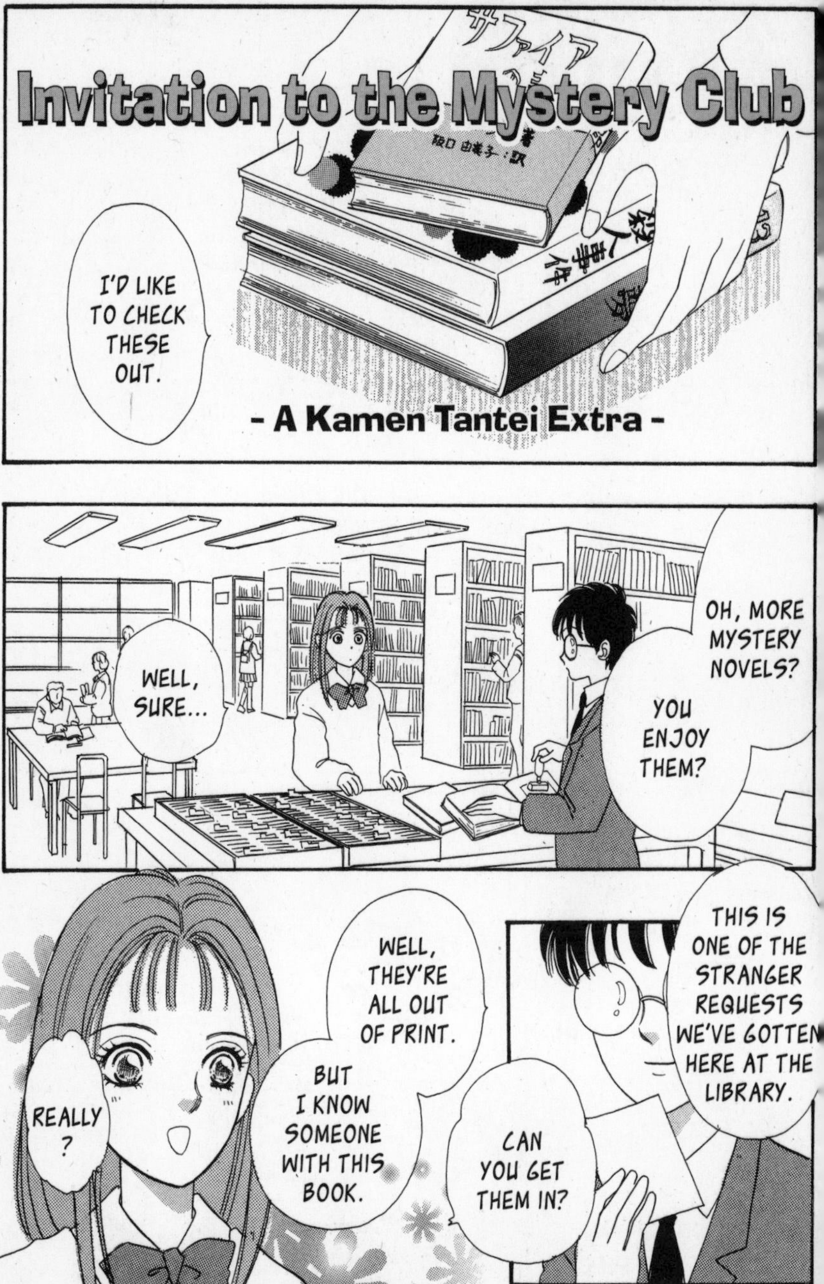
Invitation to the Mystery Club
I'D LIKE TO CHECK THESE OUT.
- A Kamen Tantei Extra -
OH, MORE MYSTERY NOVELS?
YOU ENJOY THEM?
WELL, SURE...
THIS IS ONE OF THE STRANGER REQUESTS WE'VE GOTTEN HERE AT THE LIBRARY.
CAN YOU GET THEM IN?
WELL, THEY'RE ALL OUT OF PRINT.
BUT I KNOW SOMEONE WITH THIS BOOK.
REALLY?

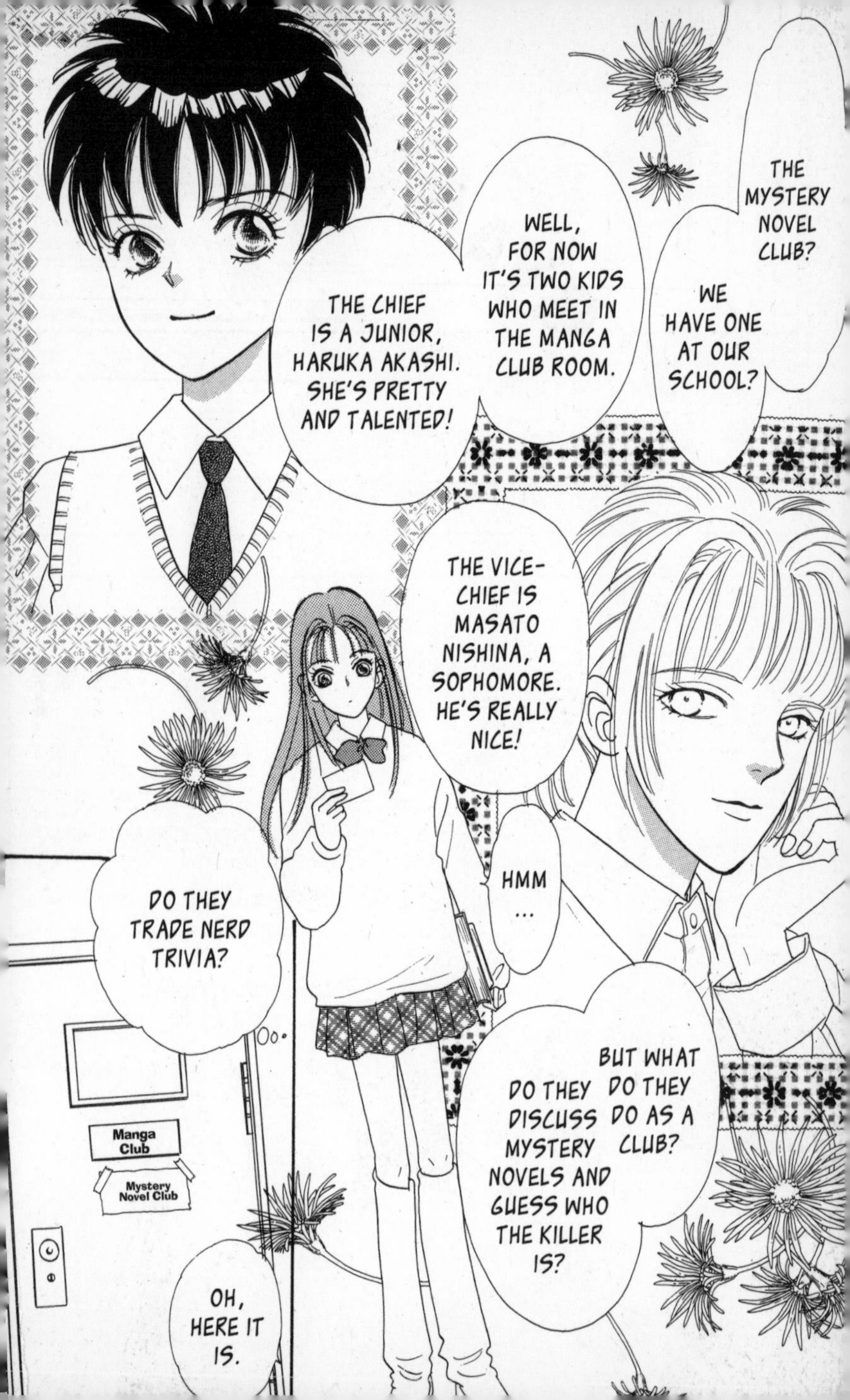
THE MYSTERY NOVEL CLUB?
WE HAVE ONE AT OUR SCHOOL?
WELL, FOR NOW IT'S TWO KIDS WHO MEET IN THE MANGA CLUB ROOM.
THE CHIEF IS A JUNIOR, HARUKA AKASHI. SHE'S PRETTY AND TALENTED!
THE VICE-CHIEF IS MASATO NISHINA, A SOPHOMORE. HE'S REALLY NICE!
HMM...
BUT WHAT DO THEY DO AS A CLUB?
DO THEY DISCUSS MYSTERY NOVELS AND GUESS WHO THE KILLER IS?
DO THEY TRADE NERD TRIVIA?
Manga Club
Mystery Novel Club
OH, HERE IT IS.

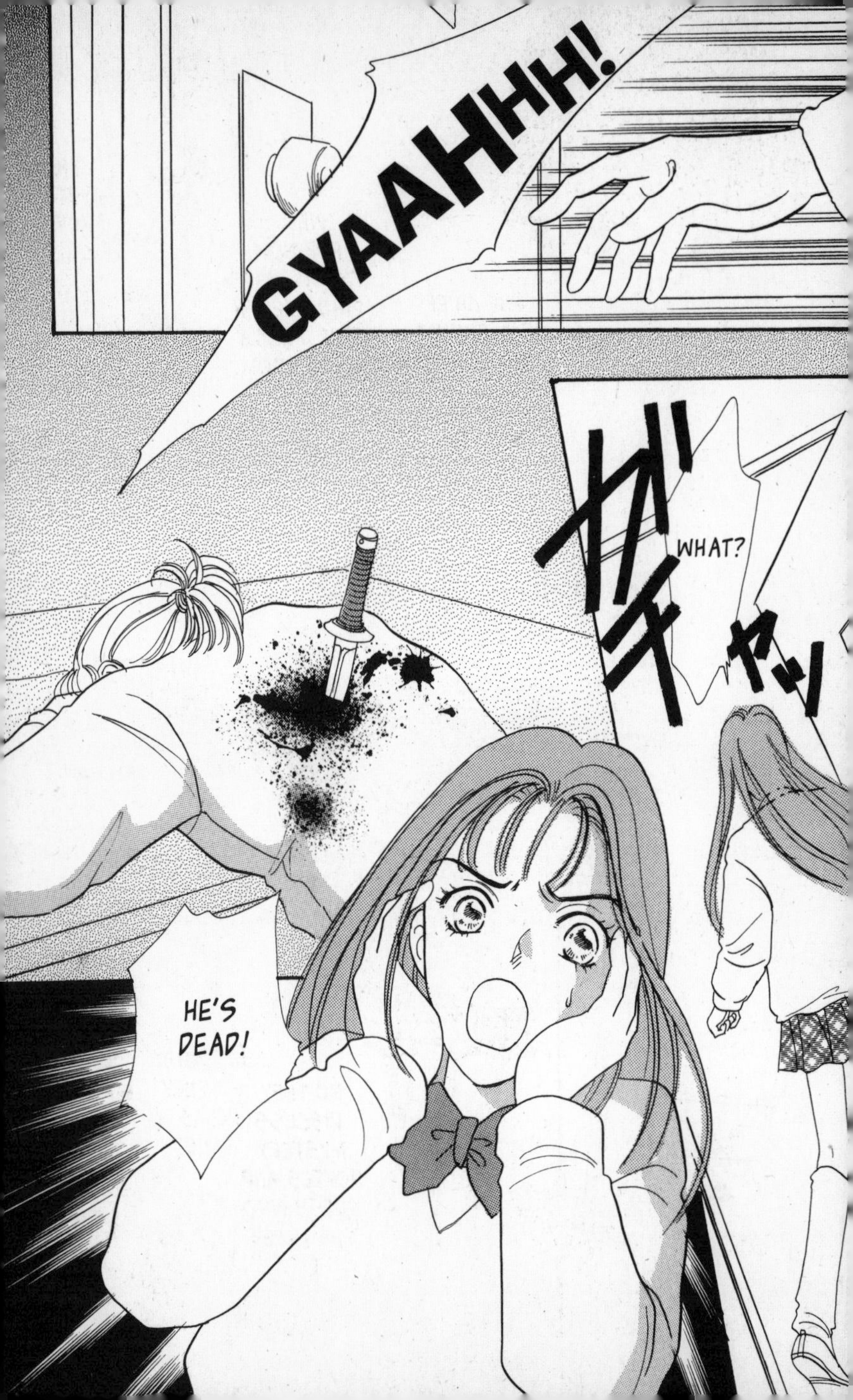
GYAAHHH!
ガチャッ
WHAT?
HE'S DEAD!

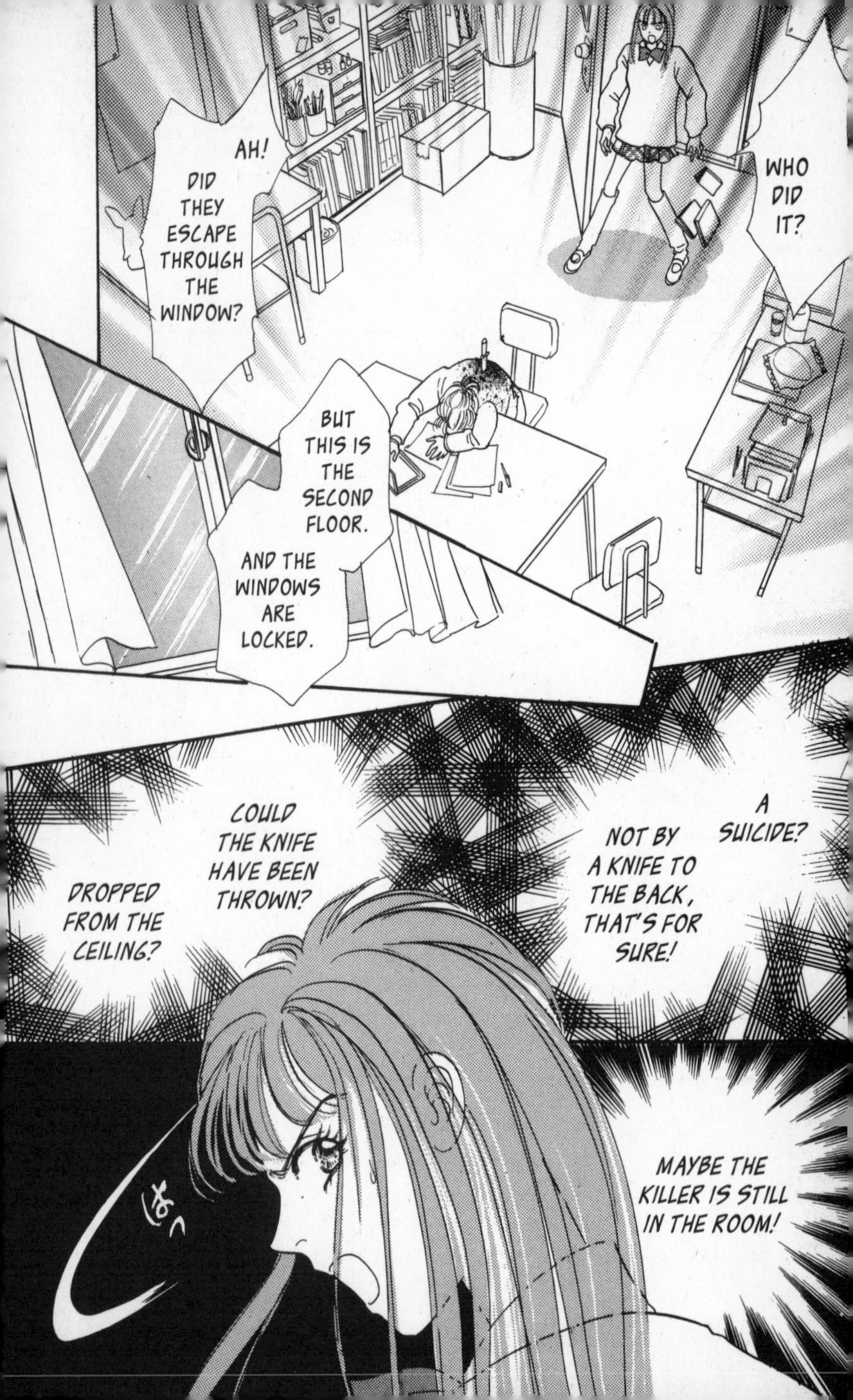
WHO DID IT?
AH! DID THEY ESCAPE THROUGH THE WINDOW?
BUT THIS IS THE SECOND FLOOR.
AND THE WINDOWS ARE LOCKED.
A SUICIDE?
NOT BY A KNIFE TO THE BACK, THAT'S FOR SURE!
COULD THE KNIFE HAVE BEEN THROWN?
DROPPED FROM THE CEILING?
MAYBE THE KILLER IS STILL IN THE ROOM!
はっ

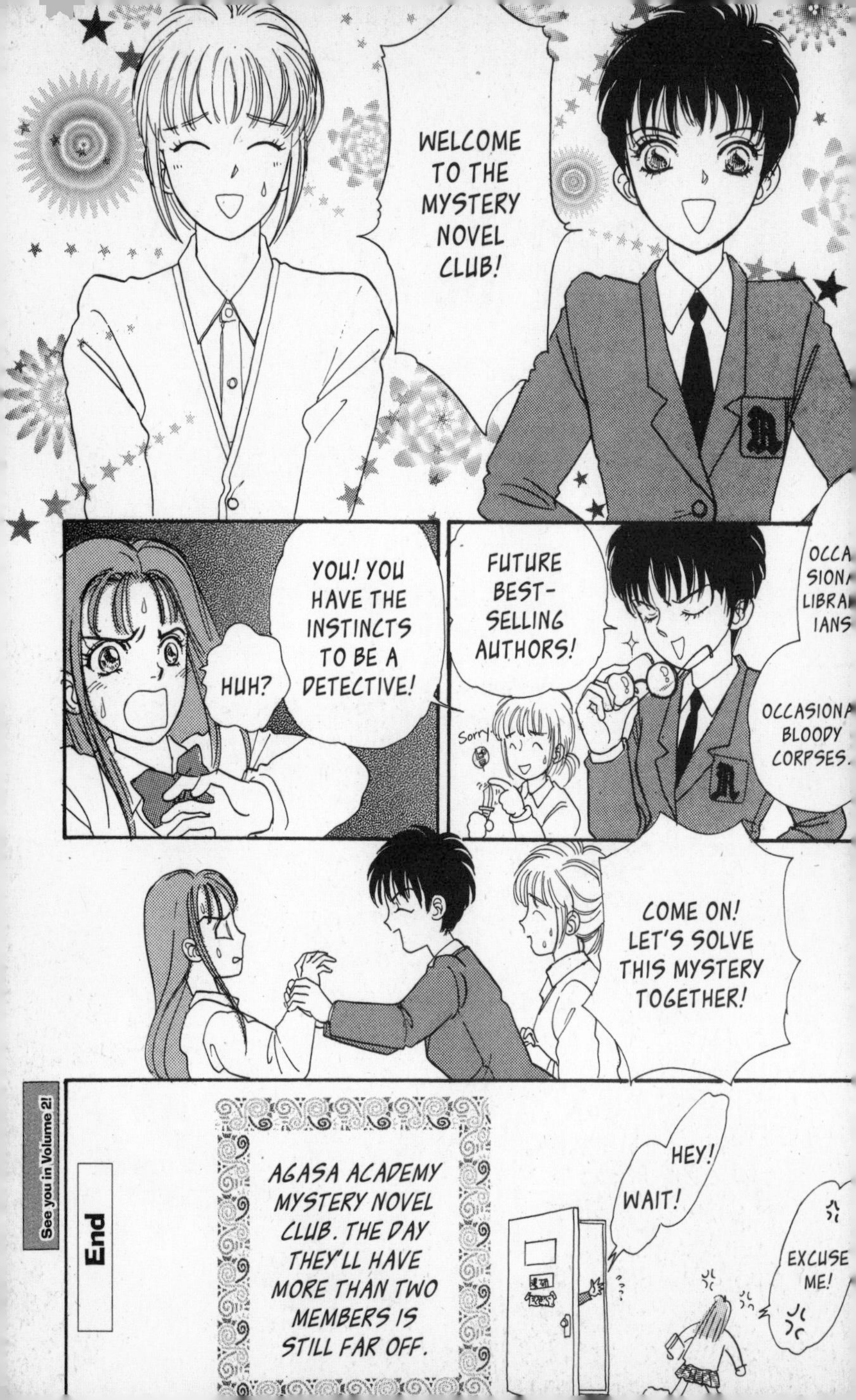
WELCOME TO THE MYSTERY NOVEL CLUB!
OCCA SIONA LIBRA IANS
FUTURE BEST-SELLING AUTHORS!
OCCASIONA BLOODY CORPSES.
Sorry.
YOU! YOU HAVE THE INSTINCTS TO BE A DETECTIVE!
HUH?
COME ON! LET'S SOLVE THIS MYSTERY TOGETHER!
EXCUSE ME!
HEY!
WAIT!
AGASA ACADEMY MYSTERY NOVEL CLUB. THE DAY THEY'LL HAVE MORE THAN TWO MEMBERS IS STILL FAR OFF.
End
See you in Volume 2!

In the next Mystery Novels Club meeting!

On behalf of the Chief and Vice-Chief of the Agasa Academy Mystery Novels Club, we'd like to thank you for joining us and helping us share our love of mystery novels! We have loads in store for our next meeting. We'll be reading mystery novels, discussing mystery novels, writing mystery novels, and err...cosplaying as mystery novels as well. (Yeah, that one was Masato's idea.)

We have one big announcement to make prior to the meeting. We've published our first book! Look for it in a few months in the pages of Akihata Mystery! So for our next meeting, we'll be brainstorming ideas for our next novel. We want this one to be even better than the first one! We'll also be discussing writer's block and ways of overcoming it, and trying to help a fellow writer work through his particular case of block. And later this week, we'll be heading down to Suzuki-san's detective agency to observe how he works cases and assist him in helping an actress deal with a slightly overzealous fan.

In short, it's a meeting not to be missed! We'll see you there!

KAMEN TANTEI™

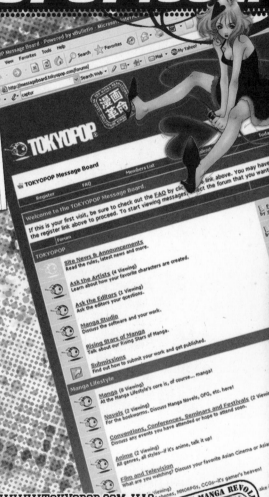

STOP!

This is the back of the book.
You wouldn't want to spoil a great ending!

This book is printed "manga-style," in the authentic Japanese right-to-left format. Since none of the artwork has been flipped or altered, readers get to experience the story just as the creator intended. You've been asking for it, so TOKYOPOP® delivered: authentic, hot-off-the-press, and far more fun!

DIRECTIONS

If this is your first time reading manga-style, here's a quick guide to help you understand how it works.

It's easy... just start in the top right panel and follow the numbers. Have fun, and look for more 100% authentic manga from TOKYOPOP®!